Outstanding SIGNET War Novels

the gunner

William Stevens

A Signet Book
Published by The New American Library

SIGNET TRADEMARK REG. U.S. PAT. OFF. AND FOREIGN COUNTRIES
REGISTERED TRADEMARK—MARCA REGISTRADA
HECHO EN CHICAGO, U.S.A.

SIGNET BOOKS are published by
The New American Library, Inc.,
1301 Avenue of the Americas, New York, New York 10019

FIRST PRINTING, JUNE, 1969

PRINTED IN THE UNITED STATES OF AMERICA

For HOLLY, MARC, HEIDI, GRANT *and* LISE . . .
helpless but cheerful hostages during the journey

PART ONE

We all did our duty, which, in the patriot's, soldier's, and gentleman's language, is a very comprehensive word, of great honour, meaning, and import.

TRAVELS OF BARON MUNCHAUSEN

1.

THE FIELD was never quiet. It lay among farms and orchards and was flanked by a sandy ridge. A perforated steel landing mat ran through its center. On one side were the tents and tufa houses of the heavy-bomber squadron, with the headquarters building and the briefing room and the field hospital built along the top of the ridge. On the other side of the mat were tents and tufa houses belonging to the service squadron —the mechanics and electricians and sheet-metal specialists who repaired broken airplanes. The two squadrons formed a single bomb group of the Fifteenth Air Force.

The nearest town was twenty miles away, and that only one of the typical sunstruck villages of Basilicata. The fighting in Italy was hundreds of miles away from the field. No German planes had been seen that far south for nearly a year. And now, in the spring of 1944, it seemed that the field had been left behind by the war, that the sandbagged anti-aircraft emplacements at its corners were pretentious. The hospital needed only pennons and a colorful fringe to become the big top of a small circus. The tents might have been the encampment of Bedouin with an eye for monotone, the lopsided tufa houses peasant shacks. There were even twin campanile, one tall and slender where parachutes were hung to dry and the other a blocky control tower. Only the airplanes and the landing strip itself were at all military.

But the field was never quiet. The men of the service squadron, the meteorologists and fire fighters and armorers, the oxygen makers and clerks and medics, all worked steadily around the clock to keep some three hundred and fifty flyers in the air. An engineering battalion had leveled the ground and laid the mat and paved taxi strips and access roads. Telephone and power lines had been strung, water tanks built, latrines dug. Thousands of troops had settled in the harsh and arid *mezzogiorno* just so that thirty-five planes could be pushed into the air each day. Thirty-five maximum, optimum. That many planes never flew. There were that many only in the scrap pile at the end of the runway.

During the blazing forenoon, while the Italian farmers were at siesta, figures in cut-down uniforms sweated and tugged at the airplanes, hammered and riveted and swung engines from the tips of manually cranked hoists. In the early evening clerks typed orders for the following day, flight plans were arranged, logistics computed. Compressors at the oxygen detachment hammered all night. Armorers loaded bombs and filled ammunition belts until dawn. Just before first light huge tanker-trailers drove to revetments and gassed the ships.

The field was never quiet, and it was hard to find a separation in either day or night which might have been considered either a beginning or an end. But there came a moment when the bulbs of the kitchen serving line went on and flashlights winked through the tent area of the flight crews, both lights paling as the sky grew brighter; a moment when the ground crews trudged sleepily to the ships which had to be warmed up, and the sun rising behind distant hills caused the runway to gleam a dull blue.

At that moment, while the Italian farmers were rising and the Americans who were to fly were being shaken awake, there would come the whine of an energizer and then a splitting cough as the first engine was turned over, a roar which might have been a trumpet. At that moment it seemed that the day began officially.

Deacon did not awaken when the CQ thumped through with his ritual call, nor when the other men in the tent fumbled with their gear and went off to breakfast. He came rushing out of sleep with the first engine's rattle, listened as others joined it until the whole area of the field snorted and exploded in a wave of noise which beat on the canvas as though on a drum. He squirmed to a sitting position on his cot and tried to breathe past the lump of phlegm caked in his throat. His stomach surged and he gagged and spat on the dirt floor.

The tent quivered and the tent pole rattled. Deacon looked with hot dry eyes at Horton and tried once again to clear his throat. Horton seemed amused.

"What time is it?" Deacon asked.

"Briefly, twenty minutes to briefing."

"Not raining, huh?"

Horton made an elaborate show of standing in the open doorway and inspecting the colors changing the sky. "No," he said, "it's not. Wasn't raining yesterday, either."

"Balls," Deacon said.

"Not the day before that, either."

10

"It was snowing then, wasn't it?"

"You mean Thursday? No, I don't think so. I think it was Wednesday that . . ."

"Never mind," Deacon said, "never mind, for Jesus sake. Fitzgerald have any beer?"

"You shouldn't be thinking about beer. You should be down getting breakfast with the rest of the troops."

"Arnie, for Jesus sake."

"A little cold champagne. What's that other stuff—spumante? Chilled spumante, Deako, brace you right up."

"Does Fitz have any beer?"

"We're out."

"Do me a favor," Deacon said, "go next door to Toole and see if he has any. Tell him I'll give it to him when I get my rations."

"What rations? You owe a case already."

The noise from the field rose in pitch as engines were pushed to their limits, and the roar became that of a monstrous angel dancing atop the pole of the tent.

"I'd get *you* beer," Deacon said.

Horton kicked the water can and winked. Deacon took it outside, filled a helmet, washed. He dried himself on a sour towel. The new day was already warm. Deacon looked through the air clear as tinted cellophane toward the range of dark blue and purple hills. An Italian sky, a religious sky, morning light like that filtering through the stained-glass windows of a church.

Horton lay on his back, blowing ragged smoke rings toward the ceiling.

"Feel better?" he asked.

"It really pains you, doesn't it, that I feel so lousy?"

"I feel for you."

"Feel yourself. I ought to move to another tent." Deacon rummaged in his footlocker and found a candy bar whose end had been nibbled by a mouse. "I ought to move in with someone like Kelleher," he said, eating.

"That'd be a howl. You and Kelleher could straighten each other out every morning."

"I could stand that better than I can this . . . what do you call this horseshit of yours, Arnie?"

"You'd better get dressed," Horton said.

"What do you call these shooting pains you feel for me? Hey, I really feel sick. I'd better go on sick call."

"Now listen . . ."

"Really, Arnie. Where are we going today? You get any poop?"

"No, and you're not sick." Horton flipped the butt through

11

the open doorway. "What's the point of sick call? You'll only have to go through it all tomorrow again. You already lost a mission."

"I never thought of that," Deacon said, "tomorrow. I never thought of it, you nursing pain in the ass, I thought the armistice was going to be signed tonight." He stood in the doorway. The sun had appeared, rolling like a wheel of fire along the tops of the hills. Deacon stretched lazily. "Tomorrow and tomorrow and tomorrow, and all our yesterdays . . ." He turned. "Hey you, Edward Everett Horton. Snap shit, soldier, pop to."

"Come on, let's go," Horton said irritably.

"What a nursing pain in the ass you are, what a man." Deacon got into a pair of dirty flying coveralls. "What a gunner. Edward Everett Red-Hot Horton. Rat-tat-tin."

"They're really coming this time," Horton said.

"Don't start that."

"They'll catch us. Pingo, right out of the sun."

"Knock it off."

"Pingo."

"Knock it off, I told you."

"Pingo, pingo."

Deacon threw his mess cup. Horton ducked.

"Chicken day, Deke. Pingo, pingo."

Behind Deacon's ear a pulse began to pound. It sent ripples across his scalp. He held a clenched fist toward Horton, the fascist salute horitontal. "Knock it off now, knock it off."

The fist was blurred by a tremor. Horton looked away. "You ready?" he asked indifferently.

"Go on down, I'll see you later."

"I'll wait."

"I don't need you to wait. I know the way."

"Somebody might ask you to drop in for a beer and you'd get lost."

"Get lost yourself." Deacon tugged at his clothing. "This zipper's broken."

"I'll get it," Horton said.

"I can jerk a zipper, Arnie. I still know how to pull up and down on a zipper."

Horton handed Deacon his cap and sunglasses. They left the tent. Deacon paused to make a small circle with his toe in the dust before the doorway. Horton erased it with his heel. They called to one of the jeeps and piled in with the crewmen already aboard.

Some walking and some in jeeps, men came from all over the bomb squadron's area, climbed the sandy ridge, and headed toward the church where briefings were held. There were not three hundred and fifty of them because there were not thirty-five operative aircraft. Crash crews and fire trucks were on standby, ground crews tinkered with the bombers parked at each revetment. The control tower's full staff was ready and all the weathermen strained their eyes toward windsocks and anemometers. Hundreds were alerted to duty for the takeoff, but only nineteen airplanes were operative. A hundred and ninety men were to fly.

The church where the briefings were held was more properly an ex-church. Cross and bell and alterstone had been removed. Perhaps it had been deconsecrated before the Americans' arrival, or perhaps grown ungodly through disuse, too far from any town to attract more than a handful of peasants for Sunday mass. The men who had planned the field had been sensitive enough to consider a church—even one without a chalice—no fit place for a briefing, had not thought it proper than any of the clever people from Operations who explained the attacks should stand behind the altar rail and conduct the preliminaries to a different kind of sacrifice. The nave of the church was kept neutral through use as a storeroom for parachutes and medical supplies and flight clothing, things which would succor and comfort.

The basement—the *vault*—was more appropriate. The church was so old that there must certainly have been martyr's blood ground into the dirt floor, perhaps the blood of heretics—the blood of some kind of victim, at any rate. Briefings were held down there beneath the tiled floor, beneath the remnants of censer ash, of holy oil blown to dust. If the men had been as sensitive as the field's planners they might have considered their descent underground symbolic, the room uncomfortably like a catacomb, Valhalla subterranean.

But no one was bled there. The American flag and the bomb group's escutcheon bracketed a platform, the briefing itself had fallen into nearly ceremonial patterns, but the men had only to sit on stools made from bomb-fin casings and listen to a story. While the story indicated that a certain amount of bleeding might be expected later in the day, nothing but spit and cigarette butts was added to the dirt on the floor.

Deacon and Horton had their names checked against a list held by a corporal at the door and then they went down the long narrow flight of stairs. Officers and enlisted men sat on different sides of the aisle, all going on the same trip, traveling in the same class, but separated by the distinction between shoot and salute. There were six gunners to each airplane's four officers. Deacon and Horton joined the rest of their crew.

"Hey, old kid *vino*," Quinn said to Deacon. "I didn't think you'd make it." Quinn, the tail gunner, had just turned nineteen and looked pinker and fresher than the others.

"I had to promise the sport another Air Medal to get him down here," Horton said.

"You look piss poor," Cantori, the ball gunner, said.

Cantori was old, nearly thirty, and he was stumpy and dark and glowering. A *mafioso* who hung in a plastic bubble beneath the plane and traversed his guns to cover the horizon's sweep. *Mafioso*, but his hands were not black. He'd come through forty-four missions. His hands were pinched and fleshless and he had a tic in his left eye.

Deacon nodded at the last two crew members, Fitzgerald and Zimmerman. Fitzgerald was the engineer and top-turret gunner. He was a master sergeant, the nominal head of the group. Zimmerman operated the radios.

"You should have sacked in," Quinn said. "I got the poop that they loaded five-hundred-pounders and we're going clean to Regensburg."

"Jesus Christ," Cantori said, "I didn't get any kind of sleep."

"Noisy," Fitzgerald said, squinting at Deacon.

Deacon leaned against the wall and tried to light a cigarette. One of the fingers of his cupped hands crept into the match flame and he had to consciously will it away. He put the finger in his mouth.

"I'm sorry," he said around it.

"You get loaded at the bar you ought to sleep there," Cantori said.

"I said I was sorry."

"That don't make me feel better. We got to go to asshole Regensburg and I'm already beat."

"Sleep on the ship," Deacon said.

"Ah balls."

Deacon shrugged and tipped his stool against the wall. He closed his eyes and let the rough damp stone bite into the back of his neck, shifted until he was pressing against some kind of nerve, the chill and dampness freezing it, cold fingers reaching through him. He was an extension of the wall, would stay when the others left and be there when they returned the following morning. He'd grow rough and gray, weep in imitation of the stone, stay all through the years of the war until it was safe to go up into the sunlight again.

"Hey." Quinn nudged him off balance. "Don't cork off."

14

Deacon took his finger out of his mouth and put on his sunglasses.

"You okay?" Quinn asked.

"Why sure, Kenny."

"You look terrible, very bad. I had an uncle got ulcers from drinking. They killed him."

"He must have lived dangerously," Horton said.

"I'm serious, Arnie, he couldn't stop. I'll bet you'll get ulcers if you don't stop, Deke."

"I wouldn't care if he got his ass dead," Cantori said, "as long as I could get some sleep."

"How long did your uncle last?" Horton asked.

"I think he was drunk for twenty years," Quinn said. "He was a bricklayer. He got a cramp from the ulcers and fell off a scaffold."

"Better start to taper off," Horton said to Deacon.

"Don't worry about me and scaffolds," Deacon said, "I have enough trouble going up in an airplane."

Fitzgerald took a K-ration fruit bar from the zipper pocket of his coveralls and tossed it to Deacon.

"Lots of iron," he said.

"Eatin all those raisins, he'll be super-tool," Zimmerman drawled.

Their voices died on the air, died on the packed damp earth underfoot, were ground beneath flying boots and incinerated by cigarettes. They became as quiet as the other crews, all reduced to muttering and mumbling. The ceiling of the vault seemed to be descending. A giant was needed who could hook his finger in the ring of the slab and lift it. Lazarus, come forth.

Instead, a major arrived, a real dandy in Class A uniform and receding hair. He mounted the platform and switched a rubber-tipped pointer. The room grew absolutely still, the faces turning toward him nearly relaxed, nearly dead, flickering only for the answer to a single question—Where? The major cut swatches from the air with his pointer. The men strained toward him. He opened his mouth and released a clear dry voice.

"Good morning, gentlemen. We have no pictures today. Headquarters is still studying the patterns of the Friedrichshafen run. Evidently the group flying left wing did not pull in tight enough. The drop was less than thirty percent on target." He tapped the pointer against his foot and let his eyes burn over the audience. "It was *this* group flying left wing. None of you are so new to all this that you do not understand the importance of a tight formation." He made a fist. "Only a concentrated drop will take out a target. Take it out and we won't have to go back." *You're not going* was in all the faces, *but we are—Where?* "Practice missions might be the answer."

Someone in the audience laughed shrilly, nearly maniacally. The major's stick thrust through it.

"When we have the planes," he said testily. "When we have the planes and the time this group will practice until it is as tight as a fist." He held up his hand with the fingers spread apart. "A blanket run is necessary today, an umbrella. There will be two wings going, eight groups. You will fly the tail-end box. One good effort will take it out."

The major made a gesture. Two men struggled to the platform with a frame from which they hung a white screen. The pointer whipped and the room went dark. A finger of light came from the rear, became a cone blue with smoke, became moistened by half-held breaths. It rested on the screen in a bright square, a blind pupil staring back at the crews. They waited for the wink of color. The projector clicked and an unfocused skein appeared, was quickly corrected to the clear image of a web, a net for someone out there. They recognized it, but they sat hoping that the major would give the projectionist acid instructions to show the *correct* map.

"The target for today is the refinery and main marshaling yard at Vienna. You will rendezvous with components of this wing at oh seven forty hours over San Severo. You will . . ."

They were no longer quiet. There was a hiss like a ripple of quicksilver. A volunteer was needed, someone who would wipe with one quick gesture the voice from the major and the tangle from the screen. No one moved, no one awakened to leave the major and his map to die in a dream. Deacon pressed against the wall. He ground after its narcotic until his neck ached, but a wall on an Italian plain was no proof against the twist of tracks, the interminable strings of cars, puffing engines, of Vienna. And there was no wall in the sky, nothing but free fall between the airplanes and the six hundred guns ringing the trainyard.

Vienna. Fee-enn-ah, on the curve of the Danube. The cosmopolitan refuge of sad-eyed poets, the Magyars' last castle where they played always a waltz tuned to regret. To an American mind it was strudel, languorous passion, the bittersweet overtones of Strauss. To the flying American eye *Wiener Blut* had become pieces of airplanes drifting through the thin blue sky.

The major rolled on in his voice of necessity, his pointer making neat emphases against the map. It was a pretty map, probably a good map, but all the arrows ran the wrong way.

16

They pointed north. The major was giving them one-way directions, telling them how to get there, how to be effective. They would be issued survival kits, but there was no one able to tell them how to survive.

Everyone understood that there had to be a mission. That was the name of the game—Fifty. Chip away at the iron number until nothing was left. Fly Fifty and go home. Someone in the States would try to knock them into shape and send them out again, but there were ways to turn ever so slightly and wind up always at the end of the line waiting for the boat. That was a problem to be faced when the time came. First there was the iron rule to break, the iron number. Fifty. One mission flown was one less to fly.

But Vienna . . . There wasn't any point in it. If they destroyed the yard and refinery, if they curled every piece of track, splintered every tie—impossible—it would not end the war. The Germans would simply have to reroute trains to the Eastern front until they developed another marshaling yard. Then *that* would have to be destroyed. The men were willing to risk a throw at Fifty, but none of them believed that an ultimate pass could be made over Vienna. There were far too many boxcars.

Deacon didn't listen to the major's instructions and exhortations. It was necessary for him only to get into the plane and be flown somewhere. He couldn't help the pilot or make certain the escort was efficient or dim the flak. Fighters were his only concern. If any enemy plane happened to come within the narrow traverse of his single weapon, he was to aim and pull the trigger. He had no other function.

The major concluded. Pilots had their course and rendezvous, bombardiers and navigators their checkpoints. The tanks had been filled, the bombs loaded, the throttles were hot. Nothing could save them except the weather. The weather officer tacked a plastic overlay on the map, a clear sheet filled with grease-pencil markings of curved arrows and cabalistic symbols. Weather magic would save them, a successful invocation to the rain god. Or clouds. If they found a ten/ten cover over the target they could fly as high as they cared to, hide behind altitude. They could dump right through the clouds, not caring what was smashed. They would be higher than Icarus, their wings riveted fast, so high that the fighters would not be able to spin their propellers in the thin air and the flak shells would fall back to earth like popgun corks. But the weather officer had no magic, no clouds. He thought he was being reassuring when he told them that one/ten or two/ten cover was the worst they'd have to put up with.

17

A communications lieutenant tied the last knot, established the day's frequencies for the radio operators. The screen went out, the lights went on, the American flag hung windless in the air and there was a glare on the polished surface of the group's escutcheon. It was over. There was no place to hide. Sick call was not permitted after the mission had been announced. There was nothing to do but file upstairs and pick up parachutes and other flight equipment. There was nowhere to go but to the airplanes.

The crew stood in bright sunlight and sweated under their burdens, chewed lips and sweated around their eyes as they waited for transportation to the ship.

"The old sausage run," Horton said.

"The bastards," Deacon said.

"Why blame the Krauts? They don't want to see us any more than we want to see them."

"I mean headquarters. That miserable bastardly Vienna again."

"It could have been Regensburg . . . or Ploesti."

"It could have been one of those lousy peanut factories in the Balkans, too. And how about sub pens? The goddamned submarines are still a menace, aren't they? We ought to go after those sub pens, Arnie. We've been up to Vienna what . . . ten, twelve times?"

"This is the fourth," Horton said.

"This air force must have made fifty passes there," Deacon said, "and they still can't take it out. What's the short order today—ten feet? Oxygen at a hundred feet?"

"Twelve thousand."

"That's not fair, Arnie."

"What're you hollerin about?" Cantori said. "I'm closer to them than you are."

"Why don't you go screw yourself, Caesar?"

"He's about the right position, scrunched over with his head between his legs," Zimmerman said. "Must surely be a hard life when he farts."

"Get the chaff out at the right time and it might blind the radar," Fitzgerald said.

"The radar? We'll be close enough to throw out tacks and blind the Krauts."

"I'd like to make a low run sometime and get in a little strafing," Quinn said.

"Too many movies, Kenny," Horton said. "You'll be keeping your uncle company sooner than you think."

"It's not sooner," Deacon said, "it's right now and right down the barrel. They'll keep doing this until the last guy goes down. Every day until they can't count anymore. You

18

know what happened? They wrote us off as soon as we shipped out."

"Bring me your ticket," Horton said, "and I'll give it an extra punch."

"They threw away our tickets."

"Come on, let's go."

And then, clicking off a time no longer theirs, they walked to the weapons carrier where the rest of the crew waited to be taken to the field where the bomber waited squatting on its mat, and where the sky, like a maw and bigger than the world, waited to receive them.

2.

THE MORNING was clear and beautiful, the air already too warm. Their ship—*Bawl, Buster*—stood at the revetment, shimmers of heat rising from the unpainted wing surfaces, while the chief line mechanic kicked at the tires with a crafty smile on his face, as though he were unloading a shoddy piece of merchandise. For eight days the plane had dared them. The sky had been pure and unruffled, cloud fronts negligible over the Alps and Balkans. The line crew had patched flak holes, corrected small malfunctions, and kept *Bawl, Buster* operative for eight consecutive days. During that period the bomb group had lost the use of sixteen aircraft.

Any straight run of missions was bad, too tight a pull on luck. Daring day to day was mean enough; but more than a long run, more than having to fly against a scale of percentages falling away from them, Deacon's crew and his squadron and his group, his wing and his whole air force were engaged in a great plan. They had been touched by the claw of a vital strategy. In May of 1944 a campaign had been instituted to destroy the petroleum and synthetic plants of the Reich. The Eighth Air Force in England was also involved, but most of the plants were beyond the range of the Eighth, and the English weather was spotty. The Fifteenth had the reach into Austria and the Balkans, the benefit of Italy's beautiful late spring.

The Oil Campaign was not the first stratagem which had caught at them. There was always someone sweating a grand design from a plotting board, inventing martial code names to emblazon on orders. The names of the campaigns were usually stunning, their success usually moderate. Costs were also moderate—terminal, but moderate. But when a great plan came out costs were discounted. It became all fang and snarl, them or us.

Groups suffered particularly heavy losses over individual targets from time to time, but only once before had the hammer descended on the entire air force. Someone had brainstormed the destruction of the Luftwaffe right at the source, the aircraft plants. The operation had been primarily the Eighth's, but the Fifteenth—then a brand-new air force—had participated. That campaign had come to be known as the Big Week, although it lasted only five days. The Big Week had cost the Eighth tremendously. Staggering into Germany from their new Italian bases and staggering back again, the Fifteenth hadn't lost nearly as many planes, but twenty-five percent of the baby air force had been destroyed during those five days.

The Big Week had been a dazzler. Raw power, the knockout punch. Someone had been wrong. The Germans interrupted their manufacturing for a short period, dispersed their plants, and went on at a more furious pace than before the raids. The Luftwaffe had since grown weaker only because it was eaten piecemeal on the wing as it met the over-all bombing offensive. There were sufficient planes but insufficient pilots.

And now the Oil Campaign. Plants were both concentrated and exposed. The Germans bunched their diminishing fighter strength in order to protect them. Fighters formed attack lines of twenty and thirty ships and cannonaded the bomber formations. Massive anti-aircraft batteries were installed around prime targets. Only men who had flown the Big Week had ever seen anything like it before.

And most of those men were dead or home. Their legend grew obsolescent, faded. Names like Ludwigshafen, Stuttgart and Augsburg no longer rang like iron. Now there were new names, places no one had ever dreamed existed. There had always been Ploesti, a graveyard since 1943. A final strike was always being organized to take Ploesti out. And Vienna was a standard choice when the planners couldn't squeeze out a new vision—dump it on the airfields and engine works and refineries, collapse the model-train layout. But who had ever heard of Brasov, Moinesti, Odertal, Pitesti? Who ever supposed that anyone but gypsies lived in Budapest, Pecs, Bratislava?

It would hasten the end, they were told, it would get them

all home sooner. The flight crews weren't interested. If it hadn't been for great plans, campaigns, if it hadn't been for fighters and flak and mechanical failures, the flight crews wouldn't have had to splinter their nails trying to hang in the air for fifty days. Their war wouldn't have lasted more than two months.

The B-24 was a rugged airplane. It was no graceful flyaway, but it carried more bombs than anything else then in service in Europe. The body was clumsy, the wings thin, the engines underslung. Twin rudders gave it an overbalanced look. It was a mean-looking ship studded with ten guns, two in each turret and one at each waist window.

The bombardier checked *Bawl, Buster*'s load, the crew the ammunition belts. No one had forgotten anything, given them an excuse to stand down. The gunners stood in the shadow of the tail while Fitzgerald and the pilot went over the line chief's checklist. He was anxious to hand over the bird. In the control tower were men with anxious watches, one with a finger itchy to trigger the take-off flare. Everyone was eager to get the group into the air, to get the vagrants out of town.

"What's this," Deacon said, "thirty-one?"

He knew. They all knew. They were bright enough to subtract and add by ones. Whether they figured their contract by the missions they had put in or by those they had yet to make, they all carried a number in their heads.

"Thirty-two," Horton said. "You lost that one on sick call."

"You mean when they shot Levine out of the ball? I didn't lose anything."

"You got to straighten out," Cantori mumbled toward the ground.

"Jesus good Christ, Caesar."

"I only got six to go." He looked up at Deacon. "I'd kill you before I'd let you fuck me up."

"What've you got, a real hard-on this morning? Go fly your six. Rent a Piper Cub or something. Why should you be so nervous? Quinn's got another forty to sweat."

"Thirty-nine after today," Quinn said.

"Look at that boy, Caesar. He's not sweating. What kind of goddamned example are you giving the recruits?"

"Hump's the only thing worth sweatin over," Zimmerman said.

"Why don't you get laid, Caesar? Don't tell me; you're too ugly, you take too many ugly pills."

"You oughta be turned in to the Flight Surgeon," Cantori said.

"I'd turn myself in if I thought I could do any good. You don't think he'd give an experienced man like me a stand-down? I understand they're so short of crews they're trying to recruit them from the Kraut POWs."

"Somebody oughta just break your arm some night," Cantori said. "I wouldn't be surprised if you got a kneecap shot off or something."

"You goddamned replacement," Deacon said, "you don't even belong on this crew. Don't listen to him, Quinn, it's a cinch. Making thirty-nine more is like walking on air."

Deacon clapped his hands together and doubled over, as though struck by a joke. His bend became more and more acute until finally he fell. Not collapsing, but simply so contorted that he could no longer stand, he fell softly to the mat and lay like a dead caterpillar, like a curled fetus.

"It wasn't that funny," Horton said.

Deacon stretched out in the cool shadow of the tail. He was sweating. A flare went up from the control tower. Energizers whined, engines exploded. Deacon got to his hands and knees, a pulse pounding behind his ear. The navigator called time.

Once there had been one crew, one ship. They trained on the flat Midwestern plains, in untroubled skies, dropped dummy bombs and made long transitional flights. They beered it up in Lincoln, Kansas City, Cheyenne, sported coin-silver wings and corporal's stripes. One crew, forging an arrow, men and machine a single instrument to be brought to the war.

The airplane was taken away. They were jammed into bucket seats along with other crews and flown across the ocean in a C-47. They were not surprised to touch down in England. Everyone knew that it was one huge airfield, that the Eighth was winning the war, that flight pay bought a lot of action in Piccadilly. The Quonset huts were bearable, the beer strong, everyone spoke the same language. That was what the war was all about—off to a day's work, then home at five to pipe and slippers. But the Eighth was primarily a B-17 air force. The ship the crew had been trained for was being flown from Italy. Someone arranged to have waiting an airplane they could fly.

Jerry Juicer had made sixty-three missions, too many. They knew it would never take them through their tour, knew that no ship could last one hundred and thirteen missions. *Jerry Juicer* was a relic, bald spots showing through its olive-drab paint, flak patches creating crazy checkerboard patterns on the wings and empennage. It was sure to die, to take them with it. They needed a brand-new airplane, a new average to work against, new luck.

The crew took the ship up to get used to it. The pilot found the controls sluggish, the number-four engine touchy. He wanted the ship worked on, wanted an instrument fit for combat. They were put on a mission alert their second day at the field; if *Jerry Juicer* could get off the ground, it was fit enough. It took them through four missions, through a seven-hundred-plane raid on Ploesti where ships much newer glittered all the more for being torn into fragments.

Jerry Juicer was breached over Toulon. Flak shattered the nose section, cleared away the co-pilot and bombardier. It took a skilled nurse, a determined hand, to get them back. They put down at Foggia, left the ancient bird to be towed to the junkpile where it would be cannibalized and made a part of other ships. The crew was taken by truck sixty twisting miles to their own field, had their first real look at Italy: barren roads, sodden orchards, the dismal towns of Apulia. They crossed the Ofanto on a pontoon bridge stretched next to a string of bombed-out arches, came home just as the uncertain sun faded, came home to the strange corroded gullies, the bleached stones, of Basilicata, the sky turned a red deeper than that on the splotched walls of *Jerry Juicer*.

The crew got their new luck, their new airplane. Shining silver, it was christened *Peaches,* the name running beneath the figure of a flamboyant nude with fuzzy breasts. Their replacement bombardier was a recruit, their co-pilot a seedy-looking second lieutenant with twelve missions. Both were outsiders. Although their number had been diminished, there was still a single crew.

Peaches seemed to be a lucky ship—for everyone but the ball gunner. He was blown out over Salon. Caesar Cantori joined them, another veteran from a broken crew, already twenty-one missions up the ladder. *Peaches* lucked them right through a Bucharest raid where the crazy Luftwaffe put up an effort so intense they attacked the bombers over the target, braving their own flak, salvoing into the bunched formations. The enemy fighters quit only when they were out of ammunition, low on gas. *Peaches* came through it with no more than a few small holes, but the radio operator went on sick call for the next nine consecutive mornings. He was finally removed from flight duty. Zimmerman, who had been flying as a temporary replacement, became a fixture.

The original crew was down to a slim six, but they still had something of that old stateside hang-together. With their fatalities already thirty percent, they were approaching the point where the averages would begin to work for the survivors. The furious Oil Campaign kinked the graph slightly; it figured that one, maybe two, more would have to go the long way before percentages swung solidly in favor of the rest. Tough on the losers, but you couldn't have winners without them.

They lost another charter member, but it didn't count on the scale. On a raid over Vienna the sky seemed to come apart and most of the controls were shot out. Both Horton and the pilot were wounded, the pilot stiff and bleeding at the wheel as he wrestled and coaxed the ship, a piece of Swiss cheese hanging on shredded propellers. It was a marvelous performance, took them all the way home. They fell into each other's arms, a lucky crew after all. Horton and the pilot compared wounds. Both showed more blood than hurt.

Both healed during a long stand-down when the weather collapsed, but the pilot seemed to have trouble with his arm. There seemed to be a pain he couldn't bear, something in the eyes of the crew he couldn't look at. He was unable to salute the colonel who pinned the Distinguished Flying Cross on him. The pilot couldn't even wave goodbye from the back of the truck which started him on the long haul back to the States.

The seedy shavetail became a first lieutenant and the airplane commander. They got a co-pilot from a broken crew. The tail gunner came down with malaria just as the weather broke. Quinn joined them fresh from the replacement pool. They were given *Bawl, Buster*. The ship had made eleven runs, a good safe number. It had enough in it to take them through their tour.

But now they had been up seven straight days without incident and *Bawl, Buster* was daring them for the eighth. And now they were no longer a crew, or lucky. Only the navigator was left of the original officers, of the gunners only Deacon and Horton and Fitzgerald. The men of *Bawl, Buster* were sweating out individual tours, each deep in his own net of Fifty. They were strangers, riding strange airplanes. Each thumbed blindly for the catch of his own release, had his own magic number.

From the point of the navigator's calling "Time," it was like a tired old legend which aged them with each telling. The men checked in from their separate stations. The bomb-bay doors ground shut, there was a kick and sputter as each engine caught, a series of roaring pebble and dust gales while they were run up. The line chief looked relieved when the pilot made an approving sign from the cockpit. Chocks were kicked away, brakes squealed as the ship took its place in the column lurching along the taxi strip.

Bawl, Buster was among the last to go up. The crew watched for the older ships to clear the runway, concentrated on the few airplanes which had thirty and forty sticks of bombs painted along the nose. Each was an omen, talisman, proof that it could be done. *Showboat*, the group's veteran ship, had flown seventy-five missions. It was good luck for all of them.

The bombers did not float gracefully into the air. At the head of the runway throttles were jammed to the firewall, engines tested as far as possible short of actual flight. And then —the twin rudders slewing, bobbing—the brakes were sprung and the ship roared forward, trying to eat at the landing mat, pushed to maximum power. As *Bawl, Buster* came abreast of the mid-point control tower the men aboard stood on tiptoe, strained to raise the ship. It wobbled and fluttered, lifted, threatened to set down again. And then it cleared the runway, climbed slowly. A tale told many too many times.

They took position in the formation gradually assembling, charged and cleared the guns. The last airplane swung in, flight leaders verified their positions, and the group headed northwest. The land below was cut into monotoned wheat fields, dusty orchards, shot through with streaks of gray rock. From the air the bleached towns looked like piles of bone. Another bomb group flew past at a tangent, heading out toward the Balkans. There was no dipping of colors, waggling of wings. The two formations were running on different clocks, on different roads, and had nothing in common.

The men in the aft section of *Bawl, Buster* smoked and drank coffee. Quinn kept radio watch. The others sprawled on the floor and shouted at each other to make themselves heard over the noise of the engines.

"I don't mind the tail-end box," Cantori said. "They been going after the lead formations."

"With all those flak suits you stick in that ball you shouldn't mind anything," Deacon said. "Can you *see* down there, Caesar? You must think you're Al Capone riding in a bulletproof car."

"It don't bother me if you want to be a hero. I had a port gunner didn't want to be bothered putting on a vest. He got caught by a piece of flak as big as my fingernail. I swear to Christ it was no bigger than the nail on my pinkie. Got him in the back and tore his lungs."

"They jumped the middle group on that Bucharest run," Horton said.

"I'd like to thank you for your good wishes, Caesar," Deacon said.

"So wear your suit if you're worried."

"But by the time we make our run they'll have the range cinched," Quinn said.

"It don't matter," Cantori said.

"They throw up everything, Kenny," Horton said. "They bracket five hundred, maybe a thousand feet. I mean, we can't keep formation in all that shit anyway. The Krauts might as well load and fire with their eyes closed."

"Just keep an eye out for the one with your name on it," Deacon said. "The bratwurst isn't bad, but the schnitzel is terrible. What I really hate is the liver dumplings. They're loading meatballs for you, meatball," he said to Cantori.

"Come on, you gonna use your vest or not?"

"I don't know."

"For Christ sake, Deacon, if you're gonna let it lay around, let me have it. My ass is hanging outside this lousy bird."

"What the hell do you think this is, armor plate?" Deacon pounded on the floor. "It's about a quarter inch aluminum."

"You gonna use it or not?"

"I'll let you know."

Cantori gathered the unused flak suits and began lining his ball turret with them.

"You're the biggest prick I ever met in my life," Cantori said. "Why don't you put in for the rest camp until I finish up? That's what you need. I'll give you fifty dollars to get yourself laid. For fifty dollars I could probably get somebody to shoot you in the nuts. I'd like that better."

"Al Capone," Deacon said.

"Are you going to wear the suit?" Horton asked.

"Maybe. Don't tell me you're getting worried about it, too?"

"Maybe."

"This buddy system is something new. You better go down there with him and hold his hand. Caesar, check me when we come off the run; I'll let you know whether I need the vest or not."

"I hope they get you, Deacon, with all my fucking heart."

"I'll kill you if you don't knock that off."

"Pingo," Horton said.

"Shut up, you bastard."

"Forget it," Cantori said, "he's ready for Section Eight."

He climbed into the ball and began arranging the flak suits to conform to his body. Quinn twiddled the dials on the aft radio.

"You won't wear it," Horton said.

"It's mine, it's mine. I'll throw it out the window if I want to. Jesus, Arnie, for Jesus sake."

Circling above San Severo were some forty ships belonging to their wing. The two groups meshed, flew toward the Adriatic.

3.

WITHIN THE corridor of the sea there was no flak, and no fighters to range after them. The men were safe for an hour. They dozed. Deacon sipped coffee and looked at the passing sky through a skein of cigarette smoke. More than passing, the sky turned like an endless wheel. There was nothing to mark their progress against because there were no clouds, no sounds of passage, everything outside drowned by the racket of the ship's engines. The rest of the formation was suspended in blue air burned pale by the sun, only the occasional flash of propellers an indication that there was any thrust or push other than from the invisible streams of wind. They were indeed vagrants, not flying but flown, tramps traveling the infinite sky from one unmarked point to another. *Bawl, Buster* droned on, toward and away from nothing. It was nearly soothing, nearly like hanging somewhere outside of time. Only Vienna waited, an incident they could not avoid.

Quinn tapped his headphones and called out. The fighter escort was making its rendezvous. Several squadrons of P-51s arrived, rising soundlessly through the sky as though drawn by a tremendous updraft, slipping and gliding in slow motion like shapes thrown against a blue screen by a projector geared to its lowest speed. They fanned out above the bombers.

Quinn held his headset with one hand, his throat mike with the other. He spoke, jerked a thumb. *Bawl, Buster* began a nearly imperceptible climb. Deacon and Horton went on oxygen. Cantori stuffed himself into the ball, arranged the flak suits in a mantle. He closed the hatch and the turret descended with a whir. Quinn settled into the rear, slammed the armored doors behind him. Now Deacon and Horton were alone in the waist, each at a single window gun.

Still climbing, the formation turned northeast, left the protection of the sea and crossed the Julian Alps. A few token puffs of flak appeared over Klagenfurt. From the nose Fitzgerald relayed instructions over the interphone. Chaff time. Horton and Deacon took out their window panels. Icy air thundered in on the engines' roar. They threw out bundles of chaff—metallic strips like jackstraws which were supposed to confuse the enemy radar. It poured from waist windows all around them, drifted below like a net of protective tinsel and then fell behind. Radar was no factor, the sky was absolutely clear.

The bombers swung around the heavily defended rail junction at Graz. The earphones were busy now, the bombardier making his plot. Ships jerked and wobbled as they pulled closer together. More concentrated flak appeared as Wiener Neustadt was skirted. The fighter escort veered off, headed toward the point where the bombers would exit from the target run. Far ahead Deacon could see the tiny ships of the lead formation hanging stiffly in the sky, Vienna rushing toward them as though the earth's roll had been accelerated.

The first squadron entered on the target, toggled, flew past. Among the ships of the second squadron there was a flare which seemed no bigger than that of a match. Specks of airplane drifted to the earth. *Bawl, Buster* was twelve miles away, coming on at three miles a minute. Bombs fell gracefully. The first squadron's salvo hit, opening a neat string of earth flowers with yellow centers. Flak shells rose like bubbles from a lake, too many, too fast. A ship slipped down in shuddering lurches, like a diseased leaf. *Bawl, Buster* ceased evasive action and came under the bombardier's rigid hand. They drove in flat over the target, the earphones quiet except for grunts and whispers as the men sweated and swore, pleaded for the bombardier to toggle. There was another flash, no longer the size of a match, as an entire wing fell off a ship. The target was obscured by smoke, the sky dim, filled with gray streamers, exploding black puffballs. Five miniature figures danced downward not far from *Bawl, Buster*. Deacon saw four parachutes open. There was a crackling blast overhead. Spent fragments rattled against the fuselage.

Deacon choked in his oxygen mask, nearly sick, and clutched at his chute harness. Something exploded beneath them. *Bawl, Buster* rocked. Deacon closed his eyes. There was a jerk as the bombardier salvoed, the ship rising at the release of the load but not fast enough, high enough, to get out of the field of flak. They banked clumsily, moved toward the city's edge. Deacon looked over at Horton, only the eyes of both men showing between helmet and mask. Horton was

28

blinking rapidly. He caught Deacon's gaze, clenched his hands together in a victory sign and began to raise them.

Just as Horton was lifting his hands above his head a flash came, white enough to sear the eyes, then red, then dancing black. Deacon held onto his harness, was lifted and slammed against the side of the ship. Metal screeched through the aft section. Deacon put his hands over his face. The ship leveled and the sound of flak bursts diminished. Deacon peeked through his gloves, through what appeared to be a film of red cellophane. He could see nothing. There were several voices on the earphones, one squealing. A hand shook him. Quinn appeared, his face and figure pink. His earphone plug was disconnected.

The voices in Deacon's ears gabbled furiously. Quinn was shouting unintelligibly into his own oxygen mask. Deacon made a gesture with his hand. The glove was smeared red. He looked at it, saw it come near his face and felt one finger tap against his headset. He tried to speak. His mouth was filled with a salty fluid. He pushed aside the oxygen mask and spat blood. Quinn was no longer pink, his face now bleached against the dark flying suit. Deacon tapped his headset again.

Quinn nodded, plugged in. Deacon looked at his glove, already changing color, becoming glacé in the frozen air. Quinn was chattering, his hand in a strangling grip around the throat mike. The hatch to the bomb bay opened and Clark, the navigator, struggled in. He edged around the ball turret mechanism, staggered against it, closed his eyes, then knelt next to Deacon. There was the drone of engines, a piercing whistle through the aft section, but there were no longer any flak explosions.

"Are you all right, Deacon? Are you all right?"

Because Clark shouted, his words came through the earphones blurred. All the other voices went off the line except for one which continued to moan and squeal. Deacon recognized Cantori.

"Okay, okay," he croaked.

"Are you hit?"

Deacon held out his smeared gloves as though pleading. Clark touched his face.

"Your nose is bleeding," he said. "His nose is bleeding," he repeated into his mike. "Anything else? Can you stand up?"

Deacon pulled himself to his feet, dizzied, clung to a stanchion near the window and stood in a pillar of cold air for a moment. Both Clark's and Quinn's eyes were anxious. Deacon nodded. Clark patted him on the shoulder and turned away.

There was a hole in the shape of a rough figure eight mid-

29

way between the starboard waist window and the ball turret, its ragged edges curled inward. There was another, smaller, hole in the roof. Horton was lying on his stomach with his arms beneath him. The fleecy collar of his flying jacket was spattered pink, but there was no head. There were pink and gray clots around the window. Three teeth clutched by a piece of jawbone lay on the catwalk. Deacon clung to the stanchion and spit blood, phlegm and coffee into the slipstream.

Cantori was still babbling. He was hit in the leg and the ball mechanism wouldn't function.

"Crank it up, crank it up," he pleaded.

"Do you need a hand?" Fitzgerald asked from the nose.

"Stay in your turret," the pilot ordered. "Can you get it up, Clark?"

"Sure you can," Cantori said. "Get the crank."

Their voices were thin, scratchy, cast along wires running through the sky.

"Okay," Clark said into the phones. He looked at the flak holes. "No serious damage. One of the hydraulic lines must be cut."

"Pressure's good," the co-pilot said.

"Controls clear," the pilot said. "How about stations?"

"Tail and port okay." He paused. "Starboard negative."

"For Christ sake, help me," Cantori squealed.

They took the crank from its clip and placed it in the socket of the ball's manual gear. At Clark's signal all three men strained. The ball moved a fraction, then froze. They heaved again, feet nearly in the air, the ship in the air, Cantori hanging below it. Drops fell from Deacon's nose, bile rose to his mouth. The crank wouldn't budge.

"It's jammed," Clark said. "Cantori, how bad are you?"

"My leg's bleeding but I can move it. Try again."

"It's no use," Quinn said, "something must have happened to the gears."

"I'll freeze down here."

"We'll be letting down soon," the pilot broke in. "It'll warm up a little."

"Try to get a strap around the outside of your leg," Clark said. "The fleece ought to work like a compress. Shoot in some morphine."

"Negative," the pilot said. "Cantori, do you hear me? Negative. I need that ball another forty-five minutes. Can you hang on?"

There was no reply.

"Can he traverse?" the co-pilot asked.

The ball machinery clicked, whirred, but the turret didn't move.

"I'm hung up at nine o'clock," Cantori said. "Isn't there some way to get me up?"

"It's better than nothing," the pilot said. "Cantori, we need another forty-five minutes. We'll be blind underneath. At this altitude the wound's going to congeal fast. It might even get numb."

Clark and Deacon looked at each other briefly. Having spent a long time in the States training together, a whole lifetime flying in Italy, they were still unable to do any better than skid their eyes past at the thought not of Cantori's leg but of all Cantori turning numb.

"Cantori?" the pilot called.

"Yeah, Lieutenant. Okay, I'll try it."

"Clark, take that starboard station. Now let's simmer down. We're in good shape and we've still got a formation and we're getting this bird home. Keep the pipe clear. Cantori, give a yell if you need anything."

Deacon smiled sourly into his mask. Only a frigid angel would have been able to reach the ball gunner with anything he needed. Deacon poured coffee into his cup, gagged, kept it down. The heel of Horton's boot had been split by a flak fragment. Deacon removed a glove and placed the jawbone and teeth on Horton's body. They were cold and slimy, like gristle. Clark bit his lips, wrestled out a tarpaulin and covered Horton. The wind continued to pipe through the aft section. There was a puddle of red hydraulic fluid beneath the catwalk.

They droned on. Clouds appeared intermittently below. Deacon strained for a sight of Graz, Klagenfurt. The ships had made an attempt to regroup but they were badly strung out. A bomber with an elevator in shreds mushed along on their port side. The four-ship box above them seemed intact. Another beyond that had two airplanes with dead propellers hung at mad angles. Through a break in the clouds Deacon saw the gray splotch of a large city to the west. He pointed it out to Clark. The navigator removed his face mask and shouted into Deacon's ear.

"Zagreb." Deacon frowned. "We're going straight down, too many cripples," the navigator said. "Can't hit the slot at Monfalcone. Too long."

Deacon gestured at the ball turret.

"He's got another hour. Won't be out of Yugoslavia for another hour."

"Banja Luka," Deacon shouted.

There was a fighter field at Banja Luka. Clark shrugged.

"How long?" Cantori called through the phones. No one answered. "Hey," he said, "hey. Am I plugged in?"

"Hang on," the pilot said.

"My leg ain't getting numb. How much longer?"

"Not much."

"I didn't make Klagenfurt yet. Are we by it?"

"Won't be long," the pilot said. "Hang on."

It *was* long, Yugoslavia unrolling piecemeal below. They sneaked past Banja Luka, but still weren't able to put down because of the crests in the Dinaric Alps. All the earphones became filled with the sound of Cantori making spasmodic whimpering noises. Deacon unplugged his headset. He thought about nothing, particularly did not think why they were struggling to get back, what point there would be in trying to sleep that night when morning would only shoot them out once again after the brass ring of a declining number.

The wind whistling through the ship wasn't as forceful as that which had taken Horton, slashed Cantori. If it had been wind, if there had been a gale in the exploding puffball, the wrenching of metal. The fist came out and selected without plan, squeezed without rancor. Ships died because they were ugly copies of birds. The fist swept all imitations as it raked the skies. Eyes gouged, metallic feathers plucked, wings broken—the ships died. Men disappeared, came back only after they had been clouded by memory's discolored shadow. Flight without sound, war between machines. The enemy was hidden by the mountain creases below. The enemy might be flying wicked sticks in pursusit. Deacon smoked and thought about nothing.

Bawl, Buster peaked the Alps, trundled toward the coast. They could swoosh down the slopes of the mountains, glide over the curve of the sea. Billows in the Adriatic would see them home, each wavelet backlighted by the fire of the declining sun. They let down, propellers chewing fiercely as they lunged toward the safety of the blue plain.

Clark became agitated, his eyes crinkling, his hand circling the throat mike. Deacon fumbled with the interphone plug, but his hand became arrested when he saw what should not have been there. Hairlines, weak crosses, about two dozen moving in from the east. There were no enemy fields that close to the coast. The formation should have been beyond the range of fighters. Deacon dropped the intercom plug and gripped the handles of his gun. The fighters broke into four groups, then rose in a steep climb, dove toward the center of each of the tail-end boxes. Lines of white fire screwed up toward them. Clark's gun hammered. There were deeper thumps from the fighters' cannon as they passed through the formations. The bombers held steady.

Deacon watched the FW-190s make a graceful tight turn below, and then come on in a diagonal run, climbing rapidly, arriving instantly. Quinn's gun went off, Deacon's swept back and forth. Slugs ripped through the aft section. A spurt of hydraulic fluid blinded him. There was an explosion. Deacon felt the blast of heat and air. He screamed. *Bawl, Buster* shuddered and bucked. Deacon wiped at his eyes, saw a trail of smoke and a flutter of debris drifting behind them.

The box on their right came under attack. A Focke-Wulf exploded. Another flamed, cartwheeled into a bomber, both going up in a fireball which rolled across the sky and nearly engulfed another ship. The flight which had attacked Deacon's formation came on again, only four now, the P-51 escort buzzing after them. Engines went at full snarl, cannon popped, machine guns hammered. *Bawl, Buster* was not hit. A Focke-Wulf climbed straight up, hung momentarily on a dead propeller while a P-51 poured after it. The German's canopy disintegrated, his cowling flew apart. The plane fell over on its back. The remaining fighters regrouped and headed east as the bomber escort clawed at stragglers.

A bomber off *Bawl, Buster*'s wing began losing altitude. Two engines had stopped, the propellers windmilling slowly. It slipped off on one wing and went into a skidding dive. Figures boiled from the hatches. Deacon counted four chutes.

He was trembling, his face covered with hydraulic fluid, his underwear soaked with sweat. *Bawl, Buster* had come down below oxygen altitude. Deacon tore away his soggy mask. The ship sputtered, vibrated, as the number-three engine alternately choked and ran away. Clark had removed his mask. He stood breathing deeply, nearly panting. There were new holes in the aft section, none serious. The puddle of hydraulic fluid was larger. An electrical conduit had been severed but there was no sparking. Deacon plugged in his phones. They were dead. He tapped his headset, heard only his own finger.

Quinn burst grinning from the tail turret. "I got one, I got one," he shouted. "You see it? I got one."

"The pipe's dead," Deacon said.

"I know," Clark answered.

Wind moaned and whistled through the holes. The canvas covering Horton snapped back, exposing his feet. Deacon sucked air through an open mouth, his nose sore and clogged.

"You saw it, Deke," Quinn said. "He must have gone off practically outside your window."

"You nearly killed me, you stupid bastard," Deacon screamed.

"Me, *me?* It was the Kraut. He would've killed you."

"How about Cantori?" Clark asked. "I didn't hear him firing."

They pounded on the ball, shouted. There was no response.

"Maybe he used the morphine," Deacon said.

"I don't think he caught anything," Quinn said.

"He's been down there an hour and a half," Clark said.

The navigator looked out the window. There was no longer any pretense of a formation, each plane limping home on its own. They were skipping over the Yugoslav islands, the coast of the mainland only a blur. No fighters would ever follow them out that far.

"I'd better go forward," Clark said.

"You'll tell them, won't you, Lieutenant?" Quinn asked. "You'll confirm I got one?"

Clark opened the bomb-bay hatch and was nearly catapulted backward by a blast of wild air. One of the bay doors had been blown off. The catwalk was exposed on one side, a ladder extending horizontally through space. Clark braced himself and struggled into the bay, closed the hatch behind him.

The bad engine spun completely out of control, wrenched the plane over on one wing. The engine mount sagged and the propeller flew into fragments. There was a huge puff of oily smoke, but no fire. The engine hung dead and crooked in the sprung nacelle.

Deacon and Quinn clung to stanchions. The ship leveled, held altitude. Small soft clouds had appeared. The sky was once more serene, raked clean of debris and hacking lead and parachutes. An echelon of specks marked the fighter escort heading back to base. The string of bombers stretched far ahead. *Bawl, Buster* wobbled and pitched, droned on.

"We ought to turn back," Deacon shouted. "We ought to put down in Yugo." Internment, some crowded *stalag* on lean rations, but the peaceful sun bound to rise someday.

"Should make Manfredonia another half hour or so," Quinn said.

"Suppose we have to ditch?" Quinn shrugged. "We'd never get the boats out. This goddamned leaky bird would never float long enough."

"Caesar'd drown," Quinn said.

Cantori frozen to death, bled to death, shot to death; what harm could drowning do?

"Where's that goddamned Clark?" Deacon asked.

"Maybe he had to make a plot."

34

"Even those boobs in the cockpit know they only have to point the nose due south. You'd better go up forward. Tell them we ought to turn back to Yugo."

Quinn bit his lips.

"Now that's a direct order," Deacon said. "Tell them we'll never make it across."

Quinn opened the bomb-bay hatch, struggled against the slipstream. The pure blue of the Adriatic flowed below. He looked back. Deacon waved him on. After Quinn had gone he slumped to the floor. The smell of hydraulic fluid was very sharp. Three engines drummed an uneven background. Deacon's eyes were heavy. He closed them and fell into a nightmare unconsciousness which was nothing like sleep.

Quinn had to shake him several times. Deacon, staring numbly from behind a half-veil of vicious coruscations, looked intently at Quinn's face for a moment. The lips were nibbled and the eyes red with windburn and there were the beginnings of creases no nineteen-year-old should have had.

"Oh, boy," Quinn said, "I thought something happened to you."

"They going back?"

"He's going to bring it in. The trim's holding and there's enough gas." Quinn twitched his shoulders. "Brake pressure's gone. We're going to have to use the chutes."

"That dumb trick out the window? Don't be stupid, it'll never work. We ought to come in close and ditch."

"Caesar'd drown."

"Fuck Caesar, he's dead."

"Zimmerman's hurt. They caught a shell in the nose. The bombardier bought it."

"Oh Jesus, Kenny, holy Jesus."

"We're going to have to do it by ourselves, Deke. They're both wrestling the wheel and Fitz is at the gauges. The chutes ought to work. We did it once in gunnery school."

"Shit on you and gunnery school. That airplane you got didn't do us any good. You'll be some big wheel when they paint that swastika on the box they ship you home in. Holy Jesus, Kenny, couldn't Fitz and Clark help? How are we going to get the chutes out?"

"Fitz can't leave the cockpit, he has to back them up." Quinn looked around the aft section. "Did Clark come back here?"

"Clark's up front, you dumb ass."

"No he's not. He never got there."

They looked blankly at each other for a moment, but then their eyes turned hot and they looked away again. Clark in clumsy boots on the catwalk, the tearing wind, the ship's lurch when the number-three engine had tried to wrench loose.

"Did he have his chute on?" Deacon asked.

"I don't know. I think he had on his Mae West."

"Nobody saw anything?"

"No."

"Well," Deacon said, "well, well. Do you think he was holding his nose when he hit the water, Kenny?"

He grinned fiercely at Quinn. The other looked sick. Deacon tried to force a laugh from behind his clenched teeth, but prisms of water sprang into his eyes instead.

"We have to do it ourselves," Quinn said.

Tears ran down Deacon's cheeks. He sat with his hands in his lap, choking.

"Somebody's got to do it. I'll have to get Fitz, then. Deke, there're only five of us."

Five out of ten. Five left from the sixteen men Deacon had flown with since his tour began. The numbers were finally working for him, the averages shifting in his favor. There was only so much dirty luck; he'd reached his capacity. Fitzgerald and he would be able to walk through the rest of the tour.

"Deke," Quinn said.

"Go screw yourself, Kenny." Deacon wiped tears into his oily cheeks. "I'll never fly with you again. You've got too far to go. Find yourself another crew, buddy. Fitz and I are going to stick together from now on."

"Come on, Deke, I don't want to make two more trips through that bomb bay. Come on."

"Never mind." Deacon got to his feet and removed his parachute. "Show me how you did things by the numbers in that lousy gunnery school."

Each buckled his chute to a gun stanchion. They passed over the Italian coast. Manfredonia, then Foggia slipped by. Deacon recognized a white town hanging on a hill. They approached the Ofanto.

"We have to touch first," Quinn said. "We have to touch and be rolling. And then on the word we let go."

"You give it."

"Okay, but we have to go together. Okay, Deke? When I say, we get the pilots out the window."

They pulled the rip cords and dug out the pilot chutes, careful to keep them out of the wind. The complex of runways centering on Spinazzola came into view, then their own fields, precise with geometric detail of runway and revetment and tent. A colored flare arched from *Bawl, Buster*'s cockpit. The emergency trucks were still parked at the control tower although the rest of the group seemed to have landed. The ship turned sloppily and began the descent. Deacon's hands were white around the shroud lines.

Bawl, Buster seemed to come in very fast. The ground rushed up and tore at the wheels. They bounced. Deacon gritted his teeth and waited for a tire to blow. They touched again, began to roll. Quinn yelled. Both men threw their pilot chutes into the slipstream. They blossomed, pulled the main chutes after them. Quinn's caught first. The ship jerked, then righted as Deacon's chute opened.

He could see daylight through one panel, a ragged hole torn by flak. Daylight as big as his fist, then a triangular strip as the panel blew out, then half the sky as the chute tore straight across. The ship swerved sharply, tore off the starboard wheel strut. They smashed down on one wing, crumpled it like tinfoil, snapped the nose wheel and swung around in a mean arc. The tail came down, flattening the ball turret. A thin stream of blood bubbled from the hatch. A montage of sky and wrinkled aluminum danced before Deacon's eyes. His mouth was strained open, but it was the metal which screamed. He bounced against the extended shroud lines, was caught for a moment, then went hurtling out the window and rolled across the slick mat, its steel blue alternating with the blue overhead. There was a final grating screech and then a heavy silence.

The control-tower disaster horn went off, then came thinner wails from the ambulance and fire engine, the noise growing as they sped down the runway. Deacon got to his feet, fell down as his right leg twisted under him. His mouth filled with dust. He gagged, got up and hobbled toward the ship, barely moving, his hands paddling the air as sirens screamed in his ear and a line of rushing figures crossed diagonally toward him. Their mouths were open, their eyes popping as they ran silently on the pulsating waves. A hand clutching at him. He twisted away, jerked himself onto the shattered wing and clambered toward the escape hatch.

Fitzgerald filled the space, caught by the door which had crushed his chest. The pilot's bare head lolled through the splintered cockpit window, the glass having bitten into his skull. A fan of red washed over the yellow bomb sticks painted beneath the window. The co-pilot hung transfixed by part of the steering wheel. Deacon saw his hand twitch, then grow still. Inside the ship, sprung ribs and spars crossed like spears. Someone lay crumpled in the gloom.

A number of hands pulled him from the window and forced him to the ground. While drops plopped from his nose he sat on the runway and watched the tattered leg of his flying suit being torn off. A long filthy scrape oozed blood. The disaster horn stopped, the sirens whined dead. Faces appeared, excited voices. Someone shook his shoulder. Deacon flailed at him, absently began cleaning the bruise with fingers moistened in his mouth. Rough hands gripped him under the armpits and lifted him into an Operations jeep.

The landing mat bounced before Deacon's eyes, then the taxi strip, then the sandy ridge as they shifted gears, climbed. At a turn in the road he looked down on the field, saw a crew of mechanics attaching a tow bar to the ship, saw four dark shapes lined up in a row at the edge of the mat.

There was a stretcher waiting at the field hospital. Deacon struggled, tripped over it and fell, then got to his feet and limped into the tent. He was forced to a table, his flying clothes stripped away. A doctor pushed and probed. Deacon grunted. His bruise was washed with stinging green soap and merthiolate, the crusted blood swabbed from his nose and lips. The doctor extended a hypodermic. Deacon flung his hand out, sent the needle squirting through the air.

"Interrogation," he said. "Interrogation first."

"Lie still."

"It's important. I'm all right." He sat up. "I'm not hurt, I just want to go to interrogation."

"Lie down and rest for a little while."

The medics gripped Deacon's arms. He looked over the doctor's shoulder, saw the face of an officer from Group headquarters.

"Captain," he said, "I should see the colonel. I'm all right."

The doctor paused while fitting another hypo. He looked at the captain.

"He seems to be all right," the doctor said, "but he should have a sedative."

"It's important," Deacon said.

"Maybe it is," the captain said.

The doctor shrugged. Deacon hopped off the table and stood in his underwear. They gave him his boots and a maroon bathrobe. The captain drove him to Group headquarters. There was a buzz when they passed through the orderly room. Lieutenant Colonel Passerant waited, a young man with tired lines cut into his face.

Passerant indicated a generous shot of American whiskey. Deacon shook his head. The colonel pointed at a chair and Deacon sat, the captain hovering in the background.

"I wouldn't have believed it," the colonel said.

Deacon took a cigarette from the desk. Instead of lighting it, he sat shredding the paper and tobacco between his fingers.

"It didn't seem possible anyone could have walked away," the colonel said. "What happened?"

"No brakes," Deacon mumbled. "We caught fighters on the way back. Two of the crew were dead before we even came in. Maybe three."

"The other crews confirmed FW-190s."

"That's right. I didn't think there were any fields near where they hit us."

"There'll be a phot-recon going out to check at first light," the captain said.

"Nobody knows where Clark is, the navigator. He probably fell out just after we crossed the Yugo coast. I don't know about a chute. You ought to look for him."

Deacon reached for the whiskey, drank it down, choked.

"What part of the coast? Could you get a fix?"

"Nobody saw him go. Past Split, probably past Vis, too. One of the bay doors was shot off and he probably . . . Quinn said he had on his Mae West."

The colonel nodded and rubbed his forehead. "We'll check it out. Now, you're who?"

"Me? I'm Deacon, Thomas Deacon, 11104449. I'm the port waist gunner." He smiled. "Did you think I was on the mat out there?"

"Okay, Deacon. It's a miracle, but you're all right. Is that it, now? Is there anything else?"

"Cantori was stuck in the ball over two hours. The pilot wouldn't let him take any morphine for his leg."

The colonel said nothing.

"The pilot wanted him to use the turret, but he couldn't traverse or depress because the motor was out. I don't know if he was alive when we hit." Deacon looked up at the colonel. "The ball got flattened. Maybe he was frozen. Can a popsicle bleed?"

"Do the medics want him?" Passerant asked the other officer.

"They think he should have a sedative and sack out for a while," the captain said. "He's all right otherwise."

"I don't want to go in there," Deacon said. "All I want to do is go to my tent. You know how it is, Colonel."

Passerant had been a lieutenant in the Mediterranean Allied Air Force, a captain when the first Ploesti strike was made, a major leading a squadron during the Big Week. Now he was a lieutenant colonel and he knew how it was, but he was restricted to the ground and he had only wrinkles in his face to show what he knew.

"Can I have some whiskey?" Deacon asked.

The colonel opened a desk drawer and took out a bottle nearly full. Deacon stood, put it in a pocket of his robe.

"I'll make out now," he said.

"Okay, Deacon, let's see how it goes. Come in and see me in a couple of days."

"There was a flak hole in the chute," Deacon said, "it ripped."

"Tough break."

"Probably the last one. It's got to start working for me now. One out of ten for today, one out of sixteen for the tour; the swing's got to be the other way." He saluted awkwardly. "Thank you very much, sir."

A spasm ran across Passerant's face. He patted Deacon on the back and thrust him gently through the door. The men in the orderly room were subdued.

Deacon took a pull from the bottle and then got into the jeep. An ambulance rocketed past them as they rolled down the hill. *Bawl, Buster* had been towed off the mat and was lying in the dust. Several mechanics were hacking at the twisted wing.

"Alert for tomorrow?" Deacon asked.

The captain's eyes cut at him from behind his flying glasses.

"Counting ours, three from the group went for sure," Deacon said. "Any unaccounteds?"

"Showboat."

"I knew they'd never make it. That airplane should've been retired. Only fifteen for tomorrow."

"Two replacements came in today."

"That's a big help," Deacon said.

The captain didn't answer. A few men nodded tiredly to Deacon as they passed through his squadron area. He indicated his tent and the jeep stopped. Deacon got out stiffly.

"You're not going tomorrow," he said flatly.

The captain blinked green-shaded eyes. He was in Intelligence or Operations, a groundgripper. The captain flew a desk.

"You didn't know who I was," Deacon said, "not any of you. I might as well be out there on the mat with the rest of them." He hefted the bottle. "Doesn't make a shit's difference, does it?"

The captain shifted into gear and drove off. Deacon watched the jeep until it turned into the road leading to headquarters, then he walked toward the empty tent.

4.

THERE CAME screaming through the next morning the sound of airplane engines, chattering explosions which caused the glass of the empty whiskey bottle to ring. Although Deacon arched and twisted, he slept on.

He came awake long after the ships had gone, his eyes popping open, the heat of the day pressing down on them like sweaty thumbs. He couldn't force his eyes closed again. Tinny sounds came from the direction of the field, but the castle of the tent was still, the canvas taut and rigid. There was no wind to rattle the pole, no rain to drum on the tent's skin. There were no voices.

Deacon had realized that there wouldn't be any even before he swung his legs over the edge of the cot and sat up. No voices, but the four empty cots nearly creaked, the lidded footlockers nearly boomed like drums. He inspected his leg, found the bruise glazed an angry red. The leg was stiff. Deacon hobbled around the tent, then grasped the pole with both hands and swung as though around a maypole, as though on a carousel, seeing at each turn a cot. Only one was warm. At each turn a cot and footlocker flew within the walls of the tent, only his own not grown strange and cold.

Deacon sat down and pressed his hands against his mouth. He said something into them, couldn't understand what he'd said. Four sets of uniforms hung headless, legless, with empty sleeves. He scuttled along the dirt floor and opened Fitzgerald's locker, found nothing in it, nothing in Zimmerman's. He passed over Horton's, found a bottle of wine in Cantori's.

The wine was warm and fusty. Deacon gulped it down, stained the maroon robe a deeper red. His stomach heaved. A liquid bubble rose to the back of his throat. Deacon drank again. The tent was growing hot. He sat panting on the floor, drank again. Through the open doorway he could see a sky burned nearly white. Another day perfect for flying. He heaved himself upright, went to the doorway and saluted the sky, turned and addressed a ponderous salute to each of the empty cots. No dim bugle was needed, no stained flag had to be run up. The salute was not intended to be military, only a sort of goodbye to the people who no longer lived there.

Deacon lay on his cot and drank the wine. It was tart and warm, left an acid taste in his mouth. A crank and wallop came from the field, an airplane engine coughed alive. It was being tested, revved until it shrieked and thundered. A lizard scurried into the tent, scurried out again.

He got up and vomited through the open doorway, then clung to the guy ropes, the sun burning his face. When his eyes cleared he looked toward the range of hills, hazed and pale gray in the harsh light. They were the hump everyone had to cross, the final ridge to be topped before the green valley could be entered. He did a clumsy about-face. The empty whiskey bottle glinted like an image in a twisted mirror, like a fish—dead and silver—floating just beneath the surface of a pool. The cots were very still, looked very cold. Deacon turned toward the sun again, squinted his eyes closed and shouted drool and spittle. No one answered. He opened his eyes and heaved forth a belch which burst in rainbow colors and knocked him backward.

A hexagon of sky revolved slowly around the top of the tent pole, a bleached canopy held upright by a spear. Then nothing moved, not even the flat darkness.

There was an eagle in the dream which came. It clawed his lip, an eagle first German black and yellow whose wings were marked with the doubled cross, then America's white-mantled bird. When he awoke Deacon saw the eyes of a lizard peering from beneath wrinkled lids. One small talon gripped his lip, the other his chin. Deacon spit. The lizard ran into a fold of his robe. He tore it off and danced out into the sunlight. A swarm of alarmed flies arose from the spot where he had been sick.

The tent area was deserted. Men were puttering near the mess hall and the squadron orderly room, but the clump of tents where the crews lived was still, heat waves shimmering over the peaked roofs as tough vigil fires burned inside. Deacon looked at his watch. The crystal was webbed. Crash time. The watch would keep crash time forever. He looked into the sky, where both time and direction were kept by the compass points of a clock dial. Only those spatial hours were real, only the interval between takeoff and touchdown. The sky was empty. There were no o'clocks to be seen.

He went into the tent and fell on the cot, closed his eyes. Sweat ran down his forehead, crept under the lids. He touched the notches cut into the cot's frame. Thirty. He could make an addition: thirty-one. Nineteen more missions and he'd be safe. Better safe. Better safe than sorry that you'd volunteered to fly and fight with the greatest team in the world. See the young man on the poster, wrapped in glittering bandoliers, the hawk in his face searching the sky, the dove eyes of the girl behind him aflame with love and lust. *You'll be sorry,* they chanted in basic training and gunnery school. No one chanted when they arrived overseas. No one said they'd be safe.

He rummaged through the footlockers again until he found a box of breakfast K-ration. Slime eggs on a cracker, the fruit bar for iron. He poured tepid water into a dirty mess cup and added the soluble coffee, then dragged a stool outside, sat in his stinking underwear and let the sun wash him.

Nearby was an almond grove, trunks twisted and gray, leaves dusty. The grass in the tent area had been worn away and the ground was baked smooth. A detail of Italian laborers raked the gravel around the squadron orderly room. They were diminutive men, some no larger than children. Many wore the knickerlike pants of the Italian Army. The PFC in charge sat in the shade, sweating splotches into his fatigues.

A dry wind blew across the wheat fields and the almond groves, carrying a fragile dusty scent. Deacon watched the sky, telling time not by the sun or by the ellipitcal creep of the trees' shadows, but by ear. There was desultory clinking and clanking from the field, the sound of chain winches, vehicular motors. The sky was quiet. Deacon listened intently for a long time.

They were late. It was nearly four when he caught the first thin drone. Up there was chaos, banks and banks of pistons crashing in their cylinders, propellers pounding at the air exhausts roaring. The dry wind carried nothing more than an uneven drone.

The ragged box formations came into view. Work at the field stopped, cooks and mechanics wiping their hands in identical gestures, clerks lounging at the orderly-room door. Jeeps were pulled off the road and the men in them sat with their faces turned up. The bombers lumbered through the air. They were neither elegant nor impressive, but they had flown perhaps a thousand miles in their search for the war, and everyone on the field watched them come home. Looking into the northwest were acres of eyes shaded by glasses and hands and peaked caps.

The ships turned in a clumsy traffic pattern, each treading air as it waited its turn to begin the descent. There were no flares to indicate wounded. The bombers fluttered down one by one, lurching across the mat with a squeal of brakes. They were noisier on the ground, sputtering and thundering along the taxi strips, clearing engines after they'd reached the revetments. Fourteen ships landed, parked, and became silent. There was a final explosive cough. Quiet flooded the field. For just a few moments it was still, and the sky was clear, and something like a benediction hung in the ancient Italian air.

Mechanics began unsnapping cowlings, bomb trucks arrived with armorers, jeeps and weapons carriers picked up the flyers. It was another half hour before the crews arrived in the squadron area. They'd been at interrogation, told what they had or had not seen. The officers went to the tents on the north side of the mess hall, the gunners to those on the south. All were subdued. They were colorful raffish figures, their conglomeration of flying outfits catching at the eye, stirring the heart. They made a picture to which a thousand words could have been added, band music, large flags. But their eyes were red and bleary, their faces drawn. They were tired and dirty. No one smiled or tried to stage a wisecrack.

The crews disappeared into the tents, popped out again to wash in helmets, roll up the side canvas so that the heat could escape. A single figure strode toward Deacon—a technical sergeant with drawn cheeks, his feet still in flying boots.

"Hello, Tooley," Deacon said.

"You're a sight in those drawers, Preacher. You look like a Neapolitan whore advertising her ass. How you feeling, okay?"

"Okay."

"You came out of it all right, huh?" Toole smiled uncertainly, kicked at the spot in front of the tent where Deacon had made the ritual circle each morning, Horton the erasure.

"You can't steal my luck, Tooley," Deacon said.

"Your luck?" Toole frowned. Deacon smiled, lit a cigarette. "You were lucky all right, Preacher. You couldn't buy that kind of luck."

"Where'd you go today?"

"Up to Ploesti again. That goddamned place . . ."

"Holy Jesus, Tooley, they've really got the hammer out. How'd it go?"

"Not bad. We only lost two in the whole group. *Big Blaster* had to put down around Foggia somewhere. Penney and his gang caught it going in on the run and so did one of those replacements they flew in yesterday."

"They didn't have to sweat long."

"Yeah, might as well get it over with right away." Toole's teeth showed. "That was some shot you came in on yesterday. I don't know how you didn't burn."

"My luck's strong now, Tooley."

"Quinn got out, too. Did you know that? He broke two legs and he's up at the field hospital. We're going up to see him tonight. You want to come?"

"Nope."

"Kenny's all right. He's a good kid. I thought you two might want to . . . nobody should have walked away from that ship."

"Quinn must have had a hard time doing it with two broken legs."

"Yeah." Toole's voice was flat. He looked at Deacon. "Nobody in the tent anymore, huh?"

"They all died yesterday."

"Shit, Preacher, I know that. I told you it was some rough shot. Listen, they're bound to shove in a bunch of recruits on you. I don't know about Kenny coming back, but we've got an extra empty sack since Martinez went home. You could just shift right over."

"I don't think so, Tooley."

"It's up to you. That other recruit we have is all right. Frank'd like you to come over, too."

"Let's let it slide for now."

"Whatever you say. Any time you're ready, just buzz us and we'll help you with your stuff."

Deacon sat and smoked.

"I'll stop by on the way down to chow to pick you up," Toole said.

"Okay, Tooley."

He shuffled off, John Toole of Harrisburg, Pennsylvania; of Basilicata, Italy. Deacon went into the tent. He tucked the blankets tight on all the cots, picked things from the floor and put them on the proper shelves, then swept out the tent. He washed and shaved from a helmet, put on a fresh pair of khakis. He sat on his cot and waited. There were sounds of talk from the other tents. The dry afternoon wind became the equally dry but cooler wind of a Mediterranean evening. Mess kits clanked.

Toole stopped by. They walked to the feeding line together. It was a combat mess, officers and enlisted men eating from the same trough, waiting in the same line. Deacon passed before the counter and held out the two halves of his mess kit, received Vienna sausage, dehydrated potatoes, fresh squash, half a canned peach. The sausage was a staple, a joke. On each Vienna run one of the ships was supposed to be assigned to take out the sausage factory. It was a cook's joke. None of the flyers laughed at it.

They moved into the dining area and sat at a long steel table. Officers and enlisted men tended to sit apart. Flies which had eluded the screening shifted and buzzed over the food. There was a lot of talk in the tent—talk of the sky, of violence, hands moving in awkward patterns to indicate the positions of airplanes. The voices of the newer men were louder than those of the veterans.

In spite of the cliques of rank, all of them shared a single life. They were crews before they were persons. Each day they mounted the same winged horse—that rod, arrow, which was the only thing able to take them from the zero side of the number right through to its conclusion halfway to a hundred. They might live together, eat together, but the thing they most shared was the steel bird which waited sleepless all night for them.

Deacon ate the soggy meat and floury potatoes, drank the bitter coffee. He lit a cigarette and watched the men coming into the tent. They had no age except that between one and fifty, and they had no expressions or attitudes except those standard for the particular number which happened to be working on them. The men above the fortieth spasm were almost burned out, in their faces a lunatic hope that they might luck out simply by putting one foot before the other, by bearing each new sun as one less confrontation. The recruits within the brackets of the first missions looked frightened but undaunted. They found the spear heavy but were going to beat their way through with it. And anyone who had made ten or a dozen looked mollified, convinced that what was inside the skin was vulnerable after all, that immortality was subject to the sharp edges of chance stones flung into the sky. And even on top of the typical marks all bore, there were some—who might have climbed down from their first or from their forty-ninth mission—whose faces looked permanently stricken.

Deacon watched the men without any real interest. In a sense they were all ciphers. In a sense there was only one Great Crew, and it had flown every mission over every target and was indestructible. When a man from that Great Crew either went the long way over or went home, someone else would assume his features and the crew would go on. No vacant chairs were reserved, no empty glasses turned over, no toasts written in wine and tragedy. If someone had gone the long way a replacement could be whistled out of the cipher pool. Names were not important.

They were not important except as they were known, and John Francis Toole of Harrisburg had a name. He'd come from that time when Deacon had not actually been at war. Toole's crew had been billeted with Deacon's in England, they'd made the boat trip to Italy together. But Toole's crew had been broken up into replacements. Nevertheless, he'd managed to prosper. He had thirty-four in his pocket. Toole had a name because there were so few at the field whose names Deacon knew.

Things were bad all over; that had to be expected. You couldn't get to glory without straining a little. The props and men were supposed to be singing and everything ready on the right, ready on the left, all along the firing line. That was the script. They'd all seen it in Technicolor, some bit player buying a fadeout before the epic closing. The hero was sometimes even dirtied by blood. Both Toole and Deacon knew the score, the melody, even the contrapuntal winds of instruments which filled the air with poison needles. They'd sat at dinner before, and through the Spam or hash or corn-willy seen the reflection of some figure who'd been left to dangle in the jaws of the sky. Toole had been at Vienna the day before, he'd just returned from a Romanian strike. There it was. You had to get up in the morning and go to bed at night and someone had to disappear nearly every day.

But fair was fair. Nine straight days' work on a master plan like the Oil Campaign didn't even come close to parity. To have eight of your crew gone the long way and one with broken legs was bad; bad even if all of them had really been no more than simple replacements for the one Great Crew, products of the cipher pool. But Clark and Fitzgerald and Horton—they'd had real names, faces which weren't replaceable.

There was no longer a sun in the sky by the time they'd finished eating, but the air was bathed with a beautiful luminous light. Toole stopped at the mail hut and collected the letters from his tent's compartment. There were some stuffed in the slot belonging to Deacon's tent. He didn't touch them.

Toole asked Deacon to stop for a beer. Inside, Frank Gruber sat on his cot cleaning a stripped-down automatic. Gruber had been in Toole's original crew and they'd been assigned to the same ship, Toole as radioman, Gruber in the tail. They continued to fly together, to prosper. Kenny Quinn had been bunked in with them. Deacon looked at Quinn's cot. It didn't appear as cold as the empty ones in his own tent.

"Hi Deke," Gruber said. "How the hell are you?"

Toole kicked back a board from a square hole cut in the earth. From it he took two bottles of beer and uncapped one and handed it to Deacon. The bottle was not quite cool.

"That was some shot you come in on yesterday," Gruber said. "I never saw anybody crawl away from anything like that."

"Here's how," Deacon said, drinking.

"And Kenny, too. A couple of broken legs is cheap. We're going up and see him later. You didn't get knocked at all, huh?"

"I cut my leg."

"You get it verified? I mean, did somebody see it?"

"The medics."

"It's a good thing, or you wouldn't get the Heart. You might even get a DFC on account of yesterday. They been giving out medals like aspirin pills."

"Was it the flak or the fighters?" Toole asked.

"We caught some of the flak. The flak got Arnie." Deacon blinked, drank. "The FWs really gave us the fix, though."

"Those old airplanes, those 190s, why don't the Krauts ground them?" Gruber asked. "Where'd they come from, anyway? I bet there's an underground field somewhere. Or maybe a pocket aircraft carrier, like they had those pocket battleships."

"Oh for Christ sake," Toole said.

"Well, where'd they come from, Tooley? There must of been three full squadrons. And where was our escort? Those Krauts were in and out before any of those meatball fighter jockeys could get their fingers out of their asses."

"Just as long as we didn't have to look at them today," Toole said.

"You know it wasn't because that escort hurt them yesterday. The Krauts were probably all drunk celebrating today. Or maybe they were assigned to knock out some other group. Listen, the Krauts know there's so many guns around that fucking Ploesti they don't need fighters. You'd figure it was all burned out by now, wouldn't you? Maybe it's all just guns camouflaged to look like a refinery."

"If we're still hitting them," Toole said, "they must still be operating."

"You couldn't tell through all that shit and smoke. Every time we go up there we just dump. I know for a fact there's no oil, Tooley, because I got a newspaper from my mother and it says we're squeezing the Krauts out because their oil production is stopped dead, period. They have to quit running their airplanes and tanks because they don't have any oil. I figure they must have invented very big rubber bands. That's what hit us yesterday, Deke, these old 190s with giant rubber bands instead of engines.

"You know what the trouble is with that fucking Ploesti, don't you? We been trying to break even ever since last year when some horse's ass thought he invented skip bombing and they lost all those ships there. Here we got this great bombsight that you can drop on a shithouse from twenty thousand feet, and they went and figured it out it was best to go in there so low you'd actually be taxiing if you put the wheels down. This horse's ass is still trying to make his point. He's got to keep losing ships to prove it's an important target. The more he loses, the more important it gets, and the only oil up there is this Kraut guard who's got a can of it he uses for his bicycle."

"Why don't you get off that rack?" Toole said. "Every time we go up there I get it all night."

"You're lucky to see night when we go up there, buddy. They got twice as many airplanes in the junk heap as the whole Fifteenth Air Force got flying. I bet they got Orville Wright's airplane they knocked down. You know what the Krauts are working on? A mystery air force. They throw away half the junked airplanes they got at fucking Ploesti and they still got enough to rebuild a whole another air force as big as this one. But we know about it and that's why this horse's ass in Intelligence or something is still running missions up there. He figures he'll let the Krauts put all those twenty-fours together, even though they do it better than we do, because all he's got to do is get the whole Kraut air force up in these twenty-fours and they'll start to fall apart just like ours and all the Krauts'll get killed. It's our secret weapon."

"For Christ sake, Frank," Toole said.

"No, I was only shitting you," Gruber said. "They got one twenty-four, see, just one, and he's the flying mystery Kraut, the Heinie Lone Ranger. And he's got a cap with a zillion-mission crush and a zillion bombs painted on his A-2 jacket and those PX boots, because the Krauts dress him up just like the movies. And he's got a white silk scarf a mile long. This guy flies all over looking for groups on a mission, and there's a sign on the back of the ship just like those jeeps on the taxi strips back in the States—Follow Me. This is The Lone Fritz, Tooley, and he catches up with a formation and he flashes the sign and they follow him because they don't know where they are anyway, and they know anybody who dresses like him has to be the world's champion pilot. So he leads the formation to Italy or North Africa or something and he gives them another sign, for the togglers who don't know what they're supposed to drop on anyway, a big red sign even those blind bastards can see and it says Toggle and they dump. He blows up the whole Fifth Army and he blows up Eisenhower and he blows up the Pope. Then he sees a formation on the way to fucking Ploesti and he turns them around and they blow up Texas instead. And nobody ever gets wise, because we been dumping on our own troops all this time anyway and everybody figures it's standard operating procedure."

Toole lay back on the cot and closed his eyes. The light outside was turned nearly silver as it washed into the tent, and in repose Toole's face seemed to be cast in the death mask of a corrupted youth.

"Help yourself to another beer, Preacher," he said.

Gruber took a bottle from the hole and uncapped it. He handed it to Deacon.

"Penney's gang went down today," Gruber said. "The whole right wing folded over on them. We didn't see any chutes but maybe some of the guys got out."

"Tooley told me."

"Tough shot."

"Whose tough shot tomorrow?" Deacon asked.

"We got a stand-down for a while," Gruber said. "They got no more airplanes to fly. You know those airplanes they got up this morning—there were two dummies. They were balloons with wings. It took the crews all night to blow them up. They were disguised zeppelins. I saw one crew chief had to build a giant slingshot and he put his ship in it and a whole bunch of guys pulled back real hard you know, and they let go and it got up all right, but none of the engines'd turn over. The crew chief hollers 'Tough shit, I got you up, now it's your problem flying it' and then all these arms come out of the window and start flapping. They were moving, I tell you. That airplane got up there and back an hour before we did."

"We need the refit," Toole said. "They only got seventeen lousy ships up this morning and even with fourteen of them coming back some of them need work so bad they don't dare send them out again. *Pith Dorf* needs a whole new rudder and empennage. We're supposed to get some replacements, so I guess they'll try to patch up all the sagging birds while we're waiting."

Deacon sipped his beer. Gruber reassembled the automatic and snapped the ejector, sending a fine spray of oil into the light.

"I'm gonna use this thing to hold off the Krauts," he said, "because somebody must be putting blanks in my guns. Jesus Christ, I go home and tell them I never shot down one shitty airplane and they'll think I was a conscientious objector. Oh man, when I get back and get all that fifty-mission hump that's going to waste back there. I'll wear my medals, you know, not just the ribbons, and I'll get these giant wings, maybe cost me a hundred dollars, with diamonds on them. Maybe I'll buy a Luger from some doggie and tell them I took it away from Hermann Goering while we were doing hand-to-hand in the air. I reached in his cockpit and knocked him out and took his gun."

"Frank and I figure we'll try to work a three-day pass and go up to Naples," Toole said. "How about coming along, Preacher?"

"I got an introduction to an Italian princess," Gruber said. "She's so high class I got to have two cartons of cigarettes to shack up with her. Yeah, Deke, we'll go up and catch some of those Neapolitan crabs and drink that piss wine of theirs, what the hell is it . . . Lacrima Cristi?"

"Maybe we could go to Rome. Did you hear that? . . . They captured Rome."

"That's a big deal."

"Yeah, we could get our bullets blessed now."

"Gruber . . ."

"Okay, Tooley, okay. Come on, Deke, do you good. Get your tubes reamed, get your hat blown off."

"I guess I don't need it, Frank," Deacon said mildly. "I'll just sack out here."

"Well you oughta sack in with us," Gruber said. "I don't know about Kenny coming back, but this other recruit we got, Wisnefski or Wickdick . . . what the hell's his name, Tooley?"

"Wieckzecki."

"Yeah, he's only been here a week but he's a quiet kid for a recruit. They get those replacements and they're going to shove a batch of them in on you."

"I'll be all right," Deacon said.

"You'd be better off with us."

"I'll work that out, Frank."

"Whatever you say, Preacher," Toole said. "Listen, after we see Kenny we're going over to the movies. You want to come?"

Deacon drained his bottle and got up. "Nope," he said.

"Why not?" Gruber said. "You can't just knock around in that tent."

"You make me nervous, Frank."

"Aw Deke, come on. We'll go down to the bar and get blind, then."

"Horton was a nursing pain in the ass sometimes."

"Jesus, he was a good guy, Deke."

"Bless him," Deacon said. "Bless him."

"Guys go, you know, but you and Arnie . . . shit, Deke, I know how you were buddies."

"And let him go screw," Deacon said. "You too, Frank."

"Come on, Preacher."

"And you, Tooley. Take your beer and shove it. I don't need any bleeders."

"We know how you feel, Deke. . . ."

"You don't know anything. Just get off my back. Would you give me another beer? Do you have another beer?"

Gruber took the last bottle from the hole and tossed it to him.

"You can give me all the beer you want and you can give me cigarettes and donuts if you want. I don't care if you act like a shitass Red Cross station. Just get off my back."

Deacon threw the bottle against the metal base of the tent pole. It shattered. Toole stuffed his hands into his pockets and looked at a spot over Deacon's head. Gruber pursed his lips and snapped the automatic. The sour beer smell rose through the tent. Deacon turned on his heel and walked out.

The sky was darkening, the sharp outlines of the almond orchard almost dissolved by the approaching night. Lights appeared in the mess hall and the orderly room and the tents as the power generator came on. Deacon sat outside on his stool and watched until all the shapes had become darker masses on dark, partially outlined by lights seeping through chinks. Voices were chink-screened, disappeared under the fitful hammering of the generator.

He went inside, did not turn on the light. But he could not escape the silence beneath the tent's canvas sky, the cold more distant than the vaults of the dead. The material fittings of cloth and blanket were as silent and stiff as shrouds—even as the failing parachute had had shroud lines, stalks, while the flower was the chute itself, a winding sheet of beautiful nylon.

Deacon put on the maroon robe and grabbed some money and headed for the bar.

5.

THE GROUP stood down, but there were no three-day passes. At an informal assembly held the following morning the crews were advised that they were restricted to the field even though they were not alerted. The men hooted. The squadron Commanding Officer—a major who still took his chances, flew the tough missions with them—explained that he had no idea what it was all about, that he was only reading from the sheet of paper he held in his hand. There had never before been a restriction after a run of wearing missions. The crew traditionally goofed after a lengthy goring.

The men milled angrily through the squadron area. A stone was thrown through an orderly-room window. Someone in the gunners' section fired off the full clip from his automatic. Signal flares arched from the officers' tents. A corporal scurried off in a jeep, came back with the line mechanic who tended bar in the evenings. The bar tent was opened at ten-thirty. Part of the crowd was sucked into it. The remainder broke into fragments. A volleyball game began and a knot gathered at the crude softball diamond.

Deacon stood watching at the doorway of his tent. He wore his khakis and robe, was without shoes or socks. He had been wrenched out of sleep by the gunfire, chased awake by the fear that someone was shooting at him. And now, as the sun dried his sweat and the pulse receded, he found nothing more than a gang of half-dressed men playing games. He pulled the robe tighter in spite of the heat and went back into the tent.

The footlockers held no more K-rations. Deacon found a crushed box half filled with moldy cookies. The mice had been at them. He had a bottle of cherry brandy he'd brought back from the bar the night before. The fumes were too strong and sweet. Voices approached the tent. There was the sound of shuffling feet outside. A corporal from the squadron orderly room poked his head in.

"All right to collect the stuff?" he said.

Deacon chewed steadily and looked at him.

"Personal effects, government issue," the corporal said. His own glasses were round steel-framed GI. "We're supposed to pick it all up."

A PFC peered over his shoulder. Deacon shook crumbs from the cookie box into his mouth. The two men edged into the tent, the corporal with a sheaf of papers attached to a clipboard.

"Four," he said, "right?"

Deacon lit a cigarette.

"I have four names here." The corporal rustled his papers. "Which one is which?"

"This here must be Zimmerman." The PFC kicked the footlocker with Zimmerman's name on it.

"Right. Just as well you're here," the corporal said to Deacon. "Better to have a witness. People get some very funny ideas about this detail. You'd think we were robbing graves or something." He showed yellow teeth. "All right, then, we'll start with Zimmerman."

Zimmerman was divided into two parts. Everything he'd owned was spread out on his cot. The obvious army gear went first—musette bag and useless gas mask and shelter-half, caps and hats. Next came the uniforms, each of the pockets meticulously turned out and all personal possessions set aside. The PFC called off each item of government issue and the corporal noted it on one of the sheets. The overseas bag was filled, then the barracks bag. The corporal laid out the remaining things—money, letters, a watch, some photographs, a hairbrush. He made a note of each and put them in a small canvas sack and tied it with twine.

They discovered Cantori next, separated the man from the uniform. Cantori had a lot of letters and pictures. He'd had a wife and a three-year-old daughter. Fitzgerald's turn came. Deacon watched silently until they began to remove the ribbons and wings from Fitzgerald's blouse.

"Give me the wings," he said.

"Everything GI has to be checked in," the corporal said. "Maybe you can stop in at the supply office and see about some kind of personal memento."

"They were bought at the PX at Chanute Field," Deacon said. "They're coin silver."

The corporal stepped to the door of the tent and tilted the wings so that the sunlight caught them. It seemed that he held cold fire in his hand.

"You really can't tell . . ." he began.

"Give me those wings, you goddamned dog-robber."

The corporal turned, mouth open, the rims of his glasses glinting. The PFC became busy with Fitzgerald's barracks bag.

"I want Horton's, too," Deacon said.

The corporal tossed him Fitzgerald's wings. "I'm putting them on my sheet," he said. "Don't blame me if the supply officer comes around later. You're not supposed . . ."

His voice trailed away. The PFC began calling off items of Fitzgerald's gear. Fitzgerald was partitioned. They began on Horton. The corporal handed over Horton's wings. A needle spray of perspiration broke out on Deacon's forehead.

"Don't touch any of my stuff," he said. "Don't put your lousy hands on it."

The corporal mumbled something but kept his head down over the list. The PFC didn't look up. Deacon went out of the tent. He kicked at the dirt, stubbed a bare toe. The soft-ball game was in full swing. Deacon threw stones toward the diamond, couldn't reach it. The men in the tent broke off

54

their recitation and began throwing out the barracks bags. They appeared carrying the canvas sacks almost daintily, walked away.

In a little while the PFC came back with a detail of Italian laborers. They took the bags, collapsed the cots and shouldered them. Deacon went into the tent. It seemed much larger. The spaces where the cots had been were darker than the rest of the trampled floor. They formed irregular outlines very much like graves. From the diamond came the sound of men shouting and swearing. Deacon found a lapel button with the air-force insignia and put it at the head of the rectangle where Horton's cot had been. He left.

The enlisted-men's bar was an old supply tent which had been braced at the sides and screened in. There were stools of bomb-fin casings and crude tables made from armor plate and in one corner was a battered upright piano. The bar counter was a simple affair of raw lumber liquor-stained red and purple and brown.

Deacon's costume didn't draw much attention. He was the only maroon robe, but there were other men in bare feet and some wearing perforated cut-down GI shoes and hand-made Italian sandals. There were a lot of faces in the bar, but not many names. Gruber's was among them, a few other old sports. The first couple of rounds had gone by, and those who'd had a drink just to protest the restriction had already left.

The bartender, a buck sergeant, still wore his oily coveralls. Deacon nodded, ordered whatever it was the Italians put into a bottle and labeled cognac. As bright as the sun was, as intense the glare outside, the liquor in his glass was flat and didn't reflect any light. Deacon drank, saw through the thin film at the glass's bottom the distorted tent walls and ceiling, the bartender's face possessed of one huge eye. He set down the glass and pointed at it.

"How's it going?" the sergeant asked, pouring.

He didn't know Deacon, knew only a familiar face, one like all those he saw every night, like the even larger number of faces he'd seen climbing in and out of airplanes during the two years he'd been overseas.

"Okay, Hobby," Deacon said.

"Some shit, huh, no passes?"

"Some crock," Deacon said.

"It's all the same to us. Ground crew wouldn't get them anyway."

"That so?"

"Twenty-four hours every ten days, that's all we get. In

55

fact, when you guys are standing down we have to work harder. We get more time off when you're up."

"That's tough," Deacon said.

"Well . . . I don't mean that. I don't want to switch with you or anything, but I'm just about to get a chance at the rest camp. I'm going on twenty-five months overseas and they're going to give me five days off."

"You'll need the rest," Deacon said.

"Are you kidding? I'm going to be either drunk or straddling for five days. I got all my life to rest."

Someone down the bar wanted service. Deacon sipped his cognac, long sips, sipped it right out of the glass. He called. The bartender returned, poured.

"As I was saying . . ." he began.

Deacon walked away. A man was trying to play the piano. The instrument's facing was gone. Deacon watched the hammers bow and nod, saw the strings vibrate. One of the men recognized the music and began to sing. Deacon sat on a stool. Gruber was talking not far away.

"I tell you," he said, "we're going home. They don't want any more of these sad sacks in the States, these combat fatigues who finished their tour or some doggie running around who had his knockers shot off. This whole group is going home as an example of a prime combat unit, and the airplanes, too, but they're gonna ship them by boat because they know they'd have to follow them up with a garbage scow if they ever tried to fly them over the ocean. But we're going home in these luxury DC-4s. And they'll be a parade with the whole group going up Broadway and they're towing the airplanes with us in them while we wave out the windows and they're throwing these pieces of paper at us. Some of the feather merchants throw five- and ten-dollar bills."

"Ain't goin nowhere," someone said. "They got some motherin big idea. Them mechanics're working breakass down on the line. Soon's they get this outfit put back together we're goin on somethin big."

"I'm telling you," Gruber said. "We'll be in these little stands like where they give away kisses for a dollar and we'll be selling bonds. They're gonna make special bonds with our pictures on them and we're gonna autograph them. The hump'll be lined up a mile to buy a bond and kiss our medals."

"I hear we're supposed to get right up to full strength again."

"Aw no, they wouldn't do that to us. You can't keep formation now without some recruit jockey slicing your tail off. It's bad enough now when they feed them in one at a time."

"We're shipping out for the Canal Zone," Gruber said. "Panama."

"I was in Panama City."

"This is Pan-a-ma," Gruber said, "not Florida. Sub duty, but all the subs are gone, so you run around dropping coconuts on these big fish and then you call it a kill and paint it under your window. Maybe a whale. They got these special twenty-fours with bunks in them and even curtains and you get some pilot that's had some combat time and it don't bother him if you bring a broad along. You cruise along under oxygen level and all the time this Spanish broad is tickling your ass with one of those ruffled skirts."

"You ought to write comic books, Gruber."

"I got one. The Adventures of Super-Cal. He's the only gunner in the whole air force can handle a three-hundred-caliber gun. They got to build an airplane with two sets of wings and eight engines just to handle the recoil. He . . ."

From the kitchen came the clang of a steel bar being beaten, the signal for the noon meal. The men stirred.

"Might as well."

"Yeah, if you don't eat you can't shit."

Gruber's audience drifted out. Gruber looked over at Deacon, his eyes heavy and lips parted, his face gripped by both drink and weariness. He smiled wanly. Deacon took Horton's and Fitzgerald's wings from his pocket and pinned one set to each shoulder of his robe. Gruber opened his mouth as though laughing and then threw an exaggerated salute. The piano and voice continued to render popular songs, unknown words garbled, unknown melodies glossed over. Deacon went to the counter and called for a drink. The bartender feigned astonishment at the wings.

The midday sun turned the bar's screening nearly phosphorescent. Seen through it, the men moving toward the mess hall seemed to be walking in a field of white fire so intense that the light reflected from the clanking mess kits was pale. But there was still not the faintest spark on the surface of the liquor in Deacon's glass.

"A little Christian music, if you will," someone shouted from the bar's entrance.

Deacon did not turn. The pianist and his vocalist footed doggedly after the thread of the celebrated musical legend of sitting under apple trees, the fruit of their own music green and sour.

"Mavournee, Londonderry Air, When Finn McCool Met the Katzenjammer Kids," the voice continued.

Deacon didn't have to turn to picture Kelleher, an assortment of red knobs—ears, nose, his wrists knobbed and blistered, his bare feet in tattered straw scuffs, the ankles bulging.

"Stack O'Barley, Danny Boy, The Pratie and Kevin Shapiro. Good day to you, Frank Gruber. 'Tis not a fit instrument you're playing, men. The Harp That Once Through Tara's Halls."

Kelleher put an arm around Deacon, nuzzled his cheek momentarily. He had a mop of hair the color of a peeled carrot.

"Tommy my boy, my bucko."

"Hello, Skip," Deacon said. "What's up?"

"We are not, and that's worth a drink. Did you hear me, Hobby? Jameson's or Bushmill's will do. Failing those, I'll taste of the Eyetalian grape. A little grappa."

"I told you a dozen times we don't have any."

"Did you not know that Lieutenant Henry always drank grappa? He had his dirty way with a nurse, a gorgeous girl, English though she was. Some of that Yugoslav rum then, Hobby. It's fresh, isn't it?"

"It oughta be, I don't think it's two weeks old."

"I'll drink to that. And what have we here, a full chicken colonel?" He inspected Deacon's wings. "Officers drinking with other ranks? Disgusting."

"It's a new rank," Deacon said, "Brigadier-Pistoleer."

"Our answer to the Eighth's greatest celebrity—who shall be nameless—that fearless, peerless hero of missionless warfare, Major Himself Mustache, Major Movie Himself Mustache. He'll have to stand away to you, my boy, raise his hand in a salute to the better man."

"I'm Irish and I'm beautiful," Deacon said.

"You are indeed, my bucko. More brave than me, more blond than you. Hobby, put your back into it, man, or our sail won't raise Cork before dawn."

The natural flush to Kelleher's nose was complemented by a fine web of broken capillaries which extended to his cheeks.

"To our health," Kelleher said, "to my magic number, my ninety-ninth mission. When I go up on that one, the Great Conductor in the Sky is going to punch my ticket."

"How many more to go, Skip?"

"I'm safe for another sixty. Did you know the Dorchester Civic Association is planning to beautify Codman Square with a statue in my honor? Did you know that they haven't fixed on a final pose yet, waiting as they are until my tour is completed? There's some question as to whether the eagle will be represented with defiant claws raised or flat on his back as he exhibits a substantially shattered ass."

"I'd better close for chow," the bartender said.

"Get a grip on yourself, man. Brigadier Deacon will give the orders here. Pour, Hobby."

"I don't know how you can fly," the bartender said.

"Sure, 'tis a miracle, though feathers are the very devil to sleep on."

"These are angels," Deacon said, pointing to his shoulders.

"Are they, now?" Kelleher's bright blue eyes clouded. "But of course they are—Arnie and Fitz watching over you."

"That's right."

"You're a lucky kid." Kelleher ruffled Deacon's hair. "The Great Conductor has seen fit to smile on you. Tommy, there must be a touch of green somewhere in your blood."

"Like Fitzgerald."

"Ah, Tommy . . . ah. His nation's blue-eyed pride. We'd better rest our elbows for now and go sample some of that fine noontime swill."

"No," Deacon said.

"No, then. It's as good an answer as any, probably better than most. No I will not, no I cannot."

"Come on, I have to close up," the bartender said.

"No," Kelleher said.

"No," Deacon echoed.

"By all the saints, that was the answer all the time. Instead of the soldier's oath—no."

"Everybody else is gone," the bartender said. "I'll sell you a bottle and you can get pissed somewhere else."

"Well, now, we should be judicious with our noes, Tommy. I realize that you're acting strictly against regulations, Hobby, and that the price will reflect the risk. But I ask you to consider for a moment before you whip your greed to a froth. Consider that while you were sacked out on your dead unreconstructed ass the good brigadier was trying to hold the pieces of an airplane together with his teeth; that he brought in a crippled ship, crashed it, and walked away. Consider, Hobby, how much you're in debt for not having been in *Bawl, Buster*."

"Boy, I saw that. And you were the guy that got out?"

"He was. And of course you'll want to pass him a bit of cheer on the house."

"Come on."

"Yes you will, Hobby, as the least gesture you can make."

"It's bad enough if I get caught selling you a bottle."

"I'll save you from that, Hobby. No money will change hands."

"Yeah?"

"You have appointed yourself chief delegate for all the groundgrippers. This one time you have decided to make a gesture of condolence. For once you will not scratch your balls and pick your nose and wonder what's for dinner after someone comes in smeared all over the mat. Hobby, you will give in the name of all. There but for the grace of someone who volunteered goes you. Celebrate this man's luck and you'll insure your own."

"Oh yeah?"

"You'll be smiling and lucky, Hobby, and not have to be working here some night when a crowd of the boys on flying status are in and someone suggests that you didn't care to help one of their comrades, that you don't think much of the day's work they put in, that you do a big business in rings and watches and religious medals with the dog-robbers."

"That's not true. None of it is."

"The very reason I will *not* say it. Surely you'd rather pledge a bottle than have lies like that repeated before a crowd of drunken, bitter and war-weary troops. I suggest that you spring, you unmitigated bastard, in the name of everybody like you who turned his back and farted when this man's ship came in."

"It's for Horton," Deacon said.

"What do you want?" the bartender asked feebly.

"Tommy?"

"Wine. To carry us through the afternoon, Skip."

"That's simple enough. We'll have two Aleatico, Hobby. Aleatico to play Alecto's part. You are herewith purged and purified."

"Don't think you're getting away with something."

"Just this once, Hobby. I give my word, better than any bond you could ever post. You'll sleep better tonight."

Kelleher tucked a bottle under each arm. They started out of the tent, but Deacon paused at the piano.

"A bit of jig and reel," Kelleher said.

Deacon pressed the keys at either end of the board. He willed music, but none came. The hammers made mushy sounds against the strings. Deacon pressed more firmly. Nothing happened.

Kelleher began to pick out a tune with one finger. Deacon brushed his hand away. He wandered at random over the discolored keys, searched for any one of the melodies within the piano. Each key, black or white, was the wrong one. Deacon raised his hands to his shoulders and made fists and brought them down with all his strength. A hammer splintered and fell to the floor.

Kelleher pulled him away gently, then picked up the hammer and tossed it back into the piano's works. The sun nearly staggered the two men as they stepped out of the tent, the southern sun rolling from bleached Greece and barren Africa.

Kelleher handed the bottles to Deacon. "We need a little something with the wine," he said. "Will it be strawberries, Sebastian? Figs, thin wafers? You wait here and I'll find a greedy cook to fix us up."

Deacon sat in the shadow of the bar tent. The serving line had closed down, but there were still a few men eating in the mess hall. There was no wind, no dust, and the outlines of nearby objects were so sharp that they cut at the eye, while those farther off were warped by the quivering air. Deacon shielded his eyes so that from beneath the canopy of his hand he could see nothing but the feet of men meandering away from lunch, the drops of water from their mess kits evaporating as soon as they touched the ground.

The tent area grew quiet, the crews sweating prone through digestion or stubbornly marching slippery pens and pencils across sheets of paper. From the field came a steady tinkering as though at the forge of a gigantic furnace. There was a final walloping of pots and pans as the Italian KPs finished their cleanup, and then the kitchen grew still.

Kelleher returned. He led Deacon to the shade of the wooden platform which supported the shower tank. The tank's corrugated sides creaked in the heat, and trickles of water ran down the wooden posts. It was a little cooler beneath it.

"Fraises," Kelleher said, holding out thick sandwiches of cold Spam. " 'Tis a good thing the beverage was complimentary, for the boyos in the kitchen put on a heavy bite indeed."

"Hey Skip," Deacon said, his mouth full, "how come the comic Irishman?"

"Is it fun of me you're making now?"

"Hey, Skip."

Deacon chewed mechanically, stuffing as much as he could into his mouth and washing down the soggy wads with wine.

"For many a lightfoot lad who found this brook too broad for leaping," Kelleher said. "But don't include me in their company yet. I made that leap from Dorchester to Cambridge, born to be a slave but determined to be a gentleman."

"This bottle's for Arnie," Deacon said.

"Don't discount me yet. In our new life I won't have a chance to be Irish, Tommy, for the colonel's lady and Judy O'Grady will walk naked all the time. In our new life everything is going to be penumbral."

"You really put it to Hobby, Skip. If he ever leaned on you he'd crush you."

"He's scared shitless like the rest of them. He's afraid that the time's going to come when those trucks start rolling *back* from the cemetery. He's afraid a general order will come out instructing him to change places with us. And is this the sacramental blood of James Fitzgerald I'm supposed to be drinking?"

"Not blood."

"To forfeit all pay, allotments and allowances for the rest of his natural life."

"Arnie would be just as happy that we emptied a bottle for him." Deacon held it up to the glare, saw it backlighted ruby. "Holy Jesus, not blood. You're not getting religious, Skip?"

"I've forgotten the rubric. Tommy, what will you do now? A game of chess and lidless eyes?"

"Why, I nearly finished my sandwich."

"So you did."

"Come on over to my tent. They're all gone. The dog-robbers came by this morning."

"Do you know, I believe that in the States there must be a line a mile long waiting for those clothes. Nobody here wants them, but back home there must be a dozen feet for every shoe."

"I saved the wings," Deacon said.

"Certainly you did. They'll lift you to paradise as well as a Chinaman's pigtail would. They're the very wings a Viking would wear on his helmet."

"A Viking's funeral," Deacon said.

"Wasn't it *Digby* Geste they buried?"

"Let's go to the tent," Deacon said.

"Discourse with the shades, that's penumbral. Certainly, Tommy, if you want to."

They left greasy scraps of paper beneath the tower, carried the wine with them. The lapels of Deacon's robe curled in the windless air, Kelleher's slippers slapped in the dust. The field was hidden behind a curtain of pulsing air, sounds of cranks and winches were veiled. The tents baked in the sun.

Deacon had not raised the sides of his tent, and all the heat of the day was trapped inside. Kelleher sat outside on the stool while Deacon rummaged among his things until he found a trench knife. He dug at the spot where he and Horton had made their marks. The earth was very hard, but Deacon pried and chopped until he made a small hole. He sat back and closed his eyes.

"I can't remember which one." He brushed at each shoulder. "I mixed them up in my pocket. We all got them at the same time, so I can't tell the difference." He unpinned the wings and held them out in the palm of his hand. "Which one do you think, Skip?"

"Oh, these have a very faint greenish tinge." Kelleher took a pair. "Must be a reflection of the old sod. I'll save them for Fitz and some St. Patrick's night."

Deacon dropped the other pair into the hole. He scraped the dirt into it and tamped it down, then poured cherry brandy over the mound. He tried to light it.

"It has to be heated first," Kelleher said.

Deacon went back into the tent and, nearly blind with sweat, raked his hands over the shelves, finally found a can of lighter fluid. He drenched the mound. Several matches broke in his fingers before he succeeded in lighting one. When he touched it to the ground a flame puffed up and caught at a spot on his robe which had been splashed by the fluid. Kelleher beat it out. Both men watched the flame intently for the few moments it danced over the ground.

As soon as it died Deacon began squirting the tent with what was left of the lighter fluid. Kelleher pried the can from his hand. Deacon fell to his knees and pressed his cheek against the dirt mound, but he couldn't tell if the heat he felt was from the sun or from the fire. A pulse pounded behind his ear and he sobbed. Kelleher knelt next to him and put an arm across his shoulders and began to croon softly.

6.

AT MIDNIGHT Deacon walked through the fields. It was not a dream, but a real midnight, with the sky at last partially obscured by a few clouds, the stars pale, the moon half dark. He passed through the almond orchard and crossed the irrigation ditch which ran parallel to the squadron area, came upon a stand of wheat. Although there was no real breeze, eddies of wind brushed the stalks into patternless swirls which were touched faintly silver each time the clouds parted.

The oxygen-making detachment was shut down and the armorers' section was quiet, their trucks parked in a neat row. Deacon was too far from the field to hear the hammering of the generator which furnished power at the ships' revetments, but he could see the drop lights of line crews working through the night. Jeep headlights circled the taxi strip.

Even at midnight the wind was dry, the air clear. Beyond

the wheat was another field, one of scrapped airplanes, a plain of refuse which glittered whenever the sky cleared. Weak starshine was reflected from shattered turrets. The half-moon streaked long empty fuselages and crumpled wings. The ships of silver and the old ships of olive drab were all merged in a single outline of humps and jagged shapes when a cloud covered the face of the moon.

And then the sound of an energizer traveled across the dark like the cry of a feeble tomcat, and there was an explosion as a ball of orange fire burst at one of the revetments. The engine coughed, spewed yellow, then steadied and trailed a scarf of beautiful blue fire. As powerful as the roar was, it was distant, and the wheat continued to nod softly in the little fits of wind. When the engine was pushed to its limit the trail of fire became longer and finer, and the roar took on a pulsing undertone.

Deacon's whole attention was drawn to the field and his eyes fixed on it. He started when the engine was cut off, backfired. The exhaust died. He continued to watch as the drop lights came together, went out one by one. A jeep's headlights blinked on, then disappeared in the direction of the line crews' quarters.

Deacon stood rooted during the time a long finger of cloud was edged by the moon's light. When it had passed he began to walk toward his tent, faster and faster, until by the time he crossed the irrigation ditch he was trotting.

Bleintrube, the squadron first sergeant, made a call the next morning. Deacon had not yet had a drink, nor had he eaten. His robe and khakis were soiled and he had a two-day beard. His hands shook slightly. Bleintrube looked glumly around the tent.

"How you been?" he asked.

"Okay."

"What do you think, you want to go back on the duty roster?"

Deacon pinched the cuff of his robe between his fingers and held it out as though he were exhibiting a threadbare garment.

"What're you, sick?" Bleintrube asked.

"I don't know if I'm supposed to go up."

From outside came calls and whistles for church. Deacon wondered why—he didn't think it was Sunday. The same jeeps and weapons carriers which had carried the crews to the real church for briefings were now ready to take them up the hill to hear services under a fly extended from the hospital tent.

Deacon pressed his lapels. "Are we alerted?" he asked.

"Not yet."

"I don't know. What do you think?"

"You can go on sick call if you want to."

"I feel all right." Deacon hugged himself. "It's just that I don't know."

"It won't matter unless we get an alert. Suppose we let it hang?"

"Okay," Deacon said.

The first sergeant paused in the doorway and looked at the sky.

"Jesus," he said, "it's a shame you guys are missing all this good flying weather."

Deacon was eating breakfast when the recruits arrived. He'd bought a half-dozen K-rations from the mess sergeant and he was washing the food down with warm beer which had cost a dollar a bottle. The recruits carried cots on their shoulders and dragged their overseas bags after them. There were three, all corporals, all wearing gunner's wings.

"They told us to move in here," one said.

"Must be a mistake," Deacon said.

Each of them looked at the number on the tent.

"It's the right number."

"This is the recuperation tent," Deacon said. They looked more closely at him. "Go next door and see Toole, he's got some space."

"This is where they told us to come."

Deacon uncapped a bottle of beer. It foamed over his robe and trousers.

"You combat crew?" one asked.

"Balls," Deacon said.

They edged into the tent.

"We just brought in a new ship. I guess it's a replacement. You been here long?"

"Depends on the time," Deacon said. "What time do you have?"

"You mean what day is it," one said with a smirk. He began to unstrap his coat.

"Now just knock that off and go find yourself a tent with some other yo-yos in it," Deacon said. "No goddamned sprogs are allowed in here."

"Listen, there's room . . ."

Deacon snatched the protecting mattress cover from his dress uniform. Staff-sergeant's stripes, the Distinguished Unit Citation, the ETO ribbon with battle stars, the Air Medal with a cluster. And a pair of silver wings brighter than any the recruits wore. They began to chatter.

"How many missions you got? How long before you get your full rank? How long before you get the Air Medal?"

Deacon finished his beer.

"Now just haul ass out of here," he said. "Tell whatever stupid clerk assigned you that I'm on temporary stand-down and I'm supposed to have peace and quiet. No sprogs."

"I hope it won't be over too soon," one said.

"Over?" Deacon showed his teeth. *"You're* over, junior, that's all you have to worry about."

"But the invasion . . ."

"Yeah, suppose they wind it all up before we get a chance?"

"What invasion?" Deacon asked.

"France, they invaded France this morning, the real thing. There must have been a million men landed."

"Jesus," Deacon said, "one big deal after another. Now listen, I'm giving you a direct order. You can leave your stuff here for now, but go down to that orderly room and tell them to assign you to another tent."

"But we . . ."

"Pop to, pop to."

They retreated. Deacon opened his last beer and lay on the cot and lit a cigarette. He began to hum, then to sing. He became aware of coughing and shuffling outside.

"They told us to stay here," one said.

"If there's any problem you're supposed to see the first sergeant."

Deacon pushed past them and went out. He knew that the bar was closed. There was a murmuring in the air which might have been the sound of men singing hymns up on the ridge. The clicking of winches came from the field. He went to Kelleher's tent. Kelleher wasn't in.

"He's taking a shit," Finger told him.

"Do you have a bottle, Finger?"

"Skip's got a whole footlocker full of them but it's locked. He oughta be right back. How about this invasion shit?"

"I heard."

"Well, they invaded North Africa twice and then Sicily and then Italy twice. About time they tried that shit somewhere else."

"I've got three sprogs in my tent who're afraid they won't get their Good Conduct medals."

"We got eight new ships today and some spare crews," Finger said. "I think they must be planning some kind of shit mission."

"You hear anything about an alert?"

"I didn't hear shit."

Kelleher came into the tent.

"Tommy, my boy. Are you here to celebrate the end of the war? They're having a mass for victory up on the hill. I'm a pacifist myself, but I understand Patton's ass deep in the English Channel blazing away with both pearly pistols. The Krauts he doesn't shoot he's slapping to death."

"Hey Skip, will you sell me a bottle?"

"That I won't." Kelleher took a key from his dog-tag chain. "But though it's a trifle late to start, I think we ought to have a drop in honor of . . . what day is it, anyway?"

Deacon went to see Bleintrube early the next morning. His clothing was dirtier, his beard heavier, and his hair more tangled.

"What was all that noise about those new men?" the first sergeant asked.

"I don't want any recruits in my tent."

"Then why the hell don't you move?"

"I'm supposed to have a tent to myself."

"You're *what?* For Christ sake, Deacon, *I* sleep with four other guys. The old man's the only one has a hut to himself. I don't want to give you a hard time. Just pick out a tent with some of your buddies in it where they've got a vacancy and you can move in."

"They're all full."

"You know better than that, buster. Of all people, you *should* know better."

"Colonel Passerant probably put me in for a medal."

"Deacon, I put in for three DFCs and a Congressional last week. I'll do what I can for you, but get off my back about this tent."

"I'd better go see the Colonel."

"Why don't you leave the man alone?"

"Is the squadron CO in?"

"He's up on a practice mission with the new crews."

"Passerant said I should see him when I was ready."

"How about the duty roster, then? You ready for that?"

"I'd better see the Colonel."

Bleintrube gave up. He called group headquarters and talked to their first sergeant. Deacon was given permission to see the commanding officer.

"Is there a jeep to take me up?" Deacon asked.

"No, there's no goddamned jeep. About this duty roster. We might have an alert. Every other group in the air force but ours must have gone up yesterday. If you're not ready you'd better put yourself on sick call."

"Maybe you can assign me flying relief."

"I've got green gunners I can use for relief. I'm not going to waste someone who already has time. They need a waist gunner on *Tedeschi Blues.*"

"What happened to their regular one?"

"For Christ sake, Deacon, go on sick call, will you?"

"I don't know the crew on *Tedeschi Blues.*"

"If they knew you, believe me, they'd ask for a recruit instead. Never mind, I'll check it out with Group."

"I'll let you know what Passerant says."

"Do me that favor."

Deacon appeared at the orderly room in his last clean pair of khakis, wearing his wings and ribbons, his cheeks scraped raw. He was shown into Passerant's office, came to rigid attention, and popped a salute. The colonel was startled, saluted awkwardly in return.

Deacon did some pure soldiering—not a limber spit-polished Stateside version, but an austere and durable veteran. He was stiff and bright and correct, exaggerating the trembling of his fingers and twitching an eye from time to time.

The colonel tapped his teeth with the erased end of a pencil while Deacon explained that he needed the tent just a little while longer, that the recruits had almost put him over the edge. When the colonel said that he couldn't live alone Deacon agreed, but just at that moment he didn't want to move in with anyone—not until he got over the fact of so many of the men he'd known having been carried off the long way. The colonel would know how it was. If Passerant did know, he didn't shift his steady gaze from Deacon, and he stopped tapping his teeth. Deacon put a little break into his voice and said that he didn't want anything to get in the way of his finishing his tour.

Passerant approved of that. He was glad to hear that the whole thing wasn't some kind of dodge, that Deacon didn't want to quit right where he was. The colonel hated to see any man turning the time he'd already put in worthless, breaking the continuity of the trip through the number. In a cold and spiritless voice he asked if Deacon didn't think he owed something to his dead buddies. Deacon double-twitched as he swore to keep the faith, push all the harder. If he could have the tent for just a little while he could finish the tour, if he could have just a little time.

The colonel offered him five days—in Capri. He offered to push up his scheduled trip to the combat-crew rest camp, offered blue water and unlimited drink and the worn bosoms of whores. The Passerant who'd been a captain wouldn't have made that offer; he'd have lit a pep-rally bonfire and turned on the old fight talk. And Passerant as a major had been capable of threatening reluctant travelers with a court-martial if they didn't turn their heads to the piece of work to be done during the Big Week. But Lieutenant Colonel Passerant had spent too many nights putting broken crews together on a plot board.

Deacon mumbled that he didn't need Capri, only the tent. The colonel was afraid that Deacon would wind up being set down on a medical if he was left alone to brood. Deacon was afraid he's wind up that way if he didn't get the tent and the time. Passerant offered to let the Flight Surgeon decide. Deacon stuttered. The colonel reminded him that he could simply order him up if he wanted to. But he wanted Deacon to finish on his own, to walk right out through the other end of the pipe just to show them how it was done. He wanted Deacon to march out wearing his Purple Heart, the Distinguished Flying Cross he'd certainly receive by the time he finished his tour. Plenty of other men had done it. Continuity straight down the line, every winner keeping the faith with every loser.

Deacon didn't want to be set down by a medical, either, but if the Flight Surgeon thought that he *should* have the tent . . . Passerant didn't think that would be the case. But if the Flight Surgeon *should* think so, Deacon pressed—not a setdown, but a pause until he'd pulled himself together. If Deacon thought he'd had it, if he thought he couldn't cut it anymore, the colonel wanted to hear about it right then and there, but he didn't want him trying to slide out on some kind of medical dodge. No *sir,* Deacon said, the colonel was right about the tour not meaning anything unless he finished it. But he wanted to be *fit* enough to finish.

Passerant scribbled on a piece of paper and put it in an envelope and sealed it. They'd see what the Flight Surgeon said. Even if it meant he could keep the tent? Deacon asked. Even that, Passerant said as he handed him the envelope. Deacon sprung a perfect salute and turned on his heel.

On the way to the field hospital he prepared a series of faces. One had to fit, to show both resolve and need. Behind the troubled veil there had to show the iron will to tough it out for another nineteen missions. He had to make them understand that all he needed was a little time.

He tried the face on the orderly in the Flight Surgeon's outer office. The orderly gave him a sweet smile and let his fingers trail over Deacon's wrist as he took the note. Left alone, Deacon tried a series of contorted expressions, but they seemed to evaporate in the hot air. He felt unprepared when he marched in to the officer.

The Flight Surgeon was a major. He was new to the group, inherited from one of the big base hospitals when the group's old Flight Surgeon had suffered a nervous collapse. He had a pleasant empty face and he looked like a general practitioner doing clinic work on his day off.

Deacon told a story filled with half-starts and twisted phrases. He made it clear that the sun was still shining and the flag was snapping in the wind, but he was careful to interject long pauses and to wring his hands from time to time. Deacon felt both iron and pathos taking shape in his face. The major encouraged Deacon with a kind smile and bright eyes. He listened and nodded, asked only a few questions. Deacon tipped his answers, more and more confident that he was over the hump, on his way down a slide into the doorway of a tent of his own.

"Well, son," the major said, "you've had quite a time."

"It's all right now, sir."

"Well . . . maybe it won't ever be, but that's behind you. I'm not surprised anymore at the way you boys can bounce back. Even for young men . . . I guess the job just has to be done, doesn't it?"

"I guess that's it."

"Bad thing for you to be living alone like that. I thought the Army never left anyone alone."

"It's really better in my case, sir."

"I know that a doctor doesn't get much privacy even in civilian life, but it's what I miss most. It's the one thing I can't get used to in the service, never being left alone. But I guess you boys need your friends to help you along. That's probably your biggest trouble, avoiding your friends. You need them now." The major smiled cheerily. "Say, that's exciting news about the invasion, isn't it?"

"The invasion? Sure, I guess it is."

"I keep forgetting that you boys don't have to hang around waiting for the war to end the way the rest of us do. Just the same, it ought to be over soon. I wouldn't be surprised if we were all home by Christmas." He laughed ruefully. "And I'll probably still only be a major."

"It's going to last another two months," Deacon said, "and that's all I need to get in nineteen missions."

"I understand, son. You're anxious to get home; we all are. But I don't think Germany can hold out much longer, do you? The Russians are starting to move now, too."

"Major . . ."

"There's no reason why you can't go back on the duty roster. Colonel Passerant only wanted an informal opinion. He's not looking for a full fitness report. Not that I think you wouldn't pass if he did want one."

"But I don't know if I'm fit for flying right now."

"Don't worry so much about yourself son. There isn't any point in running you through a physical, you're perfectly all right. A little confidence is the only medicine you need. Start mixing with your friends again. Relax and have a few drinks."

"This is the first time I've been sober in five days," Deacon snapped.

"Well, that's not good." The Flight Surgeon frowned. "A few drinks is one thing, but this is no time for any of us to be going off on a bat. We're that close, son." He pinched a white thumb and forefinger together. "You can see why that tent isn't any good for you."

"I need the tent."

"You need to get out of it. Just think, a boy that's flown as many missions as you have . . . If you hadn't had the old moxie, it would have shown up long before this. We all have our jobs to do." He looked fretful. "You may be home in two months, but it's going to be a lot longer than that before I'll be able to pick up my practice again."

"I don't know if I can keep my mind on flying."

"You'll get right back in the groove as soon as you go back to duty. Just buckle down and everything will take care of itself."

Deacon felt a different kind of buckling and tried to get a grip on himself, but through the plastic window of the tent he could see only the field and the Italian landscape. The Flight Surgeon was unreal enough to be part of a dream, but, dream or otherwise, Deacon was being suffocated by the box they were trying to build around him.

"I didn't come here to get my ticket punched," he said. "You're supposed to be a doctor, not a chaplain."

The major's mouth fell open.

"You're supposed to take care of me. All you're doing is hearing confession."

"Now, Sergeant . . ."

"Up yours," Deacon said.

He walked out of the tent. The major called querulously after him. Deacon broke into a trot, stumbled down the ridge. He crossed the taxi strip and began to run hard, compulsively, as soon as he stepped on the landing mat. He skidded on the slick surface and the bluish reflection of the sun bounced back at him as he ran, running as he had once before, but through a silence rather than through a siren's cry and the sounds of a ship tearing.

Deacon crossed the mat and scuttled along the dry irrigation ditch until he came abreast of his tent. It was empty; the
new men were still up on the practice mission. His heart
pounding, sweating furiously, Deacon snatched a bottle from
under his cot. He swiveled his head to see if anyone had followed him, then clutched the bottle tight and leaped into the
ditch.

7.

THE CREWS had grown very edgy by the time the stand-down
entered its fourth day. They would have been more relaxed if
the field had been socked in, if flying had been impossible.
But each day the sun had shone had been a wasted one. As
badly as they'd needed the rest and refit, they grumbled at the
loss of four more chances to hack their way through Fifty.

The restriction wound the crews even tighter. The bar
wasn't opened again during daylight hours, and the men had
no other supply of liquor available to them. They were fifteen
miles from the nearest town where they could have gotten a
drink and forty miles from one where they could have gotten
a woman. There were no guards to keep them on the field,
but neither was there transportation other than hitching rides
along infrequently used roads. Had they reached one of the
towns they would have had to sweat out being stranded, missing an alert, a very serious offense when a restriction was on.

The old crews grew stale at their games and quarreled fre-
quently. There were several fistfights. The new crews, the recruits, were anxious and afraid. Both were relieved when a
signal for an alert came through on the afternoon of the
fourth day. The men grew slack and preoccupied. Simple ten-
sion replaced irritability.

Deacon came out of hiding after dark. He could sense the
alert as soon as he was among the tents, feel the quiet pressure among men who had no weapons or gear to prepare,
who were waiting only until it was time to sleep, and who
would sleep only until they were called. Finishing touches
were being put on the planes at the field. The armorers' section was active. There were lights on at Group headquarters
and in the operations huts of all the squadrons.

It was a soft mild night, but Deacon began to sweat. He

edged through the tent area and tried to look inconspicuous at the squadron bulletin board. His name was on the alert list, posted to a waist gun on *Tedeschi Blues*. Deacon tried to pry up the glass frame which protected the notices on the bulletin board. It was locked. He rubbed a finger back and forth above his name. The glass clouded over but the name didn't disappear.

The bartender would not serve him. An order had come down from Group, been transmitted through the squadron— Deacon was forbidden liquor by either the glass or the bottle. He grew loud and abusive and the men nearby looked at nim, his dusty wrinkled khakis, his wings and ribbons twisted askew. Deacon asked if there was anyone who would buy him a drink. They looked away. When he lunged at the bartender the men pulled him off and eased him out of the bar. He went to his tent, found only a quarter-full bottle of wine in the rubble around his cot. The recruits told him that a runner from the orderly room had been there twice looking for him, that he was supposed to report to the first sergeant before he turned in. Deacon drank the wine and left the tent.

He was still sweating, and the pulse had begun behind his ear. He went to Kelleher's tent, but Kelleher wasn't in. Finger stopped him when he tried to force the hasp on Kelleher's footlocker. Deacon went back to the bar and looked through the screening for someone who might bring a drink out to him. He called softly. The only one to hear him was a very young man, a stranger, who looked frightened and raised his own glass and drank steadily all the time Deacon was calling.

He roamed through the area, sweating harder, blundered finally into Toole's tent. The four men playing cards around a footlocker looked up, Toole lidding his eyes, Gruber giving him a tight smile. The recruit corporal wrinkled his nose. The last man, Torazzi, let white teeth show under a pencil-line mustache. He was a master sergeant and a very old sport.

"Can I get in?" Deacon asked.

"Got your loot, Deako?" Torazzi asked. "This is two-dollar limit and the sprog is stuck for a month's pay already, aren't you, junior?" Torazzi grinned at the slight pale corporal. "Got to get heavy for when we break out of this hole, got to get some so I can get some."

"I'm all right," Deacon said.

"Sure," Gruber said, "there's room."

He moved over. Deacon took some money from his pocket and sat down.

"What're you dressed up for, Deako?" Torazzi asked. "You been in town getting some? Haven't seen you around since you crawled out of that junk pile. Oh man, you had no right. They should have carted you away with the rest of the boys."

"Five-card stud," Toole said, dealing.

"I see you got posted to *Tedeschi Blues*, Deke," Gruber said.

"Man, I'm anxious to get up," Torazzi said. "They got reports on some kind of jets the Jerries're using. They're supposed to do over five hundred. Would I ever give my left nut to get one."

"You better get some new kind of bullets, then," Gruber said, "or you'll never catch them. We probably need bullets with engines in them, like airplanes. You get these bullets with little propellers on them and they fly after the jets. Maybe you have to wind them up."

"I bet you'd get a DFC," Torazzi said.

"You already got one, Razz," Gruber said.

"I'll take another one."

"I understand you wear your medals under your flying suit so the Krauts'll know you ought to have an important funeral. Razz's got this chute with double reinforcements so it won't rip under the weight of all those tin badges he's wearing. He's got springs in his shoes so he doesn't hit too hard."

"You're light, Preacher," Toole said.

Deacon turned his cards over. The red-and-white checkered backs shifted and merged. He blinked, strained to focus. As the men bent over their cards their faces came out of the shadows and into the light from the shaded bulb. Someone dealt a new hand. The cards wobbled and fluttered in the light.

"How about a drink?" Deacon asked abruptly.

"All out of beer, Preacher," Toole said.

"Give me two cards," Torazzi said. "Yeah, some of that *vino* would really loosen me up. Some of that good juice. Send the kid for it, Tooley."

"You want to go, Wick?" Toole asked.

"Give him enough money so that thief Hobby won't give him a hard time. Some of that Alley-Oop, Tooley, just right to get us loose."

"Okay," the corporal said.

"Get a couple of bottles." Toole handed him some bills. "I'll take it out of the pot as we go along."

"And one for me," Deacon said, passing the money.

"That's a real thirst, Deako," Torazzi said after the corporal left. "You'll wind up with your pecker frozen into the relief tube tomorrow. I'd like to see the looks on the faces of that recruit crew when you show up with the staggers."

"You can shut your ass, Vic," Deacon said.

"Come on, Deako, you're too tight. You want to get up again, like a guy who falls off his horse. You remember when we mushed *The Pickler?*" Gruber nodded wearily. "They wanted to set me down, you know, but I got up on the very next mission. It turned out I had a broken finger."

"Well, you couldn't pick your nose when you were wearing gloves anyway," Gruber said. "Being in a war don't mean nothing unless you get to meet a real hero. I told my mother that, Razz. She's got a candle going all the time because she knows we can't win without guys like you."

"Your bet, Preacher," Toole said.

Deacon folded. The pulse had lengthened into a gallop. He held his ear. When his turn to deal came he passed the deck to Gruber. He anted for each hand and then clung to the cards until it was time to throw them in. Between hands his empty fingers crawled along his thighs.

When the corporal came back with the wine Toole brought out three unevenly edged glasses cut down from beer bottles. Deacon took a bottle and pulled the cork with his teeth. He tilted it, took a long drink, breathed and raised the bottle again. The others filled glasses. The corporal didn't drink.

"Don't let Deako here scare you," Torazzi said.

"I don't drink much," the corporal said.

"Man, you got to get yourself loose. Get wound too tight and you'll never make it."

"This particular hero's got sixty-seven missions, Wick," Gruber said. "He signed on for the extra twenty-five so he won't have to come back on another tour."

"That's right," Torazzi said. "You boys'll get your thirty days in the States and then you'll be right back here while old Vic is getting some."

"That's all right, Razz," Gruber said, "but I have this problem that I want to see what life is like before I get retired from it. They're gonna have to catch me to send me back after I get through and before they catch me they're gonna have to find me. Like some of these guys, their mother hides them in the closet. I already sent her the plans. It's got a private entrance so the hump don't wake her up coming in and out."

"I might volunteer for the Pacific when I get through here," Torazzi said. "Those twenty-nines are supposed to be plenty hot."

"Fifty's enough for anybody," Toole said. "They should have invaded the goddamned Balkans instead of France."

"That fucking Ploesti," Gruber said.

"I'll bet a dollar," Deacon said.

His hands were trembling only slightly and his ear had stopped shuddering. He lost the pot, but he won the next, and the next after that. The level of the wine bottle was below the halfway mark.

"You'll make master master sergeant," he said to Torazzi.

"I might get warrant officer."

"They give you a testimonial," Gruber said, "like when you get a watch. But it's a bullet, a magic silver bullet. You're all set in case you run into Dracula."

"Any poop on tomorrow?" Toole asked.

"Straight up, Tooley," Deacon said. "The master master sergeant is going to lead us right into the sun. Pingo on you, Torazzi."

"When I make it, buddy, they won't say I had to jump out of a bottle every morning to get the mustard to go up."

"Right. They won't say anything. I'll bet two dollars they won't."

"What two dollars? Are you betting on your hand or what?"

"Two dollars. Any calls?"

"I'll see you," Gruber said.

"Two dollars on what?" Torazzi asked. "What the hell is he betting on?"

"I'll call, Preacher," Toole said.

"Me too," the corporal said.

"Okay, Torazzi's out. No raises? Okay." Deacon held the cards close to his face and inched them apart. "I win, Torazzi, they don't say anything."

He laid the cards on the footlocker and took a long pull from the wine bottle, then grinned at each of the faces leaning toward him. The air within the yellow cone of the bulb's light seemed to grow thicker and thicker until Deacon felt that his lips were cemented in straight lines across his mouth.

He threw his cards in. After a moment the other players turned their hands over and wordlessly compared them. The corporal won. Toole gathered the deck together and began to shuffle. Deacon drained the bottle. Torazzi's mouth opened and closed, but he said nothing. It was Finger who spoke, his head hanging in the tent doorway as though on a string.

"I got a woman here," he said, "no shit."

Deacon put his head between his hands and listened to a new sound, a ragged bow rasping across frayed cables.

"Come on, snap shit," Finger said. "I can't keep her out here all night."

Torazzi put his hands behind his head and leaned back. "What's the freight?" he asked.

"It doesn't mean shit," Finger said. "Three packs of butts. Okay?"

"What say, Tooley?" Torazzi asked. "I could sure use some. Loosen me up."

"We could use Kenny's cot," Gruber said.

Toole shrugged. Finger's head disappeared and then he pushed the woman into the tent ahead of him. She was slight and about forty, wearing a dark wrinkled dress. She carried a net bag which held her shoes and a number of cigarette packages. Dust coated her feet and legs. As she squinted against the bright light she smiled, a silver tooth glinting at the side of her mouth. A very heavy odor came from her.

"For Christ sake," Toole said.

"Don't let the wrinkles fool you," Finger said. "She screws like shit."

"Man, you must be crazy," Torazzi said. "She couldn't work me up to thirty cents' worth of butts."

The woman's eyes shifted to each as he spoke. Still smiling, she licked at the silver tooth with the tip of her tongue.

Torazzi took her arm. *"Uei, vecchia scrofa, che cosa fa? Va via.* Take her home to the rest of the pigs, Finger."

Deacon swung the bottle toward Torazzi, but it caught the metal lampshade and the bulb burst in a flash of blue. The bottle was knocked from Deacon's hand when it clunked against the tent pole. The woman screamed softly and there was a rush of warm bodies in the dark. Deacon was tipped over onto a cot. He lay with his mouth open, the place behind his ear burgeoning with each pulse of his blood.

The men grunted and swore until someone found a flashlight. The beam darted around the tent, rested on Deacon's open eyes. He could see the figures beyond the rings of light but he could not hear them clearly above the strident rasp and the booming at his ear. Someone lunged toward him and was brushed away, then the beam swung to a hand gingerly unscrewing the broken bulb. The cone of yellow light appeared again, outside it Torazzi standing in the doorway with an angry face, saying something while Gruber held a hand against his chest. Toole bent next to Deacon and moved his mouth but only warbling sounds came out. The corporal stood with both his arms wrapped around the tent pole.

Then Torazzi was gone and Toole and Gruber stood looking at Deacon, their voices spongy and distorted. Gruber left. The corporal retreated to the corner of the tent farthest from Deacon. Toole walked back and forth, his hands in the hip pocket of his fatigues.

Deacon lay so long with his mouth open it became dry. His tongue felt like a piece of wood when he tried to move it.

The rasping died away and the pulse receded to a flutter. He closed his mouth, grating one lip against the other.

"What?" Toole said.

" 's okay, Tooley."

"You okay, Preacher?" Toole sat at the edge of the cot. "You want a drink or something?"

"Hey buddy," Deacon said, "hey buddy."

"Take it slow, Preacher."

He could hear quite clearly now. The generator hammered in the distance; there were voices nearby, occasional shouts of laughter. Wind rustled through the almond trees. He could hear the musical clink of the instruments in the Flight Surgeon's bag when the major came into the tent.

The officer peeled back his eyes and felt his pulse. He articulated each leg and then Deacon's wrists and forearms. Deacon's arms and legs lay whichever way the major arranged them. The major hummed fitfully as he unbuttoned Deacon's shirt and drew a fingernail across the skin of his chest, then rummaged in his bag and took out a hypodermic.

Deacon twisted his head until he could see Toole. He held his hand out to him. Toole grasped it, turned away as the needle caught the light and swooped down.

They shipped him out dressed as he was, adding only a stringy tie knotted at his throat and a clean cap. He sat primly in the back seat of the jeep, his feet together, his musette bag held on his lap like an oversize purse. The medic in the jeep's front seat had to balance himself on one haunch because of the billy he wore on his web belt.

Quiet had come back to the field, with it different sounds. The ships had thundered out that morning and drained the field of its perpetual noises. When the medic reached over and beeped the horn several times, it cut sharply through the air. The orderly-room door opened with a creak of wood and hinges. There was a click as the driver turned on the ignition key, a squeak as he stamped on the starter. The motor was very loud, the hood clattered. Small stones rattled against the underside of the fenders as the jeep pulled out of the squadron area.

Tires thumped against the uneven surface of the black-topped road, the jeep's canvas creaked. Everything had gone up that morning—everything. The line crews were not working and there was no activity at the service squadron. The field was cleared of airplanes, the perimeter of the runway empty of vehicles. Nothing moved along the service road except the jeep carrying Deacon.

It left a cone of dust in the clear still air. Dried leaves whispered in its wake.

PART TWO

Fight on my merry men all,
I'm a little wounded, but I am not slain;
I will lay me down for to bleed a while,
Then I'll rise and fight with you again.

JOHNNIE ARMSTRONG'S LAST GOOD-NIGHT
Anonymous

8.

AS THE sky waited, as Vienna waited, the hospital waits. It is a public work, late Duce, and there are bundled axes cut into the thin veneer of white stone on either side of the imposing door. But the stone has been assaulted by gritty winds and curdled by the sun and the fasces have become little more than graffiti. As a work the hospital no longer serves the public. An American flag flies from the roof, an MP in white cartridge belt and leggings stands guard on the steps.

The hospital receives none of the wounded left behind by the advancing front. It is far from the war, tucked among the spines and ridges of the Italian toe. The patients who pass through the corroded doorway have ordinary civilian illnesses, are accident cases, the jaundiced and malarial, the victims of diseased whores—all casualties of circumstance. Only a few are treated specially, sit waiting in one particular ward.

Both the Ionian and Tyrhennian Seas lick at the Italian toe, but neither is visible from the hospital windows, which overlook a busy highway and a blue-gray jumble of Calabrian rock. In G Ward even that meager view is blurred by a mesh of chicken wire overlaid on the screening.

Neither Duce nor the image of New Rome has succeeded in restraining the Italian flair, the rococo touch. The hospital's floors are tiled in floral arabesques, the ceilings vaulted. Each ward is set between corridors and faced with ornate doorless portals. Only G Ward has a wall across one end, a desk which partially blocks the entrance. The medic sitting behind it faces into the room so that he can keep watch over the forty beds. Less than half are occupied, and only nineteen men look on as the new patient is brought in. The eyes flickering over him are empty of casual appraisal, the quick fit usually given a new man joining an established outfit. None of the men in G Ward is established—each is himself a casual, a transient in the last stage of rehabilitation. The hospital and ward are permanent, but the men are only temporary fixtures. They watch as the new man is led to a bed, as he inches toward its foot and sits with hands curled around the chipped white frame, the fingers dark against the enamel, tanned and slightly ashen. They look away when he swings hooded eyes toward them.

A patient leaves his bedside, briskly approaches the medic's desk, backless slippers flopping. He stands with hands in the pockets of the maroon robe, slim, nearly wasted, his face drawn in a pucker. There are ringlets of gray inside each of the tight curls on his head. The medic turns the pages of a magazine and does not look up.

Julian Harris is still listed as a first sergeant, but in the hospital he is rankless. He stands stiffly inside the robe, tries to lend authority to the folds, tries to stretch them into a military outline. There are cords in his wrist and neck, his cheekbones are prominent. A high white instep arches from each of his slippers—his ankles are fragile, his heels pinched. The pucker rounds his lips in the form of a whistle.

While First Sergeant Julian Harris waits, his outfit continues to pursue the war. A photo-reconnaissance squadron, they jump from one patchwork field to another, buck up as close as possible to the front in order to obtain maximum range. From early light to sunset they breeze out to fix the enemy and the terrain in their camera lenses, stripped-down P38s in which both armor and ammunition have been sacrificed to speed. The pilots take off from hastily laid mats, sleep in shanty huts which are sometimes within sound of the artillery. Skimming low, they click mile after mile into their cameras, long strips which become aerial maps incidental to grand designs at strategic headquarters, films which are enlarged to cover limited sectors and then defaced with crayoned symbols and colored pins and chopped piecemeal into the hash of tactics.

For nearly sixteen months Julian Harris was the squadron's first sergeant, their scribe, the keeper of names and records. They have left him behind, left him his memories of musters called in the stinging North African sand, in Italian mud which sucked men bootless—memories of dawns broken by whistling engines, of skies split by the wicked slewing of tail booms. And Harris with eyes straining for the sight of wings touched red by the late sun, midwife to the spools of film delivered to the courier's pouch.

He served until drained, gave until he developed an anxiety he no longer even remembers. The squadron moved up, jettisoned Harris somewhere between Foggia and Naples, part of the detritus in the wake of the rolling front. He was stuffed into the Calabrian toe, and now he is riddled with a new anxiety; he must catch up, must join the squadron. He sees it leapfrogging through Italy, into Austria and Germany, following the front right into the North Sea until ships and rusted mats and shacks drown like lemmings. Harris was part of the squadron's original complement, and he must be there when it dies.

He waits at the desk, his wiry frame bracing the robe, and he looks without interest at the bronze streaks which follow the anticlines of the medic's rippled hair. The pages of the magazine slither and crackle.

"He don't know anything about your outfit, Harris," the medic says, still not looking up.

"Never hurts to give it a try. Last I heard they were at Termoli."

"He's from some lousy bomber squadron, another Joe Balls type like Bradeway." The medic sits back and studies Harris. "All this cheap big rank the Air Corps gets and they wind up having their noses wiped by a little old corporal."

"You're not a real corporal, Geary, you're a T-5."

"And you're Top Kick." The medic pushes a package of cigarettes toward Harris. He taps one out, puts it in the medic's mouth, lights it. His hand is steady. "But I don't see any stripes on that bathrobe you're wearing," Geary continues. "I'll bet you were a good man, Top. Do you think your outfit would take you back after you've been a nut and everything?"

"I'll have to catch them to find out." Harris's pucker opens into a small round smile.

"They're probably gone. Suppose they were transferred out of this theater? Suppose they went to the Pacific or the CBI?"

"Still at Termoli the last I heard."

"They left, Harris, they went back to the States."

"Not without me they didn't."

"Forget it, Top." The medic's lips part lazily, show white teeth. "The war'll be over and your outfit'll be back in the States before you ever get out of here. You ought to start worrying about getting out *after* the war is over."

Harris's eyes dance together, threaten to cross behind the bridge of his nose and change sockets.

"I'll get out of here before you will, Geary."

"I'm in no hurry—I never had it so good, did you?"

"Never."

"That's the spirit, Top, no gripes. I can see real progress in your case. You keep applying yourself and you'll be back up there on the firing line. How's your kindergarten therapy?"

"I'm working on a belt."

"I take a size thirty-two." The medic slaps his flat stomach. "You'd never know I was really hung, would you?"

"I'd figure you for a stump, Geary."

"That WAC of Klein's loves it. Any time I want to, Top, all day and all night. They ought to let you nuts have some. I'll bet it's been so long you've forgotten what it's like. Want me to tell you?" Harris's tongue makes a semicircle around his pursed upper lip. "I'd better not, it might be too much for you—you might break down and cry. Listen, why don't you go over and brief the new nut? He's only a staff sergeant, so you can pull that great rank of yours on him. I'd like to see you shape him up like a real soldier."

"Is he right out of IC?"

"Well no, Harris, but he might be on his way into it. He's here for observation. They want me to see if he's just some rabbity Joe Balls striper or only a poor nut who needs to be put away."

"I'll talk to him."

"You do that, Top. You can carry on now, you're dismissed."

The men have been watching obliquely, all the while twining together in maroon knots, breaking and reforming as they flow from bed to bed. The beds are not GI but spindle-legged Italian, enameled white, chipped to iron. They are carefully made, unmussed, each with an olive-drab blanket whose top is turned under the collar of a sheet, each with a flat pillow. Men sit reading on straight-backed chairs tilted against the bed frames, play cards across the blankets.

The air outside is hazed with a drift of hot dust from the highway. It clings to the wire mesh at each window, but the patients are not sweating in their robes and pajamas. They are comfortable behind the thick stone of the hospital walls, under the vaulted ceiling. Their voices float upward and become garbled in the tunnel of cool air which moves overhead. Sounds carry from the corridors. Trucks grind by steadily on the highway. In the ward itself there is the clop of slippers, the scrape of chairs, the occasional rubbing of the medic's stiff whites. The patients' clothing has grown so soft from wear and laundering it is noiseless. Cloth dimples, creases silently when they turn their heads to watch Harris approach the new man. He is holding together all the parts of Harris the first sergeant, wary but confident, used to approaches.

"Might as well get this over with," he says. "I'm Julian Harris and I'm supposed to be the ward chief but I can't even take a leak without asking one of these lousy medics for permission. This house was built by the numbers, soldier, and when they tell you to shit you better squat and strain."

The new man's fingers do not really grip the bedstead—they are curled around it like the talons of a bird. Harris's hands fan out in his pockets as he tries to stretch the robe taut.

"The first thing to do is get used to the idea that you're in here and there's no way out except through the front door. The MP'll shoot your ass off if you try to go through it dressed like that." The man looks not quite at him and not quite through him. "Everything goes nice and neat and GI, no strain," Harris continues. "We all push together on work details because we're breaking our balls to get out of here so that we never have to see each other again. A shave every morning and you make your bed before breakfast and you don't get on it again until after evening chow. *Capito?*" The springs of the bed creak as the man lifts himself from it. "Geary tells me that you're here for observation. Make it good, soldier, or they'll push you up the line to IC—intensive care—and that could turn out to be a cage. You do what the medics say and you don't lean on anybody, but if you get into a real bind, I'm the man to see. You're still a soldier and you've still got your rights, and I've been a first sergeant long enough to know what they are." He pauses. "Harris, Julian Harris."

A queer wrinkle like a smile crosses the new patient's lips. Harris has seen such a variety of smiles and queerness that he doesn't question it, only dips his head and marches stiffly away. The new man lights a cigarette, breathes a cloud of smoke toward the currents carrying along the room's ceiling, calls a single word which mingles with all the sounds of the hospital, the rubber soles and rubber-wheeled carts and rattle of glassware and the flopping slippers.

"Deacon."

Harris's tuned ear picks out the name.

Time moves through the ward at the determined pace of a rickety player piano's roll, without music, hidden splines springing in an orderly pattern through the perforations. At four in the afternoon Geary is relieved by a pleasant-face medic in thick glasses whose neck bulges over the collar of his white coat. His name is Ferguson, but the men call him Pacifier. Just before six o'clock he taps a large hand against a bell like a schoolteacher's and the patients form a double file without delay. The medic counts them off. Rays from the declining sun turn the dust-coated wire mesh into a lattice of golden pollen.

The men are marched out of the ward in a loose column of twos, pass the portals of wards where there are figures in slings and braces, pass others which are quiet and have each bed separated by a screen. The column becomes the subject of grins and snickers when it marches into the mess hall. Casts and bandaged fingers are pointed in its direction.

The men from G Ward eat in a corner, separated from the rest of the patients by two vacant tables. Places are set with a fork, spoon and metal cup, a knife with a rounded tip and blunt edge. Two Italians in white jackets arrive with a serving cart. They dole out metal trays on which generous portions of food have already been placed. There is bread and milk and coffee and jam on the table.

As they eat, the patients are perfectly relaxed, talk quietly. Ferguson, at the table's head, smiles at the old jokes and chews steadily. A blond man drops his fork, drops it again, yet again, each time the fork clanging against the metal tray. A patient across from him shuts his eyes and swears in a fierce whisper. The medic looks up. The blond man takes his fingers and forces them around the fork, wraps them like putty. Someone laughs.

At the meal's end the Italians count the silver, verify that it is complete. The medic reforms the column and marches it back to the ward. A patient who has to use the latrine must first ask the medic, then find another man to go with him. They are not permitted to leave the ward except in pairs and they must return together.

At eight o'clock a movie projector and screen are brought in. Ferguson checks attendance before hanging a drape across the entrance. Lights are turned out and a tired beam marches through the dark, spills out colored images which are blotched by the peeling screen. A yellow-haired girl in mock uniform and black stockings dances to the uneven sound track, conducts other girls in a close-order drill as she marks time in high heels and flaunts her pert behind. The men snigger. A soldier and a war worker meander across the screen in pursuit of the girl. The men meander with them, listless except when she reappears with the chorus. At one point the projectionist stops the film, catches her with whirling skirt wrapped around her waist, legs blurred slightly and parted in mid-stride to reveal a sleek crotch of bald blue satin. The medic growls and the projector grinds on, the figure spinning in the skirt's descending folds.

When the story of distant lives in a distant country is over, the drape is removed and the hospital creeps back into the room. At a quarter past ten the overhead lights blink twice and the men make a last trip to the latrine and settle near their beds. Since the new man makes the ward's twentieth, there is a neat arrangement of ten patients to each side of the room, the beds alternately empty and occupied. Ferguson makes a final count. At ten-thirty the overhead lights go out and those in the corridor dim. A shaded bulb burns at the medic's desk.

Time rolls at the same pace, without music, but there is no whine of trucks from the highway and only infrequent noises come from the corridor. Sheets rustle and springs creak. A dry breeze carries the indistinct sound of night wind on rock, on the leaves of stunted trees. Calabria's moon comes out along the track of the thirty-ninth parallel, having lighted Lisbon and Valencia, on the way to Lesbos. The ward is tinged yellow-silver and the unwrinkled blankets of the beds between the humped figures take on the appearance of decayed teeth.

The screw is gone from the face of First Sergeant Harris. He no longer has to hold things together. The tears run freely down his cheeks. Harris cannot be first sergeant again until he learns how to stop crying, cannot walk through the door and begin the long trip north to where the squadron is crouching against the dawn. He tries to stop the tears with his knuckles, gathers dust from the window and blots at them. The moon's light touches the wet corners of his mouth.

Harris feels a sob rising. As he turns to stifle it in his pillow it wrenches from him and springs rattle nearby and someone begins to swear in a harsh whisper.

9.

EACH DAY that Lieutenant Jesse Klein sits behind the desk in G Ward's administrative office hairs fall from the crown of his head. The lieutenant knows that he should not be there, that he should not even be wearing the caduceus insignia of the medical corps.

His only previous administrative experience had been in a suburban school system where he had acted as an unofficial psychologist from time to time because he had concentrated on college psychology courses. The Army misunderstood his civilian function and education, fitted him with the winged healer's staff and twined serpents. While they did not make him a doctor, they treated him like one, and Klein was disturbed by both the classification and the designation. The

Army turned his protests away by assuring him that he would never have to treat anyone.

The new lieutenant's first assignment was to a training-film unit. He was bewildered until it was explained that he was to serve as a sort of specialist in black magic of the mind, expected to develop subtle prods which would reach into all the makeshift theaters where inductees in creaking boots and new fatigues sat taking instruction in what the Army wanted of them. Klein was mildly amused at the thought of trying to motivate men toward the proper gas discipline, camouflage, extended-order drill. But the major in charge had nothing so ordinary in mind; he looked on Klein as a new kind of weapon, one he was hurting for badly.

The major—a former Hollywood second-unit manager—was under severe pressure from headquarters. The troops had not been responding to a very important area of their indoctrination, were turning up with far too many positive smears. Chaplains' lectures hadn't had any effect, nor had poster campaigns featuring the sweet image of the Girl Back Home, and the men were sleeping through the VD film which was then going the training circuit. Headquarters wanted a new movie, something which would grab where the hair was literally short, discourage the boys from wallowing in the slime and get those who were undauntable to mount a GI tire-rubber device before plunging, stampede the deliberately reckless into a pro station for a lather and sear treatment after exposure.

Klein listened in a daze. If somehow, he was told, he could rig it so that these kids started to hear a steady drip every time they kissed a girl; if he could convince them that every woman was walking around with a time bomb between her legs. And all done nicely, not too raw. Headquarters was sensitive about being accused of producing dirty pictures. No real action or anything like that.

Jesse Klein, a bachelor whose romantic opportunities had been limited, was not the man to bulldoze the id, elevate the superego. But the major was counting on him, had never had anyone with his training on the staff before. And it wouldn't be so much different from school—the new troops weren't much older, it was all for their own good. When Klein sputtered the major ran up the flag on the Army's crying need for any kind of competent advice at all; if the lieutenant would not do it, who would? Klein shifted uncomfortably at duty's call, became conscious of his new rank and new uniform. He agreed to try.

The script was incredible. Klein suggested changes more for the sake of reason and continuity than for any subliminal

88

effect they might have. The major provided him with a viewer, asked his opinion on whether one or another camera angle was the more suggestive. It seemed to be the major's intention to fill the screen with closeups of fully clothed loins and backsides. Klein watched helplessly while the actors—the boy played as an obvious hayseed, the girl as a reeking tart —leered suggestively at each other but maintained a prissy distance. He was dismayed by the finale—the young man looking down out of the picture at the seepage implicitly sprung from the organ he was supposed to be holding in his hand, a dubbed background of muffled drums and bugles as though the rest of his outfit was marching off to glory while he could look forward to nothing but an endless series of healing needles. And the entire scene set in an authentic latrine, urinals and commodes thumping away.

Lieutenant Klein's dreams were broken by the thunder of rushing waters, but he saw the film through its final cutting. Headquarters found that it did not grab. The major suggested that maybe all the gimmicks couldn't be understood because they were working on the unconscious; headquarters wanted something *they* could understand. They wanted something real, a message which would have the men thinking twice before unbuttoning their flies for any reason at all. Someone came up with a grabber, a clincher. The film would be run as it was, but a two-minute Mickey Mouse would be added, a trailer of clinical shots showing diseased organs in full color.

Jesse Klein was appalled at the number of people who had been willing to have their shattered genitalia photographed. So many films were available from the medical files an entire week had to be spent selecting the most shocking. Klein was closeted with the major while they looked at a screen filled with the horrors of advanced syphilis, acute gonorrhea, soft chancres enlarged to the size of moon craters. What did he think, this one or that? Indifferent fists milked glutinous discharges from limp tubes. There was livid flesh, ruby sores. Didn't he think that one was a beauty? A six-foot corroded labia, expressly spread, hung overhead while Lieutenant Klein retched into his handkerchief.

After the trailer had been put together he pleaded for release, for a transfer to any duty far removed from the pathology of vagina and prepuce. He would even go to the war. The major reminded the lieutenant of his healer's insignia, his Hippocratic responsibilities. Klein tried to explain that he had none, that he had no special ability and could not possibly be of use to the unit. The major became ruffled, then angry, finally grew disenchanted with his secret weapon. He threw the name of Lieutenant Jesse Klein into the operations hopper and it emerged on a shipping list for an overseas which had no particular name, no need for any of Klein's particular talents.

He baked for two months in Tunis, unused and unusable, a rootless replacement blown freely by the African winds. The depot assignment center could find no one whom Klein could replace. He tried to transfer out of the medical corps into the infantry and was told that he was capable of leading men nowhere except into disaster. The hot sun and dry air began to shrivel him. It was suggested that he might be able to find a place as the depot's VD officer. Klein curled like a rind.

A vacancy filtered down through the maze of channels, the job of managing G Ward. Klein said yes to everything. Yes, it would be something like running a school system. Yes, his psychological studies would be very helpful. He knew that he was unqualified, but he was afraid that any day he might be given a grub hoe and told to work some public thicket. The assignment officer glided over Klein's lies and evasions, glad of the chance to fob him off.

Jesse Klein believed that the hospital would quickly discover that he had no business working with a ward of disturbed men, but he also believed that a place would be found where he could be of use. The uniform had to be more than a costume, the bars on his shoulders more than decorations. There had to be someplace in the war for a bright able-bodied man. Captain Marcellus agreed, thought that the lieutenant would fit very nicely into G Ward. Klein stammered about being out of his depth. The captain advised him to tread water; he was himself a bone specialist, had not encountered psychiatrics since medical school. There was no one at all in the hospital qualified to manage G Ward. Its existence was as fortuitous as Klein's assignment, the brainchild of some boob in the upper echelons who discovered a ward with forty empty beds and thought that it would make a good way station for men who were supposedly on the road back to duty. And there weren't any other openings at all, unless—the captain shuffled through Klein's service record—he could be fitted in as some sort of rehabilitation or information officer for the venereal wards. Klein stammered again, this time with an earnest protest to do his best for G Ward.

Captain Marcellus would assume all medical responsibility; Klein need only act as counselor and keeper. There would be no problems if they would remember not to meddle, not to stir the silt at the bottom of murky waters. Since neither of them was therapeutically qualified, they could only look after the general health and impose a fairly strict discipline as a test of the men's readiness for duty. Klein listened, nodded unhappily, and took the job.

Jesse Klein has been an unhappy administrator for a year, and he has tried not to meddle. He knows that most of the men have received proper professional care before arriving at the hospital, that the Army has supposedly cured most of their psychoses and judged them fit to be returned to duty. They are to stay in G Ward until they have become completely adjusted to routine again, taken on a military gloss. During Klein's tenure most of the men who entered the ward have been sent back to their outfits. A very few have regressed, a few others seem to be static. Klein hopes that he has helped and he prays that he hasn't done any harm. Nevertheless, his hair is falling out.

The lieutenant is too young to be growing bald, not young enough to be able to shrug off his responsibilities. Captain Marcellus keeps an eye on pulse and respiration, on response to the routine, but most of the time the captain is wading through splints and osteoblast in another part of the hospital. It is Klein who must bear the full pressure of dozens of minds. He spends hours in the medical library trying to fill the gaps in his knowledge and experience, wading through books which he has not been trained to understand, which are almost occult, filled with formulas Klein dares not use because he might trip a lever which will catapult someone backward.

He tries to reach out as a person, reaches softly, trying not to disturb the coiled springs and tottering balances. When he finds that his rank is a barrier between himself and the men he removes his gold bars, disguises the walls of his office with shabby Italian prints and biting anti-officer cartoons from *Yank*. He sits in his shirt sleeves, squirms on a plain chair and lets the patients use his upholstered one. The men aren't deceived. Klein encounters hostility to his rank, to his person, finds his charges hostile to their own situations. He inevitably encounters his own ignorance.

"So I guess the Flight Surgeon just didn't understand about the tent," the new man is saying. "He wasn't our regular Flight Surgeon anyway, only a doctor."

Klein is most uneasy about the cases sent in for observation, those recommended by medical officers vegetating in remote installations. They arrive without professional psychiatric evaluation, without grips or handholds—perhaps arrive with a hidden fuse ticking.

"Well, I'm afraid I'm not even a doctor—" Klein smiles—"but then maybe you don't really need medical care. That's what we're supposed to find out. If you don't, okay, no strain. You should consider the ward as just another barracks, except that we have real beds and the food is better and you're off the duty roster for a while."

The man's cheeks are drawn, but there are fatty creases beneath the eyes, as though the face had been plumped up by an undertaker. From flying, Klein wonders, from the wind, from squinting down the barrel of a machine gun?

"How long will I be here?"

"I have no better idea of that than you do," Klein says. "Some men are here two weeks or a month, some stay longer than they should. It's not as though you were serving some kind of guardhouse sentence. We'll return you to your outfit just as soon as we're sure you're well enough to go back to duty."

"I didn't know I was sick."

"Nothing would make us happier than to find out you aren't. Look, all we have to go on is your medical history . . . and your Flight Surgeon's interpretation might have been wrong. As long as you *are* here you might as well take it easy, goof off, smoke if you've got 'em." Klein's interjection of the enlisted man's vernacular draws no response. "All you have to do is what we ask you to. We're a little GI, but that'll make your own outfit seem all the more like home when you get back."

"I won't get a Section Eight discharge, will I?"

"That's one of the things you ought to get straight right away; this isn't Section Eight. The other thing is that we don't make any recommendations for discharge. This isn't a door out of the Army. If it was, I'd have found a way through it myself by now." Klein tries another smile. "But we don't want to talk about getting out or getting back right now, we just want to find out where we are."

"Suppose everything works out, Lieutenant, would you be the one to write me some kind of authorization so that I could have the tent?"

Klein feels as though he has been slapped. He has been coasting along on nothing more than patter because his prognosis has already been established and he feels that he has nothing more than a weary birdman on his hands. He has been cheating, juggling symptoms and behavior patterns which he isn't qualified to interpret. The man's question throws Klein into direct contact with the mind of Staff Sergeant Thomas Deacon, and he feels a rush of panic.

"You never know what the Army will do," he says, the evasion leaving him stiff-lipped. "Look, we all have to put up

92

with this nonsense, don't we? We're all living under some kind of big olive-drab thumb."

A sharp white edge comes into the patient's eyes, like the rim of the moon glaring from behind an eclipse.

"I didn't ask you to punch my ticket, Lieutenant."

"I'm not here to do that, only to help if I can. If I can't, we'll try to find a place where you can get help. The fact is this hospital can only recommend the kind of duty you should be put on after you've been released, but your actual assignment will be up to your CO. I know that we'd never suggest a private tent, but there's a good chance that you might not have to go back to combat again."

"I never said I didn't want to finish my tour."

"Do you?"

"Is that what that bastard put down, that I wanted to crap out?"

Klein cannot even decide how to address the man. He tries always to avoid reference to rank; he thinks it would be patronizing to use the last name, sugary to use the first.

"Your medical officer didn't pass on any judgments," he says, "it wasn't his job to. I told you that this wasn't any kind of disciplinary battalion. If you want to finish your tour, okay, we'll try to get you in shape to finish it." Klein pauses. "You've evidently had a drinking problem. Maybe it was only a case of your being too tensed up and relaxing too hard. It could happen to any of us."

The man's eyes become occluded. He has drawn the blinds completely.

"Nevertheless," Klein continues, "it's a problem you've got to beat, and we'll help you beat it because part of our job is taking the load off your back. There's no drinking of any kind permitted in the ward. If anyone in this hospital offers you liquor, turn it down. The roof will fall in if you even smell as though you've had a beer."

"Yes sir."

"I mean it."

"Yes sir."

"If you . . ." Klein struggles. "I'm nearly always here. I'd like you to feel free to come in for any reason at any time. I'm not a doctor and you don't have to feel sick to make a visit. We can talk about anything you want to talk about, anything at all. These shoulders may not look very broad, but they can carry a lot of troubles." Klein tries a final weak smile, sees its ghostly reflection bounce off the wall between them. "Okay? I'll see you again soon. If you don't call me, I'll call you."

The man gets to his feet, shuffles, jerks his arm as though

about to salute, then clops toward the door. He pauses and turns.

"Did you know who I was?"

"Why, yes."

"I mean, you must have known I'm new here, but did you know my name?"

"Yes, I did," Klein says, still unable to find a name to call him by. "I do."

The man nods, goes out. Klein looks wearily at the tired prints, at the cartoons which have grown too familiar. He takes out Deacon's folder, fingers a pencil, finds that he has no notes to make. The lieutenant speculates, becomes entwined by snaky threads, remembers something he has read in a dark book. He feels himself slipping into the labyrinth, no longer keeper and counselor but Klein the practitioner, Dr. Klein.

The lieutenant has laundry lists to verify, progress reports to write, a pass application to approve. He ignores them all, leaves his office. There is a WAC typist in the tiny anteroom, a PFC. Klein tells the girl that he's going to the library. She nods pleasantly, tries to smile around a wad of gum that shows between her teeth like a pink inner lip. Klein is carried back to the days of the training film, hurries out.

When staff members speak to him in the corridors he dips his head mechanically, busy in the turnings of an interior maze, half remembering case histories fed into it. Outside the library he meets Captain Marcellus, a rosy nearly fat young man.

"Any new looney tunes?" the captain asks.

The greeting is routine. Klein has always hated it. "I think Mamoulian can go this week for sure," he says. "I'll drop by tonight and we can go over his file."

"Tonight's my turn with the jeep, Jess."

"Tomorrow morning, then. We'll have to get the papers into the works if we're going to get him out."

"I'm in surgery tomorrow morning," Marcellus says. "All right, come by tonight, but let's get it wound up by eight. There's a lady who wants to see Reggio in the moonlight."

"I had the new man in today. I don't know, Bob, maybe he's in some kind of a state, maybe not. He seems to have a fixation on having a tent of his own. Maybe you'd like to look at him."

"Sounds as though he joost vants to be alone." Klein does not smile. "No thank you, I don't want to look at any of them unless they rattle."

"I'm afraid to shake this one to find out. Say, you weren't

looking for me, were you? I was just going into the library to check something out."

"Don't tell me one of those Zurich wheels wrote something about tent complexes."

"Not that I know of." Klein hesitates. "He's sort of . . . remote, Bob. I can't find anything to get hold of."

"Withdrawal? Sounds as though we're meddling, Jess. While you're floundering around and muddying the waters don't overlook that old combat disease, chickenitis. Next time he gets up from the chair see if he leaves an egg."

The captain goes whistling on his way. Klein speculates on the shape of egg Marcellus might lay if he were pressed into combat. Or himself. And then, no longer remembering the specific title he was searching for, he lets his fingers trail along the spines of books, finally looks dejectedly into space and wonders just how much help he can expect from the works of someone in Zurich who has never had to contend with the by-product of thirty-one missions.

10.

THEY ARE never alone. The buddy system is always in effect, the men practically holding hands. They must have a partner every time they leave the ward, must report back immediately if they lose him.

In the morning they are sent out in groups of four, allowed ten minutes to wash and shave. The medic who has come on at midnight doles out the razor blades from a community box, collects them when each quartet returns. Because the latrine is reserved exclusively for G Ward's use there is nothing of the usual assortment of half-dressed men. The room is brightly lit, very clean, and the vitreous fittings gleam in a sterile empty atmosphere where four figures in pajama trousers stand shaving before the long mirror. They are not in an obvious rush, but they move steadily. Steam rises from the basins of hot water, clouds the bright mirror. They talk to their own lathered faces.

"God damn," Pettigrew says, "I'll bet anything it was you used this blade last, Walinski. It's all nicked from those Polack hog bristles."

A burly man down the line pulls at his face and is aped by

the image in the mirror. "You got lady hairs, Pettigrew."

"Why, I thought that was Pancho's trouble. Hey, Vierra, I wouldn't shave that off, I'd let it grow." A slender man near him scrapes unhurriedly. "You get back to civilian life and you can make a fortune as the bearded lady."

Vierra rubs an appraising finger over his chin, rinses the razor. "My choice meat is anxious for you, Pettigrew. Can you whistle?"

"Only 'Dixie,' Pancho. How come you go talking dirty like that when your folks went and named you Jesus?" Walinski's head dips reflexively. "Suppose Lieutenant Klein hears you? But I don't know about Jesse . . . maybe you two have something in common." Pettigrew half turns his head toward Deacon. "Didn't it seem to you that the lieutenant held your hand just a little too tight?"

"I didn't notice."

"Well maybe he was afraid to mess with you anyway, what with you flying that glory and all the way you did. At least that's what I understand."

"That's right."

"Why, sure, you and old Bradeway. Probably have a lot to talk over with him, probably crazy for candy bars the way he is. Bradeway's due for a hash mark for ward time. Can you feature anybody being here five months? They ought to either ship him out or send him back to IC."

"Bradeway is already gone," Vierra says. "There is no one in him. How can he be shipped out when they can't find all the parts to be put into the box?"

"IC's not so bad," Walinski says.

"Hell, they were good to you because they were afraid of you, Polack. You might've gone around breaking up all those medics. You think you could take on Pacifier? Oh man, I'd like to see that. I could sell tickets to a mix like that."

"I don't want no trouble," Walinski says.

"Hey Pancho," Pettigrew calls, "I can give you about a minute if you want to go around behind that partition with me."

Vierra dabs a fragrant lotion on his face, inspects his strong teeth. Pettigrew shrugs and begins removing the blade from his razor. It falls from his fingers. He stands with his blond head bowed over the sink for a moment, his hands clenched, then picks up the blade and dries it.

"It was wet and slippery," he says, "that's what it was."

"Why is every object your enemy?" Vierra asks. "Did Lieutenant Klein explain that to you?"

"I'll tell you what Jesse explained; he told me about that female object sitting at the typewriter in his office and he told

96

me, Pancho, that he's going to let you out just as soon as you show him you can get on top of her."

"I could stand some of that," Walinski says.

"That's not for us poor boys, she's looking to get put by Jesus." Walinski's head dips. "A religious girl like that she heats like a mink every time he comes by. I see her getting ready to gysm every time she looks at that big cross he's wearing."

"Knock that off," Walinski says.

"No offense, Polack. I was only talking in a figure of speech."

"God is screwing us all in more than a figure of speech," Vierra says. *Vamanos, amigos.* Do you understand that, Pettigrew?"

"I can't for the life of me, but it must be because of that queer accent of yours."

They gather their things, dress, return to the ward. The medic collects the blades, hands out four others to a quartet which has been waiting impatiently. After all the men have had a turn Geary arrives to relieve the night watch. He taps the bell and the patients form a column of twos. He counts them off, marches them to the mess hall for breakfast.

Each of the forty beds is neatly made. Trucks are already moving along the highway. The sun burns blue-white.

Harris plays sorcerer's apprentice, directs the broom from hand to hand down the aisle. The men put on a great show of sweeping, but they aren't able to produce any significant dirt because there is none of the usual barracks litter in the ward. All papers are put into woven wastebaskets, cigarette butts into sand-filled cans. No dirt is ever tracked in from the outside. Harris puckers and points, but he isn't able to shepherd more than a thin line of dust down the side.

He next inspects the beds, tugging at loose corners, smoothing pillows. When he reports to the medic that everything is in order, Geary strolls up and down the aisle. He stops to speak to Deacon for a moment, then goes back to his desk. Harris has been watching, makes a sign which the other patients pick up. Each gathers the magazines near him and places them at the foot of his bed. Deacon wipes his hands along the skirts of his robe, then goes slowly from bed to bed and collects the magazines. He brings the sizable stack to the medic's desk and then turns to go.

"Got a minute, Sergeant?" Geary asks, moving the pile to the approximate center of the desk. "If you could put them right here next time."

Geary looks through the magazines, makes a separate heap

of those whose covers are torn or curling. He hands some half dozen to Deacon. "Those covers look ratty," he says while Deacon stands holding the pile. "What I mean is, I think they should be fixed."

"Okay."

"We want to keep things looking nice, Sergeant. You men go to a lot of trouble to keep the room neat and clean. These ratty-looking magazines only spoil the good impression you're trying to make."

"You want me to fix them?"

"I thought you understood that, Sergeant. I didn't take you for one of these nuts who has to be led by the hand." The medic looks pained. "Fix the covers so that they lay down nice and flat. Stick the ripped parts together."

"With what?"

"Well, you could spit on them, Sergeant, if that's what you wanted to do, but I don't think your buddies would like that very much." Geary takes a jar of white library paste from his drawer. "You'd better use that. I guess you can figure out how to do it."

"I guess so."

"I'm afraid somebody lost the spreader, so you'll have to use your finger. The thing is, you can't paste anything on the covers or nobody will be able to read them. We ought to be able to think of some way to beat that." Deacon doesn't answer. "I'd say you have to stick the covers to the inside pages. It spoils some of the stories, but you can't win them all, can you? Right now I'd appreciate it if you put this other bunch right here."

Geary indicates the corner of his desk. Deacon puts down the paste and magazines he is holding and moves the remaining stack from the center to the edge of the desk.

"That's fine," Geary says. "You can bring your work back here when you get finished. Try to keep from smearing the paste all over. I'd particularly appreciate it if you could keep your robe and blankets clean, Sergeant."

Deacon goes back to his bed and clears a space on his night table. Some of the magazines are as rigid as boards, have been pasted through a dozen pages. He stands shuffling the pile. Harris comes up to the bed, his face puckered so severely that his eyes have almost disappeared.

"I guess you've been in the Army long enough to know that rank's all that counts," he says, "and if it happens to be a prick T-5 has it, then that's what we're stuck with."

Harris marches off. Deacon opens the paste jar, hesitates, then plunges his finger in.

* * *

Walinski and Pettigrew are playing cribbage on the other side of the room. Spinale sits next to Pettigrew and moves the pegs for him.

"I see they got the new guy playing stink-finger," Walinski says.

"Giving him the treatment right away," Pettigrew says. "I don't know but they might be trying to get us all queer as Vierra." He plays a card. "Fifteen-two, fifteen-four. Move it along there, Eddie."

"This is some beautiful duty, being a mumble-peg helper." Spinale moves the marker along the board. "How come you're so good at this Yankee game anyway, Pettigrew?"

"Ole Jesse says I'd better be—it's therapy. I get to work these mothering pegs and I can probably go back to duty. God damn, I remember when I couldn't even hold the *cards.*"

It is not objects but Pettigrew's hands which are his enemies. The Army had no way of knowing that they were intrinsically American hands, couldn't function outside the United States. Pettigrew had been an itinerant mechanic in the Shenandoah Valley, as adept at repairing combines as making willow whistles. The Army appreciated his clever fingers, put them to work in the Signal Corps. Pettigrew learned to repair radios, to splice wire and work a telegrapher's key.

Although a country boy a long way from home, he did well as long as he was on American soil. He understood that the army he was in was a logical development of the armies which had fought up and down the Shenandoah, was able to recognize the beaten earth of a drill field as an extension of his own front yard. Even during the ocean crossing he felt secure because he traveled under the aegis of his country's flag, in a native-built hull which turned all waters it touched territorial.

But Pettigrew's sense of security evaporated in Egypt. The flag was whipped into knots by the khamsin, a wind filled with the smell of age and corruption. It blew like a wall between each man, blew the image of America away. The Army's fences could not hold out the desert, and the print of thousands of GI shoes disappeared under a second's washing of the sands. The wire was clotted with beggars in veils and tarbooshes, naked children with infected eyes.

Nor did Pettigrew find any security, reality in Taranto, in cobbled streets filled with the chattering of Italian, with children pulling at him, calling screw-Joe, suck-suck. He was quartered in an ancient building whose walls seemed to ooze a European filth, was assigned to a unit which had none of the cohesion of the units fighting at the front, became part of a collection of time-servers waiting in a sort of limbo until they could be rotated home. And Pettigrew was not even given a soldier's duty—his quick hands were shackled to a switchboard and his voice was funneled into a headset. From midnight to eight in the morning he sat next to the high open window of an Italian building and was fanned by breezes carrying traces of decayed fish and grape pressings. During the day Pettigrew dozed restlessly through heat and strange noises.

His America grew more and more distant, became limited to the artifacts of his military clothing and equipment, to the waxed paper and cardboard cups of his solitary morning lunch, the canned meat he chewed on. Pettigrew felt that he was losing touch with all his realities, wrote home for photographs, postcards, any graphic representation of the land he knew. Lying in his medieval room half stupefied by lack of sleep and the sun's haze, he thumbed compulsively through the pictures. And then went out to lie against whorehouse bodies streaked with foreign sweat, to listen to their jokes in pidgin English when his responses grew more and more feeble.

The Army could not have known that Pettigrew would be unable to function outside his country's borders, that he would stare out at the night spaces covering the sea which rolled from Gibraltar to Lebanon, stare at the *US* indented on the buttons of his fatigues, and wonder how the one could have anything to do with the other. The switchboard would buzz, flash, and Pettigrew's plug would release a mechanical American voice twisted by wires, filtered through headphones. His frames of reference grew warped beyond recognition, the exotic air enclosed him like a wall of cloudy glass. Pettigrew's loss of touch became literal. At first only a missing beat in the rhythm of his movements, a hesitation in the manipulation of the phone plugs, it grew to real clumsiness. The world already fuzzy became dense, and a corresponding numbness crept down from his elbows. Pettigrew began to nod on the night wind, on the scent of lemon blossoms now carried to his high window. The switchboard buzzed and flashed unattended at longer and longer intervals until one night it buzzed and flashed without interruption while Pettigrew sat before it, his dead hands lying in his lap.

He has been partially mended. At one time he needed a keeper to feed him, to unbutton his fly so that he wouldn't soil himself. The doctors prodded and probed and talked until the deadness ebbed down Pettigrew's arms. He didn't have to contend with Italy in the Army hospitals. Living only among Americans, he regained his frames of reference. The strange country has become no more than a series of pictures on the other side of windows. For two months he has been in G Ward waiting for the remaining tingle to disappear from the last joints of his fingers. Lieutenant Klein thinks two months is too long a time, is growing concerned.

Pettigrew plays a card, feels it slip over a fingertip which seems to be sheathed by a callus.

"And that will just about do it, Polack," he says. "Count them out, Spinale."

"I never saw such a game," Spinale says. "We ought to work up a little gin rummy or something, a little action."

"Well, I got to take a leak," Walinski says. "How about you guys?"

They shake their heads. Walinski calls to a ginger-haired man nearby who wears a rag of parachute cloth twisted in an ascot at his throat. "Hey Bradeway, how about you?"

"Clinton," Spinale says, "do you want to go to the can with Walinski?"

The man turns his head slowly and looks at them with pale eyes. "I'd like to go for a walk," he says to Spinale.

"Okay, baby, then that's just where we'll go."

"How about it," Walinski bellows into the room, "anybody for piss call?"

Deacon crosses toward him, holding his smeared finger in the air as though it were bleeding.

Mamoulian is leaving town in style, on the Saturday Special. An alert watchful man perched behind steel-framed glasses, he has moved through G Ward in only three weeks, a loner who volunteered no information. He complied with all direction, moved through whatever twisting pattern the moment brought, and he has been judged redeemed. None of the men in the ward knows anything about him, knows the extent of his redemption.

The men take one of their biweekly showers before the Saturday-morning inspection. The patients are herded down a corridor and lined up at six shower stalls. Geary hustles them through one at a time. There is neither singing nor horseplay while they are under the water. Mamoulian soaps himself like all the others, but he is the only one rinsing away pajama lint and robe fuzz for the last time. After the men dry themselves they wrap their soiled pajamas in their towels and slip naked into their robes.

They are marched back to the ward, bare chests showing, hair uncombed, a column of wild men. A laundry cart waits. They exchange their sheets and pillowcases, receive clean pajamas identical to those they turn in. Mamoulian is different,

101

receives pieces of a uniform. He assembles it slowly, becomes a sandy wren among all the wine-breasted gray-legged birds. He wears shoes, belted trousers, a tie, moves with a certain prim assurance among the flopping slippers and fluttering robes, a scrawny PFC decorated with nothing more than the shoulder patch of an undistinguished unit—but the only real soldier in the ward.

The beds are made with extra care. Harris marshals the broom and checks butt cans, wastebaskets, ashtrays. The doors of the night tables are left ajar, the personal things within them arranged neatly. Geary snipes at Harris and Harris growls at the men. Corners are pulled square, pillows flattened. The patients mill around the room, forbidden to smoke.

Captain Marcellus arrives a little after ten, Lieutenant Klein trailing him. When Geary calls attention the slippers scrape, the robes hang from stiff shoulders. Marcellus bounces down one side of the ward, in his wake an unhappy-looking Klein, Geary with a clipboard. The captain nods stiffly from time to time. The men, at attention, do not respond. He pauses a moment to shake Mamoulian's hand man to man, soldier to soldier. At the room's blind end Marcellus turns, fingers a dusty ashtray and mutters to Geary.

Klein hisses after the captain and Marcellus slows, stops before Deacon. He reaches for Deacon's hand, has to lever it up from his side. Deacon holds the hand out palm down, as though he were a child having his fingernails inspected. Marcellus turns it over, gives Deacon a tight smile, moves on. Klein has to force Deacon's hand down.

The captain assumes a military stance at the head of the ward, a wedge of pink stomach visible through an unbuttoned gap in his shirt. He commends the patients on their neatness. They stand braced, nineteen colored maroon and stone, one colored khaki. Marcellus makes a little ceremony of Mamoulian's release, a Saturday Special which is half graduation and half parole. Sun shining through the chicken wire covers the beds in a net of shadow.

Captain Marcellus gives an awkward salute to the men, another to Geary, then leaves the ward with Lieutenant Klein. The medic calls the patients at ease. They are now free of routine until Monday morning, may sit or lie on their beds. Bradeway takes the scrap of parachute cloth from his pocket and arranges it at his throat. Mamoulian quietly packs his musette bag, then slings it and walks out of the ward without speaking to anyone.

"There's one brown-nose won't be back," Pettigrew says.

"Did the captain read your palm?" Vierra asks Deacon.

"Maybe you and him could work in the same sideshow, Pancho."

"Knock it off," Harris says harshly.

The others look at him, surprised. Harris turns to a window to hide the tears blinding him.

"About time to get that new bird working," Captain Marcellus says as he walks along the corridor.

"I'm going to start him Monday," Klein answers.

"His hand was cold."

"I don't think that means anything, Bob."

"Maybe he has a warm heart," Marcellus snickers.

11.

ON SUNDAY morning the ward is filled with an eerie greenish glow, as though Calabria had at last ceased to resist the seas and had been swallowed by them. The men's pale skins are tinted the color of lichen, and they fidget on their unmade beds, scratch their unshaven cheeks. Shredded clouds like clots of gray and mustard smoke boil along the ridges.

The air is heavy, perfectly still, until a violent gust of wind whips magazines from the beds and blows a flurry of cards across the room. The men rush to the casement windows and struggle to close them, their eyes clenched, hair streaming. They secure the latches just as the first wave of rain smashes against the glass. Sheets of rain carom off the windows in a series of mottled patterns which are repeated and enlarged on the walls of the ward.

All the hospital's sounds are drowned beneath the pounding of the rain. The men watch transfixed, their eyes washed out of focus as they stare through the warped panes. A smell of damp grows in the closeted room, of dusty tile, the biting odor of fumigated robes and blankets.

And then the sun abruptly appears, lighting all the streams of water with color. It cuts through the rain, blots it up until it is no more than a dribble. The windows are pebbled with brilliant drops and the ward is hushed for a moment until a hinge creaks and the fragrance of moist earth enters the room, a breeze bearing the faint tang of the invisible seas.

The field before the hospital has been drenched a deep brown, the highway turned to a slick ribbon. Wisps of vapor soon appear and the air grows thick and oppressive while layers of steam are sucked upward. The field's surface turns powdery once again. A hot clear glare lights the day.

The men leave the windows, recover their cards and magazines. Moisture condenses on the ceiling, dries in rings. The chicken wire has been rinsed of dust. A medic arrives to accompany the patients who wish to attend church services.

Geary waits until after lunch to call the formation. The men are dozing and reading. When Geary calls them to attention they hurry to the feet of their beds, stand stiff and slovenly and swivel their eyes to see who has come into the ward. Geary is alone.

"I'm really sorry to do this on your day off," he says, "but it seems that Captain Marcellus found a dirty ashtray yesterday." Geary stands at the head of the ward and bawls in a parade-ground voice. "I don't care that the captain might consider this a reflection on me, but it's too bad that it's a reflection on you men. I can walk out of here any time I want to, but you men have to work your way out, and every time you screw up you're taking a step backwards.

"Now that was probably only an oversight yesterday, because I know you're all good workers. I believe you're going to be willing to put your backs into a little GI party today and get this place really shined up. Show the captain what you can do. We'll have a good mop job and we'll get those night tables washed down. Maybe there won't be any oversights next time. Maybe Spinale will remember to keep his ashtray clean."

"Not today, Geary," Harris says.

"You're at attention, Top."

"You can't call attention unless an officer walks into this ward, Geary."

"I called it in a manner of speaking."

"Well you'd better change your manner, because that cheap rank of yours doesn't give you command over much more than an Eyetie KP."

Although they continue to maintain a certain amount of balance, the men begin to relax.

"I don't see that there's anybody in this ward wearing stripes, Harris."

"Nobody with a commission, either." Harris deliberately puts his hands into his pockets. "If all you want to do is say something about GIing the ward, you don't have to try to

104

pull a chickenshit formation. You don't have the rank for it, Geary."

"Harris, I don't want to have to turn in a bum report on you."

"You turn in what you want to."

"I turn myself in," Vierra says and stretches on his bed with a noisy sigh.

"I didn't dismiss anybody," Geary says.

"You don't have to because you never had any right to call attention in the first place." The files are crumbling, the men turning their backs on the medic. "And if we're going to have any extra duty, I want to hear about it from Lieutenant Klein, not from you."

"You're going to hear from Klein, Top, and you better believe it."

"The lieutenant will hear about an orderly who has given himself a battlefield commission," Vierra says.

Walinski laughs hoarsely. Other patients titter. They break into knots, begin to talk among themselves. Geary scowls for a moment, then spins around to face into the corridor. The men return to what they were doing before they were called to attention. Harris, head down, marches a zigzag course until he gets behind the medic.

"Getting your ass kissed is one thing," he says, "but you can't order this ward around like it was your private army."

"You're dismissed, Top."

"Now you listen, Geary; I'll crawl over to that desk on my belly and get you a cigarette and put it in your mouth and light it if that's what you want." The medic turns and looks at Harris with cold green eyes. "What I do myself is my own business," Harris continues, "and I'll do whatever it takes to get out of this cruddy hole. I don't say anything when you go around breaking balls with these men, but when you start giving orders to the whole ward you're acting without authority of any kind. They're still soldiers and they're entitled to be treated like soldiers. You can't order them around unless you can make it stick."

"We'll see what I can make stick, Harris."

Harris nods and turns away. As he passes their beds the patients call softly to him, make the victory sign. Spinale goes from table to table, cleaning the ashtrays with a dirty sock.

Lieutenant Klein watches Deacon shifting in the upholstered chair next to the desk, and he wonders how he might catch hold of any of the shifting planes of Deacon in the abstract. But the lieutenant is not presently performing as either priest or healer; it is time for him to play administrator, to throw the patient into the mill stream, to fix him to the musicless roll of G Ward's time.

The box complicates things. Klein has already opened and closed it several times, studied the medal as though it might have a secret to give up, as though the white enameled silhouette of Washington might have a message from long-dead times—Trenton or Valley Forge. It is a peculiar medal, heart-shaped, with a field of purple and a border of gold—a military valentine. Klein has never presented one, has never even seen one except in illustrations. He had suggested a small ceremony, thinking that it might be beneficial for the rest of the men, that it might infuse the ward with a touch of the glitter of the storybook army. Captain Marcellus asked if the men were supposed to march twice the length of the ward while he and Klein and Deacon stood on beds and reviewed them. Klein abandoned the idea, but he still wants to make the presentation mean something, wants to dispel the atmosphere of burglar and fence in a hidden room about to exchange an article of illicit merchandise.

Further, Klein is—a sour wrinkle crosses his lips—meddling. He wants to turn the occasion to profit, to pass his unqualified hand over the loom and try to interweave a few threads. He thinks that awarding the decoration might give him an opening. But first he must get Deacon lurching into motion.

"And so you see," he explains, "we're not going to pretend that occupational therapy is going to solve all the problems you men have or that it's going to do you any good at all, but it *is* a kind of achievement. Just learning a new skill shows that you're well enough to concentrate. And if you actually make something, you're giving us a chance to check out your motor responses."

"What should I make?"

"That's not really important. What you make is only a token, and our tools and equipment are pretty limited anyway. You can make something you're not in the least interested in, and hate every minute of it, and still wind up getting something out of it."

Stones, Klein thinks. They sit there with eyes at first blind, eyes that gradually turn to clear glass, seeing nothing, nothing behind them, and wind up with eyes like dead stones.

"Have you ever done any handicraft work," he asks, "even whittling, anything like that?"

"No."

"That's all right; nearly everyone has to learn. You must have noticed all the wicker baskets in the ward." There is no response. "Every one of them was made by a man who spent some time here. You don't suppose there were many servicemen who knew how to do reed work before they came here, do you?"

"You want me to make a wastebasket?"

"Well no, not unless you want to. I'd like you to make something you think you might enjoy working on. Why don't you look on this as some kind of assignment—not a test, but something which would be on the plus side if you got it done."

"I don't know how to do it."

"Bradeway can show you, he's helped a lot of the men." Klein pushes at the box. "Did you know that he was a gunner too?"

"That's what I hear."

"You should have a lot in common. In the way of experiences, I mean. You might even have the same problem. Not that he's over his." Klein fidgets. "There isn't even any real indication that he's coming out of it. Perhaps you can help him while he's helping you."

"I don't know anything about him, Lieutenant."

"I can't really say that we do, either," Klein says ruefully. "It's not easy to talk to Bradeway. If I had some idea . . . you see, I don't know what it's like—flying, I mean. And Bradeway can't or won't tell me. Without some kind of communication there isn't much we can do to help. If you and I could talk about combat flying sometime it might give me an idea of Bradeway's problem."

Klein sees an oily film appear on Deacon's forehead, sees his head begin to bob slightly as though in response to a pulse. The lieutenant feels as though he has rammed a stiff finger into Deacon's pulpy parts.

"I don't mean right now," he says quickly. "I don't even mean that we *have* to, but if sometime while we *are* talking . . ." Klein's voice trails away. He grips the box, braces himself against it and tries to get some brightness into his face. "In the meantime, I think this is a hell of a way to award a decoration, but we're just not set up in the prescribed military manner here. I don't envy the way you earned this, but I envy your having it."

He hands the box to Deacon with a clumsy flourish. Deacon opens it, looks in, snaps the lid shut. He wipes his forehead.

"I suppose a review, even a small one, ought to go with it," Klein says, "but I'm afraid this is the best we can do."

"Gruber said they were giving them out like aspirin."

"That casually? We don't usually get combat troops in here, so we don't take the Purple Heart quite so much for

107

granted. Although Bradeway has one. So does Walinski, as a matter of fact."

"It's all a crock of shit."

"Do you think so?" Klein has to restrain himself from lunging after the source of the remark. "Well, I guess that comes with it, with all the confusion and the foul-ups. It's the system, and there isn't much we can do but go along with it."

"When do you want the thing, Lieutenant?"

"The thing? The, ah . . . whatever it is you make you can bring in any time. It doesn't have to be a work of art, but it should show that you made a real effort."

"I'll try."

After Deacon leaves, Lieutenant Klein takes out his file, thinks a moment, then carefully writes *A crock of shit* as the first entry on the blank notation sheet. He absently rubs the pencil point along his cheek, leaving a shadow like an elongated sideburn, then suddenly gets up and goes into the anteroom.

"Private Cusset," he says to the WAC, "did you ever go out with any flyers?"

She looks up from the V-Mail letter she has been writing. "I'm not supposed to go out with officers, Lieutenant."

"I mean enlisted men, combat crew."

"Down here? They don't even know there's a war on down here. I don't think they know what the word 'combat' means, Lieutenant."

"Thank you, I thought maybe that . . ."

"I'm sorry I can't help you." She advances a tentative smile, her mouth free of gum. "It's for one of them—" her head jerks toward the ward—"isn't it? I can't help reading the files sometimes."

"Well, I thought . . . maybe a way to get through, you see."

"I know. You sincerely want to help, don't you, Lieutenant? Even though you're an officer."

Klein is embarrassed, bobs his head jerkily and retires to his own office. She's really not so bad, he thinks, PFC Corset. He catches the displacement, feels a glow of excitement. Cusset. Or even Cosset; maybe the lady would like to be cosseted. Maybe he is coming out from under the malediction of diseased sex. Klein taps his feet rapidly beneath the desk, absently brushes dead hairs from his shoulder.

Geary will not permit them to gamble during the day but Ferguson, the evening medic, is more permissive. He keeps an amiable watch over the poker and blackjack games which break out on non-movie nights. The men play for matches,

108

settle up for money and cigarettes. They don't gamble heavily because money doesn't matter in the ward, cannot buy a tomorrow any different from yesterday. They gamble for small stakes and small excitement, hoard their money as a dowry for the time when they will be released.

The patients in G Ward are affluent. All through their hospital term they have been paid regularly according to rank, receive the usual 20 percent premium for overseas service. They are issued PX ration cards, but the overseas PX is only a sketchy shadow of the stateside general store, and the few luxuries which arrive at the hospital are skimmed off by the permanent staff. The ration cards cover a weekly allotment of cigarettes, candy, beer and soft drinks. Patients are not allowed beer, are given a doubled soft-drink allowance instead. The men in G Ward are not permitted bottled goods of any kind, are compensated by an increase in cigarettes and candy bars. They accumulate the money they cannot spend, accumulate the cigarettes which are better than money in black-market Italy. Night tables are filled with cartons.

Although the stakes are small the men take the games seriously. Spinale has installed himself as permanent blackjack dealer, but he has no real flair for cards and handles them clumsily. The players rag him, try to unsettle him. Spinale plods doggedly on unperturbed, keeps an infallible count of the bets, only occasionally tipping one eye toward Bradeway as he promenades up and down the aisle, his white hand fluttering at the parachute cloth at his neck. Deacon weaves in and out of Bradeway's path several times before actually joining him. The two men move along the aisle together, their robes flowing behind like the cassocks of clerics. Bradeway takes no notice of Deacon until he speaks.

"I understand you're supposed to be the man to see about this handicraft crap."

"Like those?" Bradeway swings his finger toward the wicker wastebaskets which line the room. Deacon nods. "They won't hold ashes," Bradeway says.

"From cigarettes?"

"Not any kind."

"Whatever they're for, can you show me how to make one?"

"Do you want something to keep?"

"To keep what?"

"Something to keep so that you can remember." Bradeway strokes his parachute cloth. "The baskets don't belong to anyone now. They were left behind."

"All I need is something to show Klein."

"If you have something to keep with you, you can be sure

that you were in that time. Then you won't look back and see a space you're not sure you've passed through. You won't find it empty and wonder why you were never in it." Bradeway's pale eyes search Deacon's face. "You're sweating," he says.

"I ah . . . understand you were in the Fifteenth."

"The Fifteenth Air Force, yes."

"I was a waist gunner."

"Were you? Were you there?"

"Where?"

"After Christmas, when it was cold."

"I wasn't overseas then."

"At Regensburg. They told us we'd never have to worry about fighters again if we could do it all at once. We tried for three days. But it didn't matter about planes they were going to build, they had too many as it was . . . and it had been snowing. Little spidery lines of roads and train tracks and all those planes they'd already built coming up and up out of all that whiteness . . ."

"Okay, okay."

"All the rear formation. There were twelve ships and then there wasn't anything. When the smoke blew away, the sky was empty and I wasn't sure that we'd passed through it. I didn't have anything I could keep, you see."

"The Big Week?"

"Were you there?" Bradeway's voice grows querulous. "We couldn't have any real time, only the sky with spaces like the numbers of a clock. You could almost see it projecting like spokes from the ship." Bradeway extends his arm. "I don't have a watch. I can't wear one."

Spinale breaks away from the game and hurries over. "Clinton," he says.

"If it isn't in space and there wasn't any time to mark it, how can I be sure? Were *you* there, did you see me?"

"Clinton, if you come over and sit down for a minute I'll give you something nice." Spinale turns to Deacon and hisses, "You want to leave him be, Doc."

"But he has to make something he can keep," Bradeway says. "There isn't any point in it otherwise. There isn't anyone left to own all those baskets."

"I'll bet I never finished that story, Clinton . . . remember? About the time when . . ." Spinale has a firm grip on Bradeway's arm, leads him toward his bed. Deacon is left standing alone in the middle of the ward. The medic watches until Bradeway is settled, then goes back to his magazine. The card players call to Spinale to hurry up.

110

Walinski saunters over to Deacon. "You wanna watch it with Bradeway," he says, "he's real bad."

"He was supposed to show me how to make a basket."

"I guess he could one time, but now he's a real nut."

"That makes him different from everybody else."

"You figure that way?"

"Did you get that Heart for getting your brains blown out?"

"I got a DCS and a Bronze Star, too, but I ain't a nut. It don't bother me so much that I'm in here."

"Why should it? It's a rest camp for all the crap-outs."

"Nothing for me to crap out on," Walinski says. "The Army's got more guys than it knows what to do with. Let somebody else take a turn shoveling guts, I had enough of it."

"So did I, pal, so did I."

"You better see Vierra if you wanna make something—he's the one knows all about it. They like to see you keep busy. I know, because I'm getting out next week." Deacon stares at him. "Yeah," Walinski says, "that's right, I'm going. Say, you always sweat like that?"

Deacon opens his mouth, closes it and chews at his lip. Spinale is back in the dealer's slot. Bradeway is lying on his bed, sucking on a candy bar as though it were a chocolate-covered thumb.

Although Walinski may be the only murderer ever released from G Ward, he has been the meekest of men while under psychiatric control, has been content to be nudged from stage to stage because he knows that being classified as a semi-lunatic has saved him from being shot by either the Germans or the Americans.

The Teodor Walinski who has been kept in back rooms and corridors for months is the same "Crusher" Walinski the Army made a minor celebrity, photographed strung with bandoliers, a fixed animal grin on his face. The Crusher was the product of a Fifth Army publicist, became an official hero after he collected the Distinguished Service Cross—his third decoration—near Anzio. The publicist was uneasy about the grin, had seen too many like it emerge from the background of bearded shadows and spent faces, but he steadied his hand long enough to freeze it forever in the lens. Walinski's picture appeared in the newspapers back home, in the Mediterranean edition of *Yank*.

Never a spectacular soldier, he killed only to survive. Survival was the only idea he had during the long grind through North Africa and Sicily and Italy. Since only death or a wound could get him out of the infantry, he had come to the conclusion that the only way to stay alive was to wade through all the Germans and come out on the other side. Walinski didn't care whether that other side was victory or defeat or a static détente; the space between the Americans and the enemy was filled with death and mutilation, but beyond that space, beyond the wire and bunkers and through the gray lines, there was a clearing. Walinski plodded toward it, destroying Germans in his path indiscriminately, with any weapon on hand. He beat one to death with his helmet.

The Army approved. Walinski was their idea of the good soldier, and they decorated him, offered promotion, command of a squad. But he was not interested in rank, only in survival. He showed his wolf grin and declined to be more than an ordinary rifleman, a PFC. It wasn't until after Anzio, after they'd created The Crusher, that the Army discovered that their good soldier didn't distinguish between killing and murder. In the long shadow of the Cassino stalemate the men became even more spent, but Walinski kept his grip through the grinding attrition, fixed his eye steadily on that space behind the enemy lines—until a new lieutenant arrived to replace the platoon leader carried away like a meal bag on the back of a mule. At first Walinski suffered him as he had suffered other replacements, eager and green and taken with their own images as soldiers. The new lieutenant grew to be a distinct liability, however, because he saw himself as a spirited leader although he didn't know how or where to lead.

There was no time to learn in the mud before Cassino. The lieutenant fumbled two patrols, caused two deaths and dragged back three wounded. Walinski decided that the officer was a greater obstacle to his survival than the Germans, that there would not be a third bungled patrol. As soon as they were clear of their lines Walinski grasped at the paratroop helmet which the lieutenant affected and stupidly wore with the showy chin strap closed, dug the trench knife first into the back and then sawed away at the choked throat until the blood bubbled freely. The rest of the patrol watched from under their shadows. Walinski dragged the body to a shallow depression and scraped mud over it.

He reported that the lieutenant had become separated from the men and must have lost his way. The company commander—himself once a platoon leader—noticed the fresh stains on Walinski's already filthy field jacket. He questioned, Walinski grinned. The other men would neither confirm nor deny the story. The company commander supposed what had happened, supposed even that he understood Walinski's motives, but official forgiveness was not possible no matter what the understanding. Walinski was sent to the rear under armed guard. Headquarters was outraged, immediately began to process papers for the court-martial. But how could they shoot The Crusher? What use could they make of a publicity still of the hood and the splintered stake? Even allowing for a commuted sentence, a hero in Leavenworth could only be an embarrassment. Headquarters began to fiddle, to hedge, finally let the machinery run down. Surmise was not proof, they reasoned; there was no possible chance of evidence from the other dim figures who'd been on the patrol. And yet they couldn't release Walinski, couldn't ever allow him to hold a knife or a rifle again. Someone suggested the all-encompassing mantle of combat fatigue; they wrapped Walinski in it and shipped him to a hospital.

It didn't take the mind doctors, the real professionals, long to discover what they had on their hands—the good soldier epitomized, a simple mechanism fitted with whirling blades which destroyed anything in the way. Like the company commander, they understood, and understood that fitting Walinski with a morality which placed a value on any human life other than his own would mean bringing him through progressive stages of guilt and chancing his discovering that killing Germans was as much murder as killing a lieutenant. Rather than risk confronting Walinski with his own truths and perhaps turning him incurably psychotic, the doctors babied him. He was calm and cooperative, a model patient, and he adapted easily to being shuttled from ward to ward, from opinion to opinion. His file thickened and the analyses grew more and more vague, Walinski's figure becoming so padded and hazed that it was decided that there was not really anyone there to treat. But discharge was not recommended.

It was left to G Ward to spit Walinski out. He was removed from the scene of the crime, passed from his army zone into the Calabrian twilight. Jesse Klein was at first delighted by his response to orders, his evident balance. Not until he unraveled the threads of the twisted language in the file, until he consulted his books, did Klein discover the assassin. After all the probing and opinion, the man who sits in Klein's office is exactly the same one who held the knife at Cassino. There is no way to help him without risking his destruction, and Klein has no competence in any case. Captain Marcellus pretends not to understand, nevertheless feels that Walinski is somehow dangerous, that there may be a nasty incident if he is held too long. The captain leaves it to Klein to work out, but he always edges in words of praise for the things Walinski makes, always remarks on his improvement.

Klein broods. Walinski grows more and more skillful.

When the captain is able to hold up an unimaginative but neat basket Walinski has completed and demands to know what else they can expect of him, Klein stirs feebly but cannot come up with an answer. Papers are processed for The Crusher's release.

12.

GEARY CALLS the occupational-therapy room the kindergarten. The men call it the souvenir shop or the chicken house. It is a small room just outside the ward. There are two mess tables, one with benches, the other strewn with hand tools and unfinished work. Strips of blank leather hang from the walls. Tin cans hold strands of reed and raffia which droop like dead stalks.

The men are expected to work the dumb material into memorials, weave into it the pattern of their salvation. The occupational-therapy room is an important part of Captain Marcellus's concept of discipline and responsibility. Its products are real proofs of improvement, evidence that the men have acquired the digital skills of children and are ready to return to soldiers' duties. The room is windowless and close and the men sometimes sweat into their work, sometimes spit on it. First Sergeant Harris has dampened his with his tears.

Only the patients from G Ward may use the therapy room, and no more than four at a time, two sets of buddies. They work without a medic's supervision. People passing in the corridor peek through the open door, smirk and make sly comments. The men plod on, fingers clenched around worn blunt tools, hands hidden in baskets as though they had been caught in wicker snares. No matter how badly the work grows, none of it is ever set aside or thrown away. Lieutenant Klein has told them that they only need make something. They make anything, leave Klein the problem of putting a label on it. They submit what they know is trash and wait for him to praise it.

Vierra is the instructor. He is qualified to teach, can spin raffia or weave reed or tool a hidalgo's belt. But the men aren't interested in learning techniques and niceties, only want to be able to put things together. They aren't impressed

114

with Vierra's knowledge and dexterity because neither has been able to get him out of G Ward.

"So you thought Bradeway would teach you," Vierra says to Deacon. "You came too late. There are things I learned from him . . . how to tie an ascot, how to look truly insane." Vierra grins. "Maybe a little more than that. And now he has left all the idiot skills to my keeping. I am a master in the grand tradition, my friend. But Lieutenant Klein must keep telling everyone that Bradeway is still teaching, he must half believe it himself. What would he do with him otherwise, a man whose parts have all been taken out, if he did not believe that Bradeway was at least some use in the ward?"

"This is horseshit."

"Then make something of it. Something for Captain Marcellus . . . carve his bust in stinking turd. Tell me, do you want to stay here with us? Do you want to spend the duration here, or are you anxious to go back to duty? I can vary my instruction to suit your needs."

"I don't know why I'd want to stay on this garbage pile."

"At least it isn't the war." Vierra begins to select reeds. "Our hospital may kill us, but at least it isn't the war. I don't know exactly what the war is, *amigo,* but maybe you can tell me. Bradeway and Walinski, they don't know anymore . . . they're already too crazy with it. But maybe you are, too, since you must have been already a little insane to ask to fly where there is a war, in the sky, that sky up there." Vierra points toward the ceiling. "Maybe you are only here to have a few parts cleaned and then to be sent back to where you can finish your work."

"I don't care if they do send me back."

"You cause my heart to swell with admiration." Vierra coils the reeds and places them in a pan of water, then takes a handful of thicker ones and snips them into equal lengths. "I can see that you will be one of the good maggots on the garbage pile. Before long you will be able to work the horseshit into a shape which will please Lieutenant Klein. Wastebaskets are his favorites. If someone had the contacts we could begin an export business with the States. Baskets made in Italy by Americans for Americans."

"If someone had the contacts, I could get a drink."

Vierra places a round wooden base on the table and inserts the thicker reeds into the pre-drilled holes. "And now we wait for the others to soften . . . but not too long, or they begin to shred. They must be kept moist enough to bend, but not to fall apart. Don't you think that's a good attitude for our hospital?"

"I think anything's good that'll get me out."

"But that's because you are such a man of merit, *amigo,* so anxious to do your part. I am no more than a poor clerk, I cannot offer to my country courage like yours. They have no use for me out there except as an office boy in some filthy hole, to get the coffee from the mess hall or sort the mail or tack notices on the bulletin board. I am in no hurry to sweat my life away in some orderly room thirty miles from a town which is itself nothing. See, I am not brave like you. But if you have a drink . . . how will you be the good maggot if you break the rules? How will you grow well enough to become the crazy man who goes up in the sky?"

"You can knock that off any time you want to."

"But it is unusual to meet a man of such merit. It is most impressive."

"They must have a regular manual they give all you groundgrippers, something you can use to shovel dirt in your mouth . . . anything so you don't want to go. You'd be impressive with somebody waking you up in the morning, pointing a flashlight and telling you it's time. Pointing it at you, pal, nobody else . . . some bastard blinding you to make sure you get up so he doesn't have to go, so he can crawl back into his sack and not have to worry somebody's going to tap him. You'd be impressive down on your hands and knees in the dirt pissing your pants."

"But they don't want a poor clerk like me, my friend. They want someone with your splendid courage."

"Nobody's going to check you out on that, pal. They'll let you go just the way you are. I'll give you my dog tags and you can take *my* place. You don't even need the dog tags . . . just be there. Just show up wearing the right kind of suit and they'll let you go up as many times as you want to. All they want is some kind of warm body, it doesn't have to have a name. They don't care about your name, Vierra . . . they've got a barracks bag full of used names you can pick from if you don't like the one you've got. All they need is a number, somebody at the window. If you're worried about getting airsick, they'll give you a pill."

"*Amigo . . .*"

"Nobody's going to be worried whether or not you can cut it. You can be scared shitless and still have the whole big deal. You want it, don't you, the flying suit and everything? You want those fancy sunglasses, and your picture with a goddamned gun belt wrapped around your neck. You want . . ." Deacon wipes his hands along his robe and places them under his armpits. He squeezes his arms against his chest and his voice grows thick. "But don't wait around for somebody to punch your ticket. Maybe they'll kill you,

116

but they won't ever punch your ticket. All you bastards shoveling dirt and rocks in your mouths so you won't have to go up, you'll kill anybody you have to just as long as you don't . . ."

Deacon's voice dies. Vierra flexes a wet reed between his fingers, shakes the water from it, then begins to weave it between the side stringers of the basket.

"There is no war after this place," he says. "They won't ask you to do anything else."

"That's all you have to worry about, who's going to ask who. You sit around sweating out rotation and winding up miles of bullshit. Nobody's entitled to ask me to do anything . . . it's up to me to decide whether I go up or stay down."

"They might not let you."

"It's my ticket now, and I'm the only one can punch it. You think some desk pilot . . . you think some cruddy groundgripper is going to run me through like a number, cut blank orders to cover me? They put together an alert, some lousy run you can take a thirty or forty percent pasting on, and they cut in on blank orders, fill in any name you want. You and you and you . . . we'll figure out your names later. Listen, when I'm in the waist I'm so close to the other gunner we almost bang into each other when we're firing. You know how much good he can do me, don't you? That's right, pal, a big nothing. If that poor son of a bitch can't help me with my ticket, who do you think can . . . some lousy Operations officer? *I'll* do it . . . when I'm ready to, when they're ready to know who it is doing it."

"Why it should matter so much . . ." Vierra looks up at Deacon, shrugs. He comes to the end of the reed and takes another from the basin, twists the two together in a neat splice. "Time for the pupil to work . . . you must let them know that you are doing this, too. Take it and see if you can make something even uglier than the others do. Maybe it will impress Lieutenant Klein. Someday I will make him his heart's desire, a beautiful whip for him to beat himself."

Deacon picks up the unwieldy reed and tries to fit it around the side stringers of the basket. Instead he makes large uneven loops. He wipes his palms against the robe and begins again. The reed vibrates in his trembling fingers.

"Pettigrew has company," Vierra says. Deacon extends the reed to him. "Oh no, my friend, this must be *your* creation. They only pay me to help start it . . . the rest is up to you."

"Screw it."

"But certainly, and then you can bring it screwed to Lieutenant Klein."

"If I was as smart as you, Vierra, I'd have been out of here a long time ago."

"But I don't have your merit, only my simple skills." Vierra fingers the reed. "It's beginning to dry out. You must remember to keep it moist. Would you like me to write a list of these little things so you'll be able to remember them?"

"I don't know how much shit I'm going to have to take from that medic, but I don't think I'm going to have to take any from you . . . Pancho."

Vierra's face takes on a darker shade and his eyes narrow. "Pettigrew has my pity because he is a cripple, but I have no pity for you. No more 'Pancho.' "

Deacon lights a cigarette with hands which tremble more than they did when he was trying to weave.

"You can get a drink," Vierra says, "but if they catch you you'll be put away forever."

"Big deal."

"Ah, courage will always show." Vierra passes the tip of the cutting pliers under his fingernails. "If you have money to match it, maybe you should speak to Spinale about a bottle."

A group of B-24s passes overhead, four boxes of four planes each. The whip and rattle of the passing trucks drown the sound of the engines even though the planes aren't very high. Deacon presses his head against the chicken wire and watches them glide silently into the path of the sun. The dull silver ships glitter like mirrors for a moment, then swing free into the open sky and disappear into the northeast. Deacon doesn't turn when Harris clears his throat, but stands with his fingertips pressed into the wire, his forehead cut into white-edged squares by the mesh.

"Think they were from your outfit?" When Deacon doesn't answer, Harris squints up at the sky. "Couldn't see the tail markings," he says, "so I guess you couldn't tell. It's a wonder those things can fly, the way they're built. Put them up against P-38s and they look like knackwursts somebody stuck the wings on."

"What's the story on Spinale?"

"He giving you some kind of trouble?"

"I mean, is he supposed to have some kind of a deal going?"

"What's your trouble, soldier?"

"Somebody told me he could get a bottle."

"What dumb son of a bitch told you that?"

"Don't work so hard at being a wheel, Top."

"Now you just pull up a minute, soldier . . ."

"Why don't you knock off that 'soldier' noise?"

"Well maybe you think you aren't." Harris stands rigid and squeezes up his face. "Maybe you think you can tell them you won't pay your bill if the service doesn't improve. Those pajamas don't make you any kind of a civilian. The only real clothes you're ever going to put on is that suit they took off you when you came in. If you're not wearing that when you get out of here, you'll be wearing some kind of restraining jacket."

"Harris . . ."

"You think these people care about any real thing? They only care about what you look like, and you'd better untrack yourself and look like one goddamned soldier."

"Like you, I suppose. Get off my back, Harris."

"I'll take care of myself, but it's not going to do me or anybody else any good if you go around fucking up the detail. What's your trouble that you want a drink all of a sudden? Sure Spinale can get you a bottle—but I'll break his balls if he does. You get drunk and they'll nail a box closed on you in IC. It'll take you six months to get back to where you can begin in the ward again."

Harris whirls in a tight circle, the skirt of his robe flaring like a military overcoat. "We had one drunk in here and he beat on Ferguson with the bottle to get at the razor blades so he could cut himself. Puny little bastard from some supply outfit beating on that big slob even after Ferguson broke his arm for him. Broke his *arm*. You could hear it snap and this drunk screaming and swinging the bottle with his good arm until he finally decked Ferguson. They had the goddamned medics wearing pistols on duty for a week after that."

Harris shuts his eyes and swallows rapidly. Deacon looks out the window.

"He finally thought enough to run in the latrine and smash the bottle," Harris continues. "They found him crawling over the floor with that arm of his flopping around, trying to pick up a piece of glass big enough to give himself a real gash. His good hand looked like he was wearing a red glove." Harris pulls at Deacon's sleeve. "You know what that chickenshit Marcellus thought, don't you? That he had himself some kind of violent ward. You ever see a real violent ward with everybody in some kind of restraint? I don't want any more of that and I don't care if I have to soldier everybody's ass off sideways to make sure it doesn't happen again. And that includes yours."

It is Harris's turn to look out the window. Deacon turns away and lights a cigarette. The smoke fans out in the dry air.

"Good Christ," Harris says, "you think this is some kind of

rest camp, that we can all just walk out of here. Doing everything they tell you is just the beginning."

"Okay, Top."

"I mean it—we go strictly by the numbers, twist-nut GI
right down the line." Harris's words become muffled. He
clears his throat. "If we can show them that we really don't
belong here . . ."

"Whatever you say, Top."

Deacon's cigarette jerks uncontrollably between his lips.
He spits it out, then picks it off the floor and carefully puts it
into a butt can. Cords stand out in the back of Harris's neck,
his shoulders are trembling slightly. Deacon takes a wadded
handkerchief from his pocket and fumbles it into Harris's
hand without looking at him.

Like Walinski, Eddie Spinale is in the hospital on a false
passport. He is in his mid-thirties, the oldest of the patients.
Nearly all his life he had schemed his way through circles of
petty grift, and he had been a steady loser until he arrived in
G Ward. As an elevator operator in cheap hotels Spinale had
been fired for selling home-made wine. He drove a taxi until
he was picked up for collecting policy bets and lost his li-
cense, worked as a bookie's bag man but was caught so often
the syndicate finally refused to pay his fines. Spinale didn't
even make it big as a lawbreaker. His crimes were never
more than misdemeanors.

The Army was able to rake him in only after he ran out of
invented dependents and displaced vertebrae and fainting fits.
Spinale stopped fighting the moment he was inducted, looked
to see how he might turn enforced service to profit. He followed the leaders, tried to organize his own crap games, but
he hadn't the touch to attract anyone except the quarter bet-
tors. On the troopship he tried to establish a sort of agency to
rent desirable bunk space, was out on deck with a wooden
box early every morning, rattling the dice and baying after
the big shooters. They passed him by. At night he prowled
the ship's serpentine passages looking into all the nooks and
crannies where real money was working.

Even with fluent sidewalk Italian he could get no further
than the nickel-and-dime edges of the black market until the
Army assigned him as a driver in a quartermaster motor
pool. Spinale had his first big chance, a small fortune in
stores riding at his back each time he shuttled from dock to
depot. The waterfront boosters sought him out, called him
paisano and advanced proposition after proposition. But Spinale could never work out a system to get the freight out of
the truck and off the shipping manifest at the same time. In

desperation he made a clumsy arrangement to have the truck pilfered during an artificial breakdown, botched the timing and wound up doing a month in a disciplinary camp. He lived in a pup tent on a windy plateau, drilled endlessly and stood spit-and-polish inspections. Spinale got through it in a breeze, all soldier all the way.

He was chastised but not chastened when he arrived back at the motor pool. They assigned him to the grease rack. Tools began to disappear. He was apprehended one night loading empty gas and oil drums onto an Italian pickup truck. His next term at the disciplinary camp was during the rainy season, a moat gurgling perpetually around the tent, the canvas leaking whenever he happened to touch it. He got through the thirty wet days nearly as easily as he had skimmed through his first tour.

On his release Spinale was detailed as straw boss for the gang of Italian laborers who did the depot's odd jobs. The supply sergeant kept a tight count on the picks and shovels he issued, but Spinale was no longer in the tool business. Each day he edged the detail farther and farther away from the depot until he had maneuvered them near an excavation being dug by an Italian contractor. Spinale hired out the labor force—fully equipped—but the deal went sour as soon as the men were pushed to turn out a real day's work instead of the stop-motion service they gave the Army. There were complaints made to the first sergeant.

When the company commander raged at him Spinale protested that he had never taken anything from any*body,* only intercepted some of the Army's enormous waste, a little here, a little there. The CO knew that Spinale would be bounced right back to the company if he was given another tour in the disciplinary camp, knew that he had never committed a grave enough offense to be locked away in a military prison. No other outfit would accept a man with his record as a transfer. The CO's only out was to have the company doctor recommend Spinale for psychiatric observation as a kleptomaniac.

The professionals soon spotted the doctor's fraud, shuffled Spinale quickly down to G Ward. Lieutenant Klein wanted to boot him back to duty, but for the first time Captain Marcellus took an interest in a case. He detected in Spinale not so much an illness as an anti-social attitude, and he developed the curious fixation that he could make a soldier of Spinale if he could teach him responsibility. The captain had no trouble getting him to adapt. Spinale slipped easily into G Ward's routine, responded completely to the discipline. Marcellus was encouraged, looked only for the completion of some kindergarten product before he would pronounce Spinale fit for duty.

Eddie Spinale has bent all his energy on avoiding participation in the handicraft program. He has developed dozens of evasions because he wants to stay in G Ward, because after all his years of hustling he has at last found a home, access to a captive market free of competition from the outside. And the ward itself is the least of his provinces; he operates throughout the entire hospital. When he finds the buddy system restricting his movements, he adopts Bradeway as his permanent partner, binds him through the other's insatiable appetite for candy bars. They move freely from ward to ward, Bradeway in tow while Spinale feeds him as he would a pet.

Spinale is not chancing the big market, taking the big risk, by trying to sell the hospital's supplies. He acts as a broker, agent, for the medics and clerks and other patients who want to establish swindles of one kind or another. The grift is small, but Spinale is interested more in the action than in the take. He arranges to have whiskey and beer and fresh produce brought in, souvenir jewelry, lighters from outside PXs. On occasion he has arranged for a woman. The Italians who work in the hospital are his carriers, call him not *paisano*, but *padrone*. The word has been spread that Spinale can get anything, but he hasn't brought anything to drink into G Ward since the incident involving Ferguson.

"Clinton," he says to Bradeway, "what say we take a nice walk today? How would you like to visit that nice fella with the busted ribs over in D?"

Bradeway is making an intricate web from bits of string and doesn't answer.

"He owes us, baby," Spinale continues, "he's keeping money out on the store. I think that might even be a phony cast he's wearing. Maybe he's trying to make a deal to stay in, you know? Like he might have ideas to get distribution of his own going. We got to protect our territory, Clinton."

"Eddie, that fellow who left . . . yesterday. Was it yesterday?"

"Which one, Clinton?"

"I can't remember. I was wondering what he took with him. It worries me when they don't take something they can keep."

"You shouldn't worry, Clinton, because that particular guy took out something very nice, one of the nicest things I ever saw. It was a . . . butterfly, yeah a giant butterfly made out of that smooth colored stuff, that . . ."

"Raffia?"

122

". . . that's what it was and real big, baby, real nice. I'll bet he could carry it with him wherever he went and, you know, he could hang it up, so that wherever he was, that's home. Say, did you ever see that movie where this kid Heinie gets shot when he's reaching for a butterfly?"

"Oh."

"Well it wasn't really so bad, baby. You got to remember this guy was only a lousy Heinie anyway. It was the butterfly I was thinking of. There was all this mud and it was sort of pretty." Spinale leafs through a handful of paper slips and wets the tip of a pencil with his tongue. "Yeah, we could go to D *and* E. Clinton, that's where they have that nice fella who plays the harmonica, remember?"

Spinale notices Deacon approaching. He slides the papers into his pocket and turns to face him with a bleak smile.

"You're not going to bother him again now, are you, Doc?"

"You're the man I want to see."

"Hello," Bradeway says.

"Clinton, you want to sit down over there a minute?"

"I remember you," Bradeway says to Deacon.

"Yeah, well here's a nice Hershey bar, Clinton . . . with nuts."

Spinale waits until Bradeway sits and begins to unwrap the candy. "Something I can do for you, Doc?" he asks.

"I understand you're the local scrounge."

"Well . . . a little here and there. You looking for something in particular?"

"I want a book on Italian."

"A book in Italian—you mean like a story?"

"A phrase book, a grammar—something like that."

"I don't know." Spinale scratches his chest and makes a face. "If you wanted to talk Italian, I could teach you. Private lessons, not too expensive."

"All I want is a book. Can you get it?"

"Maybe. I could try. How much you want to pay?"

Deacon's smile is even bleaker than Spinale's. "This is the only game in town, pal. It'll be whatever you want to stick me."

Deacon walks away. Spinale squints after him for a moment, then goes back to his slips, makes minute markings with the moist pencil. He counts twice along his fingers.

"Okay, Clinton, let's go. Put the paper in the basket. You want to take a leak or anything first? Okay, let's go then, baby."

They stop at the medic's desk, Bradeway licking the chocolate from his fingers. "I thought I'd take him for a little walk, Corporal," Spinale says.

"What's the big deal today, robber?"

"That's what we all need, a big deal so we can retire." Spinale hunches his shoulders several times. "A guy made me a crazy bet about you, Corporal Geary, that you couldn't get to that little broom closet just outside F Ward—you know?—and open it by a quarter after four."

"Is that so? What'd you tell him?"

"I know you can do it, Corporal, so I went ahead and bet him three bottles of cold beer . . . leastwise I understand they'll be cold if you get there as soon as you get off duty tonight."

"Spinale, how in hell can they be *cold?*"

"That's what I understand, if you get there right after four. Well, we'll see you in a little bit, Corporal."

Spinale takes Bradeway's arm and leads him into the corridor. "We'll save the coconut one for the way back, Clinton. How's that—I got you *coconut.*"

At that Saturday's inspection there are no dirty ashtrays; neither is anyone released after it. Sunday passes without incident, the men dozing fitfully. The heat has grown more intense, creeps into the ward at the day's zenith. While the patients do not perspire freely, they tend to pant a little in the baked air.

There is a new arrival Monday, a pale youth who seems agitated. He chews his lip all during the time that Harris gives his lecture. When Harris tries to leave, the boy tags after him, head jerking as he chatters.

"They might have to change that one's pants regularly," Pettigrew says.

"A kid like that has a better chance than a guy like me," Spinale says. "I mean, a man my age, they break up his whole life and then expect he's going to be some kind of Sergeant York."

"Appears that one isn't doing too well. Hey, Spinale, when the hell are you going to stop messing around and try to get yourself out of here?"

"It ain't like it is with you, kid. I got adjustment problems you wouldn't know about."

Harris hasn't been able to shake the boy off. Each time he moves a few feet away the other skips after him. The two are now standing in the center of the ward, Harris with his face screwed nearly shut. Pettigrew rubs his fingers together.

"Getting on to a long time here," he says. "Couple of

months, I guess. I swear, some days it seems it's gone away completely."

"You don't want to rush it," Spinale says. "I mean, you're not going to get good chow and these kind of beds the next place you go, Pettigrew."

"Old Jesse's giving me the word that he'd like to see a little more improvement. Didn't come right out with it, but he seems kind of concerned that it might go the other way."

"It'll be a long war, kid. Couple of stiff fingers is a cheap way to slide through it."

"Goddamn, Spinale, I don't care anything about the *war*." Pettigrew squirms, looks across the room to where the screening glares like burning glass. "Look at that," he says. "I tell you, I know what hot is, but look at *that* goddamned sun."

"Anyway, you got to admit it's pretty comfortable in here."

The new patient now sits next to his bed, alone, his head in his hands.

Deacon's wastebasket grows. Looped and splintered and filthy, the strands coil on one another until they form a tottering oval, half the side stringers loose in the base. The border which Vierra has taught Deacon how to make has to be held together with knots of raffia.

Deacon sits in Lieutenant Klein's anteroom, his handiwork held on his lap as though it contains eggs. The WAC seems unable to keep her eyes off it. She forces a smile when Deacon catches her staring. When he smiles enthusiastically back she colors and begins to peck at her typewriter.

Lieutenant Klein beckons Deacon in. He looks uneasily at the basket when Deacon places it on the desk between them. The lieutenant fidgets in his chair and launches a patter of small talk. Deacon responds in monotones. Klein is working around the basket, working up to it, when Deacon interrupts him.

"You don't have to say anything, Lieutenant."

"Well . . ."

"It's a lousy job."

"It's the first thing you've ever made, after all." Klein jacks himself up to enthusiasm. "Now that you know how it's done, perhaps you'll be able to take a little more time with the next one."

"If that's what you want. But that's not going to do me any good, Lieutenant."

"You're wrong—it will. Get Bradeway to give you a little more help next time."

"Bradeway isn't helping anybody anymore."

Lieutenant Klein sits back and makes a face. "Not at all? I knew that he wasn't . . . I didn't realize he'd stopped completely."

"Vierra does it all now."

"I knew that he'd been helping . . ." Klein nods his head rapidly. The basket sits between them like a symbol of insurmountable ineptitude on both their parts. "I never could get to him," Klein says in a tired voice.

"Maybe it was the flying."

"Yes, perhaps." He looks up at Deacon, concerned. "Is it still so difficult to talk about?"

"I don't think it's talking about it. It's just flying."

"You mean the strain." Klein stumbles over the last word. "I don't mean exactly that. Maybe *you* can tell me."

"Well he didn't finish his tour."

"Yes, I know . . . but do you mean that he *wanted* to finish? That you want to finish yours?"

"It's like a contract, Lieutenant, like when you enlist for the duration of the war—you're supposed to fly until you finish your tour."

"But that's absurd." Klein shakes his head, nearly angry. "It's not you personally who's needed. There are plenty of men to take your place. They must be training thousands every month."

"Nobody can fly your tour for you."

"But that's just it—it isn't *your* tour, it's *a* tour." Klein is straining physically to make himself understood.

"The number only belongs to you. You can't give it to anybody else or take theirs."

"The number of missions . . . that's arbitrary. It could be *any* number." Klein rubs the crown of his head irritably. A few hairs fall. "Suppose you hadn't been flying at all? You don't suppose that would have made any difference to the war, do you?"

"You don't understand, Lieutenant."

"I'm trying to, but you're not making very much sense. You've got to get the idea out of your head that your being in here has anything to do with bravery or cowardice—those are only terms. It was a simple case of pressure building up every day, like steam in a boiler, until it overwhelmed you. There's absolutely nothing wrong with that. In fact, it was probably better that you gave way a little rather than trying to contain it."

"Everybody else had the same thing."

"Yes, I know." The lieutenant turns moody, jabs at the wastebasket with his pencil.

"We all volunteered."

"That doesn't mean anything. Well, I should say that it indicates a certain willingness to . . . a certain willingness. Why don't you tell me *why* you volunteered?"

"I'm sorry, Lieutenant, I don't think you'd know anything about it."

"Indeed? I think perhaps it's you who doesn't know anything if you're going to assume that I'd have to have been up in an airplane or in a rifle company before I could help any of you men. I think that's a rotten attitude to take, Deacon, and I don't think you have any right to take it." Klein is momentarily upset at having let the last name slip, at having put the man in his place, but he plunges on. "I wouldn't be here, after all, if people far more qualified than yourself didn't think I could be of some use."

"You couldn't help Bradeway."

"Neither could anyone else," Klein snaps. "He's had the best professional care in this theater, and no one's been able to bring him all the way back."

"He probably wanted to finish his tour."

"Stop harping on that. We don't make sick men well by putting them back in a situation they weren't able to cope with in the first place. Do you have some sort of medical qualifications I don't know anything about?"

"You said yourself that you weren't a doctor."

"I know what I said." Klein struggles to get a grip on himself. "Let's just say that I'm a little better able to decide what's best for this ward than you are."

"All right, Lieutenant."

"We're getting pretty far off course, aren't we? Whatever Bradeway's problem is hasn't anything to do with you." Deacon is silent. "Well it doesn't, does it?"

"You mean maybe he *didn't* want to finish his tour?"

"Every one of you has a file filled with maybes. Just worry about yourself and leave it to me to worry about Bradeway and about you and about every other single man here. Take care of yourself and leave it to me to take care of the rest of them."

"But suppose you're wrong, Lieutenant?"

"What?"

"Suppose you don't let me finish my tour, and I wind up like Bradeway?"

Jesse Klein's anger shrivels. He falls back on his sincerity, feels it crumble beneath the weight of the man in the chair opposite. Klein hasn't been able to grasp him as he is; now he can see dancing behind Deacon the spectral shadow of the man he might become.

"Then all you want to do is go back?" he asks weakly.

"I think so."

"I can't send you back the way you are. There's a responsibility here . . . Deacon. You've got to be functioning . . . there are the other men you'd fly with. And we couldn't do more than make the recommendation, anyway."

"If I make a good basket, will it prove that I'm okay?"

"The basket . . . the damned basket hasn't anything to do with it."

"Should I make something else?"

"In God's name, what are we sitting here for if one of us can't understand the other?"

"I understand, Lieutenant."

"It doesn't appear . . ." Klein closes his eyes, watches pinpoints of light flicker over the inside of the lids. "I think we'd better leave it for now," he says slowly. "We can pick this up another time when we're both a little more relaxed."

"Whatever you say, Lieutenant."

"I didn't mean to pop off at you, Deacon, but I'm trying to . . . there's no way to help without some sort of minimal understanding to start with. After all, you could be faking, couldn't you? And suppose it *is* simply combat fatigue—is that all, is there something else underneath which has nothing whatsoever to do with the war? Unless I can find a place to start, I can't begin to help."

"I guess it's hard, Lieutenant." Deacon stands, picks up the basket. "Do you want me to keep this?"

"I don't care." Klein rouses himself to a weak smile. "It's not really good for much, is it?"

"Maybe the next one will be better."

Nevertheless, Deacon takes the basket, and when the door closes behind Deacon the lieutenant is shut in with the dreary walls and empty pictures. He looks at the patients' chair, begins to see it as an inquisitor's rack. Klein can imagine coils of wire, binding straps, an electrode cap. He reaches into the air and pulls an imaginary switch, jumps when there is a tap on the door. The WAC's head appears.

"Everything all right, Lieutenant?" she asks.

"Yes, thank you."

"I couldn't help but hear the voices." She shakes her head. "Was that the flyer you were asking me about?"

"Yes, it was."

"Gee."

"Did you want something, Private Cusset?"

"You ought to remember that you're really helping these men, Lieutenant, no matter how they act. I mean, some of them are probably too nutty to appreciate what you're trying

128

to do for them. After all, what more can they expect but your best?"

"Thank you." Klein stares at the WAC for a moment, then licks his dry lips. "It's nice to know that you feel that way, Private Cusset."

"Well gee, anybody in their right mind would." She tugs at her uniform skirt. "You'll excuse me, Lieutenant, but I don't see why you always have to be so formal. I mean, we've been working together a long time. It might make you feel more relaxed if you called me Vera once in a while."

Klein stares again, nods. The girl gives him a slightly roguish smile, closes the door. Not bad at all, Klein thinks, Private Cusset Corset. And then he is engulfed by a whirlwind image of her spread on his desk, issue girdle flung away with the issue stockings still attached, her sturdy legs waving in the air as Klein strains against her and their joint sweat puddles beneath them and blots out the label pasted on the folder of Thomas E. Deacon.

Klein groans, laces his fingers over his forehead and puts his head down on the desk. He finds himself grinning into his hands.

13.

WALINSKI'S NAME is on top of the list, the next scheduled passenger on the Saturday Special, but Bradeway beats him to the door.

The men knew that something had to be done with Bradeway, that particles were flaking from him steadily, almost visibly, like a pennon of snow crystals streaming from the peak of a remote mountain. Nevertheless, they are shocked when official action is taken, orders cut and transportation arranged and a bed or a cage reserved somewhere, a blank tag made ready for Bradeway's name. They can only watch with a sort of paralysis as he is sent into an irreversible twilight.

The enchantment which has kept Bradeway from the ward's realities doesn't sustain him through his last minutes there. Something seeps through—the prospect of change, the sight of the two medics cooing like bleached imps, Spinale's nervous chatter as he helps gather personal effects and stuffs a half dozen candy bars into the canvas musette bag. Something fissures the layers of insulation, causes Bradeway to question querulously. Spinale answers with winks and twitching shoulders, chatters more urgently, tries to cram the last of Bradeway's things into the bag. Geary's clinical pose gives way to impatience. He calls for Spinale to hurry it up. Bradeway grows alarmed, clamps both hands over the mouth of the sack.

Geary beckons to Ferguson. The Pacifier approaches carrying no restraining devices other than his arms, rumbling mildly in an undertone to Geary's edgy cackle. Spinale has not stopped talking, but he is inching away, his head more thrust forward and his voice growing louder with each backward step he takes. Bradeway tries to turn to him, finds himself blocked by Ferguson, slides along the medic and meets arms extended like brackets. They close in a firm hug. Bradeway stiffens and grinds his naked heels into the floor, skids, tilts rigid against Ferguson. The other grunts, lifts him until he is forced up on the tip of his toes, steered toward the door in a jerky dance. A contorted eye shows over the medic's bulging shoulders as Bradeway strains his head toward the words still gushing from Spinale, who has retreated to the middle of the ward.

Spinale does not shut up until Bradeway disappears around the portal, and then his voice cuts off abruptly, leaving a half-finished sentence echoing along the walls. Geary's head wags in exasperation as he finishes the packing. The last thing he puts in, the thing he pinches like a soiled handkerchief and allows to flutter into the bag, is the scrap of parachute cloth.

The men seethe for days after Bradeway's removal. The air is charged as though with sulphur and brimstone, the damnation of Intensive Care. Captain Marcellus's smile is distinctly glassy during the Saturday inspection. Lieutenant Klein has a guilty look. Only Geary is undisturbed, struts as usual in their wake.

The patients' files seem to sway on the verge of disintegration, seem to be held together only by the rocklike figure of Walinski. The Crusher is in uniform, his Combat Infantryman's Badge glinting, ribbons strung across his chest in a gash as lurid as a wound. He exposes his wolf grin while the captain recites in a forced voice, looks smugly from side to side as though seeking approval from the other patients. They avoid his eye, manage to avoid shaking his hand, pounding his back through the archway. Walinski sets his teeth and marches away, still sustaining himself as the good soldier.

After lunch the patients move restlessly between beds,

form drab maroon rosettes which change shape and size with every moment. Although they are free of strict routine until Monday, there is a rush to use the handicraft room. Geary has to shout to keep order, has to set up a rigid schedule.

Dodds, the new patient, is not reluctant to discuss his problem. He is a Dear John victim, a young bridegroom who was practically combing the rice from his hair as he walked up the troopship's gangplank. His bride has not been able to wait for him. Her letters cooled to doubt, grew to petulance, then to anger at Dodds for having harnessed her youth, swindled her freedom. Their ten days in a shabby motel are all the love Dodds has to sustain him. They will not sustain her. In a burst of destructive honesty she tells him that he has become nothing more than a jailer to her, that she will hate him if she doesn't go out with others while he is away.

Dodds's chaplain can only counsel prayer. His commanding officer—himself nineteen months removed from a marital bed, dreaming each night of sheets soiled by a different stranger—has heard the story before, tartly refuses Dodds's request for an emergency furlough home. Dodds sinks, emerges blinking in the light of G Ward.

His fellow patients cluck when Dodds begins his sad story, offer him bland words while they snicker at each other over his bowed head, trade sweaty reminiscences of consolations they've given lonely wives. Dodds is left nearly entirely in Harris's care. The first sergeant plays father and nurse, tries to stiffen Dodds with a soldier's brace.

"If they'd only let me go back," Dodds says in the handicraft room, "everything would have been all right."

"I guess there's more than one would like to get back to the States, Norman." Harris's tongue protrudes slightly between his teeth as he stabs at a strip of leather with a dull tool. "The thing is to do what you've got to do."

"Read him the Articles of War," Vierra says.

"I don't know why this had to happen to me." Dodds shudders. "My God, some of the people I've been put in with. In Naples . . ."

"Well, Norman, you're not there now, and what you want to do is concentrate on getting out of *here.*"

"That fellow—what was his name?—they prodded him out of here like a . . . like a chicken. *He* certainly wasn't going anywhere I'd like to go. You'd think he was being bundled up for the guillotine."

"Think about Walinski, instead."

"Certainly," Vierra says, "and about our friend here who is so anxious to get back to the war."

Deacon is sweating lightly, struggling to weave reed around an empty tin can.

"But this is supposed to be a recuperative ward," Dodds says. "How are we supposed to make adjustments if they're always threatening to send us back to one of those terrible places where people are *really* ill?"

"Nobody's going to send you anywhere if you'll just do what they tell you to. That's all you have to do."

"No matter who is telling," Vierra says, "Captain Marcellus or Lieutenant Klein or the *cabron* Geary."

"Don't be giving him ideas," Harris says.

"My idea is to slit that animal's bags and stamp on his balls when they fall out." Vierra looks over at Harris's work. "Is that some kind of decorated truss you're making?"

"They could at least give you *tools*."

"But then there would be no excuse, Harris. Now you can blame it on the tools. Lieutenant Klein can tell you that you would do much better work if you had better equipment."

"I think it's ridiculous," Dodds says primly. "I don't see any connection between this idiotic nonsense and my state of mind. If the Army hadn't been so stupid I would never have been put in a place like this. I don't know why they think it's doing me any good, anyway."

"Goddamnit, Norman, they're not about to do anything *for* you, but they'll sure as hell do something *to* you if you don't get on the stick and get started."

"I don't care."

"Well they don't care either, sonny boy." Harris throws down the belt and wipes his forehead. "Goddamn place doesn't have to be this hot, does it? I've had just about as much as I can take."

"I hate it in here."

"Just don't wait on getting to like it, Norman," Harris says, "because if it comes to them deciding you're not doing too well nobody's going to care much whether or not you like whatever it is they figure on doing with you. Come on, we might as well go back."

"The point is, I don't see why we should accept some haphazard program no one really believes in," Dodds is saying as they go out, "particularly if we don't feel we even *belong* in here . . ."

His voice trails away into the corridor. There is an irritated bark from Harris, and then the individual tones of the two men become lost in the general sounds of the hospital—whispers, rattles, the squeak of rubber tires, the pad of rubber shoes. A nurse's laughter carries into the room. Vierra and Deacon glimpse parted lips, a shower of curls thrown back in

132

response to something a medical officer is saying. The couple passes from sight.

"He doesn't believe it," Vierra says.

"What?"

"Dodds can hardly believe he is in our hospital—he doesn't believe at all there is any reason for him to be here."

"What the hell, Vierra."

"Another one? Do you think you are in some kind of comedy?"

"I don't think I ever heard so much bullshit about what everybody's supposed to be doing, and all the time they're doing nothing."

Vierra draws his legs up and sits with his chin resting on his knees. "You need to understand something very important, my friend—no matter how foolish this seems, none of it is a mistake. Not Dodds and not Harris and not you. If you can think how this Army throws men into itself like potatoes into a peeling machine, with the bad spots already cut away and the eyes gouged out, into the machine to have what is left of the recognizable skins scraped off, and if you can remember that this Army has done everything it can to make us look like each other and has discovered that we do not suit it . . . what are we, then?"

"You, too."

"Certainly. Do you think I am only Pettigrew's joke?" Deacon's fingers squeak along the reed as he squeezes out the excess water. "Do you want me to confess?" Vierra continues. "I confess. It was an adventure and then an accommodation and then it became a distinct taste. Do you think it is so rare? Only in that I was discovered . . . myself and my adjutant. Our commanding officer was so filled with disgust he would have had both of us shot if he could have found a regulation permitting it. Disgust . . . for something he didn't even begin to understand. And then what was he to do? *Two* unsuitable discharges? A remarkable coincidence. Where my friend was sent, I don't know . . . but I am here. Maybe he's in a place like this for officers."

"I don't have your problem, Vierra."

"*Tal vez* . . . perhaps. Do you know the Italian for that?"

"*Forse.*"

"Your book is doing you some good. Will *forse* be enough when you get out, when you cannot understand whether they have washed something out of you or into you? Myself, I'm no longer sure of my taste. In here, nothing . . . but Italy is filled with beautiful boys, and maybe I would love them. I don't care which way it turns, if the entrance to love becomes front or rear or both, but I care that I do *not* know. And you

133

must care also, you must understand that you're in no comedy or accident here, before you'll grow well enough to become the crazy man who goes up in the sky."

"Don't start that again." Deacon has squeezed the reed too dry. It snaps in his hands. "You could get out of here if you really wanted to," he says, "if you stopped giving everybody a hard time."

"For what? What would I get out to?"

"You don't have to go back to being a clerk." Deacon begins peeling strips from the broken pieces of reed. "If you don't want to, you don't have to go back at all."

"Your meaning escapes me, my friend."

"To any outfit, I mean."

"Not to any outfit. To leave and simply go out there . . . is that what you mean? To go over the hill?"

The edges of Deacon's teeth show. Vierra looks at him closely. "You may not be as well as you think," he said. "You have a plan, of course."

"There's a way. And if you don't change your uniform or remove your dog tags, it isn't desertion. I checked with Harris."

"Is he going, too?"

"No, Harris isn't going. What the hell would anyone want with Harris? I checked with him, made it look like just a question about the regulations. If it isn't desertion, they can't shoot you. If you turn yourself in, you might even get away with just company punishment . . . they could break you and give you a fine and restriction."

"There is nothing for me to be broken from . . . but I don't understand. If you already have a plan to go back, then why must you go over the hill?"

"I didn't say I was going back, Vierra, or going over the hill or going anywhere. I only said how it could be."

"Beautiful, touring the ruins of Italy . . . the latest ones, I mean. And there would be money."

"Black market."

"Certainly. For you there is evidently some particular reason in all this, but why should I go?"

"To get away from all this horseshit . . . to find out just where you are. You said yourself you didn't know."

"You and I will go together, is that it? And if I find out that I don't like you, that I like Italian boys better? There is bound to be one who will help me take your money and your clothes and leave you behind in a hill village. Tell me, is it still not desertion if you are naked? Are you safe from being shot if your ass is bare?"

Vierra shakes his head, lifts his hands in a helpless gesture.

He takes a length of reed from the basin, flips water from it, then begins to splice it to the broken end jutting from the tin can.

"You have a marvelous plan," he says, "what a pity Bradeway was sent away. You could have flown together, two brave birds. But there's still Spinale. He could be your guide and interpreter. Spinale would have your money and your clothes an hour after you started. But the biggest plan is for you to get out of here first." Deacon doesn't answer. Vierra lets the spliced reed fall. "This must be part of it. Does it have a name?"

"It's a pencil holder for Klein."

"So he can make his notes more precisely?" Vierra looks critically at the work. "He will have it on his desk each time you visit, but otherwise he will keep it in his desk drawer because it is so ugly."

"Will you help me with it?"

"Something this bad? Never."

"For Jesus sake . . ."

"For my *sake,* for the sake of Jesus Vierra I will never make anything just to please that poor rabbit or the fat doctor."

"It's for me, not for them."

"It's for them. Nothing you do is for yourself."

"You won't go because you know they'll never *let* you out, you goddamned . . ."

"And you think this ugly mess will help you to become the lunatic tourist? Tell me why it will convince anyone that you should be let out."

"Maybe because I'm not queer for assholes, Vierra."

The blood already risen beneath Vierra's skin now tinges the corners of his eyes. He makes a move toward Deacon, but then goes rigid, spins on his heel, and starts for the door. Deacon calls after him.

"Yoo-hoo, Pancho, wait for your buddy."

Eddie Spinale enters Lieutenant's Klein's anteroom briskly. He says a polite good morning to the WAC, asks if the lieutenant is in.

"You can relax," PFC Cusset says. "He just left for the library and won't be back for about an hour."

"Never hurts to be on the safe side, Vera. You don't want to be put in the position you never know. I got a little thing for you to do maybe a couple of pages at a time, like when he's out."

"Is this some crazy deal like those laundry slips?"

"It's nothing like that, Vera, but you got to remember that

135

really wasn't such a bad idea . . . only I couldn't locate the right personnel."

"I don't know why I ever believed there could be such a thing, a special laundry for ladies' underclothes. I must have been crazy."

"You got to admit it looked good, Vera, and you were in there for a full ten percent. You could've been a rich lady going out of this army. You're still getting your clothes back from that GI laundry with about a pound of starch in everything, right? I bet you even get your stockings back starched."

"I do my own stockings, thank you. Whatever I send to the GI laundry at least I get back most of it. That one of yours they stole half of it and they sent the other half back it looked like somebody had been washing it with sandpaper."

"Yeah, well that's the way they do it, beating clothes on a rock. And we wouldn't have lost so much stuff if we had better control on those laundry slips. Forget it, Vera, it's all bygones. What I want now is a little thing hardly needs to involve you. I just want to get a name typed on a few three-day passes."

"Lieutenant *Klein's?*"

"I don't need that dumbbell and that's why there's nothing to it, just a phony name I made up, a captain somebody."

"You want to get me court-martialed or something?"

"When he's not here, Vera, a little bit at a time. You don't think I'd ask if there wasn't something in it for you?"

"What?"

"I got some of this nice stateside perfume. Real name stuff in fancy bottles."

"I don't exactly have to buy my own perfume, Eddie. That's a gift a gentleman very often gives."

"I'm happy to hear somebody thinks so much of you, Vera, although the stuff I got smells better than what you're wearing. How about some soap, that fancy kind looks like a dime around the edges?"

"You've been hustling those wops so long, Eddie, I think you must be a little out of touch. American girls don't go for that kind of handout."

"Cigarettes?"

"And then I turn them back to you so you can sell them for me and take your cut? No thanks."

"All I want to do is the right thing by you, Vera, if you'll just tell me . . ."

"Exactly what *is* this deal?"

"Like I said, you fill in the name of some captain or other on the bottom of maybe thirty three-day passes. You wouldn't have to do anything like sign them. I'd take care of that."

"Thanks loads."

"Then there's the name of the guy's supposed to be on pass, and a phony outfit. Also, there ought to be dates. In order, you know, consecutive-like."

"You don't want much."

"I don't, Vera, believe me, and if I could still move around the way I used to, I wouldn't even trouble you."

"Poor Eddie went and lost his dummy."

"That's like speaking evil of the dead to talk that way, Vera. The poor guy didn't know which end was up. And they didn't do him any good taking him away from me. At least I kept him quiet."

"What're you going to do now?"

"That's something I wanted to talk to you about. I was wondering if you had a line on anybody coming in, somebody all right but not too good—sort of half asleep without being really batty. It ought to be somebody who'd be in there awhile."

"We never know what kind of garbage they're going to send us, Eddie."

"No idea, huh?"

"If they bring them in with chains wrapped around it's the first idea we have what we're getting. Why don't you team up with one of the regulars, somebody like Harris?"

"He's too GI. I bring him around with me and he'll start reciting by the numbers about the regulations I'm breaking."

"That spic's not going anywhere right away."

"It's not too good for your reputation to be seen with somebody like Vierra all the time. I mean, people start getting ideas. How about Pettigrew?"

"If he doesn't get better, he's going to get worse. Why don't you try that flyer, that Deacon? Maybe he's too much of a screaming nut."

"You think so? He looks like a guy with too many angles, anyway. Maybe that new kid, Dodds?"

"That big baby?"

"I can handle that kind, Vera. I'm *simpatico, amichevole* . . . you know? You think he'll be here for a while? The thing is, if I can't make a connection I got to get out myself. I got to get into a new game if my action here's dead."

"Maybe you'd better anyway, Eddie. You could wind up back in IC."

"That's why I got to be cozy. But look, what about these passes?"

"Two dollars."

"You want more than that, Vera. I could give you . . ."

"Two dollars *each*, Eddie."

"For a couple of minutes' work? Come on, how do you think I'm gonna be able to move something at that price? If it was for me, I'd pay it gladly."

"Who's it for?"

"I'm only the broker, Vera, I got to respect my confidences."

"Well that's the deal, take it or leave it."

"I could maybe give you a *dollar* . . ."

"No dice, Eddie."

"I can see how much our friendship means, but I'm not gonna let hard feelings interfere. You do thirty passes and I'll give you fifty bucks . . ."

"That sounds more . . ."

". . . but you got to give me a little bit more, lady, and put that same name on these five ration cards here, and all that other information, too."

"*Ration* cards?"

"Fifty bucks and maybe it'll take you an hour, maybe a little more. If I wasn't in my present situation, I can tell you it wouldn't be such easy money."

"I don't think you can afford to shop around, Eddie."

"I'd appreciate it if you wouldn't give me an argument. Just tell me if you're in or out."

"Fifty dollars for sure?"

"If you get it done in the next couple days. And I'd advise you to be careful, because if this stuff gets picked up I'm out a nice buck and I'll be looking to get it back. *Capito?*"

"Don't worry, Eddie, he don't know the day of the week half the time. What should I write?"

"It's right here on this piece of paper. Just copy exactly what I put down. And don't leave *this* laying around, either."

"How about the dates?"

"The dates?"

"You have to start somewhere if you want them in consecutive order. What's the first day?"

"Yeah, that's right. It's hard to figure. What the hell, start it with Fourth of July, that's a good date."

"Okay, Eddie."

"Noon to noon, every three days. Be sure you count right."

"I made these out a hundred times in my regular work, Eddie."

"Payment on delivery."

"Okay." The WAC pats at her hair. "I'll probably make corporal any day now. Did you know that?"

"Good for you."

138

"And I wouldn't be surprised if I got to go out in a jeep once in a while. He's been paying certain attentions lately."

"It's too bad you couldn't score before this, Vera. You could've made some real money dropping a few things off if you'd have had a jeep available."

"There's other considerations. You don't think it's everybody an officer wants to take a chance going out and breaking regulations with, do you?"

"Look out that's not all he breaks."

"Just keep your dirty mind to yourself."

"I don't care what you do as long as you get that assignment finished. And none of those lousy strikeovers, either. This has to look legit."

"You're going to be so worried, you'd better get that fairy clerk to do it for you."

"Vera . . ."

"Okay, okay. I'll be extra careful."

"That's what I'm paying for."

Spinale goes out. The WAC looks at her watch, then puts one of the passes into the typewriter, sets the margins. She pops a wad of pink gum in her mouth and begins to type.

14.

ALTHOUGH THE pencil holder is as grotesque as the wastebasket, Lieutenant Klein is touched and nearly moved by Deacon's obvious attempt to butter him up with a personal gift, by his inability to produce anything better than rat work. The weaving sags, would collapse if it were not supported by the can. Klein sighs. He honestly believes that the effort involved is far more important than the product, but in this case the outcome is doubly irrelevant. The receptacle will hold pencils with blunt tips and chewed erasers, but it will hold no part of Deacon.

Worse than having nothing to hold parts, Klein has no parts to deal with, and he is near despair because a second medal has arrived—the Distinguished Flying Cross. It is as though Klein is giving it to Deacon in exchange for the pencil holder, for a mess of broken reed wrapped around a tin can. Klein is fascinated by the ribbon, a restrained but patriotic red, white and blue. He fingers the propeller imposed upon the Maltese cross, would spin it if it were not fixed, would watch the whirling blades the way a child might watch a toy. He reads the commendation over and over, finds an understated glory between the sketchy lines. Klein isn't soldier enough to realize that he's dealing with a sixth-ranked decoration. He believes that he has a confirmed and illustrious hero on his hands, one whom he has put to work making playthings of straw.

The lieutenant hasn't learned anything about heroes from the few who've passed through G Ward. Walinski was delivered to him already degenerate, Bradeway had already begun to sing in ghostly halls. There aren't any studies of blood-eaters in Klein's books and Deacon hasn't revealed anything. His time is growing dangerously long and Klein is running out of both time and references. How can he begin to weigh the value of a shoddy tin can against the DFC? The lieutenant comes to a stop at dead center, his scales inoperative. He finds himself with nothing left to balance his own person, lurches in his chair. Rousing himself to a final effort, Klein gets out Deacon's file and goes through his service record word by word, his fingers tracing each line and his lips moving.

Born after the end of another war, in Hartford, Connecticut. *Modified Yankee city . . . aircraft parts . . . insurance.* Father a lathe operator, former soldier, wounded in 1918. *Passed into the son's blood traces of shrapnel, the mark of the stiff collar, rings from the wrapped puttees?* Mother dead. *Who consoled the little boy . . . did the father drink, chase around . . . was he a protective hen, a pal?* An older brother currently in the Navy. *Shield and refuge . . . or a bully?* High school education, grades average to good. No organizations, non-leader. Four years with local aircraft instrument firm, blue collar to white, tool crib assistant to shop expediter. Responsible job. Draft deferred, but enlisted. *Why . . . guilt, tradition . . . boredom, duty?*

Klein's questions are unanswered because they are unasked. He cannot write them down, must carry them in his head. Captain Marcellus will not permit prying into the patients' civilian backgrounds. He is afraid that some beast might be prodded out of the silt, that it might rise to devour both keepers and charges. Klein feels that the answers would be absolutely useless anyway, that in Deacon he has a sort of Jack Armstrong, youth replying *I will* for no discernible reason. Give or take a year or two in Deacon's age and education, subtract or add a parent, and he would be half the men in the service. He has medals but no distinctions. Klein goes on to the army career.

Enlisted 1942, AAF. GCT above average. No effort made to apply to OCS. Basic training. Assigned to instrument school. Completed course satisfactorily, then volunteered for aerial gunnery school. *For God's sake, why?* Marksman, excellent mechanical knowledge of weapons. Graduated. PFC. Transitional flight training. Physical fitness above flight standards, mental attitude good. Functioned well as part of crew. Corporal. Good Conduct Medal. Overseas assignment immediately upon completion of flight training. Air Medal. *Pride?* Sergeant. Distinguished Unit Citation. Second Air Medal. *???* Staff Sergeant. Three campaign stars, a list of missions. *One, two, three . . . all the way to thirty-one.* No further report on physical fitness or mental attitude until incident which caused Flight Surgeon to recommend him for observation. Purple Heart. *Contempt.* Distinguished Flying Cross.

Klein reviews his own written observations. The first entry is still *A crock of shit*. Klein erases that, sucks the end of his pencil. There is a note that Deacon hasn't received or sent any letters since he's been in the hospital. They might be a family of non-writers, the mail might be slow. There are a few other scrawls, all worthless. Klein cannot draw any conclusions, cannot even find a place to begin. Deacon is a round tight ball, and Klein must either keep all of him or send all of him back. There are no parts he can deal with. He must either put Deacon in the ward's cold storage or return him to duty.

The lieutenant gnaws at himself, finds the old brittle skeleton of inadequacy. He doesn't know why Deacon stopped flying or if he wants to go back to it. The whole concept is beyond his grasp—the idea of volunteering, of anyone being willing to go up and meet the claw. Klein doesn't even know if Deacon will be *able* to fly. But he's sure that G Ward's vaulted ceiling isn't high enough to let him test his wings. The lieutenant begins to write slowly and carefully. If a depraved Walinski can be released, what harm can Klein do tossing an odd ball back into the game? He prepares a devious out-bound ticket, hides his recommendations in a welter of words which adds up to no recommendations. Jesse Klein lets Deacon roll from his hands, stretches his sincerity to its

141

limit hoping that there will be someone out there to catch him.

The rumor goes bouncing among the vitreous fittings in the latrine, is confirmed. Deacon will be released. He is a short-timer, hasn't been an obvious brown-nose, but he's on his way. The patients buzz, check the wastebaskets lining the ward. None of them is Deacon's. The men are so conditioned to the standard routine of salvation they decide that Deacon must have made something special to spring the lock, that he must have minted magic from the trash in the therapy room. They ask Vierra. Vierra is amused, tells them about the pencil holder. There is increased handicraft activity.

And then another rumor goes singing among the urinals and commodes. Deacon is only the first; Pettigrew is to follow, then an unnamed third person. The patients boil and chatter, crowd Geary so he must set up a schedule for the therapy room. Ashtrays appear, leather book covers, paper-clip receptacles which look like frazzled birds' nests. The men spy on each other's work, hide their own, search frantically for a particular totem to please Klein.

If Deacon is one and Pettigrew is two and there is to be a third, there must be a plan to clear out the ward. A final song goes roaring along the sinks and mirrors, climbs over partitions; there *is* a plan, the ward is to be gradually closed down. Everyone will be shipped out, and none to IC. There will be releases even for those beyond the range of Lieutenant Klein's doubts. When the number of patients falls below a certain practical level, even the dregs will be flushed out.

"Yeah, it looks bad," Spinale says. "I better get knocking on something."

"A basket for bread," Vierra says, "a cradle for bottle of wine."

"You think that's what he'd like? How about you? You got something special in mind?"

"I have made *everything,* my friend. Now I wait."

"It don't pay me to stay here even if they keep the ward open, what with Clinton gone . . . If there was only some way I could organize this place from the outside . . . you think I could transfer permanently into this hospital, Vierra? You know, like a conscientious objector or something? I mean, if I'm here on regular duty, I got it made."

"The bed-pan rental agency," Vierra says. "How much for the crutches, Spinale, a dollar an hour?"

"Nothing like that. I'm not out to screw anybody, just to get a little piece of what's around."

"I guess I'm ready," Pettigrew says. "I guess I'd better be."

"If you think about it, it wouldn't hurt for them to keep

you on a little while. I mean, how do we know we shouldn't be sent to another place, a kind of recuperation from this?"

"Please God no," Vierra says.

"Maybe Eddie's right," Pettigrew says. "Maybe . . ."

"Maybe it is already too late," Vierra says, his eyes pressed shut. "Maybe I have spent too much time with you animals."

"Why, you're just eager to get back to your loving, Pancho."

"I don't think we oughta talk like this," Spinale says. "I think we oughta respect each other's troubles."

"Mierde," Vierra says.

"If that's what I think it is, I don't see how you can do it," Pettigrew says. "I don't see how you can make that poor tired old bung of yours move things the other way."

Even Harris, tears unstoppered, leaking through eyes screwed nearly closed, begins to look on Deacon as the forerunner of an exodus.

"And I see they're not going too good in Normandy," he says. "Just about able to keep their feet dry."

"You sound like a couple of recruits I had who were afraid the war would be over before they had a chance to get themselves shot up."

"Goddamnit, Deacon, you know I don't want any more hurt than has to be. But if it's going to keep going on, I want to be where I should be."

"Okay, Top."

"Well that's where you're going, isn't it, back to your outfit?"

"That's what Klein tells me."

"And you're going back on combat status?"

"He didn't tell me that, Harris. What's the matter, are you afraid I'll miss something?"

"Don't go getting your balls in an uproar. Nobody would blame you."

"Nobody would blame me what? For being a crap-out like the rest of you in here?" Deacon rummages in his night table. "I've got just the thing for you, Harris, just what you've been crying for all this time."

"You just watch . . ."

"If I can find the goddamned thing. Here it is, Harris, go pin it on your handkerchief."

Harris looks into the box, then closes the lid and holds it out to Deacon.

"I've seen more than one of these where there wasn't anybody around to wear it."

Deacon pushes his hand away. "It's yours, Harris, keep it."

"Nothing to do with me, Deacon. I don't know whether you earned it or not, but it's on your service record."

"You don't want it?"

"It's not mine."

Deacon throws the case into the wastebasket nearest his bed.

"Now just a minute . . ." Harris says.

"Do you want it?"

"Lot of good men gone who ought to be wearing that DFC. You don't have any right . . ."

"You nursing pain in the ass, Harris, do you want it or not?"

"I won't let you throw it away."

"Then pick it up."

Harris reaches into the wastebasket and takes out the box. He brushes a powder of cigarette ash from it with the sleeve of his robe.

"Deacon, you oughtn't . . ."

"I'll shove it down the crapper."

Harris's pursed lips work in and out. For a moment he seems to be marching in place, then he does a neat about-face. Deacon watches Harris go to his own bed, place the box beneath his pillow.

Saturday comes and they stand in rows again, once more finding an obtrusive figure in khaki, this one with ribbons and glittering wings. Marcellus shakes Deacon's hand, Klein nods and looks haunted, Geary snickers. After a little speech, after the officers have departed, Deacon goes. He moves on the noiseless wheels of the Saturday Special, and seems to leave something like a film of ashes in his wake.

Now Pettigrew is number one. The patients turn shifty eyes toward him, watch him hold one hand up and rub the fingers together in a curiously Italian gesture. Number three is now number two, but he still hasn't a name. The men are furtive, as though trying to protect their identities. Even though they are free after the inspection, they crowd around Geary and clamor to be put on the schedule for the therapy room.

Harris waits until the desk is clear and then approaches it with his second legacy, a medal other than the tear-stained cross he now flies every night. It was given to him to be given, and as Harris stands before Geary pinpoints of malice flicker from the puckered rings around his eyes.

"He left this for you to have," he says, placing the box on the desk.

Geary looks at the Purple Heart without interest. "That's

very funny, Harris. That guy was more of a nut than I thought."

"It wasn't my idea. I think he figured you might need it if they assigned you to a pro station after they shut down the ward."

"He figured or *you* figured?"

"I'm just passing it on, Geary. He said something about you'd probably be glad to have something to show people how you fought the Battle of Clapville."

"Is that right, Harris? Did he give you something to show you've been a nut?"

"I don't need anything."

"You're a good man, Top. You're what we need here to keep the troops on the ball. You do a terrific job, Harris. I must have a dozen guys lined up for kindergarten this afternoon."

"There won't be much more than that left after Pettigrew goes."

"That's right . . . if he goes. You're whipping them into such good shape you'll be working yourself out of a job."

"I could stand that."

"Aw no, Harris. You're a leader, a natural leader. We need you to shape up these new men coming in Monday." Geary sits back and feigns astonishment. "You mean you didn't *know?* You don't mean to tell me an old soldier like you actually *believed* all these latrine rumors, Top."

Harris seems to have lost control of his levers and cables, seems to have let his strings go slack. His shoulders are rounded beneath the robe. The cuffs of his sleeves overlap the pockets where his bunched hands are working. He clears his throat twice.

"How many?"

"Only two, Top. That's a good sign, isn't it? That'll make one less than we had a month ago. Things keep going this way they might close down the joint after all."

"They might."

"It's something to think about, Top. Say, if you ever run into your buddy again, you can thank him for the Heart. I know a babe might just be impressed by it. I'll let you know how I make out. I'll tell you if I get any."

Harris takes a few shuffling steps from the desk, stops, and for a moment appears to be trembling. And then, as though filling with a rising yeast, his shoulders snap back and his head tilts erect, and as he moves briskly away the flop of his slippers takes on the regular beat of a military cadence.

*   *   *

A driver is waiting for Deacon at the hospital desk. He is not the one who brought Deacon from the field, and there is no one with him carrying a club. The driver is very young; his clothing has the stiff newness of a recruit's. Deacon completes his checkout and the two men step toward the hospital's glass door, toward their own brilliantly lit images.

They are met outside by the whole force of Calabria's summer heat, an echo of parched Sicily, burning Africa. No breeze drifts from the seas which lie dead under the July sun. Deacon lurches and the driver catches at his arm. The guard at the door, sweating under his white helmet liner, watches them.

"You all right, Sarge?" the driver asks as he guides Deacon to the jeep. "This is a pretty rough trip. You going to be able to take it? There's nothing isn't healed, is there?"

"No."

"Boy, it looks like you sure got it." The driver is staring at Deacon's ribbons. "Wow. I'm surprised they didn't send you to Naples, fly you up the way they usually do. Must have been something special, huh?"

"Sort of."

Deacon squints, shades his eyes, trying to escape the sun. The driver puts on flying glasses, stuffs Deacon's service record into a pocket next to his seat, then starts the jeep and pulls away. They pass the baked field before the hospital. Deacon cranes his head back for a moment. A tunnel of brown dust follows the jeep.

"How long you been in there?" the driver asks.

"A month."

"Yeah? That's as long as I've been overseas. That's something, you being in a hospital for as much time as I've been over. I bet you got more flying time than I got in the Army."

"Don't forget to stop at headquarters."

"Down here, you mean?"

"I have to make my last checkout there."

"It won't take too long, will it? We got a long way to go."

Deacon doesn't answer. They wait until there is a break in the stream of vehicles moving along the highway, become part of the miles of grinding trucks and lorries and *carro-matti* carrying produce from Messina, hard goods from Liverpool, from across the Atlantic. The highway's dust has been ground to a powdery gray-white, and the two men are quickly streaked with it. The hospital disappears into the gray haze flung behind them.

The driver watches the road signs, turns off when he finds one pointing to the area's headquarters. When they pull up before the building the MP on duty at the door waves them away from the restricted parking area. Deacon steps out of the jeep.

"I'll take my service record and get it cleared while you go around the block a couple of times." He holds out his hand.

"I can't do it, Sarge, strict orders. Got to keep it on my person at all times unless I hand it over to an officer."

"What if I gave you a direct order?"

The MP is shouting to them to move on.

"I don't think I could. I don't . . ."

"Give me that goddamned . . ." The MP has started down the steps toward them. Deacon closes his eyes and wipes at his forehead. "I'll wait here."

"Sure, sure. I'll find a spot and be right with you."

The driver has to circle the narrow streets twice before he can find a place to park. Clutching the service record, he hurries back to the building. He is too young, too much of a recruit, to have had the sky, Vienna, the hospital waiting for him. And now, as he puffs up to the hospital steps, he finds that Deacon hasn't waited.

PART THREE

Orestes: *You don't see them, you don't—
but I see them: they are hunting
me down, I must move on.*

CHOEPHOROI

15.

EVEN IF his wings were folded, Deacon had to have some kind of balance. The hospital had taken his old one away; they'd furnished walls he could lean against, cracked ceilings he could take bearings from. No matter how the outside world tilted, G Ward stayed level on unalterable gimbals. Deacon was able to catch up to the time he'd been lurching after only because all the clocks were stuffed and wadded. When the glass door snapped closed it locked him out in an Italian summer ticking its own time, and as he skipped and jigged trying to catch its rhythm, he found that it was easier to fall than to stand. It was no world of murmurs and squeaks and delicate whispers, there were no walls and crutches and other props—only the burning sun, gusts of raw hot wind.

But even without a balance he had to keep moving, to crawl away from the headquarters building and the headquarters town. He pulled himself erect and tottered through La Sila and out of the Calabrian toe, stood gasping at the edge of the Italian arch and looked over the humped wastes to a place where balance wouldn't matter—the hazy curve of the beach along the Gulf of Taranto. He'd be able to stretch prone there, dig his fingers into the sand while the sea wind wore away the hospital bloat and the sun blistered the pallid skin until it peeled off.

The arch wasn't safe, there were too many soldiers. They'd come panting out of the noon of the *mezzogiorno* to shed their sweat-stained uniforms and their thirsts in the little towns along the gulf's edge. MPs followed them, picking up the litter of drunk and unruly. The entire stretch had become a dinky army Riviera where everyone was drenched in wine or water. It was no place for a man to try to lose the hospital shakes. Deacon had to turn away from the southern coast, stagger through the shadow of Monte Pollino and into the mountain country of the meridional.

There was no way but up, even for the wingless. Italian trucks took him part of the distance. He topped the higher crests on foot and in two-wheeled carts, came to places where there was nothing but the thin air to lean against, only the

151

sky incandescent over lines of ridges stretching like a sea of petrified waves. He didn't have to worry about MPs or any other kind of authority in the mountains. The war had never come close and the civil government had broken down. The people weren't concerned, kept the old laws they'd always kept no matter whose voice had been bellowing from Rome. They went on pressing wizened olives and milking thin flocks and honing wheat from rock. Italy and Germany had been fighting the British and Americans, but it had been the Germans who had captured both Rome and Naples, and now Italy had declared war on Germany and was fighting on the same side as the British and Americans. None of it made any sense, none of it mattered in a land which was so remote even the bishop's crozier had been warped to the herdsman's crook.

The people didn't trust uniforms of any kind. No one wearing a uniform ever came into the mountains except to collect taxes or confiscate property or drag the young men away to military service. They watched Deacon carefully, hid their faces under broad-brimmed hats and carried their knives where he could see them. He wasn't wearing a weapon, but they were sure he had a pistol hidden in his musette bag. As soon as he caught them off guard he would take it out and demand a goat or a young girl or the *soldi* buried in the dirt floor.

When Deacon tried to approach them, to make himself understood, his broken Italian broke a second time against an incomprehensible dialect. And then with all his assurances that he only wanted a place to sleep, something to eat, he offered to pay with queer-looking money, crisp new occupation lire colored as vividly as the toy bills in a child's game. They turned their heads away and sniggered. *Fa fesso,* he was playing them for fools. No paper money was thought to be much good, but the people were at least familiar with the ornate notes of the Bank of Italy. Deacon was forced to barter his cigarettes for a meal of curded cheese, bitter bread made from mixed grains, for a sack of straw. Eyes watched him while he ate, while he shivered through the cold mountain nights.

He found it best to keep on the move, not to stay too long, to try the people too much. He trotted from ridge to ridge while the bloat was gradually pared away, while his skin colored from the sun and from the wind which blew the earth dustless. His inner ear made micrometric adjustments and his spine unkinked until he was no longer tottering or staggering, could stand upright and close his eyes without swaying. When that time came he was ready to leave the mountains. There

152

was no point in hiding from the military only to risk being murdered by civilians. No one would even know what had happened to him. The dog tags would rattle among bones growing bleached in some hidden ravine, and the Army would list him as missing forever, but not MIA—only as an indifferent question mark in their archives.

It was certainly best to turn east, toward the source of the white sun. With chapped ears and eyes tearing in the wind, he descended in a self-avalanche of dirt and loose stones, picked his way down the slopes to where the Bradano trickled at Basilicata's edge.

Deacon knew the squadron wouldn't have remembered his name just because he'd gone over the edge, become inoperative. They'd carry him on a down list, the way they would a damaged airplane. If he was repairable he'd go back on the operations board, if not they'd find a suitable scrap pile. But now they knew who he was.

He'd been on the squadron's roster from the moment his records were released to the driver at the hospital, and he'd be carried as part of the official complement as long as the organization was active. They'd probably fretted for a few days waiting for him to come back from a drunk, waiting for a keeper to bring him in wrapped in a butterfly net. By now they'd have concluded that he was a continuing non-presence. The name of Thomas Deacon would appear like a stain on each day's morning report—AWOL. He grinned at that. Each day they'd know he wasn't there. They'd reach into the replacement pool to fill a vacancy on the one great crew and they'd fumble around the empty compartment, find one of the marbles missing. And they couldn't just scrub him, replace him with someone else. His cot would be collapsed and issued to a recruit, but the uniforms and personal belongings would have to be packed in his barracks bags and stored. Some clerk would keep typing his name, someone in the supply tent would keep stumbling over the stenciled bags. Where was that goddamned Deacon, when was he coming back? Once they'd only wanted a warm body to throw into the sky —now they wanted *him*. All the groundgrippers would grow furious because he'd gotten away. They'd begin to beat their drums, pass on the name and the description to the MPs, ask them to loose the dogs and begin the hunt.

The MPs would file the report with all the others. They had a thousand or ten thousand names, all the infantrymen and tankers and artillerymen, all the cooks and clerks who'd skipped and were in or out of uniform somewhere in Italy. The MPs couldn't carry photographs or descriptions. Some central section undoubtedly kept track of all the AWOLs in the theater, compared the names of men who were pulled in for any offense with those on the master list. Deacon could be tied to the grand roster of absentees if he happened to be picked up, but there wouldn't be any MP patrols specifically looking for him. If he were stopped for a routine check he'd give them a pass, show a dummy. He grinned again. While the squadron howled for the body and blood of Thomas Deacon he'd be hidden inside Joe Rico.

Spinale had put a heavy price on the alias, gouged most of Deacon's money and cigarettes. He'd been all winks and nudges—"What's a better name for a GI? You wouldn't forget it, and you give the wops a little Italian they'll think you're a *paisano*, right?" Joe Rico had five ration cards, and he'd originally had thirty passes, a life expectancy of ninety days. Some of that time had been used up in the hospital and in the mountains, but he was still a healthy young man. A replacement could be found even if he happened to drop dead. There were an additional twenty passes which were blank, which could be assigned any identity hidden in the keys of the nearest typewriter.

The ideal Joe Rico would have been a nonentity, a foggy-eyed PFC recruit whom people would trip over before they'd notice. But if Deacon had to stuff himself inside and work the levers, he wanted a dummy who would at least look like him. And now he could step back and see what that image should be. He'd caught up in the hospital, whatever dross had sloughed away hadn't been replaced by any new growth. Now he had a real chance to reach back and find something concrete to hold on to. He could reach clear out of the Army and gather pieces of a child or an adolescent or a young man. Deacon reached, found nothing back there but shadowy forms, hollow voices. It was all fantasy and imagination, a life he might have dreamed. The real world began when he lifted his hand and took the soldier's oath. He could nearly hear the *snick,* the ratchet engaging. It had clicked steadily in only one direction, had taken up all slack as it carried him into the hard beat of marching cadence and then into the thunder of engines and finally into the rhythms of gunfire. Deacon spread his fingers like a blind man and reached as far as he could, but the only person he could find was Uncle's blue-eyed boy, a mothering thirty-one-mission old sport.

He dressed the dummy in staff sergeant's stripes and wings and ribbons, installed the new balance, and set out to see what more there was to Italy besides tents and airplanes.

*   *   *

154

If the clock at the field had been in the sky, and the hospital clocks had been dead, the foothill villages must have done without clocks altogether, used sundials or grains of sand. The Italian summer wasn't ticking among those tumbled blocks of stone. There was no sound of time at all, nothing for Deacon to match his step to.

There might as well have been only one village, and only one road. It passed through fields of pale wheat or twisted almond or olive orchards, became a street with a brief clutter of white houses, a wider place where there was a fountain, became a street again and then the road, wheat fields and parched orchards. Sometimes there was a café—not a real one, but an opening in the wall with three tables of chipped marble and a zinc bar; a place where Deacon could hide from the stifling afternoon and drink warm faintly gaseous vermouth while flies edged through the curtain of beaded glass which hung across the doorway. The prismatic glass shimmered with reflections of the houses and crumbling fountain, bursts of gray and yellow from dust and sun. Two women sat at the fountain's edge, empty water jugs at their feet.

Deacon tried to practice his Italian on the café's drowsing proprietor. The man seemed to understand nothing, responded only when Deacon raised his empty glass and cried *Bella Italia . . . ancora.* Deacon toasted Italy until he grew dull without ever having gotten drunk. He left the café, stood outside in the beating sun while the smells of wine lees and horses and manure pulsed over him. On the other side of the village square was the narrow open stall of a barbershop where an apprentice was slowly lathering a face tilted to show nothing but a set of flaring nostrils, the barber standing to one side while he picked at his own mustache before a mirror whose silver had a run. A heap of stone looked something like a store, had something like dry goods tumbled behind a window filmed with gray powder. The steps of the church were broken, its door was locked. All the village houses were shuttered against the heat. The women at the fountain were dressed in uniform black, had black shawls over their heads and appeared to be saluting each other, their hands slanting across their brows as shelves against the sun.

Deacon felt that he would be baked unconscious, drown in his own sweat, and then the terrifically slow movement of a two-wheeled cart broke the still life. The driver dozed and a panting dog shuffled in the shade beneath the wheels. Dust streamed from the rims in a fine rain, like water falling from a mill wheel, and a weary tinkling came from the bells of the ornate harness. Wheels grating, the unsprung body creaking, the heads of driver, horse and dog all nodding to the same rhythm, the cart somehow crossed the square. Deacon, nearly mesmerized, trudged after it and set his feet on the road to the next village.

When he was caught between villages he was left with no light other than a moon tinged slightly green. He had to tap-tap like a mendicant at a farmhouse. Dogs snarled, a man with a closed sullen face peeked through a crack of smoky light along the edge of a door, said nothing in reply to Deacon's *mangiare, dormire* until Deacon shook out a few bills. Thereupon the door closed in his face and from behind it came garbled words and a brief scurrying as any girls were hidden in another part of the house. When the door opened again the farmer half blocked the entrance, as though he hoped Deacon wouldn't try to come in.

Mangiare, dormire—the dinner fried potatoes and an oily vegetable, the room not much more than a pen with a door, cheesecloth tacked across the window against flies and mosquitoes, the window itself like an embrasure in the thick stone wall. Light sputtered from a wick burning in a saucer of oil. Deacon called for *vino* to get more light, to speed the limping time. There was a flicker from behind the farmer's clouded eyes, he demanded cigarettes. Soldiers were willing to pay anything for bad liquor, wine freshly cured between callused toes, flavored with toenail quick.

Deacon took his foaming pitcher and lay on the stiff old bed with its single coarse blanket. The moon had lost its color, was only a dim blur through the cheesecloth. Dry leaves rattled in a nearby orchard. The growing things which had been dormant under the day's sun sucked deep into the cracked earth, siphoned off the faint traces of moisture on the night air. He lay listening to Italy growing in the dark, siphoned juices himself and created a fine acid mix with the oily potatoes and the stalky vegetable. He'd had to give up cigarettes because it was like smoking money, but he kept his lips busy with a glass while the time passed which he could not hear, until the oiled wick guttered and the pall in the room became so deep it closed his eyes.

Or in another place which was really the same place, the same pitcher and the same bed, he lay in his underwear, rings of cold dust around his wrist and neck and ankles, while his uniform was being laundered and pressed. Frothing as briefly as the wine had, he wrapped himself in the scratchy blanket and went into the kitchen. The man looked up from the table where he sat mixing finely chopped straw with the tobacco from the cigarettes. The woman paused with her iron in the air, charcoal flickering blue from the heating chamber. Deacon's *Buona sera* brought grunts in dialect The couple's eyes shifted to the passageway which led to the room where the girls were hidden. They expected him to drop the blanket and reveal a voracious erection. *Mi chiamo Giuseppe Rico. Io sono italiano.* He wanted to talk, offered the dummy as a blood brother. But Joe Rico was a continent and too many generations removed. A gush of light threw the kitchen into high relief for a moment, froze the rough table and cabinets and rusted pump as though they were made from the same stone as the walls. The cold hard eyes seemed to flash. Deacon went back to his room trailing the blanket as though he were a defeated Indian.

If no one would listen, there wasn't any point in trying to speak Italian. Deacon would have to find Americans to talk to, soldiers. He came down onto the hard plain, nimbly skirted the military installations and wandered through the nearby towns. Most of them were off limits, but the men who'd been baking in the outlying depots and airfields were willing to take their chances. They put in ten days of duty before getting a twenty-four-hour pass, and then they were given the legitimate choice of spending the day off either lying half dead under a canvas roof or visiting a headquarters town with a rocky pool table and old magazines and bitter canteen coffee, a town which was all chicken, complete with MPs.

The men chose the illegitimate, fled just over the horizon to places where pavements were hot and dusty, deserted except for starving animals, figures bundled in rags. They leaped from the tailgates of trucks, popped in and out of side streets like targets in a shooting gallery. Children took them by the hand, led them to courtyards where they giggled and shuffled in a line which wound past manure piles and washing and up to a landing where a broken-faces mistress of ceremonies stood exchanging brass checks for thousand-lire notes. The checks represented ten dollars' worth of on and off, fifteen minutes in a room with blotted sheets and a cracked douche bowl, some practiced stranger to bleed them and afterward lie back and pick her nose. The children then led them to an alley where they could buy and drink a bottle, and perhaps next to a musky room for a fifty-dollar all-night special. Or on to other bottles and a dreamless sleep on stones. In the morning, sick and drained, the men got into trucks and took the kidney-wracking ride back to their bases.

Those Americans might listen to Deacon, but he had no desire to talk to them. They were strictly non-combat, more an army than soldiers. While the infantry pumped away without removing uniforms grimed with blood, drank whatever they could get their hands on, and the flight crews hitched airplane rides to Naples to burn away the hours of the stand-downs, these garrison troopers scuttled through back streets and waited in line for sloppy seconds of fifths or tenths, staggered around alleys trying to get drunk. And they weren't really randy, didn't have honest thirsts. Most of them weren't even wearing the sleeve bar indicating six months' overseas service. Recruits who hadn't been within hearing distance of the war, they piled up the days of donkey duty until they had enough for a pass, then made believe that it was the night before the big barrage, that they'd be cutting the wire and sprinting into the guns before sunrise. Kiss me quick, honey. *Addio, domani morrò.*

Deacon couldn't be bothered telling them what it was really like, what guzzling and screwing was really worth— telling them how it was to take off from that slingshot runway and have that stinking tent and mealy food and corroded land fall away to nothing, to next touch the earth along the beautiful curve of Naples' bay. How it felt to be living with a thin wire threaded right through your guts and out your bung, turned in a loop at the outside so that some goon from Operations could give it a tug whenever he had the urge. He and Horton and Fitzgerald set down still quivering, Naples not long free of the Germans and the Fifth Army, half ruined from shellfire and demolition and bombs dropped from airplanes like theirs, the people ragged. But somehow a tremendous life force in the air, the bay glittering under the first sun of the spring.

And not to sit in some hole where the whore's hands were busy under the table, to slush yourself into lead eyes and ringing ears—but to go walking, to stop and drink and then walk, tippling and strolling all through the afternoon until the quiver disappears. To eat and enjoy a good black-market meal, try not to notice the women and children outside scraping through the garbage. Separate rooms in what used to be a luxury hotel, a tub of lukewarm water, sleep naked and alone behind a closed door. The sun rising at noon, and the previous day's wine and food purging away the wire, erasing a few wrinkles. *Spuntino per tre,* then each on his own for the afternoon, not one of these clutch-me kiss-me buddy arrangements. Meeting later without anyone having to report where he'd been or what he'd done. A pocketful of money and a bagful of cigarettes buying a tremendous meal at a restaurant with an even larger crowd of scavengers around the back door. Strega, a stroll through the Neapolitan evening, a check of the Galleria whores. Horton brings two back to the hotel and there's a lot of traffic between his and Fitzgerald's room. You sit with a bottle of Lacrima Cristi, let Christ's tears lave your insides while you watch Vesuvius bounce under the moon.

All three are red-eyed the next day, Horton and Fitzgerald are sniggering. You plan something spectacular for the last twenty-four hours, but nothing happens. The afternoon drifts by and you're content to drift with it. More food and more drink and early to bed to let it soak in, to stretch the hours of privacy. But the armistice ends twelve hours early, at midnight when you're wrenched out of some sweaty horror, the pulse banging ice-cold behind your ear. Not even Christ's blood will help. A call to the desk brings the only remedy. She's thin and hard, looks at you bitterly while you use her. Vesuvius swims indistinctly as you try to erupt free of the earth. Both of you are still there when it's over, and you begin to hate her because she'll be there tomorrow night and you won't. But your hatreds somehow become lost in the warm bed, are rubbed away between soft skin, and you sleep in a comfortable tangle. The next day an airplane takes you back to other airplanes.

Those town commandos, those piddling yardbirds, would never understand. Deacon couldn't even tell them what it was really like looking down the barrel at *domani morrò*, how peaceful it was lying drunk in a puddle of rime-tinged mud outside a tent. He threaded his way through the towns, but he didn't go near alleys or courtyards, left the boys to their games. He found dingy bedrooms, sat at vacant windows and watched until the last trucks were gone and the Italians came out of their holes to promenade the streets they'd abandoned to daylight. He thumbed through his phrase book while they filled the mellow Mediterranean night with a murmuring he couldn't understand.

16.

ARMIES HAD moved through Italy for centuries and had barely disturbed the nearly endless stillness of the long *mezzogiorno* summer—the Americans destroyed it. The rubbish at Salerno hadn't been rotting for a year, but the plain was already plastered with steel mats and concrete. White-starred vehicles roared along nearly every road. There were jeeps and weapons carriers and a variety of specialty rigs, but mostly two-and-a-half-ton trucks, six-by-sixes.

As well as finding only one village and one road, Deacon found that there was really only one truck. It moved in its own envelope of dust and noise, fenders and hood rattling, engine whining. If he sat in the high open cab the dust boiled in and gummed his lashes together; and if he rocked in the canvas-covered oven of the body, a pool of gritty sweat formed at the base of his spine. The truck was everywhere, bouncing and swaying as it kicked past kilometer posts marking the distance between nowheres.

And there was really only one driver. The sleeves of his fatigues were chopped off at the shoulders and his arms jutted from a nest of frayed threads, the cords delicately powdered by dust. He wore his fatigue cap with the bill curled back, his eyes were screwed up behind sunglasses. He wrenched the wheel savagely, leaned on the horn and stood on the accelerator, made time as he blasted along the supply routes between field and town, town and depot, depot and port.

Deacon stood at the stone fence of a road which ran between here and there, watched the truck pull away. It left a wake of granular air and wildly fluttering leaves. Deacon's feet tingled and he could still hear the roar of hot wind past his ears. The truck dragged its whine and rattle after it like a tail. He licked the grit from his teeth and walked to the break in the fence, looked down the side road fluttering and heaving in the heat.

They's a rest camp, all right, the driver told him, *but I don't know as it's the one y'all're lookin for.*

The air cleared and a stifling silence fell with the settling dust. There was no wind in the trees, no sound of birds or insects. Deacon slung his musette bag and pushed off down the side road. The sun beat moisture from his skin. Splotches grew under his armpits, down his back.

Understood they was somethin special for flyin crews. The driver's eyes flickered over Deacon's ornaments. *This special place y'all get sent . . . wasn't it Cap-ri?*

Was and is, a haven for flyers trying to heal their ragged asses with sitz baths in the Blue Grotto. A yawl was what Deacon needed to get to Capri. He walked on for an hour. The light grew a little less intense and the road stopped dancing so violently. It dipped, disappeared around a bend. He shaded his eyes, made out a blur on a hill several miles ahead, a dreamlike huddle of buildings fired by the sun.

160

Far's I know there's no combats in that there rest camp, no doughfoots or nothin like that. The driver mustered an incredible blob of something wet and spit it out the side of the truck. *Fact is, they's no ways y'all're about to get in lessen you got authorization.*

He nearly walked into the roadblock hidden behind the bend. The barrier was painted in vivid stripes, and an MP was leaning against it, his back to Deacon. Another lay sleeping under a tree. He retreated around the bend, found a hummock which ran between the fields and the town, crouched behind it and scuttled until he was well away from the road. He sat hidden in a stony depression, panting.

What I mean's those ole boys in there got theyselves some time. The driver noticed that Deacon hadn't any gold overseas bars, that all his glory was on his chest. *Ever'body's supposed to git to go, but they ain't hardly got to men been over a full two years. Ole boy'n our outfit went had twenty-eight months . . . said he like to come inside out ever day all the five days he stayed.*

That was the whole damned point, that the ole boys in there had some time. The rest camp might be for the rear echelon, but it was for the oldest rear echelon in the Mediterranean theater. They'd come overseas when there was a real submarine menace to sweat out, hustled supplies and driven trucks and built roads in the wake of the North African landings, grown worn and hard living in the desert. They'd been in Sicily, had been waiting in the wings at Salerno and Anzio. And now they were the old guard. While some had been bombed and strafed, they weren't really combat troops—but all of them were certainly soldiers.

Seems they git their pick now . . . comin down here or going to Rome iffn they druther lookit statchis'n churches'n such. Don't know why anybody'd pass up five pure days've likker'n pussy to get hot feet walking around Rome. The driver put in the clutch, shifted, then held the pedal chattering on the edge. *Probly know what y'all're doin, but come on by here same time tomorra iffn y'all're lookin for a ride.*

Deacon wouldn't need a ride tomorrow or the next day or the day after that. He could stay five times five days if he wanted to. As he sat watching the sun fall the stillness was occasionally broken by the grind of trucks from the road, by faint shouting and singing. The heat lessened when the sun touched the rim of the hills, and a dusty breeze sprang up as though it had been lying in wait. He left his stony couch and picked his way along the hummock until he saw a farmhouse. A man was stoking manure in the yard. He watched Deacon approach, extended the pitchfork, tines clotted with dung.

Deacon stopped, shouted that he only wanted something to eat. The farmer waved him away. Deacon held up his hands, money pinched between each thumb. The Italian lowered the fork slightly.

He didn't want Deacon's money, he wanted cigarettes. Deacon had only a little more than a carton left. He tried to bargain but the farmer shook his head stubbornly and demanded a full pack. Deacon threw it to him. The Italian inspected the cigarettes, then went into the house and left Deacon standing in the yard. In a little while a boy brought out a pitcher of goat's milk and a tin plate of tired bread and hard cheese. He put it on the ground as though Deacon were one of the stock, squatted at a distance and watched him eat. At first the boy wouldn't talk, but he finally gave his name. Deacon had his routine ready—*Giuseppe Rico, sono italiano*. The boy wasn't impressed. Trying to eat and smile at the same time, Deacon asked if he could get to the town through the fields. The boy grudgingly pointed out a faint path. Deacon offered a cigarette, asked to be guided. The boy held up three fingers.

They followed the track over the hummock, into a ravine, turned off on another path which meandered through fields choked with rock and weed. When they came to a small rise the boy pointed out a faint line curling up the hill. Deacon handed him three cigarettes. The boy put up four fingers. Deacon chased him back along the path.

He put his wings and ribbons into his shirt pockets, checked to see that he had a pass properly dated. The dummy now looked like tens of thousands of other staff sergeants in Italy. Deacon glanced back, couldn't see the farmhouse in the dusk creeping through the fields. The track was becoming indistinct in the failing light. He hurried along it.

When the wind blew from a certain quarter he could hear a drumming on the air, faint cries. A generator pounded in the distance, the Army evidently furnishing electricity while the old guard cured their aching GI backs. The path snaked upward across the face of the hill and through the town dump—clouds of flies, the stench of rotting animal carcasses, kitchen slops, freshly emptied chamber pots. There was a low stone wall at the top of the bluff, the beginning of a street. It was dark, with only splinters of weak light showing around the shuttered windows. A glare came from several blocks away, outlined Italians in capes gliding by like bats. As Deacon approached the light the drumming became a rumble of noise. He came to a corner where bulbs were strung from

162

loops of wire tacked along the buildings. Someone called his name. He stiffened, was called again.

"Hey Joe . . . you."

He turned slowly. The MP stood slouched against a wall, the white stripe like a corona around his helmet liner.

"Off limits, buddy." He moved his head toward the blaze at the town's center. "Whatever business you got belongs in there. Stay on this side of the street."

Only the core of the town was illuminated. The spokes of light stopped at corners all along the curve of the lateral street. Deacon looked at the name painted on the wall—Via dei Miracoli. His lips twitched, he nodded to the MP. The other waved his club, and Deacon crossed over into America. He began to pass soldiers who were drunk or noisy or walking aimlessly. One was spreading a stain of urine against a wall. Another had a purple swollen face, wore a green ribbon tied in an enormous bow at his neck. Some wore correct clean uniforms, others had shirts open to the waist, trousers splotched with wine. The shoulder patches were principally air corps or the service forces, the hats piped to match or with the braid of military police, quartermaster, engineer, signal corps. Nearly everyone had at least three overseas bars on his sleeve.

The square was strung with a lattice of bulbs, and the men beneath it moved in a net of multiple shadows. Instead of a café there was a trestle of rough planking where Italians served drinks under the supervision of a buck sergeant. The cobbles were covered with tables and chairs which were puddled with wine, cluttered with bottles. Men sat along the fountain's rim, trash floated in the water. There was a constant din, a steady succession of booming voices.

Deacon had to shout to make himself heard. The Italian behind the trestle shouted back, gave him a half tumbler of brandy and dropped his change onto the drenched planking. Deacon cleared a small place at a vacant table, sat down. The brandy burned. It was the first hard liquor he'd had since leaving the field. He hunched against the noise as he sipped. Uniforms lurched past, sprawled in chairs, blotted up spills with their sleeves. Deacon sipped the glass empty, picked his way between the tables, rubbed other khaki arms and shoulders along the way. Everyone was talking, the argot broken with African French, crude Italian. There was a force behind the words, shades of the entire Mediterranean campaign. Desert and wadi, bony Sicily, Italy sodden with mud.

He brought a full tumbler back to the table, sat down and no longer hunched or sipped, but washed the taste of Italy out of his mouth with raw Italian brandy. A group nearby began to bellow the story of mamma packing her pistol. Deacon hummed with them. A man without hat or belt or chevrons came to the table. He looked directly at Deacon for a moment, then sat down and swept most of the bottles away with a large hand. Only a few faces turned when the glass splintered against the cobbles.

"Nobody sittin here, was there?" he asked.

The man's cuffs were turned back over rocky forearms, and the shoulder seams of his shirt looked as though they were about to split. He tilted a green long-necked bottle to a red face and squinted into it as though into the bore of a gun.

"Hey, there still somethin in there?" He turned to Deacon. "Stuff'll kill you for sure . . . pure rasselass. Want some?"

Deacon held up his half-filled tumbler.

"Well that ain't exactly what I axed you . . . Sergeant. You some kinda cook? You the sergeant a the guard? If you ain't anythin like that I'll have a drink with you."

Deacon extended the glass, had it filled. He drank and coughed. The other put the bottle to his mouth, swallowed.

"Sorry I can't do you no better, but what with this war goin on and all, we just got to take what we can get." He looked around the square. "I been laid three times today and I'm still goin, still after it. Hey, you come across any really good places . . . anywhere's, you know, sorta private? My name's George Albert Trueblow?"

Deacon sat the dummy on the lap and opened his mouth.

"My, if that ain't a fancy unusual name. Old Sergeant Joe. I'se comin, I'se comin . . . so am I can I find the right place. How many times you been laid today?"

Laid end to end, he'd stretch . . . he'd just gotten in, was still stretching his aching back.

"I oney been here two days and I found a home already. I ain't never goin back to that there guard squadron, never. Tell you what, I'll show you around this here installation. All's you got to do is get it up, and I'll show you where to get it rubbed."

Deacon mumbled something about being in no hurry, about having time enough to get all he needed. And in fact he'd caught the beat of *that* time, was marching in perfect cadence. Marching right to the bottom of the glass.

"Well you just don't understand the kinda restin we supposed to be doin in this here camp . . . Sergeant. Why don't you set that glass down a minute and I'll tell you." Trueblow tipped the bottle into the glass, emptied the rest into his mouth, then held the bottle out at arm's length and bombarded the stones. "I'll show you where's the best place to

164

start, and then you can work up to where they got these three girls goin on you at once. *Beaucoup* . . . what I mean, I like to turned inside out. Get some a that shit outen your blood, old Joe buddy. You think I got a funny name?"

Deacon had forgotten it. He had to think twice before he could remember the dummy's.

"I *told* you . . . George A. Trueblow. G-A-T, the Big Gat. I'm the chief gunner in this here town, old Joe buddy, old chicken Joe."

The big gat appeared to be hairy for some reason. Deacon didn't particularly care what his problem was, but he asked.

"Well I done bought you two drinks, ain't I? Not many's likely to give you that kinda welcomin hand. Here I am just a P-poor F-friggin C buying drinks and you the one drawin all that big pay. We goin to be buddies, it ought to be fifty-fifty, but here you actin like some damn old stateside staff just got off the boat. I been over twenty-three months exact, and I can prove it. Nothin but vetrins in this here rest camp, but you sittin there ain't even got one teeny old bar on that there sleeve. You some damn old cook, some truck driver snuck in for the night?"

Deacon's glass was empty. He looked up beyond the glare of light, the noise bellowing between the grid of electric wire, and said something about a hospital to the open sky.

"A what? You mean you just got cured from some clap you caught stateside? Reckon you had hole blisters from sittin around some orderly room."

Deacon's first impulse was to snarl at Trueblow, but then he thought that this was a poor ragged soldier worn sharp by two years of stony life. And then, because he wanted Trueblow to know that he was in the company of another good soldier, he dried a place on the table and fumbled the largest ribbon bar out of his pocket and laid it down.

"What's these here, candy wrappers?" Trueblow picked up the ribbons and studied them suspiciously. "You buy these from someone was in that hospital with you? By God, my brother got a Purple Heart, but got hisself killed doin it. By God . . ."

By old guard or new, no one was going to snow Thomas E. Deacon under, because he was the chief gunner, not George A. Trueblow, and he could throw a pair of wings on the table to prove it. Trueblow peered at the wings, ran a finger over the grain of the ribbons.

"You trying to tell me this here is so? I ain't about to . . ."

It was believe it or not thirty-one times so, and he didn't give a rat's ass what Trueblow was about to.

"There ain't no combat crew in here."

There was for sure one member of the Great Crew. Deacon's lips and nasal passages appeared to have dried up. His tongue was beginning to feel like wood.

"Don't seem likely you'd be comin in here. Why would . . . my brother was a bombardier, in the Eighth. He didn't put in but four missions, never even got hisself promoted. Second Lieutenant Edward F. Trueblow. Wasn't overseas but a month. And here you say you got thirty-one missions . . . by God, that's *beaucoup*."

It was the will of the Great Ticket Puncher. The dryness had spread and turned him to the consistency of guncotton. He waited for a spark to shoot from his blood.

"Oney a month, and here I am over here twenty-three, sittin around with a rifle up my ass guardin some pisshole headquarters." Trueblow edged the wings and ribbons toward Deacon. "Didn't mean nothin personal, but what with all these damn recruits . . ."

Deacon tried to suck the last drops from the glass.

"Never no mind, anybody flies like my brother Eddie's got just as much right's anybody to be in here. I'll tell you, let's just go get us a drink, just you and me, have one for old Eddie. I'll buy *you* a drink, that's what."

Trueblow took Deacon's arm and lifted him out of the chair. He used one shoulder like a plow to turn men out of their path. The men looked after him angrily, but no one said anything. Trueblow bought a bottle of cheap rum and cut back through the crowd, talking all the time.

". . . and that's what it is, no sense to what this here whole mess's about. There's old Eddie, and me doin nothin in a guard squadron. Before that I was oney bustin my kidneys in a motor pool. I went and *volunteered* to get up in the line . . . tried the paratroops, the infantry, everythin. But it's in my record I did a little stockade time . . . nothin serious, just beat up on some chickenshit corporal . . . and don't nobody want to transfer me in now."

They sat along the curb of one of the streets off the square. There was a steady shuffle of feet along the sidewalk at their backs. Voices caromed off the walls. Trueblow twisted off the cork and threw it away. He passed the bottle to Deacon.

"Don't know why you want to come in here when there's supposed to be a place . . ."

Let them go screw, all the weary birds sagging in one great family tree. The rum was awful, but it was wet. Deacon felt the juices spreading.

". . . but long's you here you ain't likely to get by too long without somebody's goin to ask to see your papers. Got to

166

show them if you want a sack, even in the whorehouse. We could likely buy you a pass somewheres if you got the *danaro*."

For Jesus sake, Deacon couldn't even afford to smoke.

"That's all right, now. We goin to do somethin. You got to have a pass and that's just what we goin to get. Some old boy'd do the same for Eddie was he here. Say, you all right? I mean from the hospital."

Deacon tilted the bottle. Now that he was no longer under the grid of light he could see a smear of stars overhead. He had a million-dollar wound—alcohol deficiency.

"Won't be no problem findin that remedy." Trueblow nudged him, nearly knocked him over. "You all right, old buddy Joe. We's comin together, wait and see."

It was Deacon.

"Deacon? You got a gospel to preach? We goin to have to turn that there collar around before we get you fixed up, Deacon Joe."

Deacon, Thomas. And if Trueblow doubted, let him put his fingers in the wounds. Deacon felt thoroughly moist, almost plump.

"Never no mind, a little rub-dub's all you need. But we got to get that there pass. MPs come through the whorehouse and find your poor naked ass wavin in the air they'll be lookin for you to be strictly GI, humpin by the numbers."

Fifty was the number that humped. It screwed indiscriminately.

"Better let loose a that there bottle, Preacher. We got a little work to do right now."

Trueblow helped him to his feet. For a moment Deacon felt that he might continue to rise and rise, that Trueblow might have to hold tight to keep him from floating off. They moved away from the square through the side streets, turned and turned again until they came to a short stoop flanked by two stone lions. Deacon listened a moment, hoping they would roar. The building had an official look, like a police station or a town hall.

"This here's the main whorehouse," Trueblow said. "They got girls some a them ain't fifteen and some a them ain't fifty. We just sit us down here a spell."

Deacon lowered himself carefully to a step. There were other men tilting bottles, snapping cigarettes into the street. Deacon suddenly wanted a smoke, but he thought of the long road he had to pave with cigarettes, felt a little noble at being able to resist the temptation. The building's doors creaked against the regular push of bodies, fanned out a musky blend of sweat and disinfectant and perfume. He reached for the rum. Most of it dribbled down his chin. He felt himself swelling, smiling. All was well in nighttime America. The dust had been laid by cool winds, familiar voices were muttering in the dark. He sat back, elbows against the steps, and stretched his legs. It was a fine summer night—someone should go down to the corner store for a pint of ice cream. He began to drift.

"Don't cork off now," Trueblow said.

No corks or stoppers of any kind. The men coming up the steps were edgy, too loud. Those leaving croaked like spent nightingales. Deacon blessed them all.

"Here we go now," Trueblow hissed.

Deacon opened his eyes, was momentarily dizzied by a series of doubled images. He needed the help of a large hand, was in danger of toppling if he didn't place his feet just so. A heavy figure in khakis was staggering a little way ahead of them.

"Reckon he musta knowed just what we needed," Trueblow said.

Trueblow stopped to empty the rum bottle, his eyes still on the man ahead, and then set the bottle down gently on the curb. The man came to the end of the lighted street, lurched to a stop and stood looking into the darkness across the way. Deacon wanted to call to him that he wasn't allowed to cross, that Italy was off limits. The man turned, and Deacon saw his staff sergeant's stripes. Trueblow moved up quickly.

"Well," he said, "you lost, soljer, that's what."

The man's eyes were red in a fleshy face, his mouth was slack. "Hey," he said, "this the 'merican part? Don't know . . . hey, this the right way?"

"That's just where we goin, me and my buddy, to that new whorehouse."

"I just . . . I been there. The *new* one? I jus' . . ."

"That there was the old one," Trueblow said. "We goin to a place oney opened up tonight."

The sergeant tried to look past him. "The lights're . . . got to go back that way."

"This here's the short cut."

Trueblow took several shuffling steps, edged the man around the corner and into the shadows. Deacon knew that the MP was going to tell them to go back. There wasn't any MP.

"Hey, hey, what're you . . ."

"Well now just wait a minute," Trueblow said. "Just hold on there, you goin to see."

He continued to shuffle until all three of them were well away from the corner. The sergeant was trying to brace himself against a wall.

"You kinda fat," Trueblow said, "some fat old sergeant a the guard."

"What . . . what? Hey, who're . . ."

"I bet you some fat old cook."

Trueblow's arm moved very quickly, but everything registered in stop-motion to Deacon. He saw Trueblow's fist half buried in the sergeant's dimpled shirt front and the man's eyes rolling white in the gloom. A gush of sour breath came past. Trueblow shifted his feet, hit the sergeant lightly on one side of the head, then on the other as he began to fall. The sergeant slipped straight down the wall and lay on his back. He jerked, gurgled, began to vomit. Trueblow used his toe to nudge the man's head to one side so he wouldn't choke. The retching subsided to a groan, then to hoarse breathing. The sergeant's cheek was lying in a pool of spew, his eyes were closed.

Still moving in that same jerky stop-motion, Trueblow squatted and turned the body slightly, went through the pockets, then gingerly lifted the dog tags. He wiped them on the man's hat.

"Fat old cook bastard. Sure don't smell so good. He ought to be more careful what he drinks."

Deacon shook his head, tried to break the picture sequence. It couldn't really have happened. He looked back toward the corner, tried to see if he was on the Street of Miracles. Trueblow was counting the money.

"Eighty dollars ain't much, but it's more'n we had. Here's your pass and dog tags."

Deacon couldn't put those tags on—he'd be shot.

"You got to show a pass and dog tags to get a sack."

Deacon clutched them in his hand, wondered if the man was dead.

"Can't hurt them fat old cooks, they too mean. MPs'll find him and put him in the lockup."

He'd say who'd attacked him, tell them Deacon's real name.

"He won't remember nothin. And they won't hardly believe who he is he don't have no identification. By God, I feel plumb wore out. Ain't no place to get a drink at this hour. Let's go find us a sack."

Deacon still had difficulty believing what was happening, thought he might still be on the lion steps, sleeping. But the night suddenly turned much colder and congealed all his juices. He tilted his eyes to look toward the stars, nearly fell backward. Trueblow's arm steadied him, held him in a lover's grip as they walked on and on, finally turned into an alley and came on a large courtyard.

"Watch them stairs," Trueblow whispered.

Deacon couldn't see any, but he immediately raised his knees and took jerky steps. A match flared ahead and the banded arm of an MP moved to light a cigarette. He and his partner were standing at the foot of the stairs. Deacon started to tell Trueblow about the pass in his pocket.

"Howdy," Trueblow bellowed to the MPs.

"Keep it down. There's men sleeping, for Christ sake."

"Just what me and my buddy was figurin on doin."

A flashlight snapped on, the beam playing at their feet. Trueblow held out his pass, pulled his dog tags from under his shirt. The MP grunted, shifted the light toward Deacon. Deacon put his lips at Trueblow's ear, began to whisper a warning about not showing the dog tags. Trueblow caught Deacon's wrist and held his hand in the beam of the flash. The sergeant's chain was wrapped like a rosary around his fingers.

"My buddy's a little drunk," Trueblow said. "Like to choked hisself with that there chain, so I had to go and take it off."

He pried the pass from Deacon's clenched fist. The MP smoothed the piece of paper, turned the tags so he could read them. Deacon started to laugh, thinking that the dummy had a dummy of its own now, but an acid belch rose to the back of his throat. The MP jerked back, waved them on. Deacon had to force each leg to bend, straighten and push all the way up the stairs. Their steps made hollow sounds as they moved along the wooden platform. Trueblow opened doors into rooms where there were thick body odors, heavy breathing. He closed the doors again and they moved farther along the platform.

At last he led Deacon into a room and down an aisle be-between rows of cots, found an empty one and eased Deacon down. Deacon curled into a ball, hands tucked between his knees, and he whimpered for a few seconds before he fell asleep.

There was only a pinpoint of light at first. It became a ring, and then there was a ring of noise and one he could smell. All three began to repeat, like signals from a transmitting station, growing stronger each time. Something heavy settled on the cot, gave off clouds of perfume.

"Hey, Joe."

The voice was shrill, female. Deacon thought she was calling someone else until he remembered who he was. The rings went on and on. He opened his eyes to slits and looked directly into the face of a woman with violent orange hair and a silver tooth.

"Hey, Joe baby. You happy, baby?" She stretched a hand with broken red nails and cradled his crotch firmly. "Hey, you honey baby."

Deacon stared at her. His head pounded, he was having difficulty breathing. She began to squeeze rhythmically. He groaned, thought he was going to be sick, but a flood of warmth spread through his groin and the massage produced a rapid stiffening. The woman patted it and grinned, her silver tooth glinting.

"We maka lotsa good times, Joe. Fig-fig, suck-suck."

She released him, took off her wooden clogs and began to hike her skirt. Deacon tried to sit up, grew dizzy, swung his legs over the side of the cot and fell on the filthy tile floor. The woman sprawled across the cot, her skirt twisted to reveal a pale olive ham.

"Watchyou think, Joe? I gotta no crabs, no clap. You honey baby, I maka you feel like you gotta two-feet dick."

Someone across the way laughed. Deacon tried to speak, his mouth thick and gummy. He sat up. The pattern of tiles whirled. He gagged.

"He's still hung, sweetheart," the voice across the way called. "*Sta ancora ubriaco . . residuo.*"

"*Porco—*" the woman sniffed—"*ubriaconzol'.*"

She put on her clogs, straightened her skirt and clumped down the aisle. There was a line of cots on each side of the room, some unmade, some with men still sleeping. The unpainted plaster walls were scarred, the floor littered with empty bottles, cigarette butts, parts of uniforms. At one end of the room was a window paned with layers of dirt, patched with newspapers and cardboard. A hot diffused light came through. Deacon knelt at the edge of the cot, his head in his hands.

"Say one for me," someone called.

There was laughter. Deacon struggled upright, swayed, asked the way to the latrine. Still smiling, they showed him out the door, pointed to the end of the gallery running along the building's second floor. He gripped the railing and made his way to a doorless cubicle where there was a sink and a dripping tap and a hole in the floor bracketed by metal footrests. The rim was foul, swarming with flies. He dropped his trousers, squatted, screwed up his eyes against the harsh light from outside, felt the flies crawling over his skin. His colon griped, voided. The pure voices of children floated up in song. He put one hand down to steady himself, soiled it, held

171

his trousers up with his elbows while he washed in tepid water from the tap. The children continued to sing.

He shuffled to the railing, gripped one of the posts and leaned over into waves of hot air rising from the courtyard. They baked the roof of his open mouth. The lower story was ringed with doors and open windows. Deacon tried to swallow, salivate. Another group of children began a recitation in counterpoint to the singers. An adult voice came through in measured beats. There was a *school* below. From along the gallery came the sound of a bottle breaking. A woman's piercing laugh rang out, someone swore.

Deacon threaded his way back. There were identical doors all along the gallery, and Deacon twice stood blinking inside before he realized that he was in the wrong room. He finally found it, the whore with the orange hair wrapped in a blanket, playing a different kind of Indian as she sat astride a young corporal who was completely dressed except for his trousers. The corporal whooped and the whore giggled. A poker game had begun at one end of the room. Deacon was invited to sit in. He picked up his cap and musette bag, stood on the gallery and fumbled at the open pack of cigarettes, no longer noble or at all concerned with the road which had to be paved with butts. The smoke made him feel lightheaded. He sucked stubbornly until the cigarette began to vibrate between his fingers, fell to the floor. He ground it out and started toward the stairs. Halfway down he saw the team of MPs, stood frozen until a voice bellowed.

"Well, you all right now? Thought you was goin to die in that there sack."

Deacon descended slowly, tried to smile as he passed between the MPs. Trueblow laid an arm like a wagon tongue across his shoulders and steered him through the alley.

"All's they checkin to see is you don't steal no blankets or nothin," he said. "Oney time you got to show your papers is when you goin up."

The American zone was crowded with Italians. The town's people had turned their lives around; they stayed off the main streets after dark, spent the hot hours of their normal *lanuggine* hustling after cigarettes and occupation money. They offered almonds, oranges, gaudy pottery and cheap cameos, home-made wine and mandolins. There were old men and women, young men in scraps of Italian uniforms, but no young girls. All were hopping and jigging in a parody of a village street dance as they scuttled among the soldiers slumped and squatting in the shade of walls.

Deacon grew giddy looking at them. He was stunned by the brilliant light, walked with his hands in his pockets, sweating, the juices of the night before streaming from his body. His uniform was soiled and wrinkled, he needed a bath. It might have been the American zone, but the smell boiling off the streets was pure Italian. He had to struggle to keep up with Trueblow, began to pant. They turned away from the square, went through a doorway guarded by a beaded curtain.

Deacon stepped in, stepped back through a hole in the past —coolness, musty tile, marble tables and slender wire chairs. An ice-cream parlor. A soldier was sprawling snoring across one of the tables. Two Italians were at another. They muttered and turned their backs when he and Trueblow came in. Still panting, Deacon lowered himself into a chair. His fingers crawled across the smooth marble, and then he pressed his cheek against it.

Trueblow called for champagne and the proprietor let slip a weasel smile of deference and contempt. He brought a bubbling white wine which was not champagne but was almost cold. Trueblow poured, nudged Deacon's head up with the neck of the bottle. Deacon picked up the glass and didn't put it down until it was empty. Trueblow poured again.

"This here ain't nothin but bellywash," he said, "but it's all right for startin the day."

Deacon finished the second glass and his breathing grew more steady. The beaded curtain cut off most of the glare and heat, almost kept out the street's odors. They emptied the bottle, ordered another. Deacon's sweat dried to a gritty film. Passing figures cast broken shadows on the curtain.

"I was waitin downstairs deliberate," Trueblow said. "Truth is, I figgered there wasn't no sense both a us gettin picked up in case the other got in trouble . . . either me *or* you." Trueblow fidgeted. "I went through that bag a yours while you was sleepin. Well I *had* to. That little foolishness I got into last night could get me some real hard times, and I wanted to know just who you was. I seen the Deacon part, what with the dog tags and that there authorization for them ribbons you got hid in your pocket. I don't understand about this here Joe Rico."

Joe Rico was just emerging from the sludge of yesterday's booze, beginning to revive in the fresh rain of today's. Deacon mumbled about nobody.

"Went to an awful lot a trouble settin him up if he's nobody. Don't worry, I didn't take nothin . . . wasn't that much to take."

The proprietor brought the second bottle, barely cool. Deacon filled his glass slowly. Trueblow must mean the passes.

"You sure got a pisspot full a them."

Deacon nodded, hid his face in the glass. When he lowered it Trueblow hadn't gone away. He . . . well, he . . .

"You got them made out way ahead."

That was correct. Joe Rico was only twenty-four days old, and half that time had been spent in a hospital incubator. He needed particular care, had to have his future planned. But Trueblow . . . George, was it George?

"That's right." Trueblow watched him over the rim of his own glass, wiped his hand across his mouth. "I come here half fixed never to go back. Ain't no sense to it, standin around guardin headquarters and empty freight cars and officers' villas and the like. Wouldn't even be a guard squadron if there wasn't this old major couldn't keep his rank if they didn't give him somethin to do. Nossir, I ain't about to spend another two years waitin on the Army's pleasure."

That was correct, too. They were stealing Trueblow's time, spending it as though it didn't matter, as though there were some way they could pay him back.

"That's just how I see it. What I'd do is just take off . . . if I wasn't worried on gettin shot for it."

Old Joe was beginning to feel good in the benign rain. Deacon sat back in the chair, relaxed, and tossed off some advice about keeping the firing squad away by wearing the proper dog tags.

"Is that right? Is that what *you* done?"

Well, he'd . . . how in hell had what *he'd* done crawled on the table? He hadn't done anything, he'd . . .

"Reckon it's none of my concern, but I don't know could it be anythin else but you was over the hill."

Deacon turned and turned the glass, looking for a corner. He wound up filling it, and bottle number two was gone.

"Don't reckon you killed nobody, and from lookin through that there bag it don't appear you cleaned out the paymaster." The noise of Deacon's drinking didn't drown out Trueblow. "Like I said, whatever reason you got's none a my concern. Had me some a them passes I'd go over in a minute myself. I coulda took some while you was sleepin."

Deacon's head had begun to fill with bubbles. An angry breath blew them away. Why *hadn't* Trueblow taken them then, for Jesus sake?

"Takin money from that old cook was one thing. Wasn't from nothin but black market anyways, I betcha." Trueblow signaled to the proprietor. "I ain't in the habit a beatin on people, but I don't see how else we coulda got you fixed up."

Deacon felt a flush of gratitude. The bubbles were seeping back. He could let old Trueblow have a few passes—three

. . . maybe five. He was rich enough to give away fifteen days.

"Don't know as how I'd make out too well by myself. There's more to it'n just carryin a pass around. What I had in mind was maybe I could go along with you a little ways."

The wine in the third bottle was almost warm.

"Maybe you ain't particularly lookin for company, but two's better'n one on the road any day. These here Eyeties'd cut you for your shoes. Specially with you just outen that there hospital and all. And I got more money'n you do by about sixty dollars. No reason we can't share fifty-fifty."

Nobody shared Fifty . . . but that wasn't what they were talking about. The bubbles rubbed together, merged, and his head rose slightly from his shoulders. He began to talk.

"That's right," Trueblow said, "we get to a PX where we could use them there ration cards, we could sell the stuff for plenty."

It was really a second head, like a balloon, and it floated slightly above the one doing all the talking. The open road was positively glittering—Naples, Rome, later a tour through the Abruzzi, Umbria.

"Don't know the outfit them passes're writ on, but there ain't no Fifteenth Air Force north a Foggia far's I know," Trueblow said. "And if you supposed to be in this here area, ain't no three-day pass good for more'n a hundred miles from Bari. Couldn't even get to Naples on them, let alone Rome."

Goddamned guardhouse lawyer, Trueblow was. They could go . . . there was . . .

"It don't matter none. We could just find us some nice place right in this here area, no need to travel outen it."

Find some beautiful ladies to wash their socks. Sit around for the rest of their lives and live fat.

"Yeah," Trueblow said. "Hot damn."

Traveling companions, a fellowship. Needed another bottle to celebrate.

"Truth is, we ain't holdin all that much *danaro,* and we want to get started, get outen here tonight before that old cook starts to remember who it was talkin to him. There's a truck goes north about seven every night."

Deacon raised his empty glass, toasted the open road.

"Don't exactly know where it's goin, but I don't reckon that matters no more. Hot damn, we get to go anywheres we want to."

Freebooters, scoundrels . . . *rakes.*

"Got to get the rest a this here uniform together. We got to be strictly GI, spit and polish, and then won't nobody stop us for nothin. Reckon we better get movin . . . Tom."

Tom . . . *Tom?*

Trueblow got up. Deacon followed the drift of the balloon, ducked at the doorway so it wouldn't be caught on the transom, separated the beaded curtain so it could pass. He nearly danced out into the street, nearly collapsed when the heat hit him and the balloon exploded. The street was crowded with figures trudging through gelatin light. He attempted to spit out something sliming his mouth, found that it was only air. Trueblow propped him against a wall, bought two oranges. Deacon sucked his greedily, the juice dribbling down his shirt front. The sweet orange roiled with the wine in his stomach. He began to pant again.

They went to the square. It was neatly divided, *sol'ed ombra*, and the only tables occupied were those in the shelves of shadow projected by walls. Trueblow led him into the edge of the shade, guided him to a chair. Deacon struggled to keep his eyes from crossing.

"Probly be able to pick up a belt and a hat and all from that mess layin all over the dormitory. You just wait on me right here, get yourself a little more rest. Reckon you want to give me about five a them passes right now so's I can get them typed up somewheres?"

No, he didn't. Shorten his life span. But there had been some sort of agreement reached, a little help for an old buddy. He struggled with the musette bag, tore off five blank passes.

"Lessee," Trueblow said, "need some kinda name. Reckon I should give myself a promotion to corporal . . . maybe sergeant?"

Staff Sergeant Joe Rico was the ranking member of the expedition.

"Won't be payin me anyways if I'm over the hill, so I might's well keep on a PFC. Listen now, you stay right here. I still got that old cook's tag and pass for you in case you might have to show them at the gate to get outen here tonight."

There was a street of miracles, a magic wall.

"That's all right, now. You just stay here. Get us somethin to eat when I come back, fix you right up."

Deacon's mouth gaped in something like a smile. Trueblow patted him on the back, moved away. Deacon's head inclined slowly until it rested on the table top. Sleep droned in his ears. The sun's line crept over the square, overtook him while the other men retreated with the shade. A hairy fly buzzed in his mouth. He opened one eye, felt his cheek slide through a puddle of rank sweat.

Deacon pushed himself away from the table, sat with his head wobbling, on fire. He sucked in the burning air, wanted a drink. Not a drink . . . he needed something to eat. When Trueblow came back . . . fellow vagabond, knight of the open road. Deacon groaned. He clutched his cap, threw the musette bag over his shoulder and stood up slowly, using the table for support. For Jesus sake, a fellow *vagabond*. He pushed off, one foot at a time right across the square, one foot and then the other. He was no more noticeable than any other drunk, staggered into the shade of a side street. It was freezing. He strained against the wall, the rough stone biting into his neck just like the briefing room. Not like it at all . . . he didn't want to forget, to sleep. Old buddy Trueblow would be there any minute . . . just what he needed, another nursing pain in the ass.

He moved slowly down the street, one arm extended to fend off the wall. Soldiers got out of the way, called after him. His fingertips scraped against the stone, grew raw. One corner. A group of Italian children gathered, pointing and laughing. He used his knuckles against the wall. They began to bleed. Another corner. He looked overhead, found the twist of electric wire, the bulbs dead white now. Still in the American zone. Just what he needed, a yahoo who'd want to sit drunk in a cathouse for a month.

Find the street to the wall, the Via dei Miracoli. Be more than a mothering miracle. It was either left or right along the lateral street, either up or down, a mile or a block away. He began to move parallel to the square. A corner. A corner. Italians drew away, muttered and spat. His stomach was griping. He wrapped both arms around his middle. A corner. And then there it was . . . pure holy magic, sorcery. Tears blinded him. What he needed, for Jesus sake, an old guardsman who'd go out and beat up on someone every time the pot was empty.

He turned down the Via dei Miracoli. At least another block before the wire ended, before he could get out of America. It was two. He stood trembling at the intersection where he'd met the MP, eased his head around the corner. There was a striped helmet down the way, but it was moving away from him. Deacon tiptoed across the road, back into Italy, and began a shambling run toward the street's end. Italian women leaned out their windows and screamed after him. He got to the wall, stood heaving for breath. Someone to share the passes with was what he'd needed, a goddamned buddy who'd leech his *time*.

Sobbing, Deacon reached particularly deep for air, felt the

177

wine and orange coming up with it. He jerked one leg over the wall, lost his balance, and tumbled retching toward the town dump.

17.

THE ROAD was running again, but this time out of the dust, out of Basilicata, and toward the sea. It was running away from mountains and villages and interior towns—from rest camps for a guard grown too old and horny, abandoned and living in exile too long. The road ran past a rusting German tank, stretched straight toward the blur of Barletta. Beyond it was the flat sweep of the Adriatic. The weapons carrier's wheels crunched over a sugary coating of sand blown off the plain of clump grass on either side.

Traces of the sea danced on the onshore winds, grew stronger as Barletta grew larger, and the air became clear. Barletta was a small city, its buildings were both white and pastel, touched with baroque façades. A wide drive edged with palm trees ran along a beach where soldiers were bathing. Out at the end of a jetty naked men were diving, their loins and buttocks banded white against their sunburned skin.

Barletta was British. Troops in neat shorts and gaiters strolled along the beach walk, lounged against the railing in the interval between the end of the duty day and the evening meal. The sea curled along the sand, but it left no trail of foam, and the water was calm except for a choppy area offshore which seemed to have been frayed by the wind. Military vehicles whizzed by.

Some were moving south. The weapons carrier left Deacon off at a corner. He stood breathing the new air for a minute, ready to move south himself, to Bari. He'd traveled most of the landward segment of his hundred-mile circle, and there was nothing left in the north but the air-corps towns of Cerignola and Foggia. Bari was the last place he *could* go. It was the largest military port on the Adriatic, had more than a hundred thousand people, a crowd large enough for anyone to get lost in. And Bari was the only place he could possibly use the ration cards.

Deacon's uniform was conspicuous among all the British.

He stood at the roadside and pointed his thumb south. The traffic was diminishing. A British lorry picked him up, but it only took him a few miles down the coast, to Trani, a small town posted off limits. The driver didn't know why—there wasn't sod all to do in Trani.

Deacon walked along the main street. Shutters had been thrown open and weak electric light shone from the rooms. Cooking smells drifted out, the liquid sifting of Italian voices, occasionally the sound of a scratchy radio. He tried to dig himself out of Trani with his thumb, but the traffic was sparse and the drivers hurrying home were unwilling to stop. Deacon passed a grassless mall where Italian men in black hats and black cloaks were striding arm in arm, their hands flying as they talked. He came to the outskirts of the town, to a low wall bordering a narrow empty beach.

He'd been sweating in the interior for weeks, washing out of buckets. In the pearly dusk which wasn't yet gloom—the *imbrunire*—he climbed the wall and shed his uniform as he crossed the beach. The sand was still warm and faintly fragrant. Deacon's skin was white, only rings of color like the marks of leg irons above his ankles, brown gloves which reached to his wrist. He fell into the shallows, felt the mildly astringent bite of the water and crawled out on his hands and knees until he could float face down. As a dead man he had only to turn his head to get his breath.

And then he began to swim with a strong beat, a flutter kick, drawing on a skill he hadn't known he'd remembered —a raft in a lake, small sails, motorboats. A chlorinated pool, some girl's torso green and foggy underwater. Now there was the whole empty Adriatic. If he could swim the seaward arc of his hundred miles he could reach one of the outlying Yugoslav islands, find a cave and write notes to put in bottles. His shoulders began to ache and his stroke faltered. He floated on his back, drifted toward the beach and watched the great sun sink into Basilicata's wastes while below him there came a faint wash of stones moving with the current. Sea sounds and sea rhythms rocked him, and only his heels dragging in the sand kept him from floating forever.

Deacon used that same sand to scour himself. He spent a cigarette while the evening breeze dried him and a cloud of darkness rolled in from the line where sky and water met. Say there'd been a lakefront where he'd built a fire, sat with someone through the night—he wasn't sure, remembered too many moons filling to the color of bone, bleaching memory's blacks and whites gray. He put on the uniform. It had a very strong smell.

As he walked back toward the center of Trani the walls

179

were washed yellow by the beams of the last passing truck, and the tail lights drew the night closed behind them. The mall was more crowded, the black figures promenading back and forth like a flock of stately crows. He discovered a road branching from the main street, followed it as it dipped and fanned out into the crescent of a quay. Dories had been drawn up at the water's edge and larger boats rolled at their moorings. There were nets hung to dry, stacks of wooden tubs smelling of fish. Women carried jugs on their heads. Men in sea boots stood talking. A thread of noisy children wandered around the legs of the adults.

There was no electricity at the quay and the shop windows were lit with candles dimmed by panes of misty glass. It was an entirely different Italy. A mandolin struck up, then a sweet tenor voice. It was the Italy of opera, the set at least a hundred years old, the cast in authentic folk costumes. Deacon went from shop to shop in his sour uniform, accumulated figs and soft cheese and wine. He sat at the base of a monument erected to some hero of the sea.

The moon was somewhere else in the sky, and the water was pricked with starlight, reflections turning to glittering streaks whenever the surface was ruffled. While Deacon ate, the performance continued—solos, soaring quartets, whole choruses. Wavelets broke briskly against the quay's stones. He rinsed his mouth with the last of the wine, spent another cigarette without giving it a thought, then sat back feeling that he might be as much a part of the set as the Italians, at least a supernumerary. In a moment a girl might come dancing by with a flower in her hair.

The moments passed. The singing subsided and the people broke into rounds of *ciaos*. Deacon chased after the last of the children, asked about a room. They looked sly and giggled. Only a room, he explained, no shack job. They understood, led him into the huddle of dark houses behind the stores.

He rose early to avoid any chance patrol of MPs, whistled as he got into the clean starched uniform. There was a good breakfast of potatoes and eggs. While he ate, the grandfather of the house sat with him and talked a sort of pidgin Italian trying to tell about the Italy which died with the murder of Matteotti. He shook Deacon's hand and wished him *buona fortuna*.

Deacon was still whistling as he stood at the roadside—Bari was waiting. But it was too early for traffic of any sort. Trani's streets were empty, the houses closed against the hot light already stabbing from the sun. He visited the quay, found that the stage had been vacated. The fishing boats were far out, heeling under sails colored in bizarre stripes. He wandered back to town, over the beaten earth of the deserted mall. Beyond it were two stone columns spanned with a filigree of weathered metal. It was the entrance to a park.

Paths were laid out in fine sand which had been freshly swept into intricate patterns. It was cool beneath the umbrella of palms and warped pine and cypress. The leaves of shrubs were still moist with an accumulation of dew and sea air. A groundskeeper rested on his broom and watched Deacon. He tipped his hat respectfully, made a gesture with two fingers to indicate a cigarette. Deacon gave him one, added a *buon giorno. Buon giorno, capo sergente.*

He drifted through the park, stood at the sea wall and watched the smooth surge of the Adriatic over rocks themselves worn smooth. The water's faint hissing was echoed by the treetops' stirring in a light breeze. Italy was at matins, behind her veil. The park had probably never been touched by any war, and now it gleamed under an untouched morning. Slightly exaggerated, the tracings in the sand slightly overdone, it was as baroque as Italy of the opera. People sang while the earth was being gouged, the wind darned the shattered air, bent the cypress.

Deacon had finally caught a fraction of Italian time. He was bemused by it, prepared to set some round idle thought adrift on the sea. But there was more than one Adriatic. He could paddle through it, sponge off Basilicata's dust and draw on a clean mantle . . . but the Adriatic was also a hard plain shadowed by fragile wings, a sea which could smash and swallow. It was filled with rubbish—the skulls of galley slaves, rotted trireme oars, rusting naval guns. And now his own war's litter.

The hours he'd spent sandwiched between the twin dooms of sky and water couldn't be washed away with an evening dip. He'd been floating idly as a dead man, but there were real dead men down there, and blind fish busy making new castles of the shattered turrets on the bottom, tunneling under broken wings. Clark might be approaching resurrection, his navigator's brain picked clean by crabs. Garlanded with weed, he might soon be carried by currents older than Dalmatia and laid gently along the stones below. Deacon's Adriatic was polluted by centuries of bloodstained debris, stained by the new ruin floating from the sky every day. It was too blue, too much the color of the empty mirror above it.

The air shuddered, vibrated, and then came a martial clanging. Deacon thought at first that the pulse had come

181

back underscored in bronze. But it was only a bell tolling from a nearby church. The leaves seemed to tremble with each stroke, and the sun's glare on the water took on a metallic sheen. They were marking some death or devotion in Trani, but when the sound passed over the sea it lost all relevance to an Italian town. It took on a diffused hollow tone, rocked all the drowned men and machines in their cradles of silt.

As the bell clanged on Deacon began to feel a different rhythm gathering, and then it *did* come, the full booming thud of the old ghost keeping time on the bone behind his ear, the blood pulsing as though it were clotted. He turned quickly from the sea wall and tried to walk in cadence to the swing of the bell. But the sound of the huntsmen's drums was too strong. There was a measured thumping from the field, a muffled roll from under the sea. As he began to jog toward the road his left heel came down hard on each beat of the pulse drumming its own time.

The groundskeeper looked after him, shrugged, then relit the cigarette he'd pinched dead. He took his stick with its skirt of rushes and retraced the delicate lines Deacon's footsteps had broken.

Bari was waiting with a four-lane boulevard split by a set of trolley tracks bracketed in elegant palms. There was a raucous welcoming chorus of horns from the military traffic. Trolleys clanged and bicycle bells tinkled when Deacon arrived nodding in time to invisible music.

The troops saluted him smartly, all the cosmopolitan rear echelon and the men on pass—American khaki, British dun and RAF blue, a sprinkling of sikhs in beards and turbans. Their neat uniforms were trimmed with hash marks and overseas bars, their pockets striped. Nearly all the decorations were for service, not for valor, and only a few chests were slashed with colors indicating cemetery duty. Deacon's presence was a welcome confirmation of a war somewhere.

The Italians were delighted to see him. Along one side of the boulevard was a broad esplanade fringed with suitcases and portable stands. The Italians offered fruit, scarves, jewelry—would repair pens, sew on patches or chevrons. They extended arms snaked into the bands of watches, stood bound in nets of camera straps. Bari had real stores with display windows and marble facings, arches of fluted stone. In the streets were Italians of all ages with welcoming *buon giornos* tucked somewhere behind their closed faces; even young girl's strolling in wooden clogs and wearing GI ankle socks, too busy to say hello at the moment, but dying to meet him.

A key to the city was waiting, entrance to the British Salvation Army and the American Red Cross, to a snack bar, a theater which offered both movies and USO shows. He could rent a bicycle, hire a sailboat, ride in a horse-drawn carriage. There was a cathedral with a Byzantine dome resting on spikes of sugary stone, a number of lesser churches, a castle and a museum. He could attend concerts and recitals. All Bari was his.

The city pulsed smoothly. Traffic was directed by Italian policemen in pith helmets, their arms pinned with sleeves of white paper. *Carabinieri* in outlandish outfits kept civil order. The troops were under the care of American and British MPs. They would help Deacon remain a credit to his uniform, guide him away from disreputable bars, low places where he might have to crouch with his flanks naked and quivering. He'd barely gotten a dozen steps from the British pickup truck before an MP team greeted him. They had shining helmets, white leggings and cartridge belts, spotless pistol lanyards. Each wore a PFC crowfoot on his arm, nothing on his chest, no overseas bars on his sleeve.

"See your pass, Joe?"

The welcome came out of a small mean mouth, was accompanied by the tapping of a club across an open palm in a tempo more insistent than the beat in Deacon's ear. It shriveled the briny film, brought the dummy to life. He took a slip of paper from his pocket. The MPs eyes flickered from the uniform to the pass as he studied it.

"Nice collection," he said, nodding at the ribbons.

The man sweating inside the dummy felt a fit of rage at the boy-scout recruit condescending to give him a pat on the shoulder, the dude who thought that his Joe Balls costume made him a soldier. Deacon's hands trembled on the levers, but he got the head to nod and nearly smile.

"Hafta be back noon tomorra," the MP said when he returned the pass.

What the groundgripper really wanted was the chance to go in Deacon's place, to wear a different costume, jam that small mean mouth in an oxygen mask while the hole pucker grew with every hundred feet he got off the ground, grew so tight it finally choked him.

"I'll make it," Deacon said.

"See you do."

The MP dismissed him with a wave of the club. Deacon turned and stared into a store window, at first blind to anything but the shimmer of the glass. Then the fit passed and he noticed a drape of gray plush bordered by scattered shells— conch and whelk and ruffled scallop. They looked like elaborate facsimiles of human bones. Laid among the folds of cloth were finely etched cameos framed in ovals of gold filigree, bracelets with gaudy stone and coral chips arranged in rosettes and linked leaves. One day he'd buy something like that, send someone a souvenir of Italy.

He turned away from the window, wiped his face with his sleeve. Two pretty girls clumped past, their legs marred by ugly clogs and dusty socks; the street vendors were chanting, a million uniforms were hustling past, there was a steady grind of traffic. He was suddenly very thirsty, badly wanted a drink of water, but not distilled from the sea. Sweet clear water from a mile-deep spring. Deacon closed his eyes and tried to get a grip, reach some kind of balance. He took a deep breath and pushed off into the crowd, on his way to a new home.

It was a cosmopolitan war along Bari's boulevard—impressive vehicles, an orderly promenade of neat uniforms and non-starving civilians. But a few blocks away was an Italy which wasn't at all exotic or baroque, Italy scrabbling and grubbing to get alone.

Uncle's blue-eyed boy was a sorry sight banging through the gloom of narrow streets, past tenements and garages and warehouses faced with iron doors. He went calling like a ragpicker *Una stanza, ho bisogno d'una stanza,* attracted nothing but swarms of children who thrust out dirty claws and demanded chocolate and chewing gum and cigarettes. A soldier's rest, a place where he could stretch his soggy frame—he hawked as though after rags and bones and bottles, scuffled through a murk of rancid food and horse droppings while the children tried to lead him into normal paths. *You come, Joe, screw my sister . . . she* virgine. Joe, the hollow man, mouth stuffed with straw and dying for a drink, wandering farther and farther toward the docks, into a new aromatic stew of tidal flats and pilings and diesel oil. Different children with the same drawn faces and solemn beautiful eyes, both boys and girls ragged and filthy. *Sigaretta . . . suck-suck, fig-fig.*

The American soldier's penile shadow ran before him, gharry drivers slowing as they came abreast, *Entrate,* and a whore with a razor grin peering out. Hump on the hoof, celestial vibrations from sagging springs, ten-cent perfume blended with horse sweat and the very particular odor the warmed leather seats gave off. *Ho bisogno solo d'una stanza, niente signorine.* Nobody believed him. Soldiers didn't take rooms, they shacked up. If he wanted a place to sleep he could go to the Red Cross, spend the night in the transients' dormitory with its rows of GI cots where he could lay his dummy down next to all the others. He could go back into the mothering *army* if he wanted a place to *sleep*. What he wanted was a room.

At last one boy understood Deacon, led him into a courtyard grained with dirt, enclosed by the three walls of a tenement. Overhead was a tangle of washlines, tatters flying bravely in blue shadows. The landlady was stout, had her hair oiled and parted, pulled into a thick bun. She looked at him with undisguised hostility, listened as the boy talked. She was obviously reluctant, but she led them up the ladderlike stairs, heaving and wheezing, her grip threatening to pull out the banister.

Five flights up, at each of the roofed landings doorways where babies were crying or women were screaming or men swearing or all three. And then, beautiful, a single large room with a frame bed, a scarred table and three chairs with splintered seats. In one corner an alcove with a kerosene stove and a tiny sink, in another a doorless stall with a pull-chain toilet. Deacon was breathing heavily and the woman's face was plum-colored.

"Good stuff, Joe," the boy said. "You don get like dis noplace else."

Then there was hope for the rest of Italy. The woman gave him a price.

"Troppo," Deacon said.

Anything had to be too much. Deacon had eighteen dollars in his pocket, eighteen hundred lire. The landlady understood what he said, but she waited for the boy to repeat it, replied with a string of unintelligible Italian.

"Donna Amelia," the boy translated, "she say not too much. Issa not jus room. Issa watchyou say . . . *appartamento.* You get good air up here."

He had a stubbled scurfy head, was shoeless, shirtless, wore a patched wool jacket and tattered short pants. Even through the fog of wash and garbage and cooking Deacon could smell the rank odor rising from the cleft where the pinched neck grew from the jacket. The boy grasped one foot behind him and hopped like a dark wounded bird.

"Troppo," Deacon repeated.

"Ow much you pay?" the boy asked, still hopping.

"Five hundred . . . *cinquecento* lire."

The woman flapped her apron in the air and rolled her eyes.

"Sigarette," Deacon added.

She cocked her head toward the boy. They talked. *"Una stecca settimane,"* he said. "Ever week."

"Mezzo," Deacon said. *"Cinque pacci settimane."*

He'd have enough money and cigarettes to pay for the rent for two weeks, to be able to eat during the first, maybe learn to live on edible garbage the second, maybe find a fat old cook in a dark alley. The woman began to flap her apron again. She paused, spoke directly to him.

"*Sette.*"

"*Non più . . . senz'altro* not another goddamned thing."

She squinted at him, shrugged and held out her hand. Deacon unslung the musette bag, broke the last carton of cigarettes and gave her five packs. The bills he took from his pocket were creased, grainy with dust. She slammed the key into his palm and then, her foot on the first step, she turned with her hand on her chest and bid him an amiable *Buon ripos'*, struggled down the stairs. Deacon gave the boy ten lire. He grinned, touched his forehead.

"*Sigaretta,* Joe?"

Deacon took the last three from the open pack and crumpled it under the boy's nose. He gave him two cigarettes, put the other behind his own ear.

"You wan piece ass, you tell me. My house dere." The boy pointed to one of the landings. "My name Carlo."

Deacon was about to introduce Italy's favorite son, but he stopped, wondered what he was doing hiding in a slum if he had to hide twice.

"Tomas," he said.

"*Sta bene,* Tomas. You tell me you wan something. *Ciao.*"

Deacon watched the boy skip down the ladders, and then he went into the room and closed the door and turned the key in the lock. What more there was to Italy was all his. He took off his cap and shoes and sprawled on the bed. It had a flat metal spring, a mattress filled with something which shifted and rustled, two frayed blankets. Jesus crucified looked with sad eyes from the wall. Deacon had a hole in the toe of one sock. He sat up and began to unpack his musette bag. It took him nearly a minute and he nearly half filled one drawer of the trembling chest next to the bed.

The sink tap hissed when he opened it, the toilet tank began to bubble. A gush of rust came from the tap, then a drizzle of blood-temperature water—all the way from a mile-deep spring. Deacon cupped his hands and drank, tasted iron. He turned the tap off. It hissed, the toilet tank bubbled briefly.

They had given him a window. The burned sky was overhead, the street below had cobbles smeared by indigo light. On the roof across the way a woman was collecting wash in a straw basket. The wind tangled her hair and blew her dress against her body. But there was more across the way, across

186

other roofs and between walls—a narrow rectangle which opened on the sea, the haze line at the horizon neatly dividing the blue piled upon blue, one glinting.

He'd been given a watchtower, and he could see them coming from either sky or water, hang out warning lanterns and try to rent a horse. Deacon pulled up one of the splintered chairs and propped his feet on the windowsill and lit the cigarette. It was dusty and bitter. Then he took out his pocketknife and carefully carved his name in block letters on the sill. The afternoon was dying by the time he'd finished. He sat back in the chair, watched the light change until the two blues became indistinguishable and were finally covered in a single dusky mantle.

18.

HE COULD go back into the mothering Army if he wanted a place to sleep, but he wasn't about to go back with thirteen dollars in his pocket and a half carton of cigarettes in his bag, go back a frazzled duck limping because he had a hole in his sock. He'd go back when he wanted to, not when he had to.

Deacon had to earn a little Italian bread in the sweat of his face, and Bari was the place to do it. The ration cards were drawn on a nonexistent squadron. Deacon didn't know how he could use them, but he was hoping that Eddie Spinale the fixer had fixed himself out of the hospital by now and could show him. Spinale had gladhanded the men whenever they were leaving, given them the name of his outfit as though he were a businessman passing out cards at a convention, told them to drop by if they were ever in the neighborhood and looking for a little action. Spinale's own action disappeared into Intensive Care with Bradeway. There wouldn't have been any point in his staying in the hospital. He'd only needed to produce that piece of handiwork for Captain Marcellus to spring the lock.

The morning after his arrival in Bari, Deacon stood spruce and a little haggard outside the quartermaster sub-depot as he gathered himself to re-enlist for as long as it took him to conduct his business. The installation was huge, the real Army in

187

the real business of supplying a war, Quonset huts and warehouses of sheet steel built around a complex of old Italian buildings with flaking stone, the whole enclosed by a chainlink fence. The sun was really booming down, the fence glittering, and a swarm of Italians with pots and pails were gathered at a side gate waiting to go through the breakfast slops. A steady stream of vehicles passed through the main gate where two MPs were checking trip tickets. Deacon sucked in his stomach and marched forward expecting to be stopped. The MPs were only interested in vehicular traffic.

There was nothing but clear sky over the depot, but Deacon felt as though he'd stepped under a red, white and blue roof, into brasses and tramping feet. He had only to move inside the gate to become one of the uniforms, part of the routine, a member of the band of brothers. It was a different Little America than the zone in the rest camp. This one was grunting and grinding, a dynamo spinning out a tremendous force of men and equipment.

He found the headquarters orderly room typical of the Army recording itself on paper, noisy with typewriters and telephones, lined with cabinets containing tons of files and directives and orders. Smooth clerks in Class A uniforms moved from desk to desk. Deacon began to sweat, and not from the heat, but he went to the railing and asked about Spinale. An agreeable corporal helped him look through the huge roster of names, all numbered, tagged and assigned occupational specialties. The corporal located Spinale's, referred Deacon to a company orderly room.

The PFC behind that railing didn't have to check any records. Spinale was on the duty list, all right. The clerk made a face, looked at Deacon's chest and asked if Deacon was there to take delivery on an airplane Spinale had sold him. Deacon gave him a big smile, waited edgily until the PFC could take the time to point out a wooden shack set by itself among the barracks and warehouses. There was no answer when Deacon knocked on the door, but he could hear the steady twanging of the country music featured by the Armed Forces Broadcasting System. He lifted the latch and went in.

The smell of pigments and mineral spirits was very strong in spite of an open window. There were dozens of small paint cans, a rack of brightly colored mixing sticks hung like the pipes of a toy organ on the wall. Slender brushes were arranged in pigeonhole cabinets. Spinale sat on a stool before a slanted table, his lips drawn back and his tongue showing between his teeth as he carefully painted in the ONE WAY outlined on a white board. Deacon had never seen him wearing anything but a robe and pajamas. Spinale in fatigue shirt and

188

pants, a cap pulled to his ears, looked old, looked like a lifer. He seemed only mildly surprised to see Deacon, waved his brush in greeting and after a moment went back to his work.

"I developed a sort of hand for this," he explained. "Not that I was doing any painting back there, but after I got around to working on some of that stuff I found out I was sort of flexible . . . artistic, you know?" Spinale dipped his brush in solvent and wiped it on a gloriously stained rag. "Only thing is, there's no kind of action in paint. They only give me all these little cans. If I could get hold of a dozen gallons, I could make out."

"I thought you might have something going," Deacon said.

"It ain't that I'm exactly retired . . . a little here, a little there. It's a tough grind when you can't get hold of anything, but I still keep my hand in. You looking for a dame or something? Maybe I could help you out."

"I want to find out how to use those ration cards."

"You still got them, huh?" Spinale turned up the radio. "Never can tell somebody's got an ear out," he said. "Nothing to me, but you ever go back to your outfit? I mean, you're dressed up like you're on regular duty and all." Deacon hesitated. "None of my business," Spinale said.

"No, I didn't."

"Yeah, well this ain't such a bad town to get lost in. Lot of stuff going around if you can get a hand on it. They ain't got any kind of PX for casuals, so you couldn't use those cards in that kind of a deal. Thing is, they got to be worth something. You couldn't get anything like that out of this outfit . . . chickenshit as being back in the States."

"I thought maybe you could work something out."

"The cards they got here they lock up and keep a record of the serial numbers and all. You could just try to bust through the PX line with what you got. Thing is, you'd be taking a chance some guy would notice them. They got these numbers and all here, and it ain't your outfit anyway. These wops'd give you a fortune if they could get hold of those cards and use them . . . but there ain't no way they'd let one of them through the line."

"Anything," Deacon said.

"Maybe I could work on it. Say, I heard about a little thing the other day. There was this guy looking to dump a load of GI gloves, the wool kind."

"In *August?*"

"These people don't wait until whatever you got's in season, they buy right now. You could make a fortune in electric heaters this time of year. I know a guy's working on a gadget to change the AC to the DC they got. Thing is with

189

the gloves, if you could finance yourself to buying the bundle I bet you could make a nice dollar peddling them around the stores."

"Jesus Christ, Spinale."

"It was only a thought. Look, you let me work on this other thing. I could see you, say . . . day after tomorrow. Yeah, day after. I don't think it's such a good idea you should come around here what with that fruit salad and all. These guys don't see much of that and you sorta stand out . . . know what I mean? They keep a pretty good eye out and I got to watch it. If they start in wondering why you're coming around to see me they might make a connection."

Spinale paused a moment, seemed about to give a tug on the connection, the thread between them, seemed about to shake down a little Calabrian dust right there in the middle of thousands of soldiers who'd never been to a place anything like G Ward.

"How'd your Italian come along?" he asked.

For just that same kind of moment Deacon thought about the hospital, wondered if they'd disassembled the chicken wire, sent Harris somewhere else to cry and given Vierra the chance to find out what taste love had left in his mouth. Was Geary still breaking balls and Lieutenant Klein still measuring skulls? He drew a deep breath.

"Okay."

Spinale looked away, dipped his brush, and began to make careful strokes.

"Glad to hear it," he said.

They arranged to meet Sunday at a little park not far from the house where Deacon was living. He plugged the interval by luxuriating in his new home, using the tap water to sluice down the indeterminable bread Carlo bought for him. He stoked up on yellow cake and lemonade at the snack bar, felt the money in his pocket growing thinner and thinner while all around him men were giving it away to begging children, buying junk, paying too much to hire bicycles and have their photographs taken. He walked all over Bari, limping a little when the naked toe became inflamed.

Bari's docks were waiting for him for the second time. The steamer from England landed them there, what was then a whole new crew, and the crew Toole and Gruber had originally been on. They'd been hotshots then, raunchy recruits wearing unused forty-fives showily in stiff new shoulder holsters. And there was Bari with a half-dozen freighters lying heeled or tilted in shallow waters, their decks awash, their hulls blown and punctured. The German air force had run repeated raids against the waterfront, and the concrete piers were pocked by bullet holes, torn by bomb blasts. Raw and dumb, the crews stood staring at the big time, the war, not knowing that there hadn't been a raid in some time, that the Germans hadn't a striking force any longer. Not even knowing that war had nothing to do with them. They'd put their feet firmly on Italian soil, but someone was waiting at the field to turn them upside down and stick them feet foremost in the sky.

The harbor was the chief Adriatic funnel not only for materiel, but for the troops who arrived almost daily in Liberty ships. The bombed freighters were still there, a little more rusted but still an effective spectacle. Deacon watched the unloading of a small contingent wearing air-corps braid on their caps, groundgrippers destined for some pothole in the interior. Not more than thirty days ago they'd been in the States, now they were coming down a gangplank on a Saturday afternoon in Italy, landing in a harbor cluttered with sunken ships, ringed with anti-aircraft emplacements. They didn't notice that the guns' snouts were plugged, that the British crews sat drowsing under tent flies. It was the real war. They carried new overseas bags, sweated in new fatigues. Armed only with trench knives, they shaded their eyes and looked apprehensively at the sky, as though the war might suddenly begin to fall on them.

A mob of children met every troop debarkation. The MPs kept them on the sea wall until the men were loaded into a string of open trucks, and then they released them. The soldiers sitting in the hot sun were suddenly overwhelmed by a cheering crowd waving tattered hats and making the victory sign. It was the sort of thing they'd seen in the newsreels back home. They were *overseas,* conquerors, liberators, and they began to cheer in return. The children screamed, egging the men on until they were nearly in a frenzy, were showering chocolate and gum into the upraised hands, ringing every truck. Suddenly they were all singing furiously, the dumb raunchy campaign ditties they'd learned in the States. The trucks began to move and the children followed, milking the last throwaways. Still the singing continued, echoed from the boulevard, the voices punctured by derisive horns blasting *You'll-be-sorry*. They were eventually drowned beneath the rumble of regular traffic, but Deacon could picture them singing out into the open road and the heat and dust until they began to boil and choke. They *would* be sorry when they were dumped out dazed and aching at some remote encampment which was all they'd see of their particular war.

The children reassembled at the pier and compared what

they'd collected from the recruits. Deacon watched them for a moment, listened for a ghostly echo of his own voice in that air which had been completely purged of the other voices and was now filled with the rub of hawsers and the rattle of booms and winches. He couldn't remember if they'd been singing. What song would have been appropriate for twenty men who'd had to train so long and come so far to fit themselves into airplanes which would try to kill them? He walked toward the center of the city. It was unmarked outside the dock area. And there were no marks on the uniforms strutting around as though they were in some overdone Florida resort, loafing in gharries and hanging out of trollies and clicking silly bicycle bells as though there'd never been a war in Bari, never one anywhere in southern Italy. Salerno not a year ago, Anzio just half that, the months of blood and shit at Cassino, wholesale drownings in the Rapido, the Big Week, the Oil Campaign—all of it worth no more than an afternoon's prancing to these drones, having their pictures taken, climbing into a carriage for a three-minute lay, seeing a movie. The graves-registration teams hadn't even finished collecting the garbage, but all that didn't mean any more than a day of sightseeing to the clerks and bottlewashers.

Deacon found a shallow alcove and leaned back and cocked his cap over his eyes. A frieze moved along its rim, a thousand khaki legs, a thousand feet in GI clodhoppers. He stood there like some fleshed memorial obelisk, his chest draped in colorful crepe, and hated every one of them. They were worse than drones—they were maggots, wingless and weaponless. Keep 'em flying, but don't get flown. Pass the ammunition, but stay out of range.

He was prepared to stand glaring at them all day, but his alcove was too shallow. They brushed against him, nudged him into the crowd, and he became part of a parade of bobbing hats and swinging arms. It was stopped at a corner by an Italian policeman, one of his paper sleeves tattered and flapping. Across the street the Red Cross building rose like a castle, windows trimmed with ornate cornices, the tile roof pitched in banks. The policeman pirouetted and the traffic stopped, and it was as though a drawbridge had come down when the feet thumped across the boulevard. Deacon let himself be carried into the plaza before the Red Cross, up the steps and through the huge doors.

There was a broad marble stairway choked with a double file of men surging up and down. Rooms opened from every landing, faded and worn but touched with gilt molding and carved wainscoat. A prince had lived there, or perhaps a lord who'd worn the black shirt, or perhaps it had been the city

192

hall. Now there was a small snack bar, a room with pool tables, rooms for reading and writing, the sterile dormitory. Uniforms were in all of them. Deacon was drawn past, sucked upward by strains of music until he stood beneath the pitched roof. A babble of voices rolled out, the harsh beat of an American dance band, a mist of perspiration and damp cloth and heated perfume.

It was a ballroom, the showplace of either prince or lord or mayor, where slippers and boots once scraped across the parquet floor while ladies and gentlemen in the old stiff poses of the South sat in delicate chairs lining the walls. Awkward waltzes, ragtime on squeaky violins. Country gentry yawning openly as they went home, red faces and stained mustaches, hands sweaty on the marble banisters, chains and necklaces of sturdy old gold glittering under the light of wall sconces. Horses stamping outside, carriages with minor crests, automobile drivers in military uniforms. Riding away into the Southern night, into history.

Now the room was lined three deep with servicemen, those in the first rank bracing themselves against the thrust from the rear. The line broke and rippled like a wave threatening the hemmed-in dancers. The music came from a phonograph. Some of the girls wore prim Red Cross blue, but most were Italians in curious dresses which looked as though they'd been pieced together from the frivolous and the old. The Italian girls' hair was swept in American styles. Some wore real shoes and some stockings which crushed their leg hair into delicate whorls. Hands arching in bridges to partners revealed shaggy armpits. They danced by rote, by imitation, while the Red Cross hostesses bobbed their heads diligently and pumped their elbows against their sides as though trying to strike a spark.

Deacon was funneled into the room, carried in and out of eddies until he was at its end and could see the whole length of the floor, over and between the whirling couples, see through the mullioned windows overlooking Bari moving steadily and silently beneath a cover of trees, its buildings edged with shadow by the declining sun.

Dancing tonight at Colt's Park . . . summer and a bus rumbling along Wethersfield Avenue.

The record ended. There was a pause while the wave broke and partners were exchanged. Deacon was pushed forward, came face to face with a young Red Cross hostess with cropped curly hair. She'd had her arms half extended to a tech sergeant, but he'd been carried away by the crowd, and her hand caught Deacon's elbow. He put out his arms and mumbled something as the music began. The girl leaned over

193

his shoulder to call to the sergeant, and Deacon could smell perfume, cosmetics, scented soap. She smiled at him mechanically and they began to dance.

Tonight at Colt's Park . . . the moon of a particular summer . . . girls who'd flocked to Hartford to work at the war plants. The men were away and the boys could play.

Couples bumped together. There were regional American accents, the accents of the Italian girls speaking English. The Red Cross hostess was relaxed, danced smoothly and held herself expertly away.

"Well hi there," she said.

They said *Hi there* when they handed out doughnuts or coffee or lemonade. She wasn't particularly pretty, but she wore a crisp white blouse under her uniform jacket and had on lipstick, and reflections of the sun's gold turned her hair into swirls of rich mahogany.

"Would you like to know my name?" he asked. "It's Deacon."

"Hi there Deacon," she said brightly. "I'm Tobin Bowles."

"At my service?"

"What? Oh certainly . . . at your service. And where are you from?

I'm from New Hampshire Maine Vermont . . . I don't know anybody in Hartford.

"Do you have to ask questions like that?" Deacon said.

"I suppose I don't *have* to. I thought you might want to talk about your home town."

"I'd rather not."

"My error. I'm afraid I'm not terribly good at this yet. It's only the third dance I've been to here. I haven't been overseas quite five weeks."

"That's long enough."

"How long have you been over?"

"Long enough, too."

"If you don't respond a little better, I'll be running out of phrase-book phrases."

"Miss Bowles, I bet if you didn't have the duty you wouldn't even be bothered dancing with me."

"Sergeant Deacon, if there were enough girls around I'm not so sure you'd ask me. I don't always get the names but I got yours, didn't I? That must be because you're the first gunner I've met overseas."

"Beautiful."

"And you're wearing a Purple Heart. I know an infantry captain who has one. He drinks too much . . . do you?"

"Will you have a drink with me?"

"Can't . . . against regulations. A pleasant face is required

194

at all times, but no preferences are to be expressed, and never two dances in a row with a partner. No sitting out and no private excursions to the snack bar. The Italian ladies will have come from respectable families, and they will have a working knowledge of English. It's all written down."

"When is this over?"

"At seven, but I won't be free then." She listened for a moment. "Our time is about half gone."

"Do you know the music that well?"

"I know *this* one." She paused. "You can ask again the dance after next."

"Maybe they'll have a break."

"Breaks are the worst time . . . I'm swamped. Group entertainment *is* one of our specialties." She tried to rearrange her smile, but brittle edges clung to the corners of her mouth. "Isn't it all just too bad?"

"It's a rough war."

"Oh please don't say things like that. I didn't mean . . . how would anyone in *Bari* know what kind of a war it was anyway?"

"I could tell you stories."

"I'm sure you could." She looked almost serious. "Would you?"

"Sure."

"Don't think I'm ghoulish, but . . . but here comes the last chorus and up brass and there we are. Sorry, Sergeant Deacon . . . you *can* try again."

The music stopped and there was a murmuring in the warm room as the men backed off the floor extending their hands for a last touch, their farewells sincere and almost final, as though they were leaving on a train or truck for the front. *Addio, domani morrò.* Deacon touched the girl's arm lightly, afraid to wrinkle her sleeve, to blot it with his sweaty palm.

"Please," she said, "Mother Superior doesn't approve of pawing." She rolled her eyes toward a Red Cross lady who was no longer young but had very red lips and cheeks.

"She looks like some general's whore," Deacon said.

The girl bit her lips and turned away. Two men were badgering her, the blank grooves of a record were already hissing on the phonograph. She held her hands up blindly and began to dance, looked briefly at Deacon over a khaki shoulder.

"Yes, she does," she said, and was gone.

He stood at the edge of the floor for a moment. Dancing that very night in Colt's Park, the men still away and the boys still playing. And dancing in Bari no different. He pushed through the room, down the staircase, stood among

195

the swarm of uniforms in the plaza—a vortex of nobodies going nowhere. Deacon turned back toward the docks.

It was dusk when he reached the harbor. He walked along the sea wall, passed a long table which contained the ruins of a wedding celebration. The bride and groom were gone and the little cakes had been destroyed. A few older people sat among scraps of puckered squid and glazed macaroni shells, drank wine and listened to the wheeze of a concertina. Deacon was hungry, would have eaten the leftovers if no one had been there. A chill wind blew off the water and whipped the tablecloth.

The forest of booms and cranes had been secured for the night. They creaked in the wind, their blocks and rigging rattled. Warehouses were closed. The ships in the harbor showed only dimmed riding lights. The moon arrived in the form of a disk of gold as pale as the late sunlight had been. Deacon came to the long pier where the troops debarked. He walked to its end and looked back toward Bari. It seemed far away, a city where a dim carnival was being held.

There was dancing tonight at the edge of the Adriatic. This summer's moon was Italian. The water was very dark, slicked by oil which gave off faint colors. He sat with his feet dangling over the pier's edge, his fingers playing around the rim of a bullet hole as he watched the half-engulfed ships perpetually drowning in the moonlight.

19.

THE ARMY provided luxuries on Wednesday, the PX open from three to seven in order to accommodate all the duty shifts. The men in line were dressed in everything from fatigues and undershirts to Class A uniforms. Deacon blended in with the others, his wings and ribbons hidden, eight dollars in his pocket and the rent due the next day. They shuffled and squatted in the blazing sun, talked without real interest of a battle at a place called Avranches. No one knew where it was. In Italy the Fifth Army was past Perugia, just out of Arezzo. They didn't know where that was either, didn't really care—it was a hot afternoon in Bari and the beer ration was on the way.

The deal was a little tricky, Spinale explained, and Deacon was all on his own. If he got picked up nobody knew nothing. The fix had to be put in with the clerk at the beginning of the line who checked and punched the cards. He'd pass Deacon through. Anything that happened after that was Deacon's business. The clerk could claim he'd simply goofed. Spinale would be absolutely invisible. Since so many men passed through the line in the four hours the PX was open, Deacon should be able to go through twice.

A little tricky about getting rid of the stuff, Spinale said. You could get busted in Bari for just peddling a pack of cigarettes black market—a chickenshit town. And Deacon wasn't in any position to get himself picked up for that and then have them find out . . . you know? Deacon should go back to that same park when he'd finished collecting, somebody would be along to pick up the stuff. Wouldn't even have to worry about the prices, that'd be all worked out in advance. Cash on delivery, but—Spinale scratching his chin—mightn't be as much as Deacon expected, what with having to pay off and all. Have to cut it half and half. The bagman would hold Spinale's cut, give Deacon his.

They were running through Arezzo, getting bloody noses in Avranches, but in Bari it was shuffle and squat until the door of the PX shed opened, and then more inching, out of the sunlight and into the shed's hot shade. For a moment Deacon couldn't see. He held out his card blindly. The corporal who took it looked it over without interest at first, but then Deacon, still blinking, could see his head give a little jerk, nearly lift to look at him. The clerk passed a conductor's punch over the card and made a hole in the first of the ten squares. He didn't look up.

No one did. There were six other clerks behind the long counter, behind them a lieutenant. The clerks watched the men's hands, not their faces, and the lieutenant watched the clerks. Deacon took exactly what the others did, a carton of cigarettes and six candy bars and a small can of peanuts—soap, toothpaste, shoe polish and four bottles of beer, two of Coke. He paid at the end of the line, passed out of the shed and into the sunlight, was momentarily blinded again.

He hadn't thought to bring a bag of some kind, and so he was standing in the middle of the sub-depot, phony card in one pocket, phony pass in the other, his arms filled with PX goodies he'd have to carry through the line again. Deacon wandered through the area, finally set his teeth and pushed through the doors of one of the Quonset barracks. It was like a tin oven inside, smelled of wool, canvas and brass—exactly like home. He thought at first it was empty, but there was a lone naked man lying sweating on a cot and watching him. Deacon walked down to the cot, hesitated just a moment conscious of his Class A uniform and laden arms, the man's almost brutal nakedness.

"Horton live here?" he asked.

The other shook his head slowly. Deacon nodded, walked out. He gathered himself again and went into the adjoining hut. No one was there. He quickly stripped off an OD pillow-case, stuffed in the rations and hurried outside, carried the clinking sack until he found a collection of empty gasoline drums. When no one appeared to be watching he hid the pillowcase among them, then sat killing time until he could go through the line again.

The duty shift changed and the sub-depot's pace slowed as most of the warehouses were shut down. Men strolled back and forth to the latrines, wiped their hands with gasoline-soaked rags. There was no formal retreat ceremony, the flag coming down to a bugle's cry, but it was unmistakably day's end, exactly like the closing of any day in any of the military homes he'd been in. He felt almost part of it, almost comfortable.

The PX line was longer the second time he went through. Clerks were perspiring, chocolate oozed through the paper wrappers of the candy bars. The corporal paused only a fraction of a second before punching his card. Deacon had hardly any money left after paying for the load. He recovered the pillowcase and added the second ration. With the bulging sack pressed against his hide he didn't feel like any part of the Army at all, felt like a tramp who'd just called at the kitchen door. There was heavy traffic at the main gate. The MPs paid no attention to him.

The park was a narrow triangle, a wedge of broken concrete set with backless benches worn smooth. Deacon sat down to wait. The sun waned and a lip of shadow marched across the concrete. Two old men waited with him till the shadow touched their knees, and then they rose stiffly and shuffled home. Children played along the benches. A woman's clear voice called several times and one of the children broke away. Two others lingered only a little longer before walking off into the gloom gathering in the streets.

Dim light had appeared in nearby windows by the time two natty young Italians entered the park. While one flicked at his brilliant shoes the other looked at Deacon across his partner's bent back. They wore striped suits with wide lapels and billowing trousers, ties twisted into very small knots. Both their hair and their thin mustaches were oiled. They approached Deacon.

"You got someting for me, Joe?" one asked.

"I guess so," Deacon said.

The Italian snapped his fingers at the bench. Deacon emptied the pillowcase and laid the rations along it, stood like a shopkeeper while the two men inspected the goods. He held back a carton of cigarettes. The Italians took everything but the beer.

"That'sa only good you wash you feet." The same one spoke. "*Quanto*, Mario?"

"*Più o meno . . . dice cinque mille*," the other said.

"Not much big deal, Joe. That'sa fifty dollar. Twenty and five you, twenty and five the friend who make the arrange."

"Is that all?" Deacon said.

"How I'ma going give you short change? You tell what I give, no? The friend get the same. I don't give you correct, he don't get. Okay? Fine as wine, Joe."

"Okay." Deacon took the money.

"Maybe you get more nex time. I take all you get. Maybe you get shoes. *Come si dice . . . mutande, camicette?* You GI drawers, Joe, make you good deal you get some."

The beautiful mothering clothesline thief, snatching pillowcases to put in pillowcases, stripping cots, collecting dirty socks and underwear.

"We all finished?" Deacon asked.

"It'sa big hurry you gotta take off? These place good make *bagatelle*, lil shit." The Italian waved at the surrounding houses. "They keep the eyes close and the noses clean. Maybe you got big deal, Joe, you want talk private?"

"No."

"Okay. You fly straight, I see you nex week." He snapped his fingers and the second man took a net bag from under the coat and packed the things. "Hey Joe, maybe you want good piece ass. I give you special deal, hot stuff."

"No," Deacon said.

"Aah . . . you already got. You *bello*, no?" The Italian pinched Deacon's cheek. Deacon flinched. "Hey, we buddies, Joe. You *paisano* me. Bring me good stuff, I make you good deal. *Fin'oggi a otto*."

Deacon watched them stroll off jabbering, disappear around a corner. He packed the beer and cigarettes into the pillowcase, started out of the park. Sitting on the last bench was a sergeant in the faded blue of the RAF. Deacon eyed him and the man gave a half salute. Deacon nodded, walked by.

"Oily bastards," the Britisher called after him. Deacon paused. "Wouldn't trust 'em an inch."

He turned. "You know them?"

"Can't say as I do. Wouldn't shout about it if I did. Nasty lot."

"You're shouting now."

"Afraid you couldn't hear me, Yank. In a terrible hurry to get home with that wallop, aren't you? Don't know why, it's not all that good." He patted the bench. "Why don't you put it down here for a minute?"

Deacon walked to the bench, but he didn't sit down.

"Name's Boyd," the sergeant said. "Yours is Tom. Nice and simple. Tom Fool, Tom O'Bedlam. You needn't look so put out about it, Yank. More than one man in this area I know by his first name. We've got mutual friends. Wouldn't shock me if we had mutual interests."

Deacon looked around the square.

"Waiting for the police van to come out of a side street, are you? Nothing to it Yank, just a little chat. Wouldn't pay any attention to the wops . . . seen too many of your films and they're dressing up to the part."

"You with them?"

"With *them?* Come off it. Can't properly say I'm with anyone except His Majesty's forces." He tugged at his uniform shirt. "One soldier to another, eh Yank? Course I haven't been the soldier you have. Understand you've a fair shower of ribbons, marvelous colors. Shame you don't wear them."

"I do," Deacon said.

"Just pulling your leg. I've seen you tricked out in all your glory, strutting down the street as though the pavement wasn't wide enough. Very impressive."

"What's this all about?"

"Well we don't know that, do we? Surprise me if we knew what this bloody war was all about. Wouldn't be here if we did. I'd heard of you, Yank, and I thought we should get acquainted."

"Do you know Spinale?"

"I wouldn't say I knew anybody. Nasty things, names. People tie them together like a chain, someone gives a pull, and off they all go. You know what they say in the press . . . 'linked to' and so forth. Sounds a bit like leg irons, doesn't it? Should do us just to know each other's names."

"And yours is Boyd."

"First or last, take it as you will. Don't care one way or the other myself. But I'm holding you up." He pointed at Deacon's sack. "Your beer's not much, is it? Wouldn't get a real pint if you boiled down a case of it. They give our fellas a tot of the real thing. Like to do the same for you some day."

"I'll look forward to it."

"We'll make it soon." Boyd stood, stretched and looked up at the sky. "Beautiful evening. Don't think you'll be making a night of it on that pocketful they gave you. Shame to have to go to so much trouble just to have a few coppers to rub together. Ought to be a better way, don't you think?"

Deacon didn't answer. Boyd gave him a mock salute and sauntered off. The sky had grown dark and there were squares of light in all the surrounding windows.

Four jugs of beer and a loaf of cigarettes didn't make for either singing or paradise, but Deacon was able to buy kerosene for the stove, low-grade olive oil to fry his bread in. When that gave him the GI trots he had Carlo get some hard old cheese to bind the wound. Carlo ran all his errands, probably charged Deacon twice what everything cost, but he knew where to get it and Deacon didn't. The Italians had food-ration cards which weren't really much more than an opening gambit for black-market haggling. Without real money and without a card Deacon couldn't even open for the few ratty things displayed on a *drogheria* counter, let alone try to deal for the goods kept hidden. He couldn't buy much more than a cup of ersatz coffee in a *trattoria*. Carlo kept him fed and took his uniform to be washed and pressed, even had the hole in his sock darned. Deacon was a big-deal runaway black-market operator in the care of a small boy.

He had hold of a certain kind of security now, but he hadn't hold of any kind of time, not even the three-day cycle of Joe Rico. The dummy belonged to the MPs. He was their toy, to be wound and inspected at their whim. Deacon didn't even have a watch. His old one had been broken at the moment of the crash, kept only all that old broken time. A watch wouldn't have helped him keep Bari's time because Bari wasn't one thing and hadn't one time. The parade of legs and GI shoes he'd seen marching around the edge of his cap was only part of the frieze. Uniforms alternated with the mufti, trucks and gharries were interspersed with bicycles—ranked and rankless, privileged and poor, bumpers and fenders were locked with hands and they all pinwheeled slowly in a closed chain which had no place for Deacon to break in.

He needed a watch to keep his own time—not Bari's and not the Army's and not America's. The snack bar was U S and A all the way, well organized and functionally furnished and efficiently run, serving yellow cake prepared to an American recipe. Deacon stood in a line where everyone wore Uncle's khaki rompers and talked his language, edged forward to the counter where Mom and Sis in the person of Red Cross ladies did the serving.

They weren't quite the family figures they were supposed to be, lost something in having been translated to Italy. Too many of the boys had hungers for more than cake, their female companionship having been limited to the minutes on a whore's meter or a quick dance with one of the approved *signorine* raised in the southern Italian tradition of no ring, no zing. The Red Cross ladies might be Mom and Sis on the fund-raising posters, they might wear uniforms to prove that they were national institutions, but the boys knew what was hidden beneath that severe cloth—America's home-town honey, the curves and dimpled hollows of Saturday night and the back-seat grapple. The boys sucked in their own typically American cheeks and looked faintly lascivious as they devoured typically American female faces. They were polite or nervy or shy, but no matter what they had to say the expressions they wore were dusted with something fervent and dirty.

The ladies were used to fielding those looks, ignored eyes straining to find a gaping buttonhole. Deacon ignored the ladies. He'd had enough vocal and edible handouts, both doughnuts and smiles a little greasy as the enlisted man got his ration of hope from the All-American girl who banged only for commissioned non-gentlemen. But there was *Dancing tonight at Colt's Park* when he saw her holding a spatula and serving cake . . . the dancing girl when there wasn't any dancing either that night or that afternoon and the whole snack bar was really nothing more than a hard-line cafeteria, Deacon dancing on tiptoe trying to attract her attention. She never looked away from the man she was serving, smiled and deposited her load and then picked up another portion and smiled at the new face. Her cheerful expression was slightly twisted by wear and her eyebrows peaked with the effort of keeping the curl to her lips.

He tried to hang back until he could remember her name, but the push from behind was relentless and it wasn't until he stood in front of her that it came to him. He blurted *Tobin* and a rush of other words just as she began to give the practiced roll to her mouth. Her eyes withdrew from a point of focus somewhere at the back of his head as she really looked at him, gave a *Hi there* in slightly puzzled recognition as he was edged past.

Deacon put the cake and coffee on a table and got in line again. He concentrated, did a few steps to jog his memory, and then the whole name came—*Tobin Bowles*. He practiced saying it, finally got the right combination of brightness and warmth, said *Tobin Bowles* just that way when he was standing before her again. Her response was more than automatic, better than practiced. She actually seemed pleased. The men on either side looked furious when Deacon leaned forward to speak to her and her head tilted slightly toward his. He asked if she would meet him. Her smile knotted and her head canted slightly. Deacon was forced to move on.

He deposited the second helping on the table with the first and rejoined the line. No dancing, and no making points at a drugstore or a bar, but here he was somehow back in a piece of America's time, two-part, room only for him and a partner. She looked around warily for the day's Mother Superior, bent forward as they both whispered, the men around them forming nothing more than the dumb walls of a confessional. Tobin Bowles marked a day and gave him an hour on that day. The faces of the men watching became glum or outraged because she had broken out of her official casing, given Deacon something when nobody was supposed to get anything.

He went to his table and ate all three pieces of cake, drank all three cups of coffee, watching a space between heads and over shoulders where her face appeared briefly. He caught her eye only once. When she waggled a finger at him the man she was serving turned to follow her gesture, and he gave Deacon an ugly look. Deacon shook a fist at him. For a moment their hatred flooded the space between and Deacon wanted to smash the groundgripper, the latrine orderly thinking dirty and getting nothing. He pulled himself together, gave a final nod in the girl's direction and left the snack bar, afraid that something might happen to spoil their arrangement, that she might change her mind.

Tobin Bowles, on Sunday, at eleven o'clock. Now he really needed a watch.

Bari kept the time for him. On Sunday the bells of the city's churches rang in different tones and octaves, and the cathedral sent forth a great bronze bonging which was like a call to heathen worship. Deacon didn't know if the chorus flattened and rolled at the sea's edge, shook the husked dead from their racks—he didn't care if it did, didn't care who might be drumming or coursing. That Sunday's bells were like a protective umbrella. He was safe beneath it, among the *Barese* who somehow made a grand processional of the walk to church, the ladies displaying their missals and rosaries, the men pumping hats up and down, even the poorest children wearing some touch of white.

Bari's Sunday air was filled with *buon giornos*, and Deacon was moving toward an American Sunday—the drugstore, colored comics, she strolling with her best hat held in her hand.

His trousers were so starched they popped each time he moved, and his shirt was tucked tight, his wings burnished by the fair light of eleven o'clock. Only a few soldiers idled along the esplanade. Deacon waited in place while the bells grew still and the city became filled with whispers, the echoes of incantations from all the churches. The time was elongated because he had no watch, and he didn't know whether she was five minutes or a half hour late, only that his throat tightened when he saw the blue figure striding along the nearly deserted walk, not with flowers in her hair as he'd nearly expected, but in a uniform cap. She offered a hand wearing Sunday's curiously appropriate white glove, and she gave off a hard bright American smell of soap and toothpaste.

"Good morning to you, Sergeant Deacon," she said.

"Good morning to you, Miss Bowles."

"Either you call me Toby or I'll make you walk a step to the left and two steps to the rear. And I like just plain Deacon . . . don't tell me your first name. Is that all right?"

"Sure. Would you like to just walk, or do you want to do something else?"

"I liked to go window-shopping back home on Sunday morning. Do you mind?"

She didn't take off her cap and hold it, and he couldn't reach for a hand wearing a white glove, but they walked along the row of closed shops. He looked at her reflection in the glass and saw that she still wasn't pretty, only fair, wished that something would catch her eye, that she'd make a comment as yearning and wistful as a child's. Deacon had exactly fifteen dollars he wasn't sure would carry them through the afternoon, but for Tobin Bowles he'd have been at the door when the store opened the next morning, bought whatever it was she wanted—the last one in Bari, in Italy, in Europe— and brought it to her bound in red ribbon. She had a child's seriousness as she peered through the glass, hands behind her back.

"Back home . . . that's just outside Worcester . . . do you know it? You sound a little Yankee yourself . . . back home some of the stores changed their windows on Saturday nights, and the next morning we'd walk past to see what was new . . . but there's never anything new in Bari. I keep expecting the displays to change but they don't. Where are all those smart Continental shops I'd always been told about?"

"You should go to Rome."

"Oh, *Rome* . . . have you been there? I'm dying to go. but it's such a big deal about transportation. Could you fly me there in your airplane?"

"I can't fly an airplane . . . I don't even fly *in* one anymore."

"I was wondering about that . . . I mean of course I knew you weren't a pilot. I am first class in military insignia, Sergeant Deacon, and all the little things they stand for. But I meant I was wondering about seeing you again the other day. Are you stationed in Bari now?"

"Yes," he said without hesitation.

"That's unusual, isn't it?"

"I'm training to go home on a war-bond tour."

"Really? You're not really, are you?"

"No. I'm on detached service."

"That sounds important, like being assigned to a commando operation or something."

"It's not."

"Secret? Parachute drops at night?"

"No." They'd walked past the shops, past the offices and municipal buildings, and now they were at the end of the esplanade. "Would you like to go to church?" Deacon said.

"To church? Not particularly. I'm not Catholic, are you?"

"No."

"Oh . . . you meant to *see* a church. I'm afraid I'm not much of the guidebook type. Do you like to visit places?"

"I didn't mean that, either," Deacon said. "I guess I just want to do something you want to do."

"Walking's fine . . . it's such a nice time of day for it. No mobs. Isn't it exciting about Florence? They captured it yesterday . . . did you know that?"

Deacon knew where *Florence* was. It had been a checkpoint on a mission they'd run against the Brenner Pass. They'd eaten a ton of flak and dropped a million bombs and left the mountains absolutely unchanged, the pass wide open. Florence was a long haul from Rome, a lot of ground to have gobbled up.

"No," he said.

"I wish I'd been here when they took Rome. Were you?"

"Yes, but it didn't mean anything."

"And how about Bari? The British took it, didn't they?"

"Last year."

"That's why *they* have all the best villas. It must have been exciting when the bombing was going on. Were you here then, too?"

"I've been in the interior."

"I feel closer to the war just being here, don't you?" She put white fingers to her mouth. "That was silly . . . I guess you've been as close as you want to get."

"It doesn't matter."

"It does matter. In fact . . . in fact what I said about feeling closer isn't exactly true. There really isn't anything happening here. There's only the feeling of something happening . . . all the shipping and the supplies and the troops, but all the bombs and ammunition are going somewhere else." She looked closely at him. "I wouldn't want you to think I was *really* silly, but I've got this idea that I want to know something about this war."

"Read *Yank* or the *Stars and Stripes*."

"Don't be mean. I came all this way and here it is not too much different from the twice-a-week dances at the local USO. I don't mean I expected to be working in a bombed-out church or anything . . . but after all, this is really only a nice dull city filled with people who've never been in touch with the war at all. And that's just the way I feel . . . completely out of touch."

Deacon walked on a moment in silence. "Is that why you're in touch with me?" he asked.

"Would that be wrong?"

They'd been walking toward the harbor. There was a fresh breeze, and the girl stopped, her hand at her hair, and looked seriously at him.

"I flew thirty-one missions," Deacon said stiffly. "They were all written down on a piece of paper, but I lost it."

"Oh Deacon, don't . . ."

"You're not even supposed to go out with enlisted men, are you?"

"Please . . . I'm not trying to use you for anything."

"Okay."

"Perhaps it's wrong, and I shouldn't, but I want to ask you what it was like."

"In the morning the CQ banged on the mess kits and put a light in your face and said 'Drop your cocks and grab your socks.'" She stood peering up at him with eyes some sort of grayish-brown—*hazel*—as though she were looking for something. "What *that* was like, Toby?"

Her eyes still reflected the best Sunday mornings he could remember. Deacon tried to get hold of the jumping parts.

"I'm sorry," he said. "I don't want to . . . Jesus Christ."

"It's all right," she said.

"No it isn't. I . . . this goddamned sun."

He took her arm and led her across the street into the shade. There was a low wall before a closed villa. She sat down and crossed her ankles and held her hands in her lap like a young girl idling on a swing.

"Toby . . ." Deacon started.

"No," she said firmly. "I want to tell you about this funeral back home . . . for a boy who was killed in the service, a flying accident right at Westover Field. They brought him home on the train, and the coffin was all draped in bunting, and there was this sergeant who'd ridden all the way with it in the baggage car. There was a delegation from town, and the depot was almost like a church . . . so solemn. I can't forget the smell of the smoke from the rifles . . . in the cemetery, later. They had a squad of real soldiers, and when the coffin went down two men recovered the flag very gracefully just at the last moment and they folded it as though they were doing a drill. Then saluting Ted's father and giving him the flag . . . he tried to stand up straight but he was all shriveled with crying. Everyone was crying. The whole town was mourning Ted, people who hadn't even known him except by sight, and he wasn't even the first one who'd been killed. It must have been because he was the only one who'd ever been brought home. Deacon, when I got back to the house and got out of my things I was lying on my bed with a wet cloth over my eyes thinking about it . . . and it hadn't anything to do with the war. A training accident . . . and we were burying Ted as though he were the Unknown Soldier, turning the place practically into a shrine. It hadn't the least thing to do with the war."

"Was he a particular someone?" Deacon asked.

"Nothing like that . . . a good friend, nothing more. But don't you see, all the noise and fire is really here, or in the Pacific, and we can't see or hear it . . . but everyone acts as though it's in the next county." She smiled wryly. "I don't know what I came over here to find out. The war *is* in the next county . . . three provinces away, to be exact . . . but now it might as well be back in the States."

"That's right."

"Deacon?"

"Yes?"

"I don't know why that name just fits you. When I was little they used to call me Toilet Bowles. Still good for a laugh around town to hold your nose and make believe you're pulling a chain." She held up her head and the wind blew her curls straight back along the edge of her cap. "It got to be like a continuous hospitality weekend back there, someone always dropping in on the way from one place to another. People you didn't even know. They knew people you knew, or even knew people who knew people you knew. All for the war . . . the battle of Worcester County." The smile she gave him was hazed. "I never got the knack of lying down wrapped in the flag when it got to be that time on Saturday night. There wasn't any victory in *this* girl."

"Come on, Toby, let's see if we can find a restaurant who'll sell us a bottle of wine."

"I can't, I'm a little behind already." *She* had a watch. "I'm sorry, but I've got to go."

"There isn't a dance today, is there?"

"A tea dance. Evidently enlisted men aren't any good at drinking tea."

"Oh."

"Even that isn't much different from home. We have an income from a family business, so most of the people in town are . . . Other Ranks. Daddy makes . . ."

"Daddy makes a bundle because there's a war on, and Baby wants to find out what the score is. Why don't you ask that dogface captain you were telling me about?"

"I did."

"Did he tell you to go up on the line and find out for yourself? Did he tell you about the Great Ticket Puncher?" Deacon clapped his hand behind his ear. "Okay," he said. "Okay, okay."

She put her hand on his arm, her white cloth and his khaki keeping them from really touching. "How about the dance after next?"

"Something that doesn't involve tea, something that isn't beneath your station in life?"

"Oh Deacon . . ."

Oh Tom darling. There was no one to say that on a rotten hot afternoon in Bari. The Italian girls were mincing along in the ritual stroll with the one and only *fidenza';* American girls were looking for a dance without any sweaty EM, for a moonlight ride in a jeep, for a lift to Rome. Deacon stood up.

"Next Sunday morning?" she asked. "Same time, same place?"

"Is that a good hour because your wheels are still shacked up with my wheels?" He took a breath. *"Fin'oggi a otto.* Today a week. Life with Other Ranks."

"No previous engagements next time . . . all right?"

"Fine," Deacon said, "let's go."

"Actually, it might be better if you didn't walk back with me. Our quarters are only a block or two from here."

"Beautiful."

"Please." She looked at him with the same hazel eyes, but there were only shards of Sunday mornings left in them.

"Addio, tesoro mio . . . domani morrò."

"I don't know Italian at all."

"Nothing, Toby. See you."

She gave him a thin smile and cocked her head and her

body seemed to turn in response to the movement. Before Deacon really knew it she was moving away, her skirt a little too long, the service shoes unflatting to her slender legs. Little girl blue gone to answer the call of the big brass. Deacon kicked at the wall.

A crapout even with Toilet Bowles. Fifteen dollars to salvage the afternoon in a town where he couldn't get a drink on Sunday unless he bought a meal, where soldier's delights were mapped out on the Red Cross bulletin board—a Mascagni concert at three in the lower hall of the Red Shield Club; join a language class; sign up to become a Weekly Guest in a Good Home (Whatever food you bring with you will be most welcome). Bicycle God's Path on a tour of the city's houses of worship.

Open my heart and find writ *Italy,* where on a Sunday afternoon fifteen hundred lire will get you into an American movie featuring people in gorgeous color winning both wars and girls. Deacon stopped a GI and asked the time.

20.

SOUTHERN FRANCE was invaded on the fifteenth of August. On the sixteenth, good soldier Thomas Deacon was standing in the sub-depot PX line muttering because they were late getting the doors open. He had a net bag tucked under his shirt and twelve hundred lire in his pocket, was gaining on the cost of Italian living. That week there was no shoe polish or peanuts. Deacon was dubious about the small jar of hard candy which appeared in their place.

The Italian buyers were happy with the candy, gave him a dollar more. They were disappointed that he hadn't come up with any *mutande* or *camicette.* Deacon really felt for them since his own GI shorts were raveling and the soles of his shoes were wearing thin. His khakis had been bleached and ironed almost white. He wondered how he'd look walking around Bari wearing the wings and ribbons on the broad lapels of an Italian suit.

· Eventually things might get bad all over, but that night he had a clean shirt to pin them on, had enough money to pay the rent and to eat for a week, would have two tens to rub together when he celebrated Sunday with Tobin Bowles. He could buy a couple of cheap drinks with his bonus dollar. After the Italians had gone he idled in the park half expecting to see the British sergeant, but no one else appeared, and Deacon picked up his sack and trudged toward the area behind the docks. He found a neighborhood café with an open front and a few tables set along the sidewalk.

It was a place where the local men gathered to gossip and play cards. Triumphant cries of *brisco'* rang out and balls of silvered spittle flew into the streets. The other customers turned shifty eyes on him when he sat down, thought he was drunk or lost. They didn't know Deacon was now a resident as Italian as the *ritrovo,* might as well have been suckled by the wolf. He broke into *buona seras.* Their eyes ceased shifting, grew glazed. Ears rotated away from him.

Fuckle the wolf suckle then, and a glass of the docker's wallop, grappa, for twenty-five lire. Next week there might be cigars in the ration, he could buy champagne. The grappa was mean and raw. Kelleher had always been asking for it. He thought briefly of grappa and Kelleher, Kelleher and the field, the field and the war. They were hotting up the goddamned war. First Florence and now Southern France. The war would be . . . different. Nobody was capturing Regensburg or Steyr or Bratislava. They had to cross the whole goddamned Alps to get to Vienna. But still . . . Florence, Southern France . . . they were moving, the war would be different. He was halfway through the second front and the second drink when the British sergeant sat down. Deacon didn't recognize him for a moment.

"Curious places you choose, Yank," the sergeant said, and then to the waiter, *"Lo stesso."*

"Well well," Deacon said.

The sergeant smiled and waited for his drink. He sipped it, made a face. "The atmosphere is bad enough . . . you don't have to drink *this,* do you? Thought you'd met with your friends tonight. Didn't they give you the usual handful?"

"A little extra," Deacon said. "That's what I'm celebrating."

"Is that what you call it." The sergeant slapped his palm hard on the table and the waiter came. "Come on, Yank, we can do a little better than whatever *that* is. Two mates over a bottle, eh? *Acquavite,"* he said to the waiter.

Deacon held up his grappa. *"Lo stesso per me."*

"Never pass a free one up myself, but it's your liver. You're not drunk, are you?"

"Just getting a little loose, pal."

"Drink's not your problem, is it Tom? Tom Fool, Tom

O'Bedlam. Or Tom Tom the Piper's Son. Stole a pig and away he run. That your problem, Yank, got a porker hidden somewhere?"

"My name's Deacon."

"Got a porker hid under his bed, afraid someone's going to find it. That's all right . . . everyone's got a little dust in some corner."

"Was it Boyd? Is your name Boyd?"

"Front and center. D'you think you'll get through the week on what your gangster friends gave you tonight?"

"And then some."

"You're looking a little shabby." Boyd sipped his brandy and Deacon didn't answer. "Hard without a change of uniform. Dear as gold in this country, cloth is. Wops'll peel a tunic in half and make you two suits from it."

"I'll make out."

"Certainly you will, Tom my lad. You Yanks are full of enterprise. Thought I'd just put you in the way of something."

"Spinale already told me about the gloves."

"Don't know what you're jawing about, but it's nothing to do with gloves. You look so much the dazzling soldier . . . ever kill a man?"

"Not that I know of."

"Heat of battle and all that? I thought those ribbons meant something. Aren't they any good?"

"Good for what?"

"Old Tom the dozy lad. When you were up there in the blue, did you ever kill a man?"

"I don't know."

"You'll have to tell me what that's in aid of."

"I don't know," Deacon repeated. "A fighter blew up once. Another one caught fire."

"Wasn't anyone in them, was that it? Those robot planes Jerry has."

"No one I knew."

"Can't have much taste for it, then. Men get that way, you know, the way a dog gets a taste for the sheep."

"Do you know what the hell you're talking about, Boyd?"

Boyd slapped the table again and the waiter brought fresh drinks.

"Trying to clear my head, pal?"

"I'm all for the right amount of drink. Never hurt anyone to get a little tight now and again." He leaned forward and placed a finger at the center of Deacon's wings. "That *is* a bullet, isn't it? A bullet with wings attached to wings . . .

frightful. You Americans don't leave much to the imagination, do you?"

"What do you want?"

"Well what I have in mind, Tom boy, hasn't a bloody thing to do with aircraft. Costumes are all right if you must make do, but there's nothing like having the real thing. I'm a terrible stickler."

"And I'm a real gunner?"

"It's the training, and there you are a fair wonder with all those pretty tin strips. Nothing like the right man for the job. Get into a tight corner and he'll pull it off every time."

"Pull off shooting somebody?"

"Wouldn't think of it myself unless they were shooting at me. Roundabout sort of self-defense if you study it for a moment. Never had to, but I don't think I'd think twice about looking out for my own if someone was trying to give me stick. Don't believe you would, either."

"Boyd, old man, you're winding up a mile of bullshit and I can't see the end of it yet."

"We do what we do best," Boyd said. "I'm a good talker. And you're the one knows something about automatic weapons." Deacon frowned. "It's not all that bad, Yank. Say there's a special shipping service, a private company with its own lorries. Daresay you know a bit about this country by now. It's not all that safe, is it? Bloody brigands everywhere."

"I don't get it."

"Tom my boy, it's that simple. You're not selling your fags to the service canteen, are you? Well there's more than a handful of coppers to be had. All you're to do is ride along in the truck."

"A GI truck?"

"So bloody many of yours on the road already, they're less noticeable. All the paper you need to cover you and the driver. Eight or ten hours of your time, a thousand lire an hour. Oh what's the point of carping with a dab hand like yourself . . . say twelve thousand flat, a hundred and twenty of your dollars. Buy a smashing uniform with that . . . promote yourself to brigadier."

"I'm just loose enough, Boyd, to think that you want me to ride some kind of shotgun on a GI truck that's working the black market."

"Shotgun, that's from your Western films, isn't it?"

"No, we're back with the gangsters. When the other mob tries to stop us we shoot up their beer truck and it comes out the holes like all the spigots were turned on. Right?"

"You're amused, Tom."

"Decidedly." Deacon grinned.

"Good sense of humor never hurt," Boyd said. "Course I don't see how that's going to help keep you in clobber very long on what you're getting from your friends. Get pulled in going through that canteen line and you'll be put inside for as long a time as though you'd copped the crown jewels."

"Boyd . . ."

"And that Red Cross bint of yours. Is she that partial to holding hands that you won't have to give her a good feed now and again? It isn't that there's no decent place to live in this city, Yank, it's that a little brass is needed. You're heading for a prison cell or worse and you're not making much more than your kip at it."

"Do you walk around *watching* what I do?"

"Try to hold yourself in one piece, Tom boy."

Boyd slapped the table again. When the waiter brought the drinks Boyd paid the check.

"No thanks," Deacon said, "I've *got* a dollar."

"Give over, Yank."

"Boyd, you could get a dummy . . ." Deacon broke into a fit of laughter. "A dummy to sit in that other seat. Dress up some Eyetie."

"You're not a good listener, Tom, not at all. Firstly, we want a passenger so it looks like the most natural thing in the world, not a gang. If we can get a man who's the very thing he's supposed to be, all the better . . . avoid those odd slips that end in a balls up. Has to know his tools. Slogger from a heavy-weapons company'd do . . . the real thing, Yank, nothing less can take it. Bit of color on the chest helps, less likely to have the redcaps giving lip. Authentic there, too, someone a bit brassy . . . the way you are. Got it?"

"Got it, Boyd. But suppose I can't cut it?"

"Not to worry, Tom. You're not the first in this, you know. Never been any trouble . . . don't expect any. This isn't some cheapjack operation. Old established firm."

"All this Limey bullshit makes it sound as though you're selling tea bags."

"Wouldn't use them on a dare. Still, say something did come up . . . wouldn't it be cut or be cut? We don't know how old Tom's going to jump, do we? Have to consider that he hasn't much to lose doing what's best for all concerned. Old Tom's taken good care of himself to date. Not much doubt in my mind which side he'd come down on if it came to a pinch."

"What's that supposed to mean?"

"Come off it, Yank. You've left the party, haven't you? Things got a little too warm and you decided to take a stroll."

"I can see the only place you've been warm is in the desert, Boyd. That Limey ribbon's the Desert Star, isn't it? You get that one if you just eat enough sand."

"When will you sod off? Listen to me, Yank, it's got to be tomorrow."

"*Tomorrow?* You expect me to . . ."

"Expect you to be up and singing with the birds. One offer and only one."

"What's the rush?"

"Pressure of business. And we don't know you all that well, do we? Short notice means less chance of advertisement. I've all the time in the world for you, Yank, but I don't want you deciding that you've problems need discussing elsewhere."

"Don't worry about that, Boyd."

"Doesn't worry me a bit. Hardly in a position to broadcast your difficulties, are you?"

"Hardly. Boyd, are *you* over the hill?"

"Well we don't know that, do we? Come on, say you're in or out. It's not going to get any better or worse while we sit here jawing."

"I'm not going to get much better for sure." Deacon turned his glass round and round, still unable to find a corner. "Okay," he said.

"Don't want you getting the wind up the last minute."

"I'll hold my breath."

"Not as though we can pick up some blackleg once we've made our arrangements, is it? You're our man or you aren't . . . no two ways about it."

"I'm your man for a hundred and twenty bucks."

"Right, payment on your return."

"Next of kin get it otherwise?"

"That's my lad. Six on the hour, in front of the Red Shield Club. Nice fresh shave, dazzling soldier. You needn't wear a gardenia or anything like that . . . you'll be known."

"Do I bring my own piece?"

"Your what? A weapon, you mean . . . no, all tools provided by the firm. Six in the bright and early . . . right, Yank?"

"Right, Limey."

"Ta."

Boyd strolled off into the evening, became a shadow among the others in the street, disappeared. Deacon stared at the last drink for a moment, saw the reflection of the café's dim lamp surrounded by a nimbus of dark sky. He left the glass untouched.

*　　*　　*

214

A rare fog hid Bari the next morning. The trees dripped and the red shield of the Salvation Army wavered overhead like the escutcheon of an evil castle. Dim hoots and whistles came from the harbor. Deacon shivered and hunched his shoulders, tried to draw some warmth from a cigarette.

He listened for the whine and rattle of a truck, heard moisture dribbling from invisible walls and branches. From far down the boulevard came a sound like the drumbeat of a funeral procession. Deacon knew better—he was chief warder of the sleeping city, knew that there were no funerals scheduled for six o'clock that morning, not even his. The sound grew into the clipclop of a cab horse, the squeaking of a carriage. It became a flurry of spongy echoes bearing down on him like a runaway in infinitely slow motion. The fog swayed, then the beats slewed to one side and withdrew down some blind street.

Deacon was holding his breath but the wind was roaring through him. The dummy was nobody's man, not even for a hundred and twenty dollars, and his balance was tottering badly. Joe Rico was forty-five days old that morning, already past middle age, beginning to jerk and wobble. Deacon heard a truck highballing in the distance. He couldn't leave the dummy behind, but he knew he couldn't trust it if there was any kind of a bind. The truck's engine whined as though it were caught in the cotton grip of the fog, but at last two dim pearl buttons appeared, grew into pinwheels of light and vapor edging along the curb. Deacon threw up his hand against the glare. The truck stopped abreast of him, stood huge and shuddering while a face half lit by the dials on the dash looked down at him. Deacon nodded. The driver made no response. Deacon put his hands against the streaming metal of the frame and vaulted into the cab. The driver shot the clutch.

The wheels hummed, shot a fine spray back out of the headlights as the truck drew away from the leaking palms and hidden sidewalks. It cleared the boulevard and nosed into the billows strung between the walls of tenements, set up curious sodden reverberations. They disappeared as soon as the tires bit into the gritty surface of the through road. Streamers of fog whipped into the cab. As the day grew, the vapor turned into a dirty gray boil and snatches of sky began to appear. There was a sudden wet rush of wind off the land. The road was blown clear except for tendrils, and as the torn wall of fog retreated to the east it uncovered first the shore and then the sea plated by a harsh light. Clots of mist drifted over the water. The sky was pale and clear.

"I thought for a while you might be living under a cloud

or something," the driver said. "I never seen anything like that before."

He wore a field jacket and fatigues, the bill of his cap turned back like a jockey's, and he fumbled in his pocket for a pair of flying glasses before he turned to look directly at Deacon. Most of his face was hidden behind the green insect eyes. Deacon stared back. The driver clucked, turned his attention to the wheel as he shifted through the narrow streets of Mola di Bari. He spoke again after they were clear.

"If we get stopped you're just hitching a ride."

"What?"

"You're going someplace. You got a pass or something?"

"Boyd said you'd have papers for both of us."

"*Who* said *what?* I got a trip ticket, Charlie, what you got I don't care. If you're in Class A's you're not on any duty, so you're on pass going someplace."

"I'm okay," Deacon said.

"Say I picked you up in Barletti and you're looking to get to Taranto or Brindisi."

"Is that where we're going?"

"Jeez bud, you're the guy hitching the ride. Where you're looking to go is up to you."

The road was clear except for carts pulled over on the rounded shoulder of the road, and the sun drew the metallic glare off the water as it climbed, left an undercoat of puckered blue. Other traffic began to appear. They swept through Polignano, came to Monopoli just as it was waking. The highway rolled steadily over embankments of brush and rock falling to the coarse sand along the shore. Traffic had grown to a stream of passing vehicles which set up a monotonous whiz and rattle. The full day arrived hot and bleached and yellow.

They took the fork toward Taranto, toward the shabby Riviera along the Italian arch, and Deacon began to worry that they'd loop along that meager coast and into the spines and nettles of Calabria. But they followed the main road only a little way before veering west. Deacon had never been in that part of Italy—it was identical to the racked land he'd traveled through, dry, monotoned, shot through with streaks of rock which stretched to the Apennine foothills on the horizon. There was the same dust and the same jittery motion of the cab. He came out of his stupor when the driver slowed, his eyes flickering along the roadside, and then broke through a thin screen of brush.

They parked in a clearing partly shielded from the road. Deacon got down and stretched, his ears popping in the sudden stillness, his feet buzzing from the vibration of the floorboards. The driver reached behind his seat and took out a sack.

"Pretty close to right on the button," he said. "We don't go off on time, we don't go off so good."

Deacon didn't know the time and he didn't know where he was. The driver waved the sack.

"Little chowdown," he said. "Don't look like you brought any."

"Nobody told me to."

"That's a shame." He took out a huge sandwich and a liter bottle of milk. "Maybe there's still some of that K-ration under the seat."

Deacon felt along the floorboards. He touched dustballs and oily rags, and when his fingertips brushed over a waxed box he shifted his position to get a better reach. Straining, his eyes screwed up, he saw the piece, a Thompson sub-machine gun. It was held out of sight under the dash in a bracket riveted to the firewall. Four of the extra-long ammunition clips were fastened next to it. Deacon stabbed after the box until he got it.

"Hey, you found one," the driver said. "What'd you get . . . breakfast, lunch or dinner?"

Deacon looked at the box. "Breakfast."

"That's the best."

The driver's mouth was flaked with rich brown crust. Deacon spooned out the fatty egg paste with the can lid and spread it on the crackers. It had a rubbery flavor. He looked at the envelope of soluble coffee.

"No cup," the driver said. "You could squirt it in your mouth and make a lot of spit." He laughed. "There's a water bag on the front of the truck." He took a long drink of milk.

Deacon threw away the coffee envelope, swigged from the canvas bag. He perched on the fender and chewed on the fruit bar, remembered how Fitzgerald used to save them for him . . . *Lots of iron*.

"Where are we?" he asked.

"You get out your map and I'll show you. No map, huh? Don't happen to have one myself." The driver finished his milk and put the bottle back in the sack. "That's real pretty, that stuff you got. If I was you I'd put in for a war-bond tour. I hear those guys get laid left and right."

"I'll think about it."

"There's something else we got to think about. It don't matter on the way out, Charlie, cause I don't have to know shit from Shinola about you. But coming in we're going to be heavy in the back, and it's just you and me against the world. I appreciate you got all kinds of decorations, but I

217

think you should show me you can use that chopper or not."

"I saw it."

"I *saw* you see it, and I was happy you seemed to recognize what it was. Fact is, I don't get so thrilled about breaking people in. They could just dress up a regular guy instead of digging up somebody like you."

"You're not a good listener either. Ask Boyd."

"Ask who? Jeez bud, you're not going to give me a whole bunch of names for recommendations, are you? Just let me see do you know your ass from a hole in the ground about that piece."

"You want me to fire here?"

"Well what we got is a secret underground range. Let me see can I find the fake bush that makes it work. Why don't you just take the chopper down and get yourself a clip? But don't put it in . . . that's against the firing-range procedure. They trained me so GI I never got over doing things by the numbers."

This is a piece and not a gun. You will all unbutton your pants and take out your gun and hold it in your right hand . . . the Moslems among you may use the left. I repeat a direct order . . . you will unbutton your pants and take out your gun and hold it in your right hand. By numbers . . . one . . . two. You are holding your gun and I am holding a piece. You will recover by the numbers . . . one . . . two.

Deacon took the Thompson and a clip from the firewall. The driver watched him, one hand in the sagging pocket of his field jacket. He picked up the empty K-ration box and gestured Deacon into the brush, followed closely. They found another clearing. Deacon stood holding the Thompson and the clip in separate hands while the driver scaled the box to the other side.

"You can hit anything further than that I'll stand around and hold it on my head like William Tell," the driver said.

"That's about maximum. Okay now?"

The driver nodded and stepped behind him. Deacon jammed the clip into his belt and worked the bolt, felt the toughness and power of the weapon as soon as he touched it. The chamber was empty.

This is a sub-machine gun, forty-five caliber, which you will continue to call a piece. It is an impractical weapon, a thundergun. It has no range. If a bull is more than twenty yards from you, you will not be able to hit him directly in the ass. But if you do accidentally hit him anywhere at all, he will fall down. If you hit a man in the shoulder, with this weapon, it will knock him down, it will break his shoulder.

Deacon slammed the long clip into the magazine and put a

218

round into the chamber. He slipped the safety and took a rough sight along the barrel. Beyond the clearing he could see a group of peasants working through a distant field, their bodies jackknifing like cheap toys. Deacon allowed his cheek to brush the stock, caught the K-ration box in the rear notch and brought up the blade sight and slipped the safety. He moved his finger into the trigger guard and curled it around the trigger.

You will not take a deep breath and hold it until you are about to fart. You will not jerk the trigger. You will take a deep breath and you will release it slowly, and as you are releasing it you will caress the trigger, you will stroke it, you will pinch it the way you would a nipple on a pretty woman's tit.

Deacon took a deep breath and exhaled slowly. The trigger felt cool against his creased joint, and as the finger crooked tighter and moved back toward him it snapped him perfectly into time and the gun exploded. Dirt and stones and pieces of the box flew into the air. He recovered, sighted, fired again, hit near the box and then on it and then skittered the shreds of the cardboard into the box.

"Okay," the driver shouted.

Deacon swung the blade to a sapling, plugged brief bursts into it. The driver kept shouting and Deacon kept plugging into the flying bark and falling leaves until the top half of the tree heeled over. He removed the clip, cleared the live round from the chamber and left the breech open, held the weapon braced on his hip, his grip at the neck of the stock, and turned to face the driver. There was no pulse, no sweat. His ears rang.

"We didn't need all that what with the price of forty-five rounds," the driver said, "but I guess I got to believe you ought to have a medal for learning how to shoot at least."

"Your ass is a hole in the ground, Charlie," Deacon said.

"Jeez bud . . ."

"You remind me of all those Joe Balls by the numbers range instructors strutting around like cowtown gunnies. They're still back there slopping up PX beer and the guys they put through school are out getting killed."

"I'm an overseas veteran myself, bud. You don't want to confuse me with some stateside DI."

"You'd shit if somebody really started to shoot at you."

"I might at that."

Deacon showed his teeth and turned the Thompson slightly. "Empty," he said.

"I know it is. That's why I'm not getting too nervous. You

got something pissing you off, bud, it's better you don't face in my direction because I got my own problems."

The driver was very still, almost like a green toad in his fatigues and sunglasses. The smell of powder pinched at Deacon's nose. He shifted his weight and cocked his head. The other man remained motionless. Deacon nodded, started back to the truck, the Thompson still on his hip. When they got there the driver threw him a box of ammunition.

"Why don't you fill that clip?" he said and stood watching. "Like I said, I don't go for breaking people in. At least it looks like you know what you're doing and I figure you probably got enough on you it don't help any they get you for armed robbery on top of it. That's good for twenty years hard just by itself. But I don't appreciate it much you're starting to break balls with me because we got no problems, bud, and all we got to do is hold hands all day."

Deacon finished loading the clip and lit a cigarette. It hung straight and still in his fingers, the smoke rising without a tremor.

"That why you're still keeping that thing on me?" he asked.

The driver smiled and waved the pocket of the jacket. "Nothing personal. Say I'm keeping my hand warm. Look, you don't want to feature this is going to be like Wells Fargo with Indians back of every rock. We got all kinds of paper to cover the load, so just stand easy. But I wouldn't advise you to kind of lose interest if we get in any kind of a bind, even if it comes to popping. Nobody's going to bother to ask which one of us is the bad guy before they start popping back. I know you're very brave and all, but you want to give that a little thought."

"I'm still thinking."

"That's good, it clears the head. I tell you what, shove that clip in and put a round in the chamber. And don't bother to put it on safe. I hope you're thinking about why we're going to be running with that piece open."

He didn't take his hand out of his jacket until Deacon fitted the clip and charged the Thompson and racked it. They backed onto the road and the driver kicked the truck into gear and went winging away. The peasants in the field were still jerking spastically.

The driver kept a steady pace, matched his speedometer against his watch. For nearly an hour they swung along lightly used roads in a great loop northeast, back in the direction they had come. Deacon felt cool and easy. It was as though working the weapon had worked something in him, as though he'd fed himself into the mechanism along with the clip, fed something into the trigger and through the trachea of the spring and into the slick works of the receiver where the bolt compressed it and the firing pin snapped thunder. A mass of shredded rags and wire had gone screaming from the muzzle, all there'd been to Joe Rico. The dummy couldn't cut it, had been blown away. The Deacon left crouching in the chamber was all steel, oil and bitter fumes. He ran the thumb of his nail in the grooved joint of his finger.

The driver let up on the accelerator and tooled along at a more deliberate pace. They topped a crest and Deacon saw the warehouses of a supply dump spread across the fields below, wheat growing right up to the barbed-wire fence. The dump was crisscrossed by blacktop streets laid out foursquare, and the access road was broader and better kept than most of the highways they'd been on. A guard in dirty fatigues waved them through the gate without inspecting their papers. They were in the kingdom of the ant army who'd scraped the land barren and then thrown up metallic mounds. The ants were bustling and banging and shouting as they worked fork lifts and hand trucks, loaded at one platform and discharged at the next. All their slavish energy went into endless labor in a remote facility which served no visible airfield or port or operational encampment. They had no queen, but there was a pretty flag winding stripes in the wind.

It was as simple as Boyd had said it would be. They backed to the ramp of a warehouse and the driver unclipped a sheaf of papers from the sun visor, got down and went into the weighmaster's shack. He came out with a tech sergeant wearing glasses, the eyes of both men hidden by a trick of the sun so that the driver's shone like a polished green shell and the weighmaster's like ground steel. Two men leaned against the building's sliding doors and very slowly walked them open. A fork lift came out of the depths like a pronged beast, another appeared balancing a stack of wooden crates. The crates were transferred from the lift to the interior of the truck while the driver kept tally against a set of flimsies he held.

Deacon sat facing out into the depot while the ants thumped and grunted behind him, struggled to lever burdens half their weight. The truck filled slowly. At noon a siren loosed a low growl and the men paused and straightened. The tech sergeant shouted at them to go on. Work had stopped at all the other platforms. The men swore and bent to loading again, their OD undershirts splotched, their shoulders shining with sweat. When they were finished there was a rattle of chains as the tailgate was fastened, the sawing sound of ropes being drawn through grommets as the canvas was tied closed.

They eased away from the platform, and Deacon looked back until he saw the warehouse doors come together. The weighmaster stood watching the truck, disks flashing around his eyes. The truck slowed for the sentry at the gate, but he waved them through. They came to a full stop at the highway while the driver looked carefully both ways, then eased out, kicked and kicked again until they were highballing along.

"What are we hauling?" Deacon asked. The other's eyes shifted behind the glasses. "Some kind of jackets, according to the crates. I don't know my stock numbers yet, Charlie. What are they, those infantry jobs . . . tanker's? There'll be a hot time in Bari while they're freezing up on the line."

"You could go up there and help them out if you felt real bad."

"It looked like that tech was in on it."

"Jeez bud."

"Okay," Deacon said. "I'm just here for the ride."

"*Now* you got it. Just stand easy until you get the nod to go into your act. Let's see can you give them MPs a good performance if you have to."

They pushed on northeast, skirted Basilicata's edge, towns like those where Deacon had spent a night or a dismal afternoon. The sun was strong enough to bleach shadows, and Deacon could find no trace of the staffless wanderer he'd once been. He was gone, and so was the dummy, and the new man was a jackbooted shotgun squinting against the dust of the trail and picking fragments of string jerky from his teeth.

They made another stop, on the far side of a broad shallow stream with a rutted ford next to the ruin of a bridge which had been blown. The water came only to the wheel hubs, and there was a rattle of stones as the truck pitched over the uneven bed. Deacon helped empty three cans of gas into the truck's tank and then, while the driver opened his fly and amused himself making patterns in the sand, stood looking at the countryside. There was a castle, small but unmistakable, crumbling along a ridge. Deacon stooped to pick at something in the sand. It was a rifle cartridge casing, but not from an American weapon. Thirty caliber, probably from an Enfield, probably a remnant of a small action at the bridge —cries in a variety of British accents, in German or even Italian, the *castello* watching and slowly disintegrating through it all. Open Italy's heart and find writ the dirty scrawls of a hundred armies.

They went on, the new man stiff and restless from the long ride, almost disinterested when a split gate appeared across the road ahead, the arms striped in railroad-crossing diagonals. Vehicles lined up on the other side of the barrier were being checked by a pair of MPs. The driver pulled up and put the truck in neutral. It idled as one of the MPs sauntered over.

He checked the trip ticket and swung around to the other side of the cab, his hand already out for Deacon's pass. The MP had a dent along his temple and the eye on that side was pulled slightly askew. He wore a combat infantryman's badge but no ribbons. His hand dropped when he saw Deacon's decorations. His mouth twisted and a queer combination of recognition and contempt came into his eyes.

"Well lookit the pretty soldier boy," he said. "That oughta get you a doughnut at the Red Cross."

"I'll take anything that's free," Deacon said.

"The only thing you ever got free was whatever the Krauts put in you. I gave up on wearing that shit. You figure it does any good?"

"Hasn't yet."

"Don't hold your breath until it does. On your way to Bari?"

"That's right."

"They're not going to stop traffic for you to cross the street, soldier boy. You'll have a club up your ass before you get your pants all the way down."

"It's a rough war."

"Rougher than a cob. Maybe you should try Corato . . . they don't run a patrol after five."

"I'll tell them who sent me."

The MP grinned humorlessly, then went to raise the barrier. After they'd passed through the driver slewed his eyes at Deacon and smirked. Deacon chipped him a stony look and the driver opened his mouth, closed it and gripped the wheel. They plowed on through the waning afternoon, picked up the coast road and cleared Mola, came into the sprawl at Bari's outskirts. Neither the fog nor Deacon's going had changed the city. Evening traffic flowed, trolleys clanked, palms rattled in a brisk wind. Street hawkers were closing their stands and soldiers were idling past storefronts. The driver stopped directly in front of the Salvation Army building. He handed Deacon an envelope.

"I wanted to get some clothes," Deacon said.

"Jeez bud, why don't you see your supply sergeant?"

"Thanks for the buggy ride, Charlie."

"If you can let me know next time you're ready for a trip, maybe I can go on sick call."

The driver held the clutch chattering at its edge, gestured Deacon out. Deacon got down and the truck pulled away from the curb, was lost in the crowd of others beating home for evening chow.

21.

THEIR SUNDAY song had to be in the singing. A private dining room with curtains billowing through open French doors, man and woman elemental while a pretty boy in the garden carried the tenor melody, the accompanying concertina and mandolin fingered by players whose smiles were brilliant and empty. A long stretch of Adriatic coast broken into rock and sand, along its edge a company in red neckerchiefs and white petticoats dipping their feet tirelessly in a tarantella. Linen and music and the spark of candles, street cries fading with the fading light, voices turned to night's calls. The bitter espresso beneath the tongue mellowed by the sweet fire of Strega, the lord in his cloak and the lady in her wrap shown by a fluttering maître d' to the great staircase, outside a coachman in glistening boots and plug hat already lighting the cab lamps which would show the way.

They were at the Adriatic's edge, but the sea was curbed by a wall of concrete broken by bombs, and the water was fitfully a hard dirty blue under clouds which flocked across the face of the sun, their edges burned silver. Not a private dining room, not much more than a small cut above the typical neighborhood *trattorie* in the dock area. The meal had consisted of an adequate antipasto, gray macaroni in marinara sauce, a squid and mussel plate which they'd both passed. The *melone* was sweet, but it didn't clear the bitter taste of ersatz coffee.

"I'm glad we came here," Tobin Bowles said.

Carlo had found the place, made the arrangements. He'd gouged Deacon, but not enough to hurt him, not enough to empty the bag of gold earned by the once-a-week badman who sat with his foot propped up on the dash, beneath his heel a mortal raspberry for anyone who dared challenge him. Not that Deacon's new image was that of a swaggering desperado. There was no new image—only an old one buried in an anonymous field, a heap of broken strings and levers unmourned and unattended, the Unknown Dummy whose only votive light had been the flicker of a Thompson.

"I've been to places so crowded with marble and gilt and palms . . . almost *fetid*. Too removed, Deacon. This is much more real."

She'd kept her promise, given him both morning and afternoon of that Sunday.

"Did you notice the wreck of that real house down the street somebody must have been blown apart in?" he asked.

"I am *not* ghoulish. I wish no one any harm and I'm sorry for the things that happened . . . but that doesn't mean we have to pretend they didn't."

They were into their second bottle of wine. Most of the wine had gone into Deacon.

"Toby Bowles goes to war," he said. "It sounds like a movie series. Torchy Blaine in Bari."

"I wish you wouldn't laugh at me."

"Tobin . . ."

"No, really. I *have* tried to make you understand. I don't know why everyone has to be so terribly terribly ironic . . . sardonic."

"That dogface captain giving you a hard time again?"

"He drinks too much . . . like you."

"I wouldn't drink too much with you, Tobin. It's only wine. We're living the life Other Ranks do *not* live, *tesoro mio*."

"Where did you learn the language? You're not Italian, are you?"

"No longer any part or parcel. I learned it from a book. But there's no profit in speaking Italian in Italy . . . nobody listens to you and nobody answers."

"It must help when you're in the interior. What's it like living at an airfield there every day?"

"Beautiful. We'll get a jeep and I'll take you on a personal tour. You can interview all the old sports. They're gone now, they all went home . . . or they went the long way." Deacon closed his eyes and tried to remember how many days had passed. He lost track. "Yep, they're all gone," he said.

"I thought everyone went home as soon as his tour was over."

"They do. Me, you mean? Except me. I didn't finish mine."

"Oh." She dipped her head briefly into the wine. "Because of being wounded?"

"Something like that. But I can finish if I want to . . . it's still there." Deacon looked out into the harbor. "I ought to take you up to . . . I have money, you know. There's no family business but I have money and we can rent a boat and sail up the coast to this place . . . Trani." He shivered. "Beautiful park . . . we can have a picnic."

"I don't understand about your tour. What's still there?"

Deacon used his finger to write the number nineteen in the air. "Waiting just the way you were waiting at that dance. How could you be sure I'd be there?"

"Never doubted it a minute."

"Tobin, I'm going to buy a watch just for you and me, just to keep the time since I met you."

"Deacon, please don't . . ."

"Never doubt it for a minute. I'm going to compete with the ranks who are not Other Ranks, get a jeep and a boat and a villa better than any Limey has. And we won't have to bother with any *real* places like this."

"It was nice."

"It *is* nice. Tobin, I'm at your service because you've been at my service."

"Then tell me about that." She put her finger against the ribbon bar.

"No story, all tale."

"Don't be like that."

"Oh Tobin . . ."

Deacon turned to look out over the water shaved white under gusts of wind. His glance drifted along the sea wall, stopped, started away, then stopped again at a figure lifted straight out of a montage of flying coveralls and whirling propellers and a welter of bottles.

"Wow," he said.

"Deacon? What's the matter?"

He hunched over the table and pointed a thumb over his shoulder. "That's Toole."

"It's who?" She craned her neck. "Who is it, someone you know?"

"Is he still there?"

"I see someone drinking out of a bottle . . . a master sergeant."

"He got promoted."

"Do you know him?"

"Jesus Christ, it's Toole. He should've gone home. What's he doing?"

"He's still drinking . . . now he's stopped. Is there something wrong?"

He turned in his seat and stared. Toole's face seemed to swim across the walk, to grow larger and larger until Deacon could make out the familiar furrows cut even deeper into the cheeks. The jetsam had floated past Trani, had come to shore right at Deacon's feet. Toole looked around slowly, right into the open café and past him. Deacon's arm went up reflexively, as though retreat or the national anthem had been played. Something rumbled in his chest and he shouted. Toole's head snapped, he began to walk toward the café. Deacon pushed back his chair and stood, felt a wave of blood rushing to his head. Toole's eyes crinkled, then lit.

"Hey there, Preacher . . . hey, buddy. Well what the hell."

His uniform was stained and unpressed, his chevrons frazzled at the edges. He needed a shave.

"Tooley . . ." Deacon began.

"Buy you a drink, Preacher." He waved a bottle, stopped and blinked when he saw the girl. "Excuse me."

"Tobin Bowles," Deacon said, "this is John Toole."

"Pleased to meet you," Toole said. "Well, goddamn, Preacher, you're doing . . . excuse me, Miss, haven't been out in polite society lately. I mean, you don't get to meet many . . ."

"Neither do I, Sergeant. Won't you sit down?"

"I don't want to . . ."

"Sit down, Tooley, sit down."

"All right . . . all right. Love to." Toole struggled with a chair. "Got some brandy here . . . good stuff. Like to buy you all a drink."

"None for me, thanks, but you go right ahead."

Deacon called the waiter and asked for glasses. The man stood stiffly by the table, his eyes cutting at Toole.

"*È vietato recare del alcool nel ristorante,*" the waiter said.

"*Che peccato. In tal caso, il conto . . . senza mancia.*"

"*Mi dispiace, signore, il legge dice . . .*"

"*Il legge dice che ho bisogno de due bicchieri, mi costa cento lire ogni.*" The waiter shrugged. "*Ed il conto, per piacere,*" Deacon added.

The glasses were brought. Deacon paid the check. It was another gouging. Deacon didn't care. He gave the waiter an enormous tip, got a withering look in return.

"That was very impressive," the girl said.

"Sounded like Torazzi for a minute, Preacher. Where'd you pick it all up?"

"Could have waved a couple of bills and got him to do the same thing." Deacon said. He watched Toole pour the drinks. "Whatever happened to him?"

"Torazzi? He went home. Last I heard they'd made him warrant officer and set him up at some gunnery school." Toole looked at the girl. "I hope I'm not interrupting anything."

"Please," she said, "I'd love to just sit here and listen."

"Old home week. Well, here's to it, Preacher." They drank. "This Torazzi we're talking about put in seventy-five missions," Toole said to the girl. "Finished up before I did, in fact. The only guy I ever knew did that, Preacher . . . the whole shot."

"He was a wheel."

"Wasn't anybody you'd be too crazy about, but he really put it on the line." Toole held up two fingers. "DFCs, and they were putting him in for all kinds of extra stuff."

"Why did he do that?" she asked.

"He was a hero," Deacon said.

"That's right . . . that's right." Toole sipped at his drink. "He . . . the hell with Torazzi. I saw the citation on the bulletin board when you got your DFC, Preacher."

"Tell me about it," she said.

"It was only a survival badge, Toby."

"That's what they gave me mine for, I guess," Toole said. "The Preacher here walked away from a real hearse . . . came in and piled up with eight stiffs. You and Kenny Quinn . . . remember? All they ever gave Kenny was the Heart. One of those legs he broke healed short. They sent him home . . . six missions."

"Lucky," Deacon said.

"That doesn't sound very lucky," she said, "a short leg."

"Well . . . I guess it depends . . . anyway you can make it looks like a good way sometimes, Miss." Toole toyed with the bottle a moment before pouring fresh drinks. "Old home week, Preacher . . . there they go, there they go. Finger got himself put in for a Congressional. Crazy guy. It was posthumous . . . posthumous. Caught a whole mess of shit over Steyr. Sorry, Miss, but I got so used to . . . it's the only way I think about flak now. Anyway, the aft section was all busted up, and Finger held off two attacks all by himself with one arm practically hanging off. Didn't have any blood left by the time they got in. Got put in for a Congressional . . . came out a DSC."

"How about you, John?" Tobin Bowles asked brightly.

Toole tried to peer down at his own chest. "Not me," he said. "The usual, whatever I was entitled to, I guess. I'm not too sorry I missed out on the Heart. Just so I came out on the other side . . . forty-nine plus one. As of July tenth there was no more room on the scorecard."

"Hey, you finished early, Tooley."

"I didn't know whether it was early or late, just so it was over. Funny thing . . . forty-nine sweats and what I finally pooped in on was a milk run to Southern France. Don't
228

know how it was with you, Preacher, but I had this crazy
. . . I had this *crazy* idea I wanted that last one to be like
gangbusters . . . fighters and all kinds of shit and everything,
so I could get down and kick that lousy bird to death. But
there it was, Southern France, no sweat no strain. I got down
and I could hardly believe it . . . it was like all of them'd
been milk runs. They had an alert the next day, and I
couldn't get drunk enough that night to get it out of my
head, you know . . . that I still had to go up, come in on a
real hot one before I was finished."

"How come you didn't go home, Tooley?"

"To tell the truth, Preacher, I wasn't too eager. Little rag-
gedy-assed, you know." Toole looked at the girl. She nodded
and smiled. "I mean, get back and get that thirty-day furlough and they might turn me right around, or send me out
to the Pacific."

"Probably could have beaten it."

"That's right . . . that's right. Just wasn't too eager to try."
Toole paused a moment, sipped at his drink. "Anyway, they
put together some kind of orientation course for the recruits
over at Wing, and a couple of us who'd finished they asked if
we wanted to be wheels . . . you know, field conditions and
all that crap, give the recruits a snow job on what they were
really getting their asses into. Tell them the truth and they'd
run out to get malaria or clap or something . . . anyway, it
was full rank and flight pay and overseas pay . . . that's how
I made Master."

"Sounds like a good deal," Deacon said.

"Remember when we couldn't even get replacements, when
they'd send those birds up tied with string? Got time for all
this orientation crap now, pay you the same as when they
were shooting back." Toole swung his head to the harbor and
a gust of gritty wind blew into the café and whipped his hair
stiff and upright. "I transferred over to Wing," he said. They
waited while he wiped absently at one eye and then turned
back to the table. "Couldn't cut it, Preacher. The duty was all
right . . . good chow, shared a room with this other guy in a
regular building. Wasn't expected to go up more than enough
to keep on flying status. Walk around in Class A's all day,
you know, like some Joe Balls big-time operator. Couldn't cut
it."

"Too chickenshit?"

"No, they didn't bother us . . . not all that many guys
around who'd finished a tour. The thing was . . . well, they
went right on combat duty after the orientation deal, and I
got to . . ." Toole pushed at his glass. "I was the last guy,
you know, the only one between them and going on combat

status, and I got to feel like *I* was the one sending them up
. . . standing there waving a handkerchief. There they go,
there they go . . . like one of those lousy funeral directors in
Operations."

"It didn't *really* have anything to do with you, did it?"
Tobin Bowles asked.

"That's right . . . that's right. They kept telling me that.
Hey . . . hey, Preacher, you were still in the hospital when I
transferred out. Looks like you got straightened out, I mean
that everything worked out all right . . . I mean, did you go
back to the old outfit to finish up?"

"No." Deacon drank down the second glass of brandy.
"You on your way home now?"

"That's right, going home. I'm over at the repple-depple,
waiting on a boat. They wanted me to *fly* back." Toole
smiled sourly. "Man, I'm *finished* . . . to tell the truth, I'm
not too eager to get started on that furlough. Probably be
here awhile . . . hey Miss, you don't have a friend, do you? I
mean, I'm a little drunk right now . . . just a little sipping
drunk . . . but I can get shined up."

"You ought to fly back, Tooley," Deacon said. "They're
not going to put you back on combat duty after that furlough."

"Sure . . . I can beat it."

Toole looked out at the sea again, not jetsam at all but a
king with a furrowed face, a worn king waiting for Charon's
ferry.

"They kept telling me I had nothing to do with it . . . the
recruits, I mean. And it wasn't as rough . . . you know how
it was, Preacher." He studied the girl. "We had a hundred
twenty percent casualties one month . . . crews, not airplanes." Toole smiled and gave a little shrug. "What the hell.
Goddamned recruits, they would've sent them up as soon as
they landed, like they did us, if it hadn't been for that orientation." He filled Deacon's glass, but not his own. "See that,
Miss? I can be a perfect gentleman at all times. It *wasn't* as
rough, Preacher, but you know headquarters. Burn one out
and they'd dig up another one . . . always somebody swinging that big hammer, always a couple of hot ones. At least
they didn't have to worry about Ploesti."

"*Ploesti*, they finally took *Ploesti* out?"

"Oh sure . . . didn't you hear about that the other day?
The Russians took it out. They captured it."

"*Infantry?*"

"That's right, after all that time we put in there. They were
still producing. What's Frank used to say . . . 'They got another whole Fifteenth Air Force up there'? Sure, they were
230

still producing when those *doggies* walked in and took it out."

"Jesus Christ," Deacon said. He felt as though the wind were blowing clear from the Balkans.

"Frank really sweated the big P, didn't he? I mean, he used to dream about it. Hey Preacher, do you know what? Old Gruber, with all that time training in the States and all that time over here, old Frank never got Kraut one . . . not even a probable. Don't know if he even got a chance to shoot at a fighter. All that crap he went through and he ended up not doing anybody any good. The doggies just walked right in and took it over."

The wind blew needles into Deacon's face, he felt a chill.

"Dreamed about it all the time," Toole continued. "Dreamed himself dead."

The girl turned her head away and held her hat. "Tooley, why don't you wind that up?" Deacon said. Toole picked up his empty glass and put his tongue in it. "Forget it, Tooley," Deacon said.

"That's right . . . that's right." Toole's eyes were dull, and his face was slack and empty. "You're the Preacher, you're the chaplain . . . punch my ticket so I can go home and say a little prayer. Son of a bitch, you sound like one. That's *Frank Gruber* I'm talking about . . . blew him right out of sight. Well not all of him, Preacher . . . when we got back they flushed the turret out with a hose." Toole leaned over and spat on the floor. "That's old Frank, like somebody hawked up an oyster on the revetment."

"I have to go now," Tobin Bowles said. Her head was still turned away.

"All right, Tooley . . ."

"Shit on you, forget it and all right. Son of a bitch, that's like me starting to think I flew fifty milk runs. I *didn't*. And it wasn't anybody *but* Frank back there looking like somebody's snot. Okay, Preacher, I'm forgetting I lived with him and I trained with him . . . but they still *got* him up there, didn't they? That *place* got him, it was after him right from the minute we started our tour. He knew it, he dreamed . . . that lousy shithole. It was that motherfucking *Ploesti* that reached up and tore his ass apart."

Toole swallowed and closed his eyes. The girl stood up. Deacon was oozing like a rock, not really sweating, and he felt as gray as the wind. He touched Toole's shoulder.

"Okay Tooley," he said.

A tear sneaked from the corner of one of Toole's lids. He wiped at it, sniffed, then opened his eyes and brushed Deacon's hand away, reached out to the girl.

"Excuse me, Miss, I didn't mean . . ."

Tobin Bowles walked out of the restaurant. Deacon tried not to watch as Toole took out a handkerchief and blew his nose.

"Balls," he said, "I didn't want her to . . . hey, Preacher, maybe you can get her to come back and have a drink."

"I've got to go, Tooley."

"Hey, now, I'm going to be here until they find a boat. Ask her if she knows somebody . . ."

"So long, Tooley," Deacon said.

He left without looking back, afraid of being pillared in the salt air, sprinted after Tobin Bowles. He took her arm while they walked briskly along the sea wall. At the first street corner they turned out of the wind.

"I'm sorry," Deacon said.

"Oh *God*."

"He was a little loaded. He didn't . . ."

"And tired and dirty."

The wine and brandy swelled up in Deacon and almost dizzied him. He nearly lurched. His hands went out and he grabbed both the girl's arms.

"Why, that's what you look like when you come out the other side, Tobin lady. That's a real soldier . . . John Francis Toole."

She looked up at him with hazel eyes drenched in their own kind of sorrow. Deacon could feel the distance between them. It was the thickness of a tear.

"God . . . and then both of you telling me you're *sorry*."

She was little girl blue used to the blaring of the brass, but shaken by the echo of the big drum. When he tried to pull her close she stiffened, and he was left with one arm awkwardly draped around her shoulder.

"It's all right, Tobin," he said. "It doesn't have anything to do with you."

"Deacon, that hearse he was talking about . . . you were in some kind of crash?"

"For Jesus sake, didn't you get enough?"

"I want you to tell me that, just that. A crash where everyone else was killed?"

"Quinn got out with me. Some of them were already dead. Our navigator . . ."

"No, I don't want to hear anymore." She took a deep breath and pulled her shoulders straight. Deacon's arm slid off. "But that doesn't mean I might not ask about it some other time."

"What can anybody *tell* you, Tobin?"

"I might ask you."

"Go ahead," Deacon said. "I might throw up the way Toole did."

She took off her glove and put her arm through his and took his hand. They began walking, the afternoon's last light shifting between clouds, the wind blocked by buildings. Something other than the wind was running in the streets. September was near, and the end of the summer of the first year of the Italian war. Deacon felt the chill again. A draft was banking Italy's sun, whipping the war into a raging circle which was growing smaller and smaller.

"I'd like to go back now," the girl said. "I don't know what time it is, Deacon, and I don't care."

"Okay."

"Not for a tea dance or anything like that. Not for someone else, Deacon."

"Sure," he said.

"Don't you believe me?"

"Sure I do."

"It doesn't make any difference, is that it? You can't win because there is no victory in this girl?"

"Forget it," Deacon said.

"I *won't*. He was *right*, Deacon. Is that why they do it, is that the only way you can get in touch . . . get into bed with the war?"

He stopped. Their arms unlocked and she withdrew her hand and turned her head.

"It still wouldn't have anything to do with you," he said. "That's like trying to punch someone else's ticket."

"It's something I can do though, isn't it?"

"If that's all that's left, Tobin . . ."

"But it *is* left, isn't it?"

She said it in a harsh whisper. Still looking over his shoulder, she fumbled her hand across his chest and touched his cheek. When he brushed her fingers with the corner of his mouth they contracted like a bloom's closing. Deacon caught lightly at her arm, but she twisted it out of his grasp and began to put on her glove.

"Is that true . . . what you said about money and a jeep and a decent place to stay? I know that sounds awful, Deacon, but it's just like Toilet Bowles to be worried about the things that really matter."

"It's . . . I can get them, Toby."

"Maybe we *should* go sailing next week, while the weather's good," she said grimly.

"Sure."

"To that place you were telling me about."

"We can find a place, Toby."

"Not just any place." A queer edgy hostility came into her eyes. She put one gloved hand into the other and stared down at them. "I might not always understand what you're saying, I might think . . ." Her head came up and she looked almost bewildered. "Deacon, we can afford one more Sunday, can't we? I mean . . . can't we see after that?"

"Sure we can. *Fin'oggi a otto.*"

She stood very straight and serious for a moment, one hand still in the other. Deacon felt his chin sag, felt as though someone were draining the blood out of him. The girl nodded sharply twice and, without their having touched, she turned on her heel and walked away.

As the war's circle grew fiercer, it grew smaller. It was drawing away from Deacon, leaving him behind as it had the scenes of action in southern Italy, as it was even now leaving guttered Normandy behind, the Russian steppe. And more, almost more than he could conceive, it was withdrawing from *his* battlefields. There had never been any front or rear in the air war, only a six- or seven-hundred-mile charge of winged cavalry into a space thousands of feet above the earth, into an area totally unmarked, artificially constructed by compass and sextant and altimeter. If the targets on the ground were being eliminated, the square-mile boundaries of limitless combat above them were being erased in fact and in memory. There was none of war's litter in the sky; it was swept clean and stainless minutes after a disaster. There would be no graves registration team of weeping angels, no field of celestial crosses, only the destructive sun and the dead moon and the totally indifferent stars.

There were nineteen missions waiting up there for Deacon. His watch had been broken, but the time etched into its face had gone on and on, stretched into nearly three months while he hid first in the tent and then in the hospital and finally in the shabby corpus of Joe Rico. The nineteen were still waiting, but not all in the same place, not all in the same time, as they once had. The war's contracting had taken both time and place with it. At least one of the missions would have been to Ploesti. Deacon could never make it up. Someone had made him a loan by flying in his place, and he could never repay it. That faceless member of the Great Crew might be dead or alive, might even have gone home, but he had been up there paying out the minutes of his life to a sky whose clock was keeping track of what Deacon owed.

All Romania had surrendered by the time he made his second trip. He had all the cigarettes he could smoke, money in his pocket and more to come. He'd brought his lunch, charged the piece without having to be told, endured a garrulous driver with a faint Western accent. All Romania had surrendered, and he found himself at a small dump somewhere near Caserta, willing to kill a man.

The truck had been loaded without incident . . . with the combined complicity of the weighmaster and the guard at the gate and the commanding officer, for all Deacon knew. He wasn't interested, wasn't involved. He sat in the cab trying to get hold of an invisible something dancing in the air. A young warehouseman wandered to the front of the truck and rubbed at the spattered bumper. He peered, squatted, then wiped his hand on the seat of his fatigues and came back to the passenger's side.

"That the 808th or 909th?" he asked. "I can't make it out."

Deacon stared at him. The man's narrow shoulders were shining with sweat, the straps of his OD undershirt were sodden. His heated scalp gave off the fragrance of hair oil.

"Where you guys from?" the warehouseman said.

The driver swung into his seat and leaned over with a sunny smile. "Tacoma, boy," he said, "the garden spot of the Pacific."

"I mean what outfit you from?"

"I tell you, there's a sweet woman waiting just outside that outfit's gate, and it's a long, long road and I'm not about to waste any of her time."

"That's what I mean . . . we never load anybody but local outfits here. This some kind of special deal?"

That was when Deacon could have killed him. He knew absolutely that if the warehouseman had suddenly pulled out a whistle and attempted to blow for all the world's MPs, he could have unracked the Thompson and butchered him in two seconds.

"Tell you," the driver said, "why don't you ask that fella back there with all the stripes? He's the one has to sign this stuff out, and he doesn't look too worried. What you want to do, son, is get some old gal to play with you awhile and take your mind off trying to make corporal."

The driver started the engine. Deacon looked down at the warehouseman with cold pity. The figure seemed to flicker in the sun, to grow luminous and take on the Christlike nimbus of a holy martyr. And Deacon was ready with hammer and nails.

"I just *made* corporal," the man said.

"No wonder it's taking so goddamned long to win this war."

The driver put in the clutch and spurted away from the

platform. Here all Romania had surrendered, and Thomas Deacon was indifferent about spilling a little lamb's blood, turning death to an advantage. *All* Romania, not only Ploesti. Brasov, Pitesti, Bucharest . . . shimmering mirages of cities in the sky. He might have owed a visit to each, and now they were all gone in a pop of gypsy magic.

There was nothing in Bari to replace lost Romany. Bari was grubby and hot, the evening breeze having failed, the palms hanging still and stiff. There was no pay envelope for Deacon. The driver didn't know what he was talking about. Deacon was overwhelmed by a rage which felt like a crown of nettles. If he was willing to kill, willing to let the Great Crew fly those nineteen missions over and over until all the target fires had been extinguished, he had to be paid. His hand jerked toward the Thompson, the driver's foot came off the brake ready to stomp on it. They stood poised with hand and foot lifted for just one beat of the city's sober life, and then Deacon was struck by the absurdity of violence in Bari, the vision of empty faces turning white and frozen, trolleys shooting sparks and trucks careening because the air had been torn apart and the boulevard stained. Deacon shuddered, withdrew his hand. The driver's open Western smile had turned icy. Deacon got out of the cab.

He wanted his money. He wanted not to be standing in the middle of a city filled with *borghesi* both military and civilian. He didn't want to be thinking Italian words. The incident and the truck had evaporated, and he might as well not have been there, might as well never have gone or come back. If a crippled child had come along and begged the clothing from his back, no one would have known the name of the saint standing naked.

A hand touched his elbow. Deacon stiffened and turned as though he were made entirely of fine wires.

"Got your packet, Yank . . . not to worry."

That bastard Boyd never told him what was going on.

"Aren't we the nasty today? As a matter of fact, that's the way it's usually done . . . the driver's not supposed to be your paymaster. First time out there was a chance you might've had to be left somewhere. Your lolly would've gone to your partner for his trouble." Boyd tapped his tunic. "Got it right here . . . but what I thought I'd do is buy you that drink I promised, if you can get hold of yourself."

Deacon could buy his own drinks.

"Not this, you can't . . . not yet. Come on, Yank, we'll shift a little wallop and talk about the good old days."

The good days in Bari, where everything was old and the hot dust smelled of Roman and Norman feet, of fervent but

236

unwashed crusaders who'd sailed away to rot in the Holy Land, of gamey ducal bootprints from the Kingdom of the Two Sicilies. Bari doddering in a feculent haze of singed trolley tracks and smoldering tires and horse droppings, flaunting its age like a faded whore while all the time the barbed ring moved farther and farther away from it.

"Touch of liver, Yank?"

He had a touch of never again being able to touch certain Balkan cities, of being able only to walk streets crowded with assholes.

"Only a bit further," Boyd said.

It was a night when window glass would be warm and the stone like tinder, when the rich would sweat into their silk and the poor into their rags, when Tobin Bowles would lie like a fragrant loaf under a single clean sheet while a drop of perspiration trickled from her scented armpit. Deacon felt as though his bones were rasping together. He felt like a rickety stick about to ignite.

Boyd led him into a passageway guarded by an Italian in a white jacket. The man gave a weasel smile and touched his forehead, said *Capo* to Boyd and allowed them to pass. They came into a courtyard set with chairs and tables. It was blind on three sides, faced on the other with arched columns which opened on a large café. The tables inside and out were occupied by men in both American and British uniforms, all sergeants of one grade or another. Some had Italian girls with them. Tobacco smoke curled beneath the arches and rose like a fuming overflow. Music from an Armed Forces Radio program came from the café.

"*Al fresco* suit you?" Boyd asked.

The air in the court was warm and still, and the chatter of voices hung lightly in it, echoed a certain amount of gaiety. They took a table against a wall. Deacon could feel the heat radiating from it. He wiped his face. Another Italian in a white jacket appeared and made a little bow. Boyd handed him a card. The man bowed again and left. Deacon tapped his knuckles against the wall and wondered if it was the one he was to be stood against. He'd expected to be led to the hidden garage, to something like the St. Valentine's Day massacre.

"You're a proper hard one, if all your talk's to be believed. Doesn't rattle me, though. I've really all the time in the world for you, Tom. Here we are now."

The waiter brought glasses and a bottle of Scotch, a bowl of ice. He returned the card to Boyd, bowed again. Deacon saw whiskey on the other tables. Scotch represented a real accomplishment in fixing, but the ice . . . *ice*.

"Don't use it myself," Boyd said. "Thought all of you Yanks did." He twisted the cork and poured. "Let me be mother."

Deacon put ice in his drink. He wasn't used to Continental café society, to men looking as though they'd just finished a day's work, as though they were having a sundowner before moving on to the night and better things.

"Sort of an unofficial sergeant's club," Boyd said. "Not that the redcaps don't know about it . . . your people, too. They're well oiled to pretend it really isn't here, and we keep things reasonably quiet so they won't be embarrassed. Membership's held down, but I think we can find room for you, Tom boy. Cheers."

The Scotch trickled fire and honey all the way down to Deacon's stomach. He closed his eyes and let the ripple spread.

"Little better than that piss you've been knocking back, isn't it?"

They'd all just finished a day's work—stealing the Army blind. Bari's Casbah, the native quarter for anyone over the hill.

Boyd threw back his head and laughed. "Old Tom, bound to find himself in the company of his peers. They're all garrison personnel . . . they're posted here. Fix you up the same way."

Cocktails at five, perhaps a spot of billiards in the club room, a questionable lady who'd let him suck on her hairy upper lip.

"You can get rid of those silly chits you're carrying. We'll fix you up with a what d'you call it . . . one of those permanent-party passes."

Deacon wanted no part of that party, didn't feel that Bari itself was at all permanent. He poured the second drink himself, a larger one.

"But don't you see . . . you're limited with those idiotic passes. As a matter of fact, you were out of bounds today, over the limit. If someone had checked you at the furthest point of the trip and had wanted to get nasty, you'd have been for it. Not really my concern, Yank, but you oughtn't to risk your neck that way."

Boyd was about as concerned as one of the funeral directors in Operations. The sky over the courtyard was like a black syrup, the stars were smeared. Deacon felt more than heat, felt as though the air was slowly being compressed.

"You know the drill, Tom . . . can't expect the firm to push you up the ladder unless they're given full use of all your talents. You need flexibility, and those passes of yours

238

just won't do. Set yourself up as part of the garrison here, and all the rest of it's a piece of cake."

Boyd would certainly give him a push, right up the creek. He'd have Deacon trying to get to the Alps before the Fifth Army did. The Krauts had dug in and stopped the doggies north of Florence. Florence didn't matter—neither did France or Russia. The Balkans mattered, Austria, southern Germany.

"Better heads than ours have thought this through, Tom boy. No reason you should have to do things the hard way. We'll make all the arrangements."

Deacon was sick of arrangements. The whole thing was a joke, bullshit . . . particularly the shotgun.

"You think that, do you? Don't suppose you found that chap you took the first ride with very amusing. Ah, you didn't. Wouldn't trust him an inch myself. And he didn't trust *you*. Keeps you both on the ready, a situation like that . . . you've got to rely on each other to get the piece of work done."

The air grew more dense and hot. The walls of the court had begun to lean in, compacting everything between. Deacon reached for the bottle, but Boyd put his palm over the mouth.

"Time for that in a moment. Nice piece of brass you're getting, then, for not doing anything. Not likely that either one of you in that truck will take it as a game if you consider the trouble we've gone to giving you something to protect yourselves and our goods with . . . comes to the same thing, doesn't it? I can't picture you sodding off in the middle of the afternoon for a drink if you think you might have to be ready to shoot someone. If it's a joke it's an elaborate one, Yank. You can give it a good laugh while you're stacking your lolly."

Boyd took his hand from the bottle, Deacon poured. The walls were drawing closer, forcing the whiskey he'd already drunk directly into his bloodstream, squeezing his breath until it leaked from the corners of his mouth.

"Course if all this is beneath you, you might think about going over completely, changing to mufti. You'd do all right if your Italian was a little better. Needn't worry about your accent . . . give a good listen some time and you'll hear some lovely German ones. Didn't think you'd invented the game, did you? Jerry's been on extended leave longer than anyone."

Deacon's eyes were tearing, he was breathing shallowly—but he caught enough wind to tell Boyd what he thought about becoming Italian.

"Still want to play the dazzling soldier, eh? As you will, then. We'll even give you a promotion to master sergeant. A little authority might be helpful. It can be fixed up to look as though you've just been assigned to some kind of duty in the city. That way you can keep all that rubbish on your chest, that pocket trim you're so proud of."

The walls were leaning over him, voices began to sound as though they were under the sea. The whiskey was turning to gel in his veins, he had hardly any breath left.

"And we'll give you a real name, Yank, one that's on the roster of a local battalion of some sort. That way you'll stand a fair chance if the redcaps take you in for anything. When they call your company headquarters to check, they'll be told that you really exist."

To have someone like Boyd give him a name, to have some lousy supply outfit verify his existence . . . pure hatred rimmed Deacon's eyes red, the pressure in the courtyard made his ears ring, the walls were beginning to topple. And then a great hot gust blew through him like a purge, not only Bari's air, but the blast compressed in flak shells, the turbulent streams in propellers' wakes, the gales raging through the deserted streets of lost ghost cities.

"Not getting tiddly, are you? Thought you'd remember to bring your lunch this trip."

Blew it all away as the dummy had been blown from the muzzle of the Thompson, all the time since his watch had been broken. The first and last links of the daisy chain of events were in his hands. He snapped them together, locked himself in and everyone else out. Deacon felt shaken, but the pressure in the courtyard had disappeared leaving nothing but a hot still Italian night, an assembly of groundgrippers, a Limey bullshit artist. He wasn't anxious, was even reluctant, but he knew he had nineteen duty calls to make, had to get knocking before he fell any further behind. The squadron bulletin board was waiting, an alert list with his name on it.

"I brought my lunch," he said.

"You've got a touch of style, Yank. If you'd learn to keep your bloody cheek to yourself you might do very well at this game."

"How about my money?"

"There's more to it than you think, more to be made than you know. Everyone's talking about the war being over . . . they haven't the foggiest, they've forgotten how long it's taken to get halfway through Italy. Two more years of it at least. Build yourself a fortune and more in that time if you've the spine for it. Don't want to go home with nothing more than a muck sweat to show for your time, do you?"

"I don't have anything to show for today, Boyd."

"All right, let's say it's over tomorrow." Boyd pounded a finger on the table. "Right here, that's where the gold is, war or no. There's more being made than you could dream of, and this is the poorest part of the country. Think about what must be lying around up there north of Rome. No one's begun to touch it. *After* the war, Yank . . . there's bound to be an occupation of some sort, years and years. You don't have all that much to hurry home to, do you? Italy's a perfect base for the whole Mediterranean. They'll all be starving, they won't have a rag to wear. Think of the military stores left behind when all the brave lads go back to their sodding castles. Smuggling . . . Greece, Yugoslavia, North Africa . . . That's the ticket."

"Does it pay more than you do?"

Boyd threw an envelope on the table. "You needn't bother to count it out, it's all there." He studied Deacon. "Think I'm arse over tip about all this, don't you?"

"The world is your Italian apple, pal."

"Old Tom the dozy lad again."

Deacon shaped his finger and thumb like a pistol and pointed it at Boyd. He pressed the thumb down slowly. "Pingo," he said.

"That's a rare amusement."

"Pingo."

"Tom O'Bedlam's the one you are. You've been bonkers once and maybe you're working your way around the course again."

"I'm beat, Boyd, my poor old GI back is aching."

"Thought we might knock back a few tonight, Yank. You can act the layabout all day tomorrow. Know a smashing girl who'll give your watch a good winding."

"My watch?" Deacon grinned. "Some other time."

"As you will. Might be able to work you in on the odd extra trip. You can have it all, Tom boy, but you've got to get it while you can. We'll be in touch."

"I'll wait to hear." Deacon rose from the table.

"Have that new pass ready for you next week."

As Deacon entered the mouth of the alley Boyd called something else, but the words echoed along the walls and were garbled. The Italian attendant touched his forehead. Deacon nodded, stepped out into the street where the air was as still and as hot as it had been inside.

All the windows in the tenement were open, and through them came a conglomerate smell which rose like a pillar from the courtyard, voices which were sharp and edgy without being loud. Shafts of light were sliced into queer patterns by the washlines. Deacon rapped on Carlo's door. His mother answered, her face wrinkled and buckling around the edges, as though her youth had been steamed out of her. She jerked her head at Deacon, called over her shoulder into the babble of children's voices inside. The boy came out wiping traces of food from his mouth. He followed Deacon up the stairs.

As Deacon put the key in the lock he was aware that he was doing it for the last time, that the door would swing inward under his touch just once more. He clicked the light switch and the bulb buzzed and tinted the room brownish yellow. It was not and had never been a soldier's rest, lacked more than nocked sword and buckler on the wall. The room had only been a place to hide, and now it was only a place to leave from.

"*Paisano,*" Deacon said to the boy, "*Lacrima Cristi, co-gnosce?*"

"You wan some kind water you get from church . . . *acqua santa?*"

"*Vino, tonto . . . vino da Napoli.*"

"I don never heard of it. My frien get good new stuff, knock you jock off. I get, Tomas."

"I don't want any of that homeade garbage, I want a real drink. Celebration, *festa.*" Deacon groped. "How about Strega? *Possibile* Strega?"

"Aah . . . don know I can get like dat. *Forse, ma molto costoso.* Charge you lef nut."

"How much?"

"*Non sa.* Ow much you pay?"

"*Ladrone.* Knock off that crap. I'll give you . . . *uno mille,* you bring back a bottle of Strega and keep the change."

"I don know . . ."

"If you can't get it, just bring the money back. But don't bring me anything else . . . *capite?*

"*Mille cinquecento.*"

"*Mille duecento,* no more."

"I try."

The boy left with the twelve dollars. Deacon looked around the room. It was just as it had been when he'd moved in; he'd marked it only by carving his name in the window-sill. He opened the window and let in air which was the same temperature as that inside the room. The rooftops blended with the dark, closing the alley to the sea. The water was invisible but unchanged. Bones were still squeaking together on the Adriatic's floor. Inside and out everything was the same. Only Staff Sergeant Thomas Deacon, coming off the longest

242

three-day pass he'd ever had, might have been any different either inside or out. He didn't know.

Deacon was going back reluctantly, for no reason he was certain of. It was less a decision than a step. He'd marched only briefly during basic training, but the shock of his heel slamming in cadence had carried through ankle and knee, up his spine and into his brain. He was going back to pay part of the bill he owed to the man who'd served in his place—to tend his respects to the exploded and the drowned—to redeem the contract he'd signed in blood—to be able to think of Toole without having to stammer explanations to himself. He was going back to be with men he was not contemptuous of—to wear a uniform which was more than a costume—to function as he'd been trained to. Altogether those reasons might have constituted a decision, but he had really only to make a simple step into a cadence not beaten by any hunter either dead or alive, or by any pulse.

It was rather the long rattling roll of snare drums setting the tempo for a dress parade of enameled tin soldiers. Arm swing and crisp step, sunlight on a reviewing stand, the guidon stiff and forceful on the flank and then dipping like a lance, eyes snapping right. Toys driven by tuba, horn and drum to ostentatious prancing, grand turns which carried them nowhere. They marched far from any war, carried weapons which were only props. Palms slapping polished stocks, butts thundering to the ground, bolts shining and chambers empty. The flag was silky and inconsequential in the wind, as casually bloodstained as a barber's pole. Show, sound, glorious sight—all of it nothing.

The time Deacon was returning to had to do with lost cities, a war burning too brightly, a ticket with nineteen unpunched squares. But the cadence he stepped out in was that of meaningless parades in a nearly forgotten country. Neither the decision nor the step was important. Like flying, none of it bore thinking or needed it. He was going back after three sour months which hadn't added up to anything more than a three-day layover like the old ones in Naples. He couldn't get any bottled tears, didn't have a view of a bay with a smoldering cone, but he was going through the same preparations for return.

Carlo arrived with the Strega. Deacon poured nearly a cupful, sipped it off and let the liquor run along his veins, the Italian witch, the prowling of a great golden panther. The boy sat on one of the splintered chairs, swinging his feet idly, and his musty odor seeped through the room as naturally as the outside air. Deacon felt the acute separation between them—poverty and progress, Italy and the soldier. He didn't

243

know anything about Carlo, simply held his money out to be snatched by an anonymous child beggar identical to every other he'd ever seen. And the boy hadn't taken the money from any person, but from a hand with a khaki cuff, the arm and the body behind the hand completely interchangeable.

"What do you do with all that *danaro*," Deacon asked, "give it to your father?"

"My mudder. My fadder dead."

"Peccato."

"Itsa two year." The boy shrugged. "Someday we get new one. My mudder got *pergamenta*, watchyou callit . . . special paper from *Duce*. They send lil money ever munt."

"Was he in the army or something?"

"Si . . . sergente, like you. He get dead in Tunisia . . . from *inglese*, maybe GIs."

"Mi dispiace."

"Sta finito. New fadder come when we get money. I got two sister, they small." The boy pulled at his jacket. "You don't should tink we *scadente* because I'ma wear these clothes. My mudder give us good food, but we save the money. Don need clothes, save the money so pretty soon my mudder got *dotazione* . . . don know how you say. The war be over, she get marry, I go to school."

"Good deal," Deacon said.

"Si, Tomas."

Deacon could have made the deal better, could have substantially sweetened the family money pot. He felt for Carlo, could nearly reach him, but he had his own marriage to think of, his honeymoon promenade beneath the arched sabers of the class of '43.

"Ebbene," he said. "Now's the time for that piece of ass you're always talking about. Not somebody's sister, Carlo, not a *virgine* or any of that crap. Just a nice clean *ragazza* who knows what she's doing."

"Good deal, Tomas, I know good stuff."

"No pigs. Maybe I'll want her all night and maybe not, but no pigs."

"You like what I bring."

"I don't like, you take her back."

"You don sweat, Tomas, I get prime pudding. Ow much you pay?"

"I'll talk to her about that . . . but I'll give *you* five hundred if you get hold of something decent."

"You good Joe, Tomas. I get watchyou like."

The boy went skipping down the stairs. The good Joe, good soldier who corrupted youth and supported vice. That was the way things went—people pimping to eat, screwing to survive, flying to live, drinking to fly. Deacon poured more of the Strega. He looked out into the hot black night. If the alley hadn't been closed by the dark he would have been able to see the water, see a faint golden trail across it, the panther's path. And Deacon could have walked on it until he was out of sight of land, stood singing as he'd never sung before until he was bathed in gold and drops of moonlit spray and was drawn up into the void, into the niche among the stars reserved for him—St. Thomas of the Shriveled Gut.

That was part of the routine, to have a pimp for an acolyte and a streetwalker as sacristan. Tobin Bowles didn't belong in any part of it, not even in a rose-dream version of the Last Night. Not even in some place better than the grubby room, a place she might find perfect, gilt and plush or the cathartic atmosphere of a hospital bed or organ music and incense. She could give sweetly and totally, tears standing like miniature pearls along the lashes of her closed lids. She could stretch on the cross she'd made for herself while Deacon stretched with her, palm to palm and toe to toe, and drove his blunt nail into her flesh. None of that belonged in the ritual—not *I love you,* letters and photographs, plans for an afterwards which supposed his tour ending, the war being over. Whatever she gave, all he'd be able to give in return would be a dicking. Wham, bam, thank you ma'am.

Deacon had to keep the old traditions, to spill himself into a random purse. He drank while he waited, felt empty and godlike, capable of sailing sunships all through the night. When Carlo arrived Deacon felt easy with him, with the curly-haired girl he'd brought. She was somewhere in her teens. Deacon didn't care. It only mattered that she seemed fairly clean, adequate in chest and hip. If she had to lie down to earn her bread, then Deacon was helping to feed her. He gave the boy not five but ten dollars, sent him on his way.

Her name was Lucia—another *Santa,* they could sing a duet. Deacon offered a drink. She sniffed at his cup and declined, sat stiff and bleak across the table waiting for him to get started, to say something about money or unbutton his fly or grab her backside. Deacon was more the gentleman than that, all *cavaliere,* knighthood flowering in bursts of Italian she didn't understand. He was kind because they were rough comrades, different kinds of whores used to different kinds of campaigns. She advanced a price. Deacon put the money on the table without comment, with all the style he could muster. Quaff and cuddle had a value beyond any cost.

She looked questioningly at the light and he reached up and turned it out. The dark took the edge off the game. He sat very still when the chair opposite scraped. Her move-

245

ments were only a blur against the other shadows. In her passing from one side of the table to the other, all pretense ebbed. They were strangers, and the whole of the hot Italian night flowed into the strange room with them. She stood a moment behind his chair. Deacon could hear her breathing, closed his eyes and felt a faint roaring behind the lids. There was the rubbing sound of clothing across flesh, and then she put her hands on his shoulders and leaned forward so that her freed breasts nuzzled his neck. They were heavy and cool. He turned to kiss the cleft between them, tasted dust, smelled a delicate version of all Italy as her small hands clutched at him mechanically.

The air was like a wash of blood over his skin, and all his body's heat seemed to have been drawn into a single tip which was not so much raging as bound and constricted. The bed rustled while her fingers kneaded his thigh and her tongue slid efficiently across his chest. It was all by the numbers, her swinging into position and enfolding him, his responsive surge, the flicker of fire dancing across his distended self. By the numbers—he felt at home in that strange land, any place he hung his hat, any tallow where he dipped his wick. The mechanical suction pump was every bit as efficient as tender loving care.

They were both sweating, their joint musk cloud slightly rank. Her breasts swung like oiled balloons. Deacon gathered himself, got ready to go. He wanted to cry *evviva* on the moment, to introduce the name of Tobin Bowles for the sake of love lost. But it came like an ore cart rumbling from a mine. The clotted sap was dredged from sluggish tubes, and there was no pleasure in the sound he made, no evocation of love in any form. As his particles were discarded into the heaving rented glove, the pulse flexed like a thumb behind his ear, and he called out his own name.

22.

SPINALE WOULD have called it a little tricky.

Deacon stood at the window of the Red Cross installation in the Wing Headquarters town, behind him clerks and drivers idling around a rocky pool table, leafing through tattered magazines. There was a file in the big building around the corner, his name in red letters on the crapout list, but he wasn't worried about being picked up. They didn't know what he looked like, didn't expect him to be drinking coffee and eating yellow cake in their own backyard.

He was right back in it as though he'd never been away—the vehicles with familiar bumper markings, the variety of uniforms, the streets choked with dust. Only the sun was different, hidden behind a hazy overcast which sometimes billowed into long spools of woolly clouds. The day's heat was unusually heavy. Deacon stood easy about headquarters, about the local MPs, but the skin behind his ear crawled from time to time and his palms were sweatier than they should have been. Lucia hadn't been able to drain all the viscid jellies even though she'd tried more than once, given him meaty handfuls to hold through the night, even a parting line to his wry *Addio, domani morrò*. Looking neither younger nor older, looking only disheveled and empty, she'd shrugged and muttered *Domani, dopodomani . . . non importa*.

He was edgy because it did matter, because it was going to be a little tricky at the field, more than a case of breezing in and sassing the groundgrippers who'd grown to know his name so well, who'd been so hot for his body. If they'd brought him in they'd have lashed him to a wing and sent him on every dirty run which came up on the operations board. But he was returning voluntarily, telling them that he was ready to fly now that they knew who it was going in place of their own lousy selves. There wouldn't be any satisfaction, any malice, in their sending him up. They'd want to forbid it, to bury him in chains and throw him in the nearest dungeon. The only way they could get even would be to suffocate him in the Articles of War.

The whole tricky business would have to turn on Lieutenant Colonel Passerant. Deacon would have to soldier him blind, stand stiff and bristling as an arrow while he stated his case. Passerant would listen with a basin of water at his elbow, ready to wash his hands of the person of Thomas E. Deacon. And all the groundgrippers, all the clerks and cooks and mechanics would form a mob crying for justice, muttering in the courtyard.

Terrific. He looks like he just beat the Guineas to a uniform somebody threw away, standing there like he's trying to make points to get into Officers' Candidate School and where he's been is over the hill six weeks, wearing all the usual shit they give them for picking their noses, trying to look like a hero while he's telling the CO he don't know what happened.

Terrific . . . I think I'll take off for Rome for a couple of weeks and tell them I didn't know what come over me.

That there, Slim, is one of the reasons we're not about to get home this Christmas, that there which is what we got to prosecute this here war with, old wino deserter even did a little Section Eight in case he might be missing something. Gives you that real confidence, we got fightin men like that, airborne Sad Sack about ready to jump back in the bottle first time anybody sneezes too loud.

Passerant would listen, water and clean towel waiting, while the Flight Surgeon and the chaplain and all the commissioned dirteaters whispered in his ear.

He walked out when the going was rough, and he's back because he thinks it's tapered off and he can coast home on milk runs. The tour he should have finished is over. . . . I'd give him both barrels.

Since he took off from the hospital, not from the field, there isn't any question of his fleeing in the face of the enemy, and we needn't call it desertion, not in the strictest sense. The charge can always be mitigated with a question as to stability, a little emphasis on the hazardous nature of the duty, his coming back on his own.

The hospital psychiatrist's report isn't as precise as it might be, but he was evidently a model patient, and there isn't any indication that he can't resume his normal duties.

To err is human etc. . . . but salvation is paramount, and he is contrite and penitent, willing to redeem himself through good works.

The first sergeant would grumble about how the hell was he supposed to keep discipline if somebody didn't make an example of this bird. The Operations officer would be concerned that his funerals mightn't have the proper tone if such a shopworn type were included. The clerks would be sullen about keeping his records and the cooks wouldn't want to feed him and the supply men would issue him shoddy equipment. Both barrels, right up the poop.

Everything turning on Passerant would find Passerant turning to look at Deacon. He'd see one of his own babies, hand raised and hand beaten on that steel mat, rocked out of sleep by the CQ's lullaby. He'd shush the mob, tell them to go back to washing their socks, tell them to leave his mothering *soldiers* alone. And then he'd throw the basin of water over all of them.

Tricky, but Deacon was sure he could cut it. There'd be some kind of court-martial, he'd be broken to private, lose pay and allowances and probably be confined to the field. Although Deacon wouldn't be lashed to any wing, Passerant

248

would certainly assign him the dirtiest relief jobs, the longest and dreariest missions . . . but out of love, not malice. He'd understand that Deacon had to jump through that hoop of numbers, and he'd put Deacon's ticket back in his own hands, leave the punching to the Great Conductor in the Sky.

The afternoon was getting on to the time when the men who'd had business at headquarters would be returning to their outfits. Deacon walked to the edge of town and stood at the fork which led west into the flattest part of Basilicata's wastes. Several vehicles passed before a jeep with the Group's markings came by. Deacon recognized the squadron mail driver. The man didn't know him, and they passed most of the hour's ride in silence, the leaves rattling and the dust boiling and the familiar landmarks moving by as though they were on a treadmill. The jeep turned in at the Group's service road. Deacon got out before it entered the squadron area.

He walked a little way up the road and sat among a pile of rusting oil drums. August had been a big month—Avranches and Florence, Southern France, Falaise, Romania. None of it seemed to have changed anything at the field. It looked and sounded as it always had. That very day there'd been news that Paris had been liberated. Paris was very far from a heavy still evening in Basilicata. The tops of the far hills were drifted over with a dark scud, and it looked as though there might be rain.

He waited until a billow of gloom rolled down the slopes of the hills and the lights in the tent area went on. There had been only a brief show of stars before the sky was sealed off by clouds. A gusty wind came up and showered grit and pebbles through the air. Deacon bent his head against it. He wasn't going to report in that night. There'd be no one but the CQ and the OD in the orderly room. They'd make a big production out of his appearance, roust the first sergeant and the squadron CO, probably parade him up the hill to Group headquarters. He knew it had to come, that the whole process would have to have a beginning so that he could pick up where he'd left off. But not that night. However much the air war had tapered off in the last three months, Deacon had only that night to taper all the time he'd been away, to whittle down patient and pilgrim and shotgun so they'd fit the waiting slot. Morning was time enough for the grand opening, the formal act of contrition.

The last of the diners moved around him, their heads down and mess kits jangling. Chains on tent poles rattled, canvas creaked. The wind went singing through the guy ropes of the bar tent. Deacon squeezed out a grin before he entered. Not for the people, for the place—the old smoked walls and the screening and the indestructible armor-plate tables. There wouldn't be any people he knew, only men who looked like them, a new generation of flying hoboes in slashed shoes and cut-down uniforms. The upright piano was still there, hammers missing, strings curling. Deacon had made a permanent mark on it, one of the empty spaces belonged to him.

He edged up to the bar, got a glance or two because of his Class A's. Only a glance. He had the right wings, the right ribbons, was probably someone coming off pass. Hobby was still bartending. Deacon called for brandy. Hobby paid no attention. Deacon waited until he was closer, then called in a voice calculated to sound familiar, a voice an old classmate might use. The bartender set a glass in front of him, poured and took his money without looking up. Waves of talk rolled over Deacon's back—women and missions and luck and the everlasting niggling Army, old sports and recruits all tied together by a numbered band. Deacon knew the luck and the Army they were talking about, but not the women. The old crews had gone back to their women or had carried them into the enduring night of the long way. And he knew of missions they did not, the targets cut away by the rolling Russian front.

He emptied his glass, a little smug, a little heroic about having made those runs, having accomplished something now beyond anyone's reach . . . although some of the men in the tent might have hit those targets. Deacon felt a chilly ripple. *Any* of them might have. The recruits of his flying days were old sports now. There were crews with a score as large as or larger than his who hadn't even been in Italy then. Any of them might have been witnesses to Finger's grand performance or pallbearers on Gruber's last flight. Any one of them might be the man who'd flown Deacon's nineteen. They'd moved as the time had, left him panting to catch up. He rapped his glass on the counter.

"How're things?" he asked the bartender.

"Okay. How's by you?"

"Hobby, do you remember me?"

The other looked at his face. Something seemed to flare briefly in his eyes and then fade.

"Sure, sure. You ain't been around in a while."

"That's right."

"They rotated you home and now you're back for another tour. What a crock."

"No," Deacon said.

"I'm on the rotation list myself. I'm going on twenty-eight

250

months, and there're some outfits shipping guys back with thirty, thirty-one."

"Maybe you'll make out."

"Yeah. Well anyway, welcome home. I'll buy you a drink."

He filled the glass, gave Deacon an exaggerated wink and moved away. There wasn't anybody to talk to, anybody who'd want to listen to an odd dodo trying to fly his way out of the past. They all had numbers of their own to worry about. No matter what the targets were or would be, they had to get up in the morning and climb into airplanes loaded with bombs. There was no such thing as a safe way station for anyone clicking along the track of Fifty.

A particularly strong gust shook the tent. The crusty warrior with a bagful of stories worth about as much as a dribble of broken wind in a gale. He slammed the empty glass against the counter, shouted the bartender's name. Hobby came over slowly, gave him a longer look.

"Hey," he said, "ain't you . . . you and that other guy, I remember. You put the arm on me for those bottles that time."

"That's right," Deacon said. "Kelleher."

"Yeah . . . you're Kelleher."

"He was the other one." Deacon struggled for a moment. "What happened to him? What happened to Kelleher . . . did he go home?"

"Beats me. He ain't been around in a while."

Hobby wiped at the bar. A wave of light drumming passed over the tent, then another, and then there was a faint steady beating. The bar was quiet while ears were cocked and eyes were raised to the roof. The rain might scrub the next day's mission.

"Then you must be . . ." Hobby began. "I remember now. You must be the guy they finally had to give the needle to."

"I'll have a drink."

"Am I right?"

"Make it a double."

"Didn't you try to brain some guy with a bottle?"

"Just a drink, and spare me all the bullshit."

"No offense, Mac. I mean, you're the one started asking me . . ."

Deacon carried the drink to the side of the tent, stared out into the rain he could only hear, could only smell as damp dust. He finished half the brandy, looked into the rest of it and suddenly wanted to get drunk, to fall down stupefied in the middle of all of them and scream his name just once before he passed out. He had to stay pure that first night, had to keep himself shining for the morning. Deacon threw the rest of the brandy through the screening and went back to the counter.

"Got a raincoat, Hobby?" he called.

"There's one around here somewhere."

"Can I borrow it?"

"I don't know . . ."

"Just for a minute. I'll get it right back to you."

"It ain't as if I knew you, Mac."

"You son . . ." Deacon clutched at the molding, then reached into his pocket and took out two bills. "Here's twenty bucks. You can keep it for a lousy deposit."

"For twenty bucks you can keep the lousy coat."

The bartender rummaged beneath the counter and came up with a musty rubber coat. Deacon grabbed it, threw down the money and went out. The wind had died away and the rain fell in a fine straight drizzle. The dampened dust was very pungent, almost acrid. He walked to the service road, headed toward the field. A jeep came bounding by and nearly brushed against him. Deacon plodded on past the hammering generator of the oxygen-making detachment. The chains and winches at the service squadron were dripping. There was a bomber with two empty nacelles parked in the work area, another with a missing rudder. A heap of discarded wings and fuselages were being cannibalized for parts, and patches torn from the skin left odd holes like the work of geometric shells. A guard lounging in the overhang of the supply hut took a cigar from his mouth and waved it at Deacon.

A black-topped road looped around the runway. There were work vehicles rattling along it, their tires whining. The next day's mission was evidently still on. Deacon had taken that ride often enough, had been bounced and jostled in a jeep while he sat watching a ship loom larger and larger in the sun. Even on foot he was right back in it, right up to the end of his spine. The whole area behind his ear seemed ready to break into a trot.

The rain diminished, drifted away entirely. He came to the landing mat, flares burning at either side to mark home for any cripple who might flutter down. The other end was lost in the night, a huge empty swatch of wet steel which might as well have gone on and on until it stretched past the earth's curve and went sailing right into the sky. Deacon walked along the edge of the mat. The perforated surface was slick, gave a little with his weight. Bombers were parked in the revetments bordering the runway, and the headlamps of passing vehicles lit the line of planes individually, flashing each out of the darkness and back again like a stroboscopic series of dusky silver crosses. There were none of the veteran olive-drab ships left.

A dim glow came from the tinted windows of the control tower. At a revetment just ahead there was a line crew working, winch draped like a steel web around one engine, droplight swaying. Deacon cut away from them, passed under a parked ship's tail and let his hand trail the length of the wet fuselage. There was a single miniature yellow bomb painted beneath the pilot's window, but the airplane had no name. It was a new ship and probably had a new crew.

He poked his head through the nose-wheel aperture, was struck by the intense smells of rubber and hydraulic fluid and battery acid, leather and canvas. They were so strong, so familiar, he could almost hear the complex series of sounds which went with them, the noise of the plane in flight. He boosted himself over the nose wheel and into the lower deck, crouched for a moment in the nearly total dark and then moved without thinking or stumbling to the top turret deck. The flight clock ticked away its twenty-four-hour watch against the night. Banks of luminous green dials gleamed in the cockpit.

Deacon moved easily along the bomb-bay catwalk, the shackles hanging empty, and into the aft section. The ball rose in a familiar hump, the waist guns jutted from the walls, the fuselage tapered to the tail turret. It was his slot. The faces of the oxygen demand regulators were spots of blurred green, rain hung in drops on the waist windows and reflected some dim light which gave a sheen to the huge cartridges in the metallic ammunition belt. Deacon put his hand on the port gun—*his*. It was a real weapon, the largest caliber short of cannon, and no one but a real shotgun could ride behind it. His palm curled around the bolt in what was nearly a lover's grip, and he ran his other hand along the barrel's outer jacket. Deacon at home, standing on the few square feet of his platform in the sky, his window looking on an infinite world. The booze and edginess drained away. He was in it up to the hilt—there was nothing more he could do.

The lights of a passing truck jeweled the drops on the window, and then a wave of hard rain arrived and set up a tinny racket along the ship's aluminum skin. Deacon's hands were wet from the gun's sweating metal. He wiped them on the coat, started back through the bomb bay. A voice sounded hollowly through the ship. He stopped, thought that someone was calling his name. The voice came again, broken by a slamming sound, and the fuselage reverberated with thumps and cries and the tearing of the rain. Deacon hurried forward. A head with a wet helmet liner was thrust through the nose-wheel aperture. Two wet green arms were banging the butt of a carbine against a stanchion.

"Hey," the head called, "what're you doing in there? Get out of there."

"On my way," Deacon answered.

"Move it, move it, before I let fly."

The head withdrew to give Deacon room to get out. He dropped to the ground, rubbed his hands together. They stank of the gun. The guard stepped back, his carbine wavering.

"What d'you think you're doing?" he said. "You got no business fooling around in there."

He was very young. Water from the helmet liner dripped onto his cheeks. He had a round face and looked like a child who'd just stopped crying.

"Take it easy, pal," Deacon said. "Just checking my station."

"Your what? Who're you?"

They'd know tomorrow who he was, all of them. But even as the answer formed he could hear an echo bouncing from far back in his old time, Passerant asking the question and Deacon's reply the same one he now gave the guard.

"Me? I'm Deacon, Thomas Deacon, 11104449. I'm the port waist gunner."

"Yeah?"

"For Jesus sake."

Deacon undid the raincoat, showed his wings and ribbons. He pulled down the coat's shoulder until his stripes showed, stood posed like a coy temptress while the rain drilled on the wing above them.

"Oh . . ." the boy said.

"You're dripping all over your piece."

When the guard looked down at the carbine water from his helmet liner trickled over it. "Rats," he said and then licked his lips. "We got orders, Sarge. You know how it is."

"Indeed I do. Forget it."

Deacon gathered the coat about him and took a little skipping step toward the road. The revetment was faced with the same slick perforated mat as the runway. Deacon's heel skidded. He staggered across the mat and into a wall of rain which suddenly blazed across the road. For a fraction of a second he saw the fine streaks lit up like colored threads, and then a voice cried behind him just as a grille caught his chest and a fender slammed into his hip. Deacon felt a tremendous blow but no pain. The back of his head bounced against the revetment's mat.

He could hear, but he couldn't see because there was a

254

prickling in his eyes as though the weather had changed and the sun was stabbing into them. The same voice was gurgling words he couldn't understand. It grew warmer, hot, and something came out of him in a great tearing rush. The voice began calling for a mother, faded away. Deacon tried to spit the meal from his mouth.

It had grown very hot and the sun was cutting cruelly into his eyes. He couldn't understand why everything had changed . . . and then there was a burst of hazy light and he realized he'd caught up to the old time, was in the old place. The chute had blown and the ship had mushed. He could feel the vibration of footsteps, they were crossing the runway, running toward him. But there wasn't any horn or siren. The mat began to sway. His fingers scrabbled at it.

The weapons carrier backed to the revetment and four men jumped out. Three wore wings and corporal's stripes, were obviously recruit gunners. All of them were shouting. The guard clung to the bomber's landing-gear strut, real tears on his cheeks, drops of water forming on the carbine's tilted muzzle. The carrier's driver sprawled flat and put his head in the dent across Deacon's chest, pressed his ear into the apron of blood fanning from his mouth. He looked up and called to the others, his ear red. They hung back. The driver began to call again, but just then there was a sharp cough from the revetment up the line and a ball of orange fire burst through the rain and into the night. He had to scream to make himself heard over the thunder of the engine.

Deacon could only hear the engine. It shouldn't be there if he was back in the old time. There should be a horn and a siren. If he was back in the old time, then all the rest had been . . . The mat was swaying badly. He dug his fingers in. The engine grew louder and louder and the mat began to tilt. All the rest had been . . . Something bubbled from the back of his throat. He choked, tried to swallow. The mat tilted sharply. Deacon felt himself slipping, and then the sound of the engine grew enormous and he fell into it and was carried away.

The guard dropped his carbine, vomited over the landing wheel. All three recruits edged closer as the driver stared into Deacon's face. He sat back and sighed.

"He run right into it," he said.

"I saw it, I saw it," one of the others shouted.

The engine trailed a stream of bright blue fire which lit their faces. Pinpoints of blue light danced in the eyes looking up into the rain. The driver closed them with his thumb and forefinger. One of the recruits shouted into the reddened ear.

"Who is he?"

Beads of moisture gathered on the closed eyelids. The driver pulled at his ear. He looked at his fingers, wiped them along the mat.

"I don't know," he said.

The open raincoat had been furled over the arms, and as the rain beat the blood into a pink froth the wings and ribbons began to show.

Edgartown, Massachusetts
April 4, 1967